SEA OF
AKERI

KINGDOM OF
VENDA

A TERR

TEUX

★ SANCTUM

FALWORTH

GREAT RIVER

KINGDOM OF
DALBRECK

REUX
LAU

CRUVAS

By Mary Pearson

The Remnant Chronicles
The Kiss of Deception
The Heart of Betrayal
The Beauty of Darkness

The Jenna Fox Chronicles
The Adoration of Jenna Fox
The Fox Inheritance
Fox Forever

The Miles Between
A Room on Lorelei Street

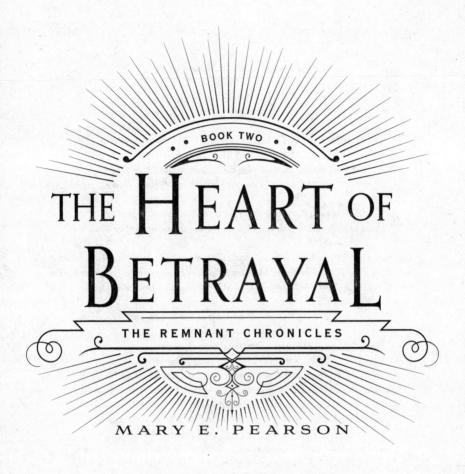

BOOK TWO

THE HEART OF BETRAYAL

THE REMNANT CHRONICLES

MARY E. PEARSON

SQUARE
FISH

Henry Holt and Company

NEW YORK

SQUARE
FISH

An imprint of Macmillan Publishing Group, LLC
120 Broadway
New York, NY 10271
fiercereads.com

Square Fish and the Square Fish logo are trademarks of Macmillan and
are used by Henry Holt and Company under license from Macmillan.

Our books may be purchased in bulk for promotional, educational, or business use. Please
contact your local bookseller or the Macmillan Corporate and Premium Sales Department
at (800) 221-7945 ext. 5442 or by email at MacmillanSpecialMarkets@macmillan.com.

Library of Congress Cataloging-in-Publication Data
Pearson, Mary (Mary E.)
The heart of betrayal / Mary E. Pearson.
pages   cm.—(The remnant chronicles ; book 2)
Summary: Held captive in the barbarian kingdom of Venda, Princess Lia and Rafe
have little chance of escape—and even less of being together—as the foundations of
Lia's deeply-held beliefs crumble beneath her while she wrestles with her
upbringing, her gift, and her very sense of self to make powerful choices that
affect her country, her people, and her own destiny.
ISBN 978-1-250-08002-8 (paperback)   ISBN 978-1-62779-470-1 (ebook)
[1. Fantasy.   2. Princesses—Fiction.   3. Love—Fiction.]   I. Title.
PZ7.P32316He 2015   [Fic]—dc23   2015000921

Originally published in the United States by Henry Holt and Company,
First Square Fish Edition: 2016
Book designed by Anna Booth
Square Fish logo designed by Filomena Tuosto

11   13   15   17   19   20   18   16   14   12

AR: 5.5 / LEXILE: HL780L

For Kate Farrell,
my friend and editor,
and Siarrah of the highest order

Her tears, they ride the wind.
She calls to me,
And all I can do is whisper,
You are strong,
Stronger than your pain,
Stronger than your grief,
Stronger than them.

—*The Last Testaments of Gaudrel*

CHAPTER ONE

ONE SWIFT ACT.

I had thought that was all it would take.

A knife in the gut.

A firm twist for good measure.

But as Venda swallowed me up, as the misshapen walls and hundreds of curious faces closed in, as I heard the clatter of chains and the bridge lowering behind me, cutting me off from the rest of the world, I knew my steps had to be certain.

Flawless.

It was going to take many acts, not just one, every step renegotiated. Lies would have to be told. Confidences gained. Ugly lines crossed. All of it patiently woven together, and patience wasn't my strong suit.

But first, more than anything, I had to find a way to make

my heart stop pummeling my chest. Find my breath. Appear calm. Fear was the blood scent for wolves. The curious inched closer, peering at me with half-open mouths that revealed rotten teeth. Were they amused or sneering?

And there was the jingle of skulls. The gathering rattle of dry bones rippled through the crowd as they jockeyed to get a better look, strings of small sun-bleached heads, femurs, and teeth waving from their belts as they pressed forward to see me. And to see Rafe.

I knew he walked shackled somewhere behind me at the end of the caravan, prisoners, both of us—and Venda didn't take prisoners. At least they never had before. We were more than a curiosity. We were the enemy they had never seen. And that was exactly what they were to me.

We walked past endless jutting turrets, layers of twisted stone walls blackened with soot and age, slithering like a filthy living beast, a city built of ruin and whim. The roar of the river faded behind me.

I'll get us both out of this.

Rafe had to be questioning his promise to me now.

We passed through another set of massive jagged gates, toothy iron bars mysteriously opening for us as if our arrival was anticipated. Our caravan grew smaller as groups of soldiers veered in different directions now that they were home. They disappeared down snaking paths shadowed by tall walls. The *chievdar* led what remained of us, and the wagons of booty jingled in front of me as we walked into the belly of the city. Was Rafe still somewhere behind me, or had they taken him down one of those miserable alleyways?

Kaden swung down from his horse and walked beside me. "We're almost there."

A wave of nausea hit me. Walther's dead, I reminded myself. *My brother is dead.* There was nothing more they could take from me. Except Rafe. I had more than myself to think about now. This changed everything. "Where is *there*?" I tried to ask calmly, but my words tripped out hoarse and uneven.

"We're going to the Sanctum. Our version of court. Where the leaders meet."

"And the Komizar."

"Let me do the talking, Lia. Just this once. Please, don't say a word."

I looked at Kaden. His jaw was tight, and his brows pulled low, as if his head ached. Was he nervous to greet his *own* leader? Afraid of what I might say? Or what the Komizar would do? Would it be considered an act of treason that he hadn't killed me as he was ordered? His blond hair hung in greasy, tired strands well past his shoulders now. His face was slick with oil and grime. It had been a long time since either of us had seen soap—but that was the least of our problems.

We approached another gate, this one a towering flat wall of iron pocked with rivets and slits. Eyes peered through them. I heard shouts from behind it, and the heavy clang of a bell. It juddered through me, each ring shivering in my teeth.

Zsu viktara. Stand strong. I forced my chin higher, almost feeling Reena's fingertips lifting it. Slowly the wall split in two and the gates rolled back, permitting our entry into an enormous open area as misshapen and bleak as the rest of the city. It was bordered on all sides by walls, towers, and the beginnings of narrow streets that disappeared into shadows. Winding crenelated walkways loomed above us, each one overtaking and melting into the next.

The *chievdar* moved forward, and the wagons piled in behind him. Guards in the inner court shouted their welcomes, then happily bellowed approval at the stash of swords and saddles and the glittering tangle of plunder piled high on the wagons—all that was left of my brother and his comrades. My throat tightened, for I knew that soon one of them would be wearing Walther's baldrick and carrying his sword.

My fingers curled into my palm, but I didn't even have so much as a nail left to stab my own skin. All of them were torn to the quick. I rubbed my raw fingertips, and a fierce ache shook my chest. It caught me by surprise, this small loss of my nails compared to the enormity of everything else. It was almost a mocking whisper that I had nothing, not even a fingernail, to defend myself. All I had was a secret name that seemed as useless to me right now as the title I was born with. *Make it true, Lia*, I told myself. But even as I said the words in my head, I felt my confidence ebbing. I had far more at stake now than I'd had just a few hours ago. Now my actions could hurt Rafe too.

Orders were given to unload the ill-gotten treasure and carry it inside, and boys younger than Eben scurried over with small two-wheeled carts to the sides of the wagon and helped the guards fill them. The *chievdar* and his personal guard dismounted and walked up steps that led to a long corridor. The boys followed behind, pushing the overflowing carts up a nearby ramp, their thin arms straining under the weight. Some of the booty in their loads was still stained with blood.

"That way to Sanctum Hall," Kaden said, pointing after the boys. Yes, nervous. I could hear it in his tone. If even he was afraid of the Komizar, what chance did I have?

I stopped and turned, trying to spot Rafe somewhere back in the line of soldiers still coming through the gate, but all I could see was Malich leading his horse, following close behind us. He grinned, his face still bearing the slash marks from my attack. "Welcome to Venda, Princess," he jeered. "I promise you, things will be very different now."

Kaden pulled me around, keeping me close to his side. "Stay near," he whispered. "For your own good."

Malich laughed, reveling in his threat, but for once, I knew what he said was true. Everything was different now. More than Malich could even guess.

CHAPTER TWO

SANCTUM HALL WAS LITTLE MORE THAN A DISMAL TAVERN, albeit a cavernous one. Four of Berdi's taverns could have fit within its walls. It smelled of spilled ale, damp straw, and overindulgence. Columns lined the four sides, and it was lit with torches and lanterns. The high ceiling was covered in soot, and an enormous rough wooden table sat heavy and abused in the center. Pewter tankards rested on the table or swung from meaty fists.

The leaders.

Kaden and I hung back in the shadowed walkway behind the columns, but the leaders greeted the *chievdar* and his personal guard with boisterous shouts and slapping of backs. Tankards were offered and raised to the returning soldiers with calls to bring more ale. I saw Eben, shorter than some of the serving boys, lifting a pewter cup to his lips, a returning soldier the same as the rest. Kaden pushed me slightly behind him in a protective manner, but I still scanned the room, trying to spot the Komizar, trying to be ready, prepared for what was to come. Several of the men were huge, like Griz—some even bigger—and I wondered what kind of creatures, both human and beast, this strange land produced. I kept my eyes on one of them. He snarled every word, and the scurrying boys ran a respectful wide distance around him. I thought that he had to be the Komizar, but I saw Kaden's eyes scouring the room too, and they passed over the burly brute.

"These are the Legion of Governors," he said, as if he had read my mind. "They rule the provinces."

Venda had provinces? And a hierarchy too, beyond assassins, marauders, and an iron-fisted Komizar? The governors were distinguished from the servants and soldiers by black fur epaulets on their shoulders. The fur was crowned with a bronze clasp shaped like the bared teeth of an animal. It made their physiques appear twice as wide and formidable.

The ruckus rose to a deafening roar, echoing off the stone walls and bare floors. There was only a pile of straw in one corner of the room to absorb any noise. The boys parked the carts of booty along one row of pillars, and the governors perused the haul, lifting swords, testing weights, and rubbing forearms on leather breastplates to polish away dried blood. They examined the goods as if they were at a marketplace. I saw one of them pick up a sword inlaid with red jasper on the hilt. Walther's sword. My foot automatically moved forward, but I caught myself and forced it back into place. Not yet.

"Wait here," Kaden whispered and stepped out of the shadows. I inched closer to a pillar, trying to get my bearings. I saw three dark hallways that led into Sanctum Hall in addition to the one we had entered through. Where did they go, and were they guarded like the one behind me? And most important, did any of them lead to Rafe?

"Where's the Komizar?" Kaden asked in Vendan, speaking to no one in particular, his voice barely cutting through the din.

One governor turned, and then another. The room grew suddenly quiet. "The Assassin is here," said an anonymous voice somewhere at the other end.

There was an uncomfortable pause and then one of the shorter governors, a stout man with multiple red braids that fell past his shoulders, barreled forward and threw his arms around Kaden, welcoming him home. The noise resumed but at a noticeably lower level, and I wondered at the effect an Assassin's presence had on them. It reminded me of Malich and how he had reacted to Kaden on the long trek across the Cam Lanteux. He'd had blood in his eye and was equally matched, but he'd still backed down when Kaden stood his ground.

"The Komizar's been called," the governor told Kaden. "That is, if he comes. He's occupied with—"

"A *visitor*," Kaden finished.

The governor laughed. "That she is. The kind of visitor I'd like to have."

More governors walked over, and one with a long crooked nose shoved a tankard in Kaden's hand. He welcomed him home and berated him for being gone for so long on *holiday*. Another governor chided him, saying he was away from Venda more than he was here.

"I go where the Komizar sends me," Kaden answered.

One of the other governors, as big as a bull and with a chest just as wide, lifted his drink in a toast. "As do we all," he replied and threw back his head, taking a long careless swig. Ale sloshed out the sides of his mug and dripped down his beard to the floor. Even this taurine giant hopped when the Komizar snapped his fingers, and he wasn't afraid to admit it.

Though they spoke only in Vendan, I was able to understand nearly everything they said. I knew far more than just the *choice* words of Venda. Weeks of immersion in their language across the Cam Lanteux had cured my ignorance.

As Kaden answered their questions about his journey, my gaze became fixed on another governor pulling a finely tooled baldrick from the cart and trying to force it around his generous gut. I felt dizzy, sick, and then rage bubbled up through my veins. I closed my eyes. *Not yet. Don't get yourself killed in the first ten minutes. That can come later.*

I took a deep breath, and when I opened my eyes again, I spotted a face in the shadows. Someone on the other side of the hall was watching me. I couldn't look away. Only a slash of light illuminated his face. His dark eyes were expressionless, but at the same time compelling, fixed like a wolf stalking prey, in no hurry to spring, confident. He casually leaned against a pillar, a younger man than the governors, smooth-faced except for a precise line of beard at his chin and a thin, carefully clipped mustache. His dark hair was unkempt, locks curling just above his shoulders.

He didn't wear the furred epaulets of a governor on his shoulders, nor the leather vestments of a soldier, only simple tan trousers and a loose white shirt, and he was certainly in no hurry to attend to anyone, so he wasn't a servant either. His eyes moved past me as if bored, and he took in the rest of the scene, governors pawing through carts and swilling ale. And then Kaden. I saw him watching Kaden.

Heat rushed through my stomach.

Him.

He stepped out past the pillar into the middle of the room, and with his first steps, I knew. This was the Komizar.

"Welcome home, comrades!" he called out. The room was instantly silent. Everyone turned toward the voice, including Kaden. The Komizar walked slowly across the expanse and anyone in his path moved back. I stepped out from the shadows to stand by Kaden's side, and a low rumble ran through the room.

The Komizar stopped a few feet from us, ignoring me and staring at Kaden, then finally came forward to embrace him with a genuine welcome.

When he released Kaden and took a step back, he looked at me with a cool, blank gaze. I couldn't quite believe that this was the Komizar. His face was smooth and unwrinkled, a man just a few years older than Walther, more like an older brother to Kaden than a fearsome leader. He wasn't exactly the formidable Dragon of the Song of Venda—the one who drank blood and stole dreams. His stature was only average, nothing daunting about him at all except for his unwavering stare.

"What's this?" he asked in Morrighese almost as flawless as

Kaden's, nodding his head toward me. A game player. He knew exactly who I was and wanted to be sure I understood every word.

"Princess Arabella, First Daughter of the House of Morrighan," Kaden answered.

Another restrained hush ran through the room. The Komizar chuckled. "Her? A princess?"

He slowly circled around me, viewing my rags and filth as if in disbelief. He paused at my side, where the fabric was torn from my shoulder and the kavah was exposed. He uttered a quiet *hmm* as if mildly amused, then ran the back of his finger down the length of my arm. My skin crawled, but I lifted my chin, as if he were merely an annoying fly buzzing about the room. He completed his circle until he faced me again. He grunted. "Not very impressive, is she? But then, most royals aren't. About as entrancing as a bowl of week-old mush."

Only a month ago, I would have jumped at the baited remark, tearing him to shreds with a few hot words, but now I wanted to do far more than insult him. I returned his gaze with one of my own, matching his empty expression blink for blink. He rubbed the back of his hand along the line of his thin, carefully sculpted beard, studying me.

"It's been a long journey," Kaden explained. "A hard one for her."

The Komizar raised his brows, feigning surprise. "It needn't have been," he said. He raised his voice so the whole hall would be sure to hear, though his words were still directed at Kaden. "I seem to remember I ordered you to slice her throat, not bring her back as a pet."

Tension sparked in the air. No one lifted a tankard to their lips. No one moved. Perhaps they waited for the Komizar to walk over to the carts, draw a sword, and send my head rolling down the middle of the room, which certainly in their eyes was his right. Kaden had defied him.

But there was something between Kaden and the Komizar, something I still didn't quite understand. A hold of some sort.

"She has the gift," Kaden explained. "I thought she'd be more useful to Venda alive than dead."

At the mention of the word *gift*, I saw glances exchanged among the servants and governors, but still, no one said a word. The Komizar smiled, at once chilling and magnetic. My neck prickled. This was a man who knew how to control a room with the lightest touch. He was showing his hand. Once I knew his strengths, I might discover his weaknesses too. Everyone had them. Even the feared Komizar.

"The gift!" He laughed and turned to everyone else, expecting them to laugh in kind. They did.

He looked back to me, the smile gone, then reached out and took my hand in his. He examined my injuries, his thumb gently skimming the back of my hand. "Does she have a tongue?"

This time it was Malich who laughed, stepping over to the table in the center of the room and slamming down his mug. "Like a cackling hyena. And her bite is just as nasty." The *chievdar* spoke up, concurring. Murmurs rose from the soldiers.

"And yet," the Komizar said, turning back to me, "she remains silent."

"Lia," Kaden whispered, nudging me with his arm, "you can speak."

I looked at Kaden. He thought I didn't know that? Did he really think it was his warning that had silenced me? I had been silenced far too many times by those who exerted power over me. Not here. My voice *would* be heard, but I'd speak when it served my purposes. I betrayed neither word nor expression. The Komizar and his governors were no different from the throngs I had passed on my way here. They were curious. *A real princess of Morrighan.* I was on display. The Komizar wanted me to perform before him and his Legion of Governors. Did they expect jewels to spill from my mouth? More likely, whatever I said would find ridicule, just as my appearance already had. Or the back of his hand. There were only two things a man in the Komizar's position expected, defiance or groveling, and I was certain that neither would improve my lot.

Though my pulse raced, I didn't break his gaze. I blinked slowly, as if I were bored. *Yes, Komizar, I've already learned your tics.*

"Not to worry, my friends," he said, waving his hand in the air and dismissing my silence. "There's so much more to talk about. Like all of this!" His hand swept the room from one end to the other at the display of carts. He laughed like he was delighted with the haul. "What do we have?" He started at one end, going from cart to cart, digging through the plunder. I noticed that though the governors had searched it, nothing appeared to have been taken yet. Perhaps they knew to wait until the

Komizar chose first. He lifted a hatchet, running a finger along the blade, nodding as if impressed, and then moved on to the next cart, drawing out a falchion and swinging it in front of him. Its *sching* cut through the air and drew approving comments. He smiled. "You did well, Chievdar."

Well? Massacring a whole company of young men?

He tossed the curved blade back into the cart and moved on to the next one. "And what's this?" He reached in and pulled out a long strap of leather. Walther's baldrick.

Not him. *Anyone but him.* I felt my knees weaken, and a small noise escaped my throat. He turned in my direction, holding it up. "The tooling is exceptional, don't you think? Look at these vines." He slowly slid the strap through his fingers. "And the leather, so buttery. Something fit for a crown prince, no?" He lifted it over his head and adjusted it across his chest as he walked back to me, stopping an arm's length away. "What do *you* think, Princess?"

Tears sprang to my eyes. I, too, had foolishly played my hand. I was still too raw with Walther's loss to think. I looked away, but he grabbed my jaw, his fingers gouging into my skin. He forced me to look back at him.

"You see, Princess, this is my kingdom, not yours, and I have ways of making you speak that you cannot even begin to fathom. You will sing like a clipped canary if I command it."

"Komizar." Kaden's voice was low and earnest.

He released me and smiled, gently caressing my cheek. "I think the princess is tired from her long journey. Ulrix, take the princess to the holding room so she can rest for a moment and

Kaden and I can talk. We have a lot to discuss." He glanced at Kaden, the first sign of anger flashing through his eyes.

Kaden looked at me, hesitating, but there was nothing he could do. "Go," he said. "It'll be all right."

ONCE WE WERE OUT OF KADEN'S SIGHT, THE GUARDS ALL but dragged me down the hallway, their wrist cuffs stabbing into my arms. I still felt the pressure of the Komizar's fingers against my face. My jaw throbbed where his fingers had dug in. In just a few brief minutes, he had perceived something I cared about deeply and used it to hurt me and, ultimately, weaken me. I had braced myself to be beaten or whipped, but not for that. The vision still burned my eyes, my brother's baldrick proudly splayed across the enemy's chest in the cruelest taunt, waiting for me to crumble. And I had.

Round one to the Komizar. He had overtaken me, not with quick condemnation or brute force, but with stealth and careful observation. I would have to learn to do the same.

My indignation mounted as the guards jostled me roughly through the dark hall, seeming to relish having a royal at their mercy. By the time they stopped at a door, my arms were numb under their grip. They unlocked it and threw me into a black room. I fell, the rough stone floor cutting into my knees. I stayed there, stunned and hunched on the ground, breathing in the musty, foul air. Only three thin shafts of light filtered through vents in the upper wall opposite me. As my eyes adjusted to the darkness, I saw a straw-filled mat, the stuffing spilling out onto the floor, a short milking stool, and a bucket. Their holding room had all the comforts of a barbaric cell. I squinted, trying to see more in the dim light, but then I heard a noise. A shuffle in the corner. I wasn't alone.

Someone or something else was in the room with me.

et the stories be heard,
So all generations will know,
The stars bow at the gods' whisper,
They fall at their bidding,
And only the chosen Remnant,
Found grace in their sight.

—Morrighan Book of Holy Text, Vol. V

CHAPTER THREE

KADEN

"SO, YOU THOUGHT SHE'D BE USEFUL."

He knew the true reason. He knew I disdained the gift as much as he did, but his contempt for the gift sprang from lack of belief. I had more compelling reasons.

We sat alone in his private meeting chamber. He leaned back in his chair, his tented hands tapping his lips. His black eyes rested on me like cool, polished onyx, betraying no emotion. They rarely did, but if not anger, I knew at least curiosity lurked behind them. I looked away, gazing instead at the lush fringed carpet beneath us. A new addition.

"A goodwill gift from the Premier of Reux Lau," he explained.

"Goodwill? It looks expensive. Since when do the Reux Lau bring us gifts?" I asked.

"*You thought*. Let's get back to that. Is she that good in—"

"No," I said, standing up. I walked to the window. Wind hissed through the gaps. "It's not like that."

He laughed. "Then tell me how it is."

I looked back at his table, overflowing with maps, charts, books, and notes. I was the one who had taught him how to read Morrighese, which most of these documents were. *Tell me how it is.* I wasn't sure myself. I returned to my chair across from him and explained Lia's effect on Vendans as hardened as Griz and Finch. "You know how the clans are, and there are plenty of hillfolk who still believe. You can't walk through the *jehendra* without seeing a dozen stalls selling talismans. Every other servant here in the Sanctum wears one or another tucked beneath their shirt and probably half the soldiers too. If they think the Vendans have somehow been blessed with one of the gifts of old, one of royal blood even, you might—"

He leaned forward, sweeping papers and maps to the floor with a broad angry stroke of his arm. "Do you take me for a fool? You betrayed an order because the backward few of Venda might take her to be a sign? Have you now appointed yourself Komizar to do what *you* think to be the wiser move?"

"I just thought—" I closed my eyes briefly. I had already disobeyed his order, and now I was making excuses, just as the Morrighese did. "I hesitated when I went to kill her. I—"

"She caught your fancy, just as I said."

I nodded. "Yes."

He leaned back in his chair and shook his head, waving his hand as if it was of little matter. "So you succumbed to the charms of a woman. Better that than believing yourself to make better decisions in my stead." He pushed his chair back and stood, walking over to a tall footed oil lamp in the corner of the room, jagged crystals rimming it like a crown. When he turned the wheel to increase the flame, splinters of light cut across his face. It was a gift from the Tomack quarterlord and didn't fit the severity of the room. He tugged the short hair of his beard, lost in thought, and then his eyes rested on me once again. "No harm done bringing her here. She's out of the hands of Morrighan and Dalbreck, which is all that matters. And yes, now that she's here . . . I'll decide the best way to use her. The governors' hushed surprise at a royal in their midst wasn't lost on me, nor the whispering of servants when she left." A half smile played on his lips, and he rubbed at a smudge on the lantern with his sleeve. "Yes, she might prove useful," he whispered, more to himself than to me, as if warming to the idea.

He turned, remembering I was still in the room.

"Enjoy your pet for now, but don't get too attached. The brethren of the Sanctum aren't like the hillfolk. We don't settle into flabby domestic lives. Remember that. Our brotherhood and Venda always come first. It's how we survive. Our countrymen are counting on us. We're their hope."

"Of course," I answered. And it was true. Without the Komizar, even without Malich, I'd be dead by now. But *don't get too attached*? It was too late for that.

He returned to his desk, shuffling through papers, then stopped to look at a map and smiled. I knew the smile. He had many. When he had smiled at Lia, I'd feared the worst. The one on his face now was genuine, a satisfied smile, meant for no one to see.

"Your plans are going well?"

"Our plans," he corrected me. "Better than I hoped. I have great things to show you, but it will have to wait. You made it back just in time before I ride out tomorrow. The governors of Balwood and Arleston didn't show."

"Dead?"

"Most likely for Balwood. Either the sickness of the north country finally got him or he lost his head to a young usurper too frightened to come to the Sanctum himself."

My guess was that Hedwin of Balwood had succumbed to a sword in the back. Just as he always boasted, he was too mean for the withering sickness of the north woods to overtake him.

"And Arleston?"

We both knew that Governor Tierny of the southernmost province was probably lying in a drunken stupor in some brothel on the road to the Sanctum and would stroll in with apologies featuring lame horses and bad weather. But his tithe of supplies to the city never wavered. The Komizar shrugged. "Hot-blooded young men can grow weary of well-oiled governors."

As the Komizar had eleven years ago. I looked at him, still every bit the young man who had slaughtered three governors right before he killed the previous Komizar of Venda. But he wasn't so hot-blooded anymore. No, now his blood ran cool and steady.

"It's been a long time since there have been any challenges," I mused.

"No one wants a target on his back, but challenges always come, my brother, which is why we must never grow lazy." He shoved the map aside. "Ride with me tomorrow. I could use some fresh company. We haven't ridden together in too long."

I said nothing, but my expression must have revealed my reluctance.

He shook his head, retracting his invitation. "Of course, you've just returned from a long journey, and besides that you've brought *Venda* a very interesting prize. You deserve a respite. Rest a few days and then I'll have work for you."

I was thankful that he didn't mention Lia as the reason. He was being more gracious than I deserved, but I took note of his emphasis on Venda, a deliberate reminder of where my loyalties belonged. I stood to leave. A draft ruffled the papers on his desk.

"A storm brews," I said.

"The first of many," he answered. "A new season comes."

CHAPTER FOUR

I JUMPED TO MY FEET AND SEARCHED THE SHADOWS OF the room, trying to see what made the noise.

"Here."

I spun around.

A thin shaft of light took new form as someone stepped forward into its soft beam.

A dusky strand of hair. A cheekbone. His lips.

I couldn't move. I stared at him, all I had ever wanted and all I had ever run from locked in the same room with me.

"Prince Rafferty," I finally whispered. It was only a name, but its sound was hard, foreign, and distasteful in my mouth. *Prince Jaxon Tyrus Rafferty.*

He shook his head. "Lia . . ."

His voice shivered through my skin. Everything I had hung

on to across thousands of miles shifted inside me. All the weeks. The days. *Him*. A farmer, now turned prince—and a very clever liar. I couldn't quite grasp it all. My thoughts were water slipping through my fingers.

He stepped forward, the beam of light shifting to his shoulders, but I had already seen his face, the guilt. "Lia, I know what you're thinking."

"No, Prince Rafferty. You have no idea what I'm thinking. I'm not even sure what I'm thinking." All I knew was that even now, as I shivered with doubt, my blood ran hot, spiking with every word and glance from him, the same feelings swirling in my belly as when we were in Terravin, as if nothing had changed. I wanted him desperately and completely.

He stepped forward, and the space between us suddenly vanished, the heat of his chest meeting mine, his arms strong around me, his lips warm and soft, every bit as sweet as I remembered. I soaked him in, relieved, thankful—angry. A farmer's lips, a prince's lips—a stranger's lips. The one true thing I thought I had was gone.

I pressed closer to him, telling myself that a few lies compared to everything else didn't matter. He had risked his life coming here for me. He was still at terrible risk. Neither of us might survive the night. But it was there, hard and ugly between us. He had lied. He had manipulated me. To what purpose? What game was he playing? Was he here for *me* or for Princess Arabella? I pushed away. Looked at him. Swung. The hard *slap* of my hand on his face rang through the room.

He reached up, rubbing his cheek, turning his head to the

side. "I have to admit, that wasn't exactly the greeting I envisioned after all those miles of chasing you across the continent. Can we go back to the kissing part?"

"You lied to me."

I saw his back stiffen, the posture, the *prince*, the person he really was. "I seem to recall it was a mutual endeavor."

"But you knew who I was all along."

"Lia—"

"Rafe, this may not seem important to you, but it's terribly important to me. I ran from Civica because for once in my life, I wanted to be loved for who I was—not what I was and not because a piece of paper commanded it. I could be dead by the end of the day, but with my last dying breath, I *need* to know. Who did you really come here for?"

His bewildered expression turned to one of irritation. "Isn't it obvious?"

"No!" I said. "If I had truly been a tavern maid, would you still have come? What was my true worth to you? Would you have given me a second glance if you hadn't known I was Princess Arabella?"

"Lia, that's an impossible question. I only went to Terravin because—"

"I was a political embarrassment? A challenge? A curiosity?"

"Yes!" he snapped. "You were all those things! A challenge and an embarrassment! At first. But then—"

"What if you *hadn't* found Princess Arabella at all? What if you'd only found me, a tavern maid named Lia?"

"Then I wouldn't be here right now. I'd be in Terravin kissing the most infuriating girl I ever laid my eyes on, and not even two kingdoms could tear me away." He stepped closer and hesitantly cradled my face in his hands. "But the fact is, I came for *you*, Lia, no matter who or what you are, and I don't care what mistakes I made or what mistakes you made. I'd make every single one again, if that was the only way to be with you."

His eyes sparked with frustration. "I want to explain everything. I want to spend a lifetime with you making up for the lies I told, but right now we don't have time. They could be back for either of us any minute. We have to get our stories straight and make our plans."

A lifetime. My thoughts turned liquid, the warmth of the word *lifetime* flooding through me. The hopes and dreams that I had painfully pushed away surged once more. Of course, he was right. What was most important was to figure out what we were going to do. I couldn't stand to watch him die too. The deaths of Walther and Greta and a whole company of men were already too much to bear.

"I have help coming," he said, already moving on. "We just have to hold out until they get here." He was confident, sure of himself the way a prince might be. Or a well-trained soldier. How had I not seen this side of him before? His troops were coming.

"How many?" I asked.

"Four."

I felt my hopes rise. "Four thousand?"

His expression sobered. "No. Four."

"You mean four hundred?"

He shook his head.

"Four? Total?" I repeated.

"Lia, I know how it sounds, but trust me, these four—they're the best."

My hope fell as quickly as it had sprung. Four hundred soldiers couldn't get us out of here, much less four. I wasn't able to hide my skepticism, and a weak laugh escaped my lips. I circled the small room, shaking my head. "We're trapped here on this side of a raging river with thousands of people who hate us. What can four people do?"

"Six," he corrected. "With you and me, there are six." His voice was plaintive, and when he stepped toward me, he winced, holding his ribs.

"What happened?" I asked. "They've hurt you."

"Just a little gift from the guards. They're not fond of Dalbreck swine. They made sure I understood that. Several times." He held his side, taking a slow shallow breath. "They're only bruises. I'm all right."

"No," I said. "You're obviously not." I pushed away his hand and pulled up his shirt. Even in the dim light, I could see the purple bruises that covered his ribs. I recalculated the odds. Five against thousands. I dragged the stool over and made him sit, then ripped strips from my already shredded skirt. I carefully began wrapping his middle to stabilize his movement. I was reminded of the scars on Kaden's back. These people were savages. "You shouldn't have come, Rafe. This is my problem. I brought it on when I—"

"I'm fine," he said. "Stop worrying. I've taken worse tumbles on my horse, and this is nothing compared to what you've been through." He reached out and squeezed my hand. "I'm sorry, Lia. They told me about your brother."

The bitterness rolled up in my throat again. There were things I never thought would happen, much less have to witness. Watching my brother be slaughtered right before my eyes was the worst of them. I drew my hand away, wiping it on my tattered skirt. It felt wrong to have the warmth of Rafe's hands on my fingertips when I spoke of Walther, who lay cold in the ground. "You mean they laughed about my brother. I listened to them on the road for five days, gloating over how easily they fell."

"They said you buried them. All of them."

I stared at the weak beams of light filtering through the slits, trying to see anything but Walther's sightless eyes staring into the sky and my fingers closing them for the last time. "I wish you could have known him," I said. "My brother was going to be a great king one day. He was kind and patient in all ways, and he believed in me the way no one else did. He—" I turned to face Rafe. "He rode with a company of thirty-two—the strongest, bravest soldiers of Morrighan. I watched every one of them die. They were outnumbered five to one. It was a massacre."

The protective curtain I had drawn around myself was torn away, and sickening heat crawled over my skin. I smelled the sweat of their bodies. *Pieces of bodies.* I had gathered them all so nothing was left for the animals, then dropped to my knees thirty-three times to pray. My words spilled loose, bleeding from somewhere inside, thirty-three cries for mercy, thirty-three good-byes. And then the earth, soaked with their blood, swallowed them up, practiced, and they were gone. This was not the first time. It wouldn't be the last.

"Lia?"

I looked at Rafe. Tall and strong like my brother. Confident like my brother. *He had only four coming.* How much more could I face losing?

"Yes," I answered. "I buried them all."

He reached out and pulled me to his side. I sat on the straw next to him. "We can do this," he said. "We just have to buy time until my men get here."

"How long before your soldiers come?" I asked.

"A few days. Maybe more. It depends how far south they have to ride in order to cross the river. But I know they'll be here as soon as they can. They're the best, Lia. The best of Dalbreck soldiers. Two of them speak the language fluently. They'll find their way in."

I wanted to say that getting in wasn't the problem. We had found our way in. The problem was getting out again. But I held my tongue and nodded, trying to appear encouraged. If his plan didn't work, mine would. I had killed a horse this morning. Maybe by tonight I would kill another beast.

"There might be another way," I said. "They have weapons in the Sanctum. They'd never miss one. I might be able to slip a knife beneath my skirt."

"No," he said firmly. "It's too dangerous. If they—"

"Rafe, their leader is responsible for killing my brother, his wife, and a whole company of men. It's only a matter of time before he goes back for more. He has to be—"

"His soldiers killed them, Lia. What good would killing one man do? You can't take on a whole army with a single knife, especially in our positions. Right now our only goal is to get out of here alive."

We were at odds. In my head, I knew he was right, but a deeper, darker part of me still hungered for more than escape.

He grabbed my arm, demanding an answer. "Do you hear me? You can't do anyone any good if you're dead. Be patient. My soldiers will come and then we'll get out of this together."

Me, patient, four soldiers. The words together were lunacy. But I conceded, because even without the four, Rafe and I needed each other, and that was what mattered right now. We sat on the mattress of straw and made our plans, what we would tell them, what we wouldn't, and the deceptions we would have to construct until help arrived. An alliance at last—the one our fathers had tried to procure all along. I told him everything I already knew of the Komizar, the Sanctum, and the halls they had dragged me through. Every detail could be important.

"Be careful. Watch your words," I said. "Even your movements. He misses nothing. He's sharp-eyed even when he appears otherwise."

There were some things I held back. Rafe's plans were metal and flesh, floor and fist, all things solid. Mine were things unseen, fever and chill, blood and justice, the things that crouched low in my gut.

In the middle of whispering our plans, he paused suddenly and reached out, his thumb gently tracing a line across the crest of my cheek. "I was afraid—" He swallowed and looked down, clearing his throat. His jaw twitched, and I thought I would break watching him. When he looked back at me, his eyes crackled with anger. "I know what burns in you, Lia. They'll pay for this. All of it. I promise. One day they'll pay."

But I knew what he meant. That Kaden would pay.

We heard footsteps approaching and quickly moved apart. He looked at me, the deep blue ice of his eyes cutting through the shadows. "Lia, I know your feelings about me may have changed. I deceived you. I'm not the farmer I claimed to be, but I hope I can make you fall in love with me again, this time as a prince, one day at a time. We've had a terrible start—it doesn't mean we can't have a better ending."

I stared at him, his gaze swallowing me whole, and I opened my mouth to speak, but every word still swam in my head. *Fall in love with me again . . . this time as a prince.*

The door banged open, and two guards came in. "You," they said, pointing to me, and I barely had time to get to my feet before they dragged me away.

CHAPTER FIVE

"DOWN YOU GO, GIRL."

I was dunked into a tub of ice-cold water, my head held below the surface as forceful hands scrubbed my scalp. I came up sputtering for a breath, choking on soapy water. Apparently the Komizar had found my appearance disgusting and especially offensive to his delicate nose, and ordered a quick cleanup. I was hauled out of the tub and ordered to dry myself with a piece of cloth no bigger than a handkerchief. A young woman whom the others called Calantha supervised my humiliating bath. She threw something at me. "Put this on."

I looked at the heap of cloth at my feet. It was a rough, shapeless sack that appeared more suited to stuffing with straw than a body. "I will not."

"You will if you want to live."

There was no hint of anger in her tone. Only fact. Her gaze was unnerving. She wore a patch over one eye. The black ribbon holding it in place contrasted with her strange, colorless dead white hair. The patch itself was startling, almost impossible to look away from. It was sewn with tiny polished beads to give the appearance of a bright blue eye staring straight ahead. Decorative tattooed lines swirled out from beneath the patch, making one side of her face a piece of artwork. I wondered why she drew attention to what others might see as a weakness.

"Now," she said.

I tore my gaze from her unsettling stare and snatched the rough cloth from the floor, holding it up for a better view. "He wants me to wear this?"

"This isn't Morrighan."

"Nor am I a sack of potatoes."

Her single eye narrowed, and she laughed. "You'd be far more valuable if you were."

If the Komizar thought this would demean me, he was wrong. I was well beyond nursing any kind of pride now. I threw the cloth over my head. It was loose and difficult to keep on my shoulders, and I had to hold up the excess length to keep from tripping. The coarse fabric scratched my skin. Calantha threw a length of rope at me. "This might help keep things in place."

"Lovely," I said, returning her smirk, and proceeded to tuck and fold the loose fabric as best I could, then secure it with the rope around my waist.

My bare feet were freezing on the stone floor, but my boots

had been taken away, and I didn't expect to see them again. I tried to suppress a shiver and nodded to indicate I was ready.

"Be grateful, Princess," she said, eerily tracing a finger over her sightless jeweled eye. "I've seen him do far worse to those who defy him."

CHAPTER SIX

PAULINE

THE LAST LEG OF THE TRIP TO CIVICA HAD BEEN GRUELING.
A driving rain had overtaken us near Derryvale, and we were
forced to take shelter in an abandoned barn for three days, sharing
our quarters with an owl and a feral cat. Between the two of them,
there were at least no rodents. Every day that passed idle made
my anxiety grow. Lia was surely in Venda by now if that was
where Kaden was taking her. I tried not to dwell on the other
possibility—that she was already dead.

It had all happened so quickly, I hadn't quite grasped it at
the time. *Kaden took her. Kaden was one of them.* Kaden, whom I had
favored over Rafe. I'd actually made the mistake of nudging
her in his direction. I had liked his calm demeanor. I had told her
his eyes were kind. Everything about him had seemed kind. How
could I have been so wrong? It shook me somewhere deep. I had

always thought myself a good judge of character, but Kaden was the opposite of kind. He was an assassin. That's what Gwyneth claimed. How she would know, I wasn't certain, but Gwyneth had many talents, and pulling illicit information from tavern customers was surely among them.

We had decided it was safer to stay at an inn in one of the several hamlets just outside the city walls. While no one would know Gwyneth, they'd know me, and I needed to keep my presence hidden until I had at least arranged a meeting with the Lord Viceregent. I was a very visible figure of the queen's court, and probably facing treason charges myself for helping Lia run away. Of all the cabinet, the Viceregent had always been the kindest to Lia, solicitous, even. He seemed to understand her difficult place in court. If I explained her plight, surely he could break the news to the king in the most advantageous way. What father wouldn't at least try to save his daughter, no matter how she had defied him?

I hung back in the shadows with my hood drawn over my head while Gwyneth secured a room for us. I watched her conversing with the innkeeper, though I couldn't hear what was said. It seemed to take far longer than necessary. I felt a rolling quiver in my belly. It was a constant reminder of how much things had changed, how much time had passed, a reminder of Lia's promise, *we'll get through this together.* A reminder that time was running out. I kissed my fingers and lifted them to the gods. *Please bring her back.*

Some paper was passed between Gwyneth and the innkeeper. He eyed me briefly, perhaps wondering why the hood of my cloak was still drawn inside the inn, but he said nothing and finally shoved a key across the counter to Gwyneth.

The room was at the end of the hall, small, but with far greater comforts than the barn. Nove and Dieci were in the stable and seemed to appreciate having their own quarters and fresh barley to eat too. Money wasn't a problem. I had traded the jewels Lia gave me for coin in Luiseveque. Even Gwyneth was impressed at how easily I dealt with shady merchants in back rooms, but I had learned it all from Lia.

When I had shut the door behind us, I asked Gwyneth what had taken so long. Securing a room at Berdi's was a matter of agreeing on a price and pointing the guest to the room.

Gwyneth threw her bag on the bed. "I sent a note to the Chancellor requesting a meeting."

I caught my breath, unable to speak for a moment. "*You what? Against my wishes?* I already told you, he hates Lia."

She began unpacking, unruffled by my alarm. "I think it might be wiser to nose around through . . . more *discreet* channels, before we go straight to the second in power. If the Viceregent proves unhelpful, we're at a dead end."

I looked at her, a chill crawling across my shoulders. It was the second time she had suggested the Chancellor, and now she had gone ahead and acted without my consent. She seemed determined to draw the Chancellor into this. "Do you *know* the Chancellor, Gwyneth?"

She shrugged. "Hmm, maybe a little. Our paths crossed some time back."

"And you never thought to tell me before now?"

"I thought you might not take it well, and it seems I was right."

I dumped out my bag on the bed and shuffled through the pile, looking for my brush. I brushed my hair briskly, trying to untangle my thoughts, trying to appear in control when I felt anything but. She knew him *a little*? I didn't like or trust the Chancellor any more than Lia did. There wasn't anything about any of this that I liked.

"I've decided. I'm going to go straight to the king," I said. "You can just stay put."

She grabbed my hand, stopping my strokes. "And how would you manage that? March through the citadelle and bang your brush on his chamber door? How far do you think you'd get? Or would you send a note? Everything goes through the Chancellor's office first anyway. Why not go straight to him in the first place?"

"I'm certain I can get an audience with the king one way or another."

"Of course you can. But don't forget, you were an accomplice in Lia's flight. You might very likely be speaking to him from a prison cell."

I knew she was right. "If that's what it takes."

Gwyneth sighed. "Noble, but let's see if we can avoid that. Let's nose around first."

"By talking to the Chancellor?"

She sat down on the bed and frowned. "Lia didn't tell you about me, did she?"

I swallowed, preparing myself for something I didn't want to know about Gwyneth's past. "Tell me what?"

"I used to be in the service of the realm. I was a purveyor of news."

"Which means?" I asked cautiously.

"I was a spy."

I closed my eyes. It was worse than I thought.

"Now, don't go getting all knotted up. It's not good for the baby. My being a spy—an *ex*-spy—isn't the end of the world. It might even come in handy."

Come in handy? I opened my eyes and saw her grinning at me.

She told me about the Eyes of the Realm, spies of Civica scattered throughout towns and manors in Morrighan, who relayed information back to the seat of power. At one time, she had needed the money and was good at drawing out information from patrons at an inn in Graceport where she cleaned rooms.

"So you spied for the king?" I asked.

She shrugged. "Maybe. I dealt only with the Chancellor. He—" Her expression darkened. "He was *persuasive*, and I was young and stupid."

Gwyneth was still young. She was only a handful of years older than me. But stupid? Never. She was sly and calculating and irreverent, things I was not. In my gut, I knew her skills could be useful in finding a sympathetic ear, but still I hesitated. I was afraid to be drawn into some network of spies, even if she claimed to no longer be part of it. *And what if she still was?*

It was almost as if she could see the thoughts parading through my mind.

"Pauline," she said firmly, "you're probably the most saintly, loyal person I've ever met, which can be admirable, but also quite annoying at times. It's time to knuckle down. No more playing nice girl. Do you want to help Lia or not?"

The only answer to that was *yes*.

No matter what I had to do.

CHAPTER SEVEN

THE WALLS CLOSED IN, THE PATH SEEMING TO NARROW with each footstep. I was led through a dark hall, up two flights of musty stairs, along another hall no wider than arms' breadth, three turns, then down several steps. The inside of this fortress was as much a maze as it appeared to be from the outside, centuries of architecture mashed together.

This wasn't the path back to Sanctum Hall. I felt my heart quicken. Where were they taking me now? My hair was still damp on my shoulders, and my bare feet frigid on the cold floor. I memorized my path, certain it would matter at some point. Everything mattered. Every detail. Every flutter of an eyelash. Of all people right now, I longed for Gwyneth, so smooth in all her movements, and so good at hiding her secrets with a smile—except when it came to things she cared about, like Simone. That was when lies showed on Gwyneth's face. Even now, I was learning from her. Everything I still cared about had to cease to show on my face.

On our last turn, we walked down a drafty passageway headed toward a large double door. Its thick black hinges branched out in tangled thorns. The guards knocked, and I heard the heavy slide of a bolt unlatched within. I was thrown forward because the guards seemed to know no other way of releasing prisoners, but this time I was ready and only stumbled.

I entered a silent room. My gaze fell on Kaden first, his jaw tight, the telltale vein rising on his neck as he took in my new coarse attire. Was it shame or anger I saw flashing through his eyes? But I also noticed he had bathed—and changed. With his Morrighese disguise discarded, he looked like one of them now, an animal of a different stripe. He wore a loose shirt cut in their style, and a trail of bones hung from his weapon belt. This had been the real Kaden all along.

And then I saw Rafe. His back was to me, and his hands were shackled behind him with a guard close at his side. I looked away quickly and settled my gaze on the Komizar instead.

"Perfect timing, Princess," he said. "Your farmhand just arrived too." He waved me forward until I was standing near Rafe.

The Komizar still wore the baldrick, and now Walther's sword dangled from it too. He grinned as I took it in. I molded my gaze to steel. From this moment forward, I would make my brother's pillaged goods my strength rather than my weakness.

He stepped to the center of the room and threw his hands out to his sides. "It's a historic day in Venda, my brethren. Not one, but two prisoners." He still spoke in Morrighese, I assumed for our benefit. I didn't know if Rafe understood Vendan or not. I cursed myself for not asking when we were in the holding room together. Details like this could matter later on. The Komizar turned his attention to me and Rafe. "I hope you both appreciate your good fortune to even be prisoners. It's a rare privilege—though it may be fleeting." His voice was playful, his expression almost cheerful. He walked closer to me, lifted a strand of damp hair from my shoulder, then dropped it with distaste. "I already know why you're here. A royal with a supposed gift that my Assassin believes will be useful to Venda." He shrugged. "Time will tell."

He turned to Rafe. "But, you . . . tell me why I shouldn't slice you from gizzard to gut right now and punish the soldiers who didn't kill you on sight."

"Because I have news for you that will benefit Venda." Rafe's answer was quick and confident.

The Komizar laughed in a way that made the room grow darker. "So I've heard." He walked over to the table in the center of the room and hoisted himself up on it, sitting on its edge with his legs dangling. He looked more like a swaggering ruffian sitting in a pub than a ruler. "Chievdar Stavik told me of your claim," he said. "But the soldiers tell me otherwise. A smitten farmhand, they call you, and the princess seemed to think you showed up just for her. I understand there was an entertaining embrace."

"I was a familiar face in a foreign land," Rafe answered. "I can't help that the girl latched on to me. But I'm not a fool when it comes to women. Pleasure is one thing; business is another. I wouldn't show up on a hostile doorstep over a mere summer distraction."

The Komizar's eyes flickered to me. I glared at Rafe.

"A distraction," the Komizar repeated, nodding. "So being a farmhand was only a ruse?"

"The prince sent me to find out if the girl really fled the wedding or if it was a planned retaliation all along, for past grievances. In case you aren't aware, Dalbreck's had a long, rocky relationship with our nearest neighbors. Shall I recite the entire history of petty actions perpetrated by Morrighan? However, the king's offer of marriage was a genuine effort to bury past grievances."

"And to create an alliance."

"Yes."

"To wield more power over us."

"Isn't that what every political move is about? Power and getting more of it?" Rafe's tone was cold, commanding, and unapologetic.

It seemed to give the Komizar pause. His eyes narrowed, and then one corner of his mouth lifted in an amused grin. "You look far more like a farmhand to me than the grand emissary of a prince." He turned around, scanning the room. "Griz!" he yelled. "Where is he?"

One of the governors informed him that Griz was still in Sanctum Hall, and a guard was sent to retrieve him. The Komizar explained that Griz had seen the prince and his court when he was in Dalbreck at a public ceremony last year. He'd be able to identify Rafe as genuine or fake.

"Do you wish to change your story now? The truth would mean I could get to my evening meal sooner, and I'd be willing to make your death quick and relatively pain-free."

"My story stands," Rafe answered without hesitation.

Breathe, Lia. Breathe. I looked at Kaden and tried not to betray my panic, hoping for help. He owed me this. He returned my gaze, his head barely moving, *no*. I forgot. *Venda always comes first.* The fear rose in my chest, and I looked at the weapons belted at so many sides, the governors, the guards, the unidentified brethren of Venda. More than a dozen of them filled the room. Even if I were able to disarm one of them and kill another, what chance did Rafe and I have against all of them? Especially with Rafe's hands chained behind his back. I inched forward and then I saw Rafe flex one hand, a quiet signal. I stopped. The room remained silent, the seconds ticking by torturously, the Komizar seeming to enjoy every one. Then we heard the footsteps, the heavy tromp of a giant coming down the hall.

The door opened, and Griz entered.

"*Bedage akki,*" the Komizar called and slung his arm around Griz's shoulders. He walked him over to stand in front of Rafe, speaking in Vendan as he explained Rafe's claim. "You were at the ceremony and saw the prince and his personal court. Do you recognize this man?"

Griz squinted, studying Rafe. He shifted his footing, looking askance and appearing uncomfortable with all eyes on him.

"Hard to tell. It was a large crowd in the square. I was a long way back, but—" He scratched his head, taking a closer look. I saw the recognition in his eyes, and my stomach jumped to my throat.

"Well?" the Komizar asked.

Griz shot me a sideways glance. I stared at him, not breathing, frozen. He looked back at Rafe again, nodding in thought. "Yeah, I remember this one. He was standing right next to the prince, all fussed up in one of them frilly coats. Chummy they were. He and the prince laughed a few times." He nodded as if satisfied with his recollection and then his scarred brow twisted in a scowl. "Anything else?"

"That's all," the Komizar answered.

Griz glanced briefly at me once more before he turned and left.

I tried to let the trapped air in my chest out in an even steady breath. Had Griz just lied for me? Or did he lie for Rafe? *There are spies everywhere, Lia. One palm crosses another in return for watchful eyes.* But not Griz. That was impossible. He was so utterly *Vendan.* Still, I remembered that he had hidden his fluency in Morrighese from the others.

"So, frilly emissary boy," the Komizar said, "what's this important message from your prince?"

"As I said before, this is for your ears only."

The Komizar's eyes turned to fire. "Don't insult my brethren." The governors grumbled threats.

Rafe conceded. "The King of Dalbreck is dying. It's a matter of weeks, if not days. Until then, the prince's hands are tied. He can do nothing, but soon the hand of power will pass to him. When it does, things will be different. He wants to be ready. The prince and his father have very different ideas about alliances and power."

"What kind of ideas?"

"He's looking to the future. He thinks marriage alliances are primitive and sees an alliance with Venda to be far more beneficial to Dalbreck than one with Morrighan."

"And the benefit to Venda?"

"There's a port we want in Morrighan and a few miles of hills. The rest is yours."

"The prince has grand dreams."

"Is it worth it to have any other kind?"

"And how would we know this isn't another of Dalbreck's tricks?"

"Once his father is dead, the prince himself is coming to negotiate with you as a sign of good faith—but of course, by then he would be king."

"Here?" Kaden interjected. His tone was brittle with skepticism.

Rafe looked at him, keeping his expression even, but in the tick of a second, I saw the strain in his face. If his hands had been unshackled, I'm not sure he could have held himself back. How had I ever imagined that they were friends? "In a neutral area in the Cam Lanteux to be determined," Rafe answered, and looked back at the Komizar. "He'll send a messenger with details. But he wants you to be ready. The alliance will have to be quickly struck before Morrighan gets whiff of it."

The Komizar studied Rafe, drawing out the silence. He finally shook his head. "I've no reason to trust you or believe that the prince is any different from his treacherous father, or any of their plotting fathers before them. All of Dalbreck is enemy swine." He stood and walked around the room, his head bent in thought. "Still . . . it's an interesting game your prince plays—or that you play." He looked into the faces of the governors, Kaden, and others present as though opinions were being gathered, but no words were exchanged, only a few subtle nods. He turned and faced Rafe again. "A few weeks are little enough to play his game. It might even be amusing. If the prince's father isn't dead and a messenger doesn't arrive within a month, then his supremely foolish emissary will be sent back to the prince—a finger and foot at a time. In the meantime, I'll send my own riders to Dalbreck to confirm the king's poor health."

"I'd expect no less," Rafe answered.

The Komizar stepped closer, almost chest to chest with Rafe, with his hand resting on the hilt of Walther's sword. "What's your stake in this, Emissary Boy?"

"What else?" Rafe answered. "Power. The prince has made promises to me as well."

The Komizar smiled, and I saw a glint of admiration in his eyes.

I had listened to Rafe spill out lie after lie with such grace and ease I almost believed him myself, and I marveled at how easily he conjured them, but then I remembered how smoothly he had lied to me back in Terravin. This was not a new endeavor for him.

The Komizar told everyone our business there was finished and they should return to Sanctum Hall. He would follow shortly. A few more words were exchanged with this governor or that guard, without aid of a cabinet Timekeeper flashing his timepiece, and all done with a casual air at striking odds with the previous conversation. *Rafe would be sent back a piece at a time.* The guards led Rafe out, and the governors filed out behind him. Kaden reached to take hold of my arm.

The Komizar put his hand out. "I'll escort the princess," he said, stopping him. "We'll be along soon. I need a few minutes with her. To talk."

"I can wait," Kaden said.

"Alone." A dismissal, firm and final.

My blood ran cold. *Alone with the Komizar.*

Kaden glanced from him to me and then back again, still not moving, but I knew he'd be leaving, one way or another. It would be better if it was on my timing. My terms. *Now.* My stomach knotted in fear. *Now.*

"It's all right, Kaden," I said, forcing my words out clearly and firmly, ignoring the Komizar as if he weren't there. "You can go along."

A wedge perfectly aimed.

If Kaden left now, it would be on my orders, not on the Komizar's. The silence bore down, heavy and unexpected. Kaden looked at me, knowing what I had done. The boundary of loyalty had been pushed. He shook his head and left, the damage done, the heavy door rattling in his wake. It was a short-lived victory. Now I was alone in the room with the Komizar.

"So . . . you have a tongue after all."

I kept my eyes fixed on the door. "For those who deserve my words."

He jerked me around to face him. "For someone in your precarious position, you don't choose them wisely."

"So I've been told many times before."

One of his brows rose slightly as he studied me. "It's curious that you had no reaction when the emissary revealed Dalbreck's betrayal of Morrighan. Perhaps you don't care what happens to your own kingdom? Or maybe you saw no truth in the emissary's story?"

"On the contrary, Komizar, I believed every word. I simply didn't find it surprising. In case you aren't aware, my father put a bounty on my head because I fled from the marriage alliance. I've been betrayed by my own father, why not a kingdom? I'm weary of the treachery of all men."

He pulled me closer, his chest still decorated with the finest work of Morrighese artisans—a gift from Greta to Walther on their wedding day. Thick dark lashes lined his cool black eyes. An arrogant glint filled them. I wanted to scratch them out, but I had no nails. I wanted to draw my dagger, but they had taken that too. I glanced down at the sword at his side embedded with the red jasper of Morrighan, almost within my reach.

"So weary you'd be foolish?" he asked. "It's harder to kill a man than a horse, Princess." His grip on my arm tightened. "Do you know what happens when you kill the Komizar?"

"Everyone celebrates?"

A faint grin lit his face. "The job falls to you." He released my arm and walked over to the table, his hand resting near a deep gouge. "This is where I killed the last Komizar. I was eighteen at the time. That was eleven years ago. Kaden was just a boy. He barely stood to my navel. Small for his age. He'd been starved, but he managed to catch up under my care. A Komizar must raise up his own Rahtan, and he's been with me since the beginning. We have a long history between us. His loyalties to me run deep." His thumb rubbed the groove, as if recalling the moment it was made.

His scrutiny turned back to me, sharp-edged. "Do not try to wheedle your way between us. I'm allowing Kaden this diversion for now. My loyalty to him runs deep too, and you might make an interesting diversion for all of us. But make no mistake about it, you and your supposed gift are worth less than nothing to me. The emissary has a better chance of being alive at month's end than you do. So do not orchestrate games that you will lose."

His irritation fed me. My well-aimed wedge had hit its mark. *You are making me fonder of games by the minute*, I wanted to say. It was as if he could read my mind.

His eyes burned bright, molten with threat. "I will repeat, in case your dim royal ears didn't understand the first time, your position is precarious."

I returned his stare, knowing that soon I'd see his whole army of butchers wearing the swords of Morrighan at their hips, that for the rest of my life, I'd hear my brother's and his comrades' dying cries being thrown up a windswept cliff into my face, all because of him and his disregard for borders and ancient treaties.

"There's actually nothing precarious about my position,"

I said. "I'm wanted for treason in my homeland, and here you've taken my freedom, my dreams, and my brother's life. Everything I care about is gone, and you wear my dead brother's baldrick as proof. What more could you take from me?"

He reached up, wrapping his hand around my neck, his thumb gently tracing a line along the hollow of my throat. He pressed harder, and I felt the flutter of my pulse under his touch.

"Trust me, Princess," he whispered. "There's always more to take."

I weep for you, my brothers and sisters,
I weep for us all,
For though my days here can be counted,
Your years of struggle have just begun.

—Song of Venda

CHAPTER EIGHT

RAFE

I SAT AT THE TABLE DIRECTLY ACROSS FROM KADEN. Staring. Cutting him into small pieces with my eyes.

Why they'd brought me in here, I wasn't sure. Maybe they intended to feed me. Or perhaps let me watch them eat. My hands were still bound behind my back. Kaden sipped an ale, periodically eyeing me, stewing almost as much as I was, I guessed. He had seen Lia kiss me. It ate through him like a stomach worm.

Several of the governors milled around, some shoving my shoulder and encouraging me to drink up, then laughing at their thin joke. A full mug rested on the table in front of me. The only way I could drink was to suck at the foam like a pig at a trough. That was a show they'd have to wait a long time for—I wasn't that thirsty.

"Where is she?" I asked again.

I thought Kaden was going to answer with more silence, but then he sneered, "What do you care? I thought she was only a summer distraction."

"I'm not heartless. I don't want her hurt."

"Neither do I." He looked away, engaging a governor who stood just to his right.

A mere summer distraction. I stared at the sloshed foam puddling around the mug, thinking about Lia's glare again when I said the words, her lip lifted in disgust. Surely she was playing along. The glare was just to strengthen our position. She had to know why I said it. But if she was playing along, she played her part too well.

Something else ate at me too, something I had seen in her eyes, her movements, the tilt of her chin, something I had heard in the hardness of her voice when we were in the cell. It was a Lia I didn't know, one who spoke of knives and death. Just what had these animals put her through?

Kaden glared, his attention turned back to me again. The worm dug deeper. "Do you always take such an intimate interest in your prince's affairs?"

"Only when it suits me. Do you always dance with the girl you plan to murder?"

His jaw clenched. "I never liked you."

"I'm wounded."

A governor stumbled into the table, then righted himself. He realized it was Kaden he had bumped into and laughed. "The Komizar still holed up with that royal visitor? A blue blood has to be a first even for him." He winked and staggered away.

I leaned forward. "You left her *alone* with him?"

"Shut up, Emissary. You don't know anything."

I sat back. Strained against the shackles cutting into my wrists. Felt the burn at my temple. Wondered about all those weeks on the Cam Lanteux and everything Lia had had to endure.

"I know enough," I said.

I know when I get these chains off, I'm going to kill you.

CHAPTER NINE

CALANTHA ESCORTED ME BACK INTO SANCTUM HALL. There were pockets of laughter when I tripped on my sack dress. The Komizar took the rope belt away, saying it was a luxury I would have to earn. Yes, there was always more to take, and I had no doubt he would find things I didn't even know I valued and take them away piece by piece. I'd have to play the role he was painting for me for now, the pathetic royal getting her comeuppance.

I saw the Komizar's goal achieved, mirrored in the gawking faces that closed in around me. He had made me utterly ordinary in their eyes. Kaden pushed through a circle of governors who crowded around. Our eyes met, and something wrenched tight in my chest. How could he do this? Had he known I'd be paraded as an object of scorn—and still he brought me here? Was loyalty to any kingdom worth debasing someone you professed to love? I tugged on the sackcloth dress, trying to cover my shoulders. He pulled me from Calantha's clutch and away from the ogling eyes of the governors into the shadows behind a pillar. I pressed against it, grateful for something solid to lean on. He looked into my eyes, his lips half parted as if searching for something to say. Worry etched his face. I saw that he had wanted anything but this, and yet here we were—because of him. I couldn't make it easy for him. I wouldn't.

"So *this* was the life you promised for me? How wonderfully charming, Kaden."

Lines deepened around his eyes, his ever-present restraint tested. "Tomorrow will be better," he whispered. "I promise."

Servants hurried past us carrying platters piled with dark warm meats. I heard the brethren and governors muttering their hunger, and the low growl of heavy chairs being dragged across stone as they swarmed toward the table in the center of the room. Kaden and I remained planted behind the pillar. I saw one kind of sorrow in his eyes and felt another kind in my heart. He would pay for this like everyone else—he just didn't know it yet.

"The food is here," he finally murmured.

"Give me a moment, Kaden. Alone. I just need—"

He shook his head. "No, Lia, I can't."

"Please." My voice cracked. I bit my lower lip, trying to muster some scrap of calm. "Just so I can adjust the dress. Spare me some dignity." I tugged the fabric back over my shoulder.

He cast an awkward glance at my hand clutching a fistful of

fabric at my chest. "Don't do anything foolish, Lia," he said. "Come to the table when you're finished."

I nodded and he reluctantly left.

I bent down and ripped at the hemline, making a tear up to my knees, then tied the excess fabric up into a knot. I did the same at my neck, tying a smaller knot at my chest so my shoulders would remain covered. Hopefully the Komizar wouldn't consider knots a luxury too.

Dignity. My skin chafed under the coarse fabric. My toes ached with chill. I was dizzy with hunger. I didn't care a whit about dignity. That had been taken from me long ago. But I did need a clear, unfettered moment. That much wasn't a lie. Was such a thing possible here?

The gift is a delicate way of knowing. It's how the few remaining Ancients survived. Learn to be still and know.

Dihara's words swept through me. I had to find that place of stillness somehow. I leaned back against the pillar, hunting for the quiet I had found in the meadow. I closed my eyes. But peace was impossible to come by. What good was a gift if you couldn't summon it at will? I didn't need a quiet knowing. I needed something sharp and lethal.

My thoughts tumbled, angry and bitter, an avalanche of memory past and present, trying to find blame, to spread it around to every guilty party. I conjured a sip of poison for each one who had pushed me here, the Chancellor, the Scholar—even my own mother, who had knowingly suppressed my gift. Because of them I had suffered years of guilt for never being enough.

I opened my eyes, shivering, staring at the stained stone wall in front of me, unable to move. I was thousands of miles from who I was and who I wanted to be. My back pressed closer to the pillar, and I thought that maybe it was all that held me up—and then I felt something. A thrum. A pulse. Something running through the stone, delicate and distant. It reached into my spine, warming it, strumming, repetitive. Like a song. I pressed my hands flat against the stone, trying to absorb the faint beat, and heat spread to my chest, down to my arms, my feet. The song slowly faded, but the warmth stayed.

I stepped out from behind the pillar, vaguely aware of heads turning, whispers, someone shouting, but I was hypnotized by a thin, hazy figure on the far side of the hall, hidden in the shadows, waiting. *Waiting for me.* I squinted, trying to see the face, but none materialized.

A strong jerk pulling me to the side broke my attention, and when I looked back, the figure across the hall was gone. I blinked. Ulrix pushed me toward the table. "The Komizar said to sit down!"

Governors and servants alike were watching me. Some scowled, a few whispered to each other, and I saw some reach up and rub amulets strung around their necks. My eyes traveled the length of the table until they stopped at the Komizar. Not surprisingly, he looked at me with a grave warning plastered across his face. *Do not test me.* Had I caught their attention with a simple unfocused stare? Or when I squinted to see someone hiding in the shadows? Whatever I did, it didn't take much. The Komizar may have had zero regard for the gift, but at least a few of them were hungry for it, looking for any small sign.

The regard of a few bolstered me. I proceeded forward, leisurely, as if my torn sackcloth dress were a regal gown, lifting my chin and imagining Reena and Natiya beside me. My eyes swept one side of the table and then the other, trying to look directly into the eyes of as many of those present as I could. Searching them. Bringing them to my side. The Dragon wasn't the only one who could steal things. For the moment, I had the audience he so greatly treasured, but as I passed him to take my seat, I felt my chill return. He was the stealer of warmth as well as dreams, and I felt an icy sting at my neck, as if he knew the purpose of every move I made and had already calculated a countermove. The force of his presence was something solid and ancient, something twisted and determined, older than the Sanctum walls that surrounded us. He hadn't gotten to be the Komizar without reason.

I took the only empty seat left, one next to Kaden, and instantly knew it was the worst place to sit. Rafe sat directly across from me. His eyes were immediately upon me, cutting cobalt, bright against the grim, full of worry and anger, searching me, when all he should have done was look away. I gave him one pleading glance, hoping he understood, and I averted my gaze, praying to the gods that the Komizar hadn't seen.

Calantha sat next to Rafe, her baubled blue eye staring at me, her other milky blue eye scanning the table. She lifted the plate of bones, skulls, and teeth that had been set in front of her and sang out in Vendan. Some of the words I had never heard before.

"E cristav unter quiannad."

A hum. A pause. *"Meunter ijotande."*

She lifted the bones high over her head. *"Yaveen hal an ziadre."*

She laid the platter back on the table and added softly, *"Paviamma."*

And then, surprisingly, all the brethren responded in kind, and a solemn *paviamma* was echoed back to her.

Meunter. Never. *Ziadre.* Live. I wasn't sure what had just happened, but the tone had turned grave. A chant of some sort. It seemed to be said by rote. Was it the beginning of a dark barbaric ritual? All the frightening stories I had heard about barbarians as a child came flooding back to me. What were they going to do next?

I leaned close to Kaden and whispered, "What is this?" Calantha passed the platter down the table, and the brethren reached to take a bone or a skull.

"Only an acknowledgment of sacrifice," Kaden whispered back. "The bones are a reminder that every meal is a gift that came at cost to some creature. It is not taken without gratitude."

A remembrance? I watched as the platter was passed and fearsome warriors reached into the pile and attached bleached fragments to the slitted tethers at their sides. *Every meal is a gift.* I shook my head, trying to dispel the discord, to erase an explanation that didn't quite fit the space I had already created for it. I recalled the gaunt faces that had looked into mine as I passed through the city gates and the fear I had felt at hearing the bones rattle at their sides. My first impressions had planted dark thoughts of bloodthirsty barbarians showing off their savagery.

I didn't realize I was scowling until I saw the Komizar staring at me with a smug grin twisting his mouth. My ignorance was exposed, at least to him, but I had also caught his subtle observance of Kaden. A slow, casual perusal. It still ate at him. Kaden had followed my orders and not the Komizar's.

When the platter of bones was passed around me to a governor, I reached out and grabbed a bone. It was a piece of jaw with a tooth still anchored in it, boiled clean of every scrap of flesh. I felt Rafe watching me, but I was careful not to look his way. I stood and pulled a raveled string from my hem, then tied the bone and tooth around my neck.

"Can you recite the words too, Princess Arabella," the Komizar called out, "or are you only good at creating a show?" An invitation to speak to them in their own tongue? He had unwittingly played into my strength. I might not have known what every word meant, but I could repeat every one. A few would do. *"Meunter ijotande. Enade nay, sher Komizar, te mias wei etor azen urato chokabre."*

I spoke it flawlessly and, I was certain, with no hint of an accent. The room fell quiet.

Rafe stared at me, his mouth slightly open. I wasn't sure if he understood or not, but then Calantha leaned close to him whispering the essence of the words: *You're not, dear Komizar, the only one who has known hunger.* The Komizar shot her a condemning glance to silence her.

I looked at the long line of brethren that included Griz, Eben, Finch, and Malich. Their mouths, like Rafe's, hung open. I turned back to the Komizar. "And if you're going to address me with ridicule," I added, "I'll ask that you at least address me correctly. Jezelia. My name is Jezelia."

I waited, hoping for a reaction to my name, but there was none—not from the Komizar or anyone else. My bravado plummeted. None of them had recognized it. I lowered my gaze and sat down.

"Ah, I forgot, you royals are rich enough to have many names, just like winter coats. Jezelia! Well, Jezelia it is," the Komizar said, and lifted a mocking toast to me. Laughter rolled off tongues that only seconds ago I had silenced. Jests and more mocking toasts followed. He was accomplished at twisting moments to his purpose. He left everyone thinking about the excesses of royals, including their many names.

The meal began, and Kaden encouraged me to eat. I forced down a few bites, knowing that somewhere deep inside, I was starving, but so much already swirled in my belly, it was hard to feel the hunger anymore. The Komizar ordered Rafe's hands unchained so he could eat and then waxed eloquent on how the other kingdoms were finally taking proper notice of Venda, even sending royalty and their esteemed cabinet to dine with them. Though his tone was flippant and drew the laughter he sought, I saw him lean toward Rafe more than once and ask about the Dalbreck court. Rafe chose his words carefully. I found myself watching, mesmerized, noticing how he could go from shackled prisoner to shining emissary in a heartbeat.

Then I noticed Calantha lean in, pouring him more ale, even though he didn't ask for more. Was she trying to loosen his lips? Or was she attentive for other reasons? She was beautiful, in an unsettling way. An otherworldly way. Her colorless hair fell in long waves past her bare shoulders. Nothing about her seemed natural, including her long, slender fingers and painted nails. I wondered what position she held here at the Sanctum. There were other women in the hall, a few seated next to soldiers, many of the servants—and the slight figure I had seen in the shadows—that is, if it was a woman. But Calantha possessed a boldness, from her bright eye patch down to the delicate chains that jingled around her waist.

I was stunned to see Rafe smiling and playing up the role of the jaded emissary who only sought the best deal for himself. The Komizar soaked it up, even if he tried to maintain distance. Rafe knew just which words to drop and when to hold back with a measure of vagueness, keeping the Komizar's curiosity piqued. I wondered how the farmer I had fallen in love with could have so many sides I hadn't known. I watched his lips move, the faint lines fanning out from his eyes when he smiled, the breadth of his shoulders. *A prince.* How had I not even suspected? I recalled the scowl on his face that first night I had served him at the tavern—the bite of every word he spoke to me. I had left him at the altar. How angry he must have been to track me down all the way to the tavern—which meant he was also skilled. There was so much I still didn't know about him.

I glanced at the Komizar, who had fallen quiet, and found

his eyes fixed on me. I swallowed. How long had he been watching me? Had he seen me staring at Rafe?

He suddenly yawned, then leisurely slid his hand across the leather strap on his chest. "I'm sure our guests are getting tired, but where should I put them?" He explained at length that since they didn't take prisoners in Venda, they didn't have actual prisons, that justice was swift even for their own citizens. He weighed his various options, but I sensed he was leading us down a path he had already mapped. He said he could shove us both back into the holding room for the night, but it was damp and dreary, and there was only one small straw mattress for us to share. He looked at Kaden as he said it. "But there is an empty room not far from my own quarters that's secure." He sat back in his chair. "Yes," he said slowly, as if thinking it through, "I'll put the emissary there. But where should I put the princess where she'll be secure too?"

Malich called from the other end of the table. "She can stay with me. She won't go anywhere, and we still have a few things to discuss." The soldiers near him laughed.

Kaden pushed his chair back and stood, glaring at Malich. "She'll stay in my quarters," he said firmly.

The Komizar smiled. I didn't like where this game was leading. He rubbed his chin. "Or I could simply lock her up with the emissary? Maybe that would be best. Keep the prisoners together? Tell me, *Jezelia*, which would you prefer? I'll leave it up to you." His eyes rested on me, cold and challenging. Had my glares at the emissary been real or contrived? *There's always more that can be taken.* He was looking for something else I valued besides a rope around my waist.

My hands trembled in my lap beneath the table. I squeezed them into fists and straightened them again, forcing them to comply, to be convincing. I pushed back my chair and stood next to Kaden. I lifted my palm to his cheek, then drew his face to mine, kissing him long and passionately. His hands slid to my waist, pulling me closer. The room erupted into hoots and whistles. I slowly pulled away, looking into Kaden's surprised eyes.

"I've grown comfortable with the Assassin after the long ride across the Cam Lanteux," I said to the Komizar. "I'll stay with him, rather than that treacherous parasite." I shot Rafe one last glare. He returned it with a glance of cool rage. But he was alive. For now, he was something not worth taking from me.

CHAPTER TEN

KADEN'S ROOM WAS AT THE END OF A LONG DARK HALL. It had a small door with wide hinges frosted in rust and a lock in the shape of a boar's mouth. It didn't budge when he tried to push it open, as though the wood was swollen with the dampness, so he put his shoulder into it. It gave and swung open, banging into the wall. He held out his hand for me to go in first. I stepped in, hardly seeing the surroundings, only hearing the weighty thunk of the door closing behind us. I heard Kaden step closer and felt the heat of his body close behind me. The taste of his mouth was still fresh on my lips.

"This is it," he said simply, and I was grateful for the distraction. I looked around, finally taking in the expanse of the room.

"It's bigger than I expected," I said.

"A tower room," he answered, as if that explained it, but the room was large, and the outer wall curved, so maybe it did. I walked farther inside, stepping onto a black fur rug, my bare feet finally getting some relief from the cold floor. I wiggled my toes deep into the soft fleece and then my eyes landed on a bed. A very small one shoved up against the wall. I noticed that everything, in fact, was shoved up against the wall in a dull, orderly procession the way a soldier who only cared about practicality might arrange things. Next to the bed was a wooden barrel piled with folded blankets, a large trunk, a cold hearth, an empty fuel bin, a chest, and a water basin, followed by a line of mismatched trappings leaning against the wall side by side—a broom, wooden practice swords, three iron rods, a tall candlestick, and the very beleaguered boots he had worn across the Cam Lanteux, still caked with mud. Hanging overhead was a crude wooden chandelier, the oil in its lanterns aged to a deep tawny yellow. But then I saw details that didn't fit a soldier's quarters, their smallness suddenly larger than the room itself.

Several books were stacked beneath his bed. More proof that he had lied about not reading. But it was the trinkets that made my throat swell. On the other side of the room, bits of blue and green colored glass strung on braided leather hung from a beam. Tucked in the corner was a chair, and lying in front of it was a chunky rug woven of colorful rags and uncarded wool. *The gifts of the world. They come in many colors and strengths.* Dihara's rug. And then, lying in a shallow basket on the floor, were ribbons, a dozen at least of every color, painted with suns and stars and crescent moons. I walked closer and lifted one, letting the purple silk trail through my palm. I blinked back the sting in my eyes.

"They always sent me off with something when I left," Kaden explained.

But not this last time. Only a curse from sweet, gentle Natiya, hoping that my horse would kick stones in his teeth. He would never be welcome in the vagabond camp again.

Dread swept over me. Something loomed, even for the vagabonds. I had seen it in Dihara's eyes and felt it in the tremble of her hand on my cheek when she said good-bye. *Turn your ear to the wind. Stand strong.* Did she hear something whisper through the valley? I sensed it now, something creeping through the floors and walls, reaching up through pillars. An ending. Or maybe I was feeling my own mortality drawing near.

I heard Kaden's footsteps behind me and then felt his hands on my waist. They slowly circled around, pulling me to him.

I drew in a sharp breath.

His lips brushed my shoulder. "Lia, finally we can . . ."

I closed my eyes. I couldn't do this. I stepped away and whirled to face him.

He was smiling. His brows raised. A full, indulgent grin. He *knew*.

Guilt and anger stabbed me at the same time. I spun and walked to the trunk, throwing it open. The closest thing to a nightgown I could find was one of his oversized shirts. I snatched it out and turned. "And I'll take the bed!" I threw one of the folded blankets at him.

He caught it, laughing. "Don't be angry with me, Lia. Remember, I know the difference between a real kiss from you and one given only for the Komizar's benefit."

A real kiss. I couldn't deny what our first kiss had been.

He dropped the blanket onto the rug. "Our kiss in the meadow set the bar high, though I admit I'll always treasure this contrived one too." He reached up and touched the corner of his mouth, teasing, as if he was savoring the memory.

I looked at him, his eyes still lit with mischief, and something tugged inside me. I saw someone who, for a moment, forgot that he was the Assassin, the one who had dragged me here.

"Why did you play along?" I asked.

His smile faded. "It's been a long day. A hard day. I wanted to give you time. And maybe I hoped I wasn't just the lesser evil of your options."

He was perceptive, but not perceptive enough.

He pointed to the trunk. "If you dig a little deeper, you'll find some woolen socks too."

I dug to the bottom and found three pairs of long gray socks. He turned around for me, and I threw off the dress from hell that was lined with a thousand burrs. His shirt was warm and soft and fell to my knees, and his socks came up just past them.

"They look far better on you," he said when he turned around. He dragged the fur rug over near the bed and grabbed another blanket from the barrel, throwing it on the rug beside the other one. I used the washbasin in the corner while he prepared for bed, throwing off belts and boots, and lighting a candle. He told me that the door in the corner led to a chamber closet. It was a small room and far from luxurious, but compared to my last few nights camping amid hundreds of soldiers with barely a shred of privacy, it was perfection. It had hooks for towels and even another of Dihara's braided rugs that offered welcome warmth from the bare floor.

When I came out, he lowered the chandelier and extinguished the lanterns. The room flickered with the single golden candle, and I crawled into the narrow bed, staring at the ceiling above me dancing with long shadows. The wind howled outside and pounded at the wood shutters. I pulled the quilt higher around my chin. *The emissary has a better chance of being alive at month's end than you do.*

I rolled over and curled into a ball. Kaden lay on his back on the rug with his arms crossed behind his head, staring up at the ceiling. His shoulders were bare, the blanket only covering half of his chest. I could see the scars that he said didn't matter anymore but refused to talk about. I scooted closer to the edge of the bed.

"Tell me about the Sanctum, Kaden. Help me understand your world."

"What do you want to know?"

"Everything. The governors, the brethren, the others who live here."

He rolled over to face me, lifting up on one elbow. He told me the Sanctum was the innermost part of the city, a protected fortress set aside for the Council, who governed the kingdom of Venda. The Council comprised the Legion of Governors from the fourteen provinces of Venda, the ten Rahtan who were the Komizar's elite guard, the five *chievdars* who oversaw the army, and the Komizar himself. Thirty in all.

"Are you part of the Rahtan?"

He nodded. "Me, Griz, Malich, and seven others."

"What about Eben and Finch?"

"Eben's being groomed and will be Rahtan one day. Finch is one of the first guard who aid the Rahtan, but when he's not on duty, he lives outside of the Sanctum with his wife."

"And the other Rahtan?"

"Four of them were there tonight, Jorik, Theron, Darius, and Gurtan. The others are off meeting their assigned duties. *Rahtan* means 'to never fail.' That's what we're charged with, never failing in our duty, and we never do."

Except for me. I was his failure, unless I did prove to be of value to Venda, and it seemed that would be determined only by the Komizar.

"But does the Council really have any power?" I asked. "Doesn't the Komizar ultimately decide everything?"

He rolled to his back, his hands lacing behind his head again. "Think of your own father's cabinet. They advise him, present options, but doesn't he have final say?"

I thought about it, but I wasn't so sure. I had eavesdropped on cabinet meetings, boring affairs where decisions seemed already to be arrived at, cabinet members spewing off figures and facts in rote fashion. Rarely did a speech end in a question for my father to answer, and if he raised a question himself, the Viceregent, Chancellor, or some other cabinet member would step in and say they'd investigate further, and the meeting would move on.

"Does the Komizar have a wife? An heir?"

He grunted. "No wife, and if he has any children, they don't carry his name. In Venda power passes through spilled blood, not the inherited kind."

What the Komizar had told me was true. It was so foreign to the ways of Morrighan, and all the other kingdoms too.

"That makes no sense," I said. "You mean the position of Komizar is open to anyone who kills him? What's to stop someone on the Council from killing him and seizing the power himself?"

"It's a dangerous position to hold. The minute you do, there's a target on your back. Unless others see you as more valuable alive than dead, your chance of surviving until your next meal is slim. Few are willing to take the chance."

"It seems a brutal way to govern."

"It is. But it also means if you choose to lead, you must work very hard for Venda. And the Komizar does. For years in Venda there were bloodbaths. It takes a strong man to navigate that line and stay alive."

"How does he manage it?"

"Better than past Komizars. That's all that matters."

He went on to tell me about the various provinces, some large, some small, each with its own unique features and people. The governorship was passed down in the same way, through challenges when reigning governors grew weak or lazy. Most of the governors he liked, a few he despised, and a few were among the weak and lazy who might not be long for this world. The governors were supposed to spend alternate months in their provinces and the city, though most preferred the Sanctum to their own fortresses and extended their stays.

If this bleak city was preferable to their homes, I could only wonder how much more dismal those places must be. I questioned him about the strange architecture I had seen so far. He said Venda was a city built on a fallen one, reusing the available resources of the ruins. "It was a great city once. We're only just learning how great. Some think it held all the knowledge of the Ancients."

That was a rather lofty claim for such a wretched city. "What makes you think so?" I asked.

He told me the Ancients had vast and elaborate temples built far belowground, though he wasn't certain they had all always been below the surface and that maybe they had been buried by the devastation. He said every now and then, part of the city would collapse, literally falling in on itself when buried ruins below gave way. Sometimes that led to discoveries. He told me more about the many wings of the Sanctum and the paths that connected them. Sanctum Hall, the Tower quarters, and other meeting chambers were part of the main building, and the Council Wing was connected by tunnels or elevated walkways.

"But as large as the Sanctum may seem," he said, "it's only a small part of the city. The rest spreads for miles, and it continues to grow."

I remembered my first glimpse of it, rising up in the distance like a black eyeless monster. Even then, I felt the dark desperation of its construction, as if there were no tomorrows.

"Is there any other way to get in besides the bridge we crossed?" I asked.

He paused, staring at the beams above him. He knew what I really wanted to learn—if there was any other way out.

"No," he finally answered quietly. "There's no other way until the river widens hundreds of miles south of us and the current calms. But there are creatures in those waters that few will risk encountering, even on a raft." He rolled over and looked at me, lifting up on one arm. "Only the bridge, Lia."

A bridge that required at least a hundred men to raise and lower.

Our gazes were fixed, and the unstated question—*how do I get out of here?*—hovered between us. I finally moved on, asking more about the bridge's construction. It seemed a carefully wrought wonder, considering the hapless construction of the rest of the city.

He said the new bridge was finished two years ago. Before that there had only been a small and dangerous footbridge. Resources were limited in Venda, but the one thing they didn't lack was rock, and within rock were metals. They had learned ways of mixing them that made the metal stronger and impervious to the constant mist of the river.

It was no small task, extracting metals from rock, and I was surprised that they seemed to be accomplished at it. I had noticed the strange glint in the bracelets that Calantha wore, like nothing I had ever seen before—a beautiful blue-black metal that shone bright against her pale wrists. The circles of metal jingled down her arms when she lifted the platter of bones, like bells ringing in the Sacrista in Terravin. *Listen. The gods draw near.* For a people who discounted the blessings of the gods, the hush that had fallen when Calantha spoke had been startlingly devout.

"Kaden," I whispered, "when we were at dinner, and Calantha gave the blessing—you said it was an acknowledgment of sacrifice. What were the words? I understood a few, but some were new to me."

"You understand more than I thought you did. You surprised everyone when you spoke tonight."

"It shouldn't have been a surprise after my tirade this morning."

He grinned. "Speaking the choice words of Vendan is not the same thing as commanding the language."

"But there are still words that are foreign to me. None of you ever said that blessing over a meal in all our way across the Cam Lanteux."

"We've grown accustomed to living many different lives. Some of our ways we have to leave behind once we pass the borders of Venda."

"Tell me Calantha's prayer."

He sat up and faced me. The glow of the candle lit one side of his face. "*E cristav unter quiannad*," he said reverently. "A sacrifice ever remembered. *Meunter ijotande.* Never forgotten. *Yaveen hal an ziadre.* Another day we live."

The words bored into me and all the ways I had misinterpreted the wearing of the bones.

"Food can be scarce in Venda," he explained. "Especially in winter. The bones are a symbol of gratitude and a reminder that we live only by the sacrifice of even the smallest animal and by the combined sacrifices of many."

Meunter ijotande. I was shamed at the beauty of every syllable of what I had once called barbarian grunts. It was a strange emotion to feel side by side with the bitterness of my captivity.

There were so many times I had looked at Kaden back in Terravin and wondered what storm was passing through his eyes. I knew what at least part of that storm was now.

"I'm sorry," I whispered.

"For what?"

"For not understanding."

"Until you've lived here, how could you know? Venda is a different world."

"There was one more word. Everyone said it together at the end. *Paviamma.*"

His expression changed, his eyes searching mine and warmth lighting them. "It means—" He shook his head. "There's no direct translation in Morrighese for *paviamma*. It's a word of tenderness and has many meanings, depending on how it's used. Even the tone in which it's said can change its meaning. *Pavia, paviamas, paviamad, paviamande.* Friendship, thankfulness, care, mercy, forgiveness, love."

"It's a beautiful word," I whispered.

"Yes," he agreed. I watched his chest rise in a deep breath. He hesitated, as if he wanted to say more, but then he lay back down and looked up at the rafters. "We should get some sleep. The Komizar expects to see us early in the morning. Was there anything else you wanted to know?"

The Komizar expects. The warmth that had filled the room was swept away with a single sentence, and I pulled the quilt closer. "No," I whispered.

He reached out and snuffed the candle with his fingers.

But there was still a question stabbing me that I was afraid to ask. Would the Komizar really send Rafe home piece by piece? Deep down, I knew the answer. Vendans had cut a whole company of men to pieces, my own brother among them, a massacre, and the Komizar had praised them for it. *You did well, Chievdar.* What was one more emissary to him? All I could do was make sure he didn't perceive him as something valuable to take from me.

I turned toward the wall, unable to sleep, listening to Kaden's breathing and his restless turning. I wondered about his regret at the choices he had made and all the throats he hadn't held back from slitting. How much easier his life would be now if he had slit mine as he was ordered to do. The wind picked up, whistling through crevices, and I nestled deeper under the blankets, wondering about my own regrets to come, for the things I was yet to do.

The room closed in, dark and black and far from everything I had ever known. I felt like a child again, wishing I could curl into my mother's arms on a stormy night and she could whisper away my fears. The wind punched and thrashed against the shutters, unforgiving, and I felt something wet trickle down the side of my face. I reached up and swiped the salty wetness away.

How quaint.

How very quaint.

Like believing some things last forever.

A tear.

As if that could make a difference.

CHAPTER ELEVEN

KADEN

ENJOY YOUR PET FOR NOW.

Every aspect of the words ate at me.

Enjoy.

Seeing Lia's fear made it impossible to enjoy anything. Seeing her paraded through the hall in a sack made me sick in a way I hadn't been since I was a child. Why hadn't I thought it out? Was I as thick as Malich? Of course, the Komizar couldn't treat her as an honored guest. I hadn't expected that, but seeing her grasping at fabric to cover herself—

I slammed a cupboard shut and rummaged through another in the larder under the scrutinizing eye of the cook. She didn't approve of me raiding her kitchen.

"Here!" she snapped, slapping away my hand when I reached for a wheel of cheese. "I'll do it!" She grabbed a knife to cut off a chunk for me. I watched her move about the kitchen, gathering more food.

Your pet.

I knew how the Komizar perceived royals. I couldn't blame him. It was how I had perceived them too, but she wasn't selfish fluff wearing a crown. When she had defied all of us and killed Eben's horse, that wasn't fluff.

For now.

Temporary. Fleeting. Provisional. But bringing Lia to Venda was a forever move for me. An ending—and a beginning. Or maybe it was a return to some part of me I didn't want to die. *Don't do it.* The words had beat through me back in Terravin as I had watched her walk alone through the woods. They had tapped in my skull again as I had sat in the barn loft, drawing my knife across my whetstone.

I had never defied an order before, but I hadn't disregarded his command just because I fell for the charms of a girl. Lia was hardly charming. At least not in the usual way. There was something else that drew me to her. I'd thought just getting her here would be enough, and that once she was here, there'd be no reason to kill her. She'd be safe. She could be forgotten, and the Komizar could move on to his other plans. *I'll decide the best way to use her.* But now she could become part of those plans.

Lia's words on the battlefield had echoed through my head since the day she said them—*for evermore*—and for the first time, I was starting to understand how long that was. I was only nineteen, and it seemed I had lived two lifetimes already. Now I was beginning a third. A life where I had to learn new rules. Living in Venda and keeping Lia alive. If I had just done my job as I always had before, I wouldn't have to worry about any of this. Lia would be another forgotten notch on my belt. But now she was something else. Something that didn't fit into any of the rules of Venda.

She asks for another story, one to pass the time and fill her.

I search for the truth, the details of a world so long past now, I'm not sure it ever was.

> *Once upon a time, so very long ago,*
> *In an age before monsters and demons roamed the earth,*
> *A time when children ran free in meadows,*
> *And heavy fruit hung from trees,*
> *There were cities, large and beautiful, with sparkling towers that*
> *touched the sky.*
>> *Were they made of magic?*

I was only a child myself. I thought they could hold a whole world. To me they were made of—

> *Yes, they were spun of magic and light and the dreams of gods.*
>> *And there was a princess?*

I smile.

> *Yes, my child, a precious princess just like you. She had a*
> *garden filled with trees that hung with fruit as big as a man's*
> *fist.*

The child looks at me, doubtful.

She has never seen an apple but she has seen the fists of men.

> *Are there really such gardens, Ama?*

Not anymore.

> *Yes, my child, somewhere. And one day you will find them.*

—***The Last Testaments of Gaudrel***

CHAPTER TWELVE

I STARTLED AWAKE, GASPING FOR AIR, AND LOOKED around, taking in the stone walls, the wooden floor, the heavy quilt still covering me, and the man's shirt I wore for a night-gown. It wasn't a dream. I really was here. I glanced at the rug on the floor next to me, empty, the blankets from last night neatly folded and returned to the top of the barrel.

Kaden was gone.

There had been a storm last night, winds like I had never heard before, loose bits of the city battering against walls. I thought I would never sleep, but then when I did, I must have slept hard, drawn into dreams of endless rides across a savanna, lost in grass waving far over my head, and stumbling upon Pauline on her knees praying for me. Then I was back in Terravin again, Berdi bringing me bowls of warm broth, rubbing my forehead, whispering, *Look at the trouble you get into*, but then her face transformed into my mother's and she drew closer, her breath searing hot on my cheek—*You're a soldier now, Lia, a soldier in your father's army*. I thought I had sat up awake, but then beautiful, sweet Greta, a golden crown of braid circling about her head, walked toward me. Her eyes were blank, sightless, and blood dripped from her nose. She was trying to mouth *Walther*, but no sound would come out because an arrow pierced her throat.

But it was the last dream that actually woke me. It was hardly a dream at all, only a flash of color, a hint of movement, a sense I couldn't quite grasp. There was a cold, wide sky, a horse, and Rafe. I saw the side of his face, a cheekbone, his hair blowing in the wind, but I knew he was leaving. Rafe was going home. It should have been a comfort, but instead it felt like a terrible loss. I wasn't with him. He was leaving without me. I lay there gasping, wondering if it was only the Komizar's prediction haunting me. *The emissary has a better chance of being alive at month's end than you do.*

I threw back the quilt and jumped out of bed, inhaling deeply, trying to lift the weight on my chest. I looked around the room. I hadn't heard Kaden leave, but neither had I heard him the night he came to kill me in my cottage while I slept. Silence was his strength, while it was my weakness. I crossed the room to the door and tried it, but it was locked. I went to the window and pushed open the shutter. A blast of cold air hit me, and goose bumps shivered up my arms. A glistening, dripping city was laid out before me, a raw, smoky pinkness to it in the predawn light.

This was Venda.

The monster was just waking, the soft underbelly beginning

to rumble and stir. A horse hitched to a dray and led by a cloaked figure ambled down a narrow street below me. Far across the way, a woman swept a walk, water spraying out to the ground below. Dark, huddled figures stirred in shadows. The dim light bled onto the edges of parapets, dipped in crenelations, spilled across scaled walls and rutted muddy lanes, a reluctance to its slow crawl.

I heard a soft tap and turned. It was so faint I wasn't sure where it came from. The door or somewhere outside below me? Another soft tap. And then I heard the scrape of a key in the lock. The door eased open a few inches, the rusty hinges whining. Another soft tap. I grabbed one of the wooden practice swords leaning against the wall and raised it, ready to strike if necessary. "Come in," I called.

The door swung open. It was one of the boys I had seen last night pushing the carts into Sanctum Hall. His blond hair was chopped off in uneven chunks close to his head, and his large brown eyes grew wider when he saw the wooden sword in my hand. "Miz? I only brought your boots." He gingerly held them up as if he was afraid to startle me.

I lowered the sword. "I'm sorry. I didn't mean to—"

"You don't have to explain, Miz. It's good to be prepared. I could have been one of those monster men coming through the door." He giggled. "But that little sword couldn't knock their arse an inch."

I smiled. "No, I suppose not. You're one of the boys from last night, aren't you? The ones who brought in the carts."

He looked down, and red seeped across his cheeks. "I'm not a boy, Miz. I'm a—"

I caught my breath realizing my mistake. "A girl. Of course," I said, trying to find a way to take away her embarrassment. "I just woke up. I haven't quite brushed the sleep from my eyes yet."

She reached up and rubbed her short uneven hair. "Nah, it's the buggy hair. You can't work in the Sanctum if you've got vermin, and I ain't much good with a knife." She was willow thin, certainly not more than twelve, with no bloom of womanhood yet. Her shirt and trousers were the same drab brown as the rest of the boys'. "But one day, I'm going to grow it real long like yours, all pretty and braided like." She shifted from foot to foot, rubbing her skinny arms.

"What's your name?" I asked.

"Aster."

"Aster," I repeated. The same name as the powerful angel of destruction. But she looked more like a forlorn angel with badly clipped wings.

I listened to her distorted assessment of the angel Aster, clearly not what the Morrighese Holy Text revealed. "My bapa says Mama named me for an angel right before she drew her last breath. He said she smiled all full of the last glow, then called me Aster. That's the angel who showed Venda the way through the gates to the city. The saving angel, she's called. That's what—" She suddenly straightened, clamping her lips to a firm line. "I was warned not to prattle. I'm sorry, Miz. Here are your boots." She stepped forward formally, set them down in front of me, then took a stiff step back again.

"Where I'm from, Aster, sharing a few words isn't prattle. It's the polite and friendly thing to do. I hope you'll come and prattle with me every day." She grinned and skimmed her head again self-consciously. I looked at my boots, cleaned and neatly laced. "How did you come by them?" I asked.

I was pleased to learn that silence was not Aster's strength either. We had something in common. She told me she got them from Eben. He grabbed them just before they were being sent off to market. My clothes were already gone, but he snuck the boots out of the pile and cleaned them for me. He'd be whipped if anyone found out, but Eben was good at being sly, and she promised I didn't need to worry. "As far as those boots are concerned, they got up and walked off by themselves."

"Will you be whipped for bringing them to me?" I asked.

She looked down, the pink tingeing her cheeks again. "I'm not that brave, Miz. Sorry. I brought them on orders from the Assassin."

I knelt so I was eye to eye with her. "If you insist I call you Aster, then I insist you call me Lia. That's short for Jezelia. Can you do that, Aster?"

She nodded. And then for the first time, I noticed the ring on her thumb, so loose she had to hold her hand in a fist to keep from losing it. It was the ring of a Morrighese pageantry guard. She had taken a ring from the carts.

She saw me staring at it, and her mouth fell open. "It was my pick," she explained. "I won't keep it. I'll sell it at market, but just for overnight I wanted to feel its goldness all smooth on my skin. I rubbed that red stone all night, making wishes."

"What do you mean, Aster, your pick?"

"The Komizar always gives the barrow runners first pick of the booty."

"The governors pick after you?"

She nodded. "The whole Council goes after us. The Komizar makes sure of that. My bapa will be happy for my pick. The quarter-lords, they love rings. This might fetch us a whole sack of grain, and bapa can stretch a sack for a month."

I listened to the way she talked of the Komizar, more like a benefactor than a tyrant. "You said *always*. Are there many carts brought into the Sanctum?"

"No," she said. "Used to be just goods from the trading caravans every few months, but now there's war bounty. We've had six loads this month, but this was the biggest one. The others were only three or four barrowfuls."

War bounty. The patrols were being slaughtered. Small companies of men were riding to their deaths with no idea that the game had changed. They weren't chasing a few barbarians back behind borders any longer. They were being stalked by organized brigades. For what? Rings to give to servants? No, there was something else to it. Something important enough to send an assassin to kill me.

"Did I say something wrong, Miz?"

I looked back at Aster, still feeling dazed. She bit her lip, intent on my answer.

A sudden voice startled us. "The door's wide open. How long does it take to drop off one pair of boots?"

Neither of us had heard Kaden approaching. He stood in the doorway looking sternly at Aster.

"Not long," she gasped. "I just got here. Truly I did. I wasn't prattling." She squeezed past him, worried as a mouse with a cat on her tail, and we heard the echo of her footsteps running down the hall. Kaden smiled.

"You frightened her. Did you have to be so stern?" I asked.

His eyebrows rose, and he looked down at my hand. "I'm not the one holding a sword."

He closed the door behind him and walked across the room, setting a flask and basket down on one of the trunks. "I brought you some food so you don't have to dine in the hall. Eat and get dressed, and we'll go. The Komizar's expecting us."

"Get dressed? In what?"

He looked at the sack dress balled up on the floor.

"No," I said. "I'll wear the shirt I have on and a pair of your trousers."

"I'll talk to him, Lia, I promise, but for now just do what I—"

"He said I had to earn luxuries like clothes, but he didn't say how. I'll fight you for them." I waved the sword in circles at the floor, taunting him.

He shook his head. "No, Lia. That isn't a toy. You'd only end up getting hurt. Put it away." He spoke to me like I was Aster, a child who had no understanding of consequences. No, worse, like a royal who hadn't a grasp of anything. His tone was superior and dismissive and more Vendan than ever. Heat bristled at my temples.

"I've swung a stick before," I said. "What else is there to know?" I pursed my lips and looked at the sword with wide-eyed wonderment. "And this is the hilt, right?" I asked, touching the cross wood. "I played with these with my brothers when I was a child." I looked back at him, my jaw set. "Afraid?"

He grinned. "I warned you." He reached for the other sword leaning against the wall, and I lunged, whacking his shin.

"What are you doing?" he yelled, grimacing. He hopped on one leg while he clutched the injured one. "We haven't started yet!"

"Yes, we have! You started this months ago!" I said and swung again, hitting the same leg from the side. He seized the other sword and held it out to defend himself, hobbling in obvious pain. "You can't just—"

"Let me explain something to you, Kaden!" I said, circling around him. He limped around, trying to keep me in sight. "If this were a real sword, you'd already be bleeding out. You'd be faint, if you could stand at all, because my second strike would have cut your calf muscles and tendons and opened vital veins. All I'd have to do is keep you moving, and your heart would do the rest, pumping your blood out until you collapsed, which would be right about now."

He winced, holding his shin and at the same time keeping his sword ready to block other lunges. "Dammit, Lia!"

"You see, Kaden, maybe I lied. Maybe I wasn't just a child when I used one of these last, and maybe it wasn't play. Maybe my brothers taught me to fight dirty, to gain the advantage. Maybe they taught me to understand my weaknesses and strengths. I know I may not have the reach or the sheer power of someone like you, but I can easily beat you in other ways. And it seems I already have."

"Not yet." He lunged forward, advancing with rapid strikes that I managed to block until he backed me up against the wall. He grabbed my arm that held the sword and pinned it, then leaned against me, short of breath. "And now I have the advantage." He looked down at me, his breaths coming slower and deeper.

"No," I said. "You've bled out by now. You're already dead."

His eyes grazed my face, my lips, his breath hot on my cheek. "Not quite," he whispered.

"Do I wear your shirt and trousers or not?"

A hissing breath escaped beween his teeth. He released my arm and hobbled to the chair in the corner.

"I didn't hit you *that* hard," I said.

"No?" He sat down and pulled up his pant leg. Just above his boot, an egg-sized knot was already swelling. I knelt and looked at it. It was nasty. I had struck harder than I thought.

"Kaden, I'm—" I shook my head and looked up at him, searching for words to explain.

He sighed. "Your point is made."

I still wasn't sure that he understood why I was angered or why I attacked him. It wasn't just about clothes. "Kaden, I'm trapped in a city with thousands of people who hate everything about who I am. The Komizar demeaned me in front of your entire Council last night. The one thing I can't bear is that same derision from you. Haven't you learned anything about me yet? *Yes*, royals know how to do things beyond counting our twelve toes. You're all I have here. You're my only ally."

His eyes narrowed at the word *ally.* "What about Rafe?"

"What about him? He's a conniving accomplice to a prince

who'd probably like to see me dead more than anyone—a prince who's betraying my kingdom by proposing deals to yours, and Rafe is brokering the deal for his own benefit. Whatever I thought may have passed between us is exactly that. Past. He was an unfortunate distraction for me too and certainly not an ally. He's nothing to me but an ugly wart on my good judgment."

He studied my face and finally grinned. "And your judgment had a decidedly sharp aim."

I looked back at his growing knot. "Is there an icehouse in the Sanctum?"

He snorted. "This isn't Berdi's tavern, Lia." He limped over to the trunk and rummaged through it, pulling out some trousers and a wide leather belt. "These should do for now," he said, and he threw them on the bed.

As a precaution, I gathered up the sack dress from the floor, opened the shuttered window, and threw it out. "*Jabavé*," I grumbled after it. I brushed my hands with finality and turned back to him. At least one matter was settled—I would never again be wearing the dress of thorns.

I peeked in the basket he had brought. "What's so important that the Komizar has to see us this early?" I asked as I began eating the hard rolls and cheese. The memory of public executions in Morrighan surfaced. They had always taken place just after dawn. What if the Komizar hadn't believed Rafe's story after all?

"He's leaving to check on Balwood Province in the north. The governor didn't show, which likely means he's dead," Kaden answered. "But the Komizar has some matters here to settle before he goes."

Leaving. The word was like music—the best news I'd heard in months. Though I did worry what the matters were that needed settling. I finished eating, and Kaden stepped outside while I finished dressing. I noticed again the splintering cry of the hinges when he opened the door and wondered how I had slept through the noise when he left earlier.

It felt good to put my boots on again, *clean.* With clean socks to wear too. I would bless Eben for this tonight when I sang my remembrances. I said them every night now, almost as if I was saying them in Pauline's stead, as if she were here with me and we were on our way to Terravin about to begin a great adventure instead of me being here alone at the end of this one.

WE WALKED TO THE COUNCIL WING SQUARE. AGAIN WE passed through a maze of hallways, open courtyards, and narrow windowless paths with one lantern barely lighting the way to the next. Kaden told me the Sanctum was riddled with abandoned and forgotten passageways after centuries of being built and rebuilt, some with dead ends and deadly drops, so I should stay close. Many of the walls told stories of their ruin. The stacked rubble sometimes offered up the macabre, like a sculptured arm or a partially visible head of stone blankly staring out from the wall like an ageless prisoner, or a piece of engraved marble block with a note from another time, the letters dripping away like tears. But they were only stone, the same as any other, repurposed to build up the city, an available resource, as Kaden called them. Still, as we entered another dim passageway, I sensed something else and stopped, pretending to adjust the lace of my boot. I pressed my back against the wall. A beat. A warning. *A whisper.*

Was I simply spooked by a ghoulish hallway?

Jezelia, you're here.

I stood abruptly, almost losing my balance.

"Coming?" Kaden asked.

The thrum disappeared, but the air was cold in its wake. I looked around. Only the scuffle of our movement filled the passage. *Yes, spooked, that was all.* Kaden moved forward through the passage again, and I followed him. He was in his element, that was certain, as comfortable walking through this strange city as I was disoriented. How foreign Terravin must have been to him. *And yet it wasn't.*

He had easily fit in. His Morrighese was flawless, and he had sat back in the tavern ordering an ale like it was a second home to him. Was that why he thought I could just slip into this life as if my old one never existed? I wasn't a chameleon like Kaden, who could become a new person just by crossing a border.

We walked up a winding flight of stairs and emerged in a square similar to the one we'd arrived in yesterday, but of course it wasn't square—nothing in Venda was. On the far side, I could see stables with horses being led in and out by soldiers. Loose chickens scratched and strutted, feathers ruffling as they skipped to avoid the horses. Two spotted hogs rooted in a pen near us, and ravens twice the size of any in Morrighan squawked from their perch high on a tower overlooking the square. I spotted the Komizar in the distance, directing some wagons that were rolling through gates as if he were a sentry. For the leader of a kingdom, he seemed to have his hands in everything.

I didn't see Rafe, which brought me some uneasy relief. At least he wasn't here with a rope around his neck, but that didn't mean he was safe. Where had they put him? All I knew was that he was somewhere near the Komizar's quarters in a secure room. It might be no more than a barbaric cell. As we approached, the guards, governors, and Rahtan saw the Komizar stop and turn toward us. They turned too. I felt the weight of the Komizar's scrutiny. His eyes rolled over me and my new attire. When we stopped at the edge of the crowd, he strolled over to give me a more critical inspection. "Maybe I didn't make myself clear last night. Certain luxuries, like clothing and shoes, have to be earned."

"She earned them," Kaden said, nearly cutting off the Komizar's words.

There was a drawn-out hushed moment, and then the Komizar threw his head back and laughed. The others did too, boisterous guffaws, one governor punching Kaden in the shoulder. My cheeks burned. I wanted to kick Kaden's other shin, but his explanation kept the boots on my feet. Just like soldiers in a tavern, the governors enjoyed their coarse entertainment.

"Surprising," the Komizar said under his breath, shooting me a questioning glance. "Maybe royals do have some use, after all."

Calantha approached, followed by four soldiers leading horses. I recognized the Morrighese Ravians, more booty from the massacre. "These are the ones?" the Komizar asked.

"The worst of the lot," Calantha answered. "Alive but injured. Their wounds are festering."

"Take them to the Velte quarterlord for butchering," he ordered. "Make sure he distributes the meat fairly—and make sure they know it's a gift from the Sanctum."

I saw that the horses were hurt, but the injuries were gashes that could be cleaned and dressed by a surgeon—not mortal wounds. He dismissed her and walked over to the wagons, waving for the Council to follow him, but I saw Calantha's lone pale eye linger on him, the hesitation as she turned away herself. Longing? For *him*? I looked at the Komizar. As Gwyneth would say, he was easy enough on the eyes, and there was something undeniably magnetic about his presence. He exuded power. His manner was calculating and demanded awe. But longing? No. Perhaps it was something else I saw in her glance.

The drivers of the wagons were busy loosening tarps, and the Komizar spoke with a man carrying a ledger. He was a thin, scruffy fellow—and seemed oddly familiar. He spoke softly with the Komizar, keeping his whispers away from the governors' ears. I stepped behind the others, peeking through the backs of the Sanctum brethren, studying him.

"What is it?" Kaden whispered.

"Nothing," I answered, and it probably was. The drivers threw the tarps back, and a sickening thud hit my chest. Crates. Before the Komizar even pried one open, I knew what was inside. He pushed aside straw, pulling bottles from it and handing them out to the governors. He walked over to Kaden. "And I can't forget the Assassin, can I? Enjoy, my brother." He turned to look at me. "Why so pale, Princess? You don't enjoy the vintage of your own vineyards? I can assure you, the governors love it."

It was the revered Canjovese of the Morrighese vineyards.

Apparently raiding trading caravans was among the Komizar's many talents. This was how he secured his position. Procuring luxuries for his Council that only he seemed able to obtain: bottles of expensive wine for his governors that the Lesser Kingdoms paid great sums for, gifts of war booty for servants, fresh meat donated to the hungry.

But a full stomach was a full stomach. How could I argue with that? And my own father gave gifts to his cabinet, though he didn't raid caravans to get them. How many Morrighese drivers had died at the hands of raiders so the Komizar could indulge his governors? What else did they steal, and who did they kill to get it? The death list seemed to grow and grow.

He gave the Council free rein to rummage through the other crates in the remaining wagons and split it up among them, and then walked back over to us. He threw a small pouch to Kaden that jingled when it landed in his palm.

"Take her to the *jehendra* and get her some suitable clothes."

I looked at the Komizar suspiciously.

His brows rose innocently, and he raked his long dark locks from his face. He looked like a boy of seventeen instead of a man nearly thirty. *A Dragon of many faces.* And how well he wore them. "Don't worry, Princess," he said. "Just a gift from me to you."

Then why did it create a breath-sucking hollow in my stomach? Why the turnaround from a sack dress to a gift of new clothing? He always seemed to be a step ahead of me, knowing just how to push me off-kilter. Gifts always came with a price.

A soldier brought him his horse as a whole squad waited for him at the gate. He took the reins, called his good-byes, then added, "Kaden, you're the Keep in my absence. Walk with me to the gate. I have a few things to tell you."

I watched them walk away, the Komizar's arm slung over Kaden's shoulder, their heads nodding, conspiring. A frightening shiver skipped through me as if I were seeing ghosts. They could be my own brothers, Regan and Bryn, walking through the halls of Civica confiding a secret. The small wedge I had planted was already disappearing. They had a history together. Loyalty. The Komizar called him *brother*, as if they really were. I knew, even minutes ago when I had called Kaden an ally, that he wasn't—not as long as Venda came first.

CHAPTER THIRTEEN

KADEN

"SHE SPEAKS THE LANGUAGE WELL. HOW IS THAT possible?"

He hadn't shown his surprise last night when she spoke. He wouldn't. Surprise in front of the Council wasn't his way. In truth, I think he was rarely surprised by anything, but I heard it in his voice now. It was strange that I should feel a sense of pride. Just as I had underestimated Lia when I began tracking her, he had underestimated her too. Most royals barely knew where Venda was, much less spoke the tongue.

"She's gifted at languages," I explained, "and our time crossing the Cam Lanteux gave her plenty of opportunity to study ours."

He sighed dramatically. "Another gift? The princess is full of them—though I haven't seen evidence of the one you claim yet.

I wouldn't call that dizzy-eyed performance last night anything but a sham. Though maybe a useful one."

He left his last thought hanging in the air. A sham, his preference, because that he could control.

"I'll be gone a few weeks. No more. But if Tierny still hasn't shown by the time I get back, it doesn't bode well for him. It will be your turn to ride with a show of force and see if we have a challenger who needs to be brought into the fold. We can't have renegade governors when so much is at stake. Especially with the critical supplies we need coming from Arleston."

"Tierny is always late."

"Late or not, when I return, you go. And without her. Remember what I said. We aren't cocks guarding hens. We are the Rahtan."

The *Rahtan.* I was eleven the first time I repeated those words back to him. Younger even than Eben. By then, I had been under his protection for a year. He'd made sure I got double portions of food. At that point, my eyes were no longer sunken, the hollows in my cheeks had filled out, and meat was back on my scarred ribs. I had said the words with all the pride I heard in his voice now. *We are the Rahtan*, the united brothers, dauntless and enduring. From that moment, he had begun grooming me to become the next Assassin. I was awed and grateful for the trust he gave me.

My loyalty to him was probably greater than anyone's. He had slaughtered many to save my skinny bones. I owed him everything. He was the Assassin back then. Three Assassins had come and gone since, none of them surviving more than a few years.

At the age of fifteen, I was the youngest ever to claim the position. That was four years ago.

How much blood do you have on your hands, Kaden? How many people have you killed? I couldn't answer Lia because I didn't know the numbers. I knew only gurgled breaths. The half gasps that came too late. The hands that were too slow to draw the weapon poised at their side. I knew the startled eyes that took a piece of me with them before they closed. They had grown into one faceless blur. All I knew was that they were traitors who had infiltrated other kingdoms to escape justice, or officers at outposts, whose attacks were relentless and brutal, and who hunted down families like Eben's that tried to settle in the Cam Lanteux. But the work of an Assassin could only instill fear in the enemy, and perhaps slow the attacks. A marching army could stop them for good.

The Komizar stopped several yards short of the gate. "We can't let weakness take hold, and that brings me to my next matter," he said. "Three soldiers ran. We found them hiding with a camp of vagabonds. The vagabonds were dealt with for sheltering them, but the soldiers were brought back."

"Vagabonds? Which ones?"

"In the forests north of Reux Lau."

I took an easier breath. I shouldn't have been relieved that any vagabonds had perished, but I had a special fondness for Dihara and her clan. I knew Dihara was too smart to harbor traitors. Most vagabonds were. News of the harsh consequences meted out to a few traveled like wind through vagabond camps.

He told me the execution would be at the third bell in front of comrade soldiers, and I was to call the count.

Though a *chievdar* carried out the executions and staking, the Komizar or the Keep always gave the last interrogation, always called to the troops who witnessed for a yea or nay, always gave the final instruction for them to lay their heads on the block. Always gave the final nod. The count, it was called, the final steps that dealt justice.

"But remember, don't kill them too quickly. It goes a long way toward discouraging similar actions. Make sure they suffer. You'll take care of that, right, brother?"

I looked at him. Nodded. I always met my duty.

He gave me a hearty hug and walked away, but after only a few steps, he paused again and turned. "Oh, and make sure you feed the emissary. I think Ulrix will conveniently forget, and I don't want to return to a corpse. I'm not done with our royal ambassador. Yet."

CHAPTER FOURTEEN

I SPOTTED GRIZ LEADING A HORSE OUT OF THE STABLE. With Kaden's and the Komizar's backs still to me, I hurried over to intercept him. He saw me coming and stopped, his ever-present scowl receding.

"May I speak to you?" I asked. "Privately."

He looked to each side. "We're as alone as we're going to get."

I had no time for diplomacy. "Are you a spy?" I asked bluntly.

He stepped forward, his chin tucked to his chest. "No more talk of that," he grumbled low. His eyes darted to nearby governors talking in groups of three or four. "I did you a favor, girl. You saved my life and that of my comrades. I pay my debts. We're even now."

"I don't believe that's all it was, Griz. I saw your face. You cared."

"Don't make it out to be more than it was."

"But I still need your help."

"We're done, Princess. Do you understand that?"

But we couldn't be done. I still needed more help. "I could reveal to them all that you speak fluent Morrighese," I threatened. I was desperate for his help, even if I had to blackmail him to get it.

"And if you did that, you'd be condemning my whole family to death. Thirty-six of them. Brothers, sisters, cousins, their children. More than that whole company of men you watched die. Is that what you want?"

Thirty-six. I searched his scarred face and saw fear, true and real. I shook my head. "No," I whispered. "That's not what I want." I felt my hopes slump with another door closed. "Your secret is safe."

"And yours is as well."

At least I had confirmation that he knew Rafe's true identity. I was grateful that Griz had covered for him, but we needed so much more.

I opened my mouth to ask for one last bit of information, but he turned brusquely, his elbow deliberately catching my ribs. I doubled over, falling to one knee. He leaned down, a snarl on his face, but his voice was low and even. "We're being watched," he whispered. "Snap back at me."

"You stupid oaf!" I yelled. "Watch where you're going!"

"That's right," he whispered. "One bit of advice I can give you. You'd be wise to friend Aster. The urchin knows every crevice of the Sanctum as well as any mouse." He straightened and glared down at me. "Then stay out of my way!" he bellowed as he stormed away. A group of nearby governors laughed.

I glanced across the yard and saw it was Kaden who was watching us.

He walked over and asked what Griz had wanted. "Nothing," I answered. "He was only grunting and drooling over the haul of goods like everyone else."

"With good reason," Kaden answered. "It might be the last for a long while. Winter is near."

He made it sound like a door slamming shut. In Civica there wasn't a big difference between winter and summer, a few degrees, stronger winds, a heavier cloak, and rain. But it wasn't enough to stop commerce or traffic. And by my calculations, winter was still at least two months off. We were only just entering autumn, the last bloom of summer. Surely winter couldn't come any earlier to Venda than it did to Civica. But I felt the chill in the air, the tired glint of sun, already different from yesterday. *Winter is near.* Enough doors were already closed to me—I couldn't let this one shut too.

I FOLLOWED KADEN THROUGH THE SQUARE TO A GATE that led out of the Sanctum. He was taking me to the *jehendra* to get suitable clothes, as the Komizar had ordered. I stayed close to him, fearing the people outside the gates as much as those within. It was a mixed blessing to have the Komizar gone. It gave me breathing room—little passed his notice—but it also meant he was out of my reach. I wanted to ask Kaden about Rafe, where he was and how he had fared through the night, but I knew that would only make him doubt my pronouncement that I wanted nothing to do with the emissary, and if Kaden was suspicious, the Komizar would be too. I prayed the guards hadn't shown Rafe more of their distaste for Dalbreck swine. Maybe after last night's dinner and the Komizar's frequent attentions toward him, they would show more restraint.

We walked side by side, but I noticed an occasional limp in Kaden's gait. "I'm sorry about the leg," I said.

"As you said, there are no rules when it comes to survival. Your brothers taught you well."

I swallowed the tender knot in my throat. "Yes, they did."

"They taught you to throw the knife too?"

I had nearly forgotten about Finch and my near bull's-eye on his chest. Kaden obviously hadn't. "My brothers taught me a lot of things. Mostly just by being with them, watching, and absorbing."

"What else have you absorbed?"

"I guess you'll have to find out."

"I'm not sure my shins want to know."

I grinned. "I think your shins are safe for now."

He cleared his throat. "I apologize for my tone with you this morning. I know I was—"

"Arrogant? Condescending? Dismissive?"

He nodded. "But you know I don't feel that way about you. It's a language that's become part of me after so many years. Especially now that I'm back here. I—"

"Why? Are you ever going to tell me why you hate royals so? When you haven't ever known any but me?"

"I've known nobility, if not royalty. There isn't much difference."

"Of course you have," I mocked. "An assassin in court rubbing elbows with lords and ladies happens every day. Name names. Just one noble that you've met."

"This way," he said, grabbing my arm to lead me down an alleyway, using our sudden turn as a way to avoid my question. I suspected his answer was that he had known none, but he didn't want to admit it. He hated royals because all Vendans did. They were expected to. Especially certain powerful Vendans.

"Just so you know, Kaden, *your* revered leader plans to kill me. He told me so."

Kaden shook his head and held up the bag of coins the Komizar had tossed to him as if it were evidence to the contrary. "He's not going to kill you."

"Perhaps he just wants me well dressed when I'm hanging from the end of a rope."

"The Komizar doesn't hang people. He beheads them."

"Oh, *well*. That's a relief. Thank you for enlightening me."

"He's not going to kill you, Lia," he repeated. "Unless you do something stupid." He stopped and grabbed my arm. "You're *not* going to do something stupid, are you?" Passersby stopped and watched us. I realized they all recognized the Assassin. They knew who he was and gave him respectful distance.

I studied Kaden. Stupid was all a matter of perspective. "I'm only doing what you asked. Following your lead and trying to convince others of my gift."

He leaned in close, lowering his voice. "Use your displays sparingly, Lia, and never hold it over the Komizar's head like you did with Griz and Finch. You'll feel the backlash if you do. Let him use your gift as he sees fit."

"Help him perpetrate a sham, you mean?"

"And I'll repeat your own words: There are no rules when it comes to survival."

"What if it's not a sham?"

His expression darkened. I realized that in all our time across the Cam Lanteux, he had never once conceded that I might really have a gift, not even when I warned him about the bison stampede. Strangely, he used rumor of my gift as an excuse to keep me alive, without admitting any belief in it himself.

"Just do as he asks," Kaden finally said.

I offered a grudging nod, and we continued walking. It was almost as if he had a deeper regard for the gift than Griz and Finch. Was it the potential power it held that neither he nor the Komizar could control? Dihara would laugh at the idea of using the gift as the Komizar saw fit. She had balked when I suggested it. *The gift cannot be summoned, it is just that, a gift, a delicate way of knowing, a way as old as the universe itself.* A small sigh escaped my lips. *Delicate.* Oh how I wish it were a heavy spiked mace that I could wield instead.

Kaden went on to explain that the Komizar's threats were only his way of establishing boundaries and power with me. A little respect from me could go a long way.

"And his bag of coin is a bribe? Like the stolen wine he gives to the governors? Is he trying to buy my respect?"

Kaden looked sideways at me. "The Komizar has no need to buy anything. You should know that by now."

"The clothes I have on are just fine. I rather like your shirt and trousers."

"As do I, and my wardrobe isn't limitless. Besides, it swims on you, and if the Komizar wants you to have new clothes, you'll have new clothes. You don't want to insult his generosity. You said you wanted to understand my world. The *jehendra* will open your eyes to more of it."

Generosity? I tried to keep from choking. But Kaden had a certain blindness when it came to the Komizar. Or maybe he simply had the same unrealistic hope that Rafe had in his army of four—that together, against all odds, they could make everything right that was wrong in their world.

I trudged along next to him, swallowing my skepticism of the Komizar's generosity because understanding Kaden's world, which included the *jehendra*, just might help me get out of this godforsaken place. I probed about other things. "He said you were the Keep in his absence. What does that mean?"

"Not much. If a decision must be made while he's gone, it falls to me."

"That sounds like an important job."

"Not usually. The Komizar keeps a tight rein on affairs that concern Venda. But sometimes a quarterlord can't settle a dispute or a patrol has to be sent out."

"You can give orders to raise the bridge?"

"*Only* if necessary. And it won't be necessary." The Vendan loyalty was thick in his tone.

We walked silently, and I took in his city, its hum filling my ears. It was the sound of thousands of people pressed too close, a rising rumble of tasks that were laced with urgency. Eyes raked over us from doorways and patched-together hovels. I felt the gazes on our backs long after we passed. I was sure they somehow knew I was an outsider. When the alley narrowed, Vendans traveling in the opposite direction had to squeeze past us, and the bones on their belts clattered against the stone walls. People seemed to crowd every inch of this endless city. The stories that they bred like rabbits didn't seem far-fetched.

The alleyway finally opened up onto a wider street that buzzed with more people. The tall surrounding structures blocked the sun, and ramshackle huts balanced precariously on their ledges. The city was woven of a weft and warp that defied reason. Sometimes only a canvas wall trembling in the wind defined a living space. People lived where they could, overflowing dark smoky lanes and whittling out a space to call home.

Children followed after us, offering horse patties for fires, amulets strung on leather, or mice that wriggled in their pockets. Mice as pets? Would anyone actually pay for such a thing? But when one little boy described his as plump and meaty, I realized they weren't being sold for pets.

We walked for at least a mile before we reached a large open market. This was the *jehendra*. It was the widest open space I had seen in the city thus far, as large as three tourney fields. Only a few permanent structures filled it. The rest were sewn together like a colorful quilt. Some stalls were no more than an overturned crate to sell the smallest trinket. Bells, drums, and the strings of a zitarae strummed the air in a jangling beat that matched the city.

We passed a stall with skinned lambs hanging from hooks, flies getting the first taste. A little farther down, shallow clay pots brimming with powdered herbs were set out on blankets, women offering a pinch for free to lure us their way. Across the aisle, three-sided tents showed off piles of clothing, some of it threadbare and torn. Other stalls had freshly woven fabrics that seemed to rival those brought in on the Previzi wagons. Cages of scrawny bald doves cooed across rutted pathways to pens of fresh pink piglets. I saw row after row of wares, from food, to pottery, to darker shops in the permanent structures that offered unseen pleasures behind drawn curtains.

In contrast to this city painted in soot and weariness, the *jehendra* teemed with color and life. Though he said nothing, I felt Kaden studying me when I stopped at stalls and examined the goods. Was he fearful I would use the word *barbarian* with the same distaste as I had crossing the Cam Lanteux? Some of the offerings were the humblest of efforts, rags twisted into dolls or balls of rendered fat tied up in animal entrails.

I was tempted to spend the Komizar's coin on all manner of things besides clothing, and it was hard to walk away when earnest faces were hopeful I would buy their goods. I walked through a stall of talismans. Flat blue stones inlaid with white stars seemed to be the favored design, sometimes with a splash of red stone bleeding from the center, and I wondered if it hailed back to the story of the angel Aster.

I remembered what Kaden had said, that the one thing Venda was not short of was rock and metal. At least some Vendans didn't seem to be short on memory either. Their stories of history might not be accurate, but at least they had them—and some, like these artisans, revered them enough to fashion jewelry into remembrances.

That was one thing I hadn't heard this morning in Venda, the singing of remembrances that always greeted mornings throughout Morrighan. I'd never thought I would miss them, but maybe I just missed those who sang them: Pauline, Berdi, my brothers. Even my father never missed morning remembrances, singing of the braveries of Morrighan and the steadfastness of the chosen Remnant. I rubbed my thumb across the amulet, the inlaid star a remembrance as carefully wrought as any musical note.

"Here," Kaden said, and he flipped the merchant a coin. "She'll take that one."

The merchant put the talisman around my neck. "I knew you'd take it," he whispered in my ear. He stepped back, his gaze fixed on mine. His manner set me on edge, but perhaps it was the way of Vendan merchants to be so familiar.

"Wear it in good health," he said.

"I will. Thank you."

We continued down the path, Kaden leading the way, until we came to several tents in a row with clothing and fabrics hanging from poles. "One of those should have something for you," he said. "I'll wait here." He sat on the end of an empty cart and folded his arms, nodding toward the tents.

I walked past them nonchalantly, not sure which one to go into, especially since I had no interest in finding something "suitable" to wear. I perused from a distance, not committing to stepping inside any of them, but then I heard a small voice. "Miz! Miz!" From the darkness of a tent, a hand reached out and grabbed mine, pulling me inside.

I sucked in a startled breath but saw it was Aster. I asked what she was doing here, and she said this was her bapa's shop. "Not *his* shop proper, but he works here sometimes. Lifting things too heavy for Effiera. Not today, though, because he's sick, so he sent me, but Effiera doesn't much think that someone my size—" Aster clapped her hand over her mouth. "I'm sorry, Miz. There I go again. It doesn't matter why I'm here. Why are *you* here?"

Because I was yanked into your tent, I wanted to tease, but I knew Aster was self-conscious, and I didn't want to add to her insecurity. "The Komizar says I need suitable clothes."

Her eyes grew wide, as if the Komizar himself were standing there, and in the same instant, a squat woman bustled into the middle of the tent from behind a curtain stretched across the back.

"You came to the right place, then. I know just what he likes. I have—"

I set her straight immediately. I wasn't one of the Komizar's "special visitors." Aster enthusiastically offered more details about who I was. "She just got here! She's a *princess.* She came from a faraway land, and her name is Jezelia, but—"

"Hush, girl!" The woman looked back at me, chewing on something tucked inside her cheek, and I wondered if she was going to spit it at me now that she knew I came from the other side. She studied me for a long while.

"I think I have just what you need." She judged my measurements with a practiced eye and said she'd return shortly. She ordered Aster to keep me company in the meantime.

As soon as Effiera was gone, Aster squeezed her head through a slit in the side of the tent and let out a deafening whistle. In seconds, two bone-thin children smaller than Aster slipped through the flap. Like Aster, their hair was cut short to the scalp, and I wasn't sure if they were boys or girls, but their eyes were wide and hungry. Aster introduced the smaller one as Yvet, and the other was a boy named Zekiah. I noticed he was missing the tip of his forefinger on his left hand. The stump was red and swollen, as if the injury had happened only recently, and he rubbed it self-consciously with his other hand. At first they were too shy to speak, but then Yvet asked in a shaky voice if I had really been to other lands as Aster claimed. Aster looked at me with expectant eyes as if her reputation lay on the line.

"Yes, what Aster says is true," I said. "Would you like to hear about them?"

They nodded eagerly, and we all sat on the rug in the middle of the tent. I told them about forgotten cities in the middle of nowhere, savannas of copper grass that spread as wide as a sea, glittering ruins that shimmered for miles, meadows high in the mountains where the stars were so close you could touch their sparkling tails, and an old woman who spun star shimmer into thread on a great spinning wheel. I told them of bearded animals with heads like anvils that rode together in groups more numerous than the pebbles in a river, and of a mysterious tumbled city where springs flowed with water as sweet as nectar, streets gleamed gold, and the Ancients still cast their magic.

"Is that where you're from?" Yvet asked.

I looked at her, not sure how to answer. *Where was I from?* Strangely, it wasn't Civica that came to mind.

"No," I finally whispered. And then I told them about Terravin. "Once upon a time," I said, making it into a story as distant and removed as it now felt, "there was a princess, and her name was Arabella. She had to flee a terrible dragon that was chasing her, intending to make her his breakfast. She ran to a village that offered her protection." I told them of a bay as bright as sapphires, silver fish that jumped into nets, a woman who stirred up bottomless pots of stew, and cottages woven of rainbows and flowers, a land as magical as any princess could ever dream up. But then the dragon found her again, and she had to leave.

"Will the princess ever go back?" a new voice asked.

I looked up to my left, startled. Four more children had slipped in and crouched on their knees at the entrance of the tent.

"I think she'll try," I answered.

Effiera breezed in from behind, clapping her hands and shooing them off.

"Here we go," she said, and I turned to see three more women standing at the back of the tent, their arms piled with fabrics. Among them were soft leathers of every shade—tans, browns, and fawns, and some dyed in purples, greens, and reds. Another woman held accessories like belts, scarves, and scabbards in her arms.

My heart pounded, and I wasn't sure why, but then I knew—before they even unfolded them.

Barbarian clothes. These weren't like the ones Calantha wore, made of light and delicate fabrics, brought in on Previzi caravans. I looked at Effiera uncertainly. Her expression was resolute. I was sure it wasn't what the Komizar had in mind, but somehow these fabrics seemed right. It was the same strange feeling I had felt the first time I rounded the bend and saw Terravin. A feeling of rightness. Clothing, of course, was not the same as a home, I reminded myself. "All I need is something simple, trousers and a shirt. Clothes I can ride in," I said.

"And that you'll have, and a simple change of clothes as well," Effiera answered, and with a quick wave of her hand, the women moved in, a whirl of motion, and began measuring and pinning together a basic riding outfit.

KADEN AND I WALKED BACK TOWARD THE SANCTUM. Effiera promised to send the two outfits I had ordered with Aster later today after a few alterations had been made. The fear I had carried ever since I had crossed the bridge into Venda was momentarily lifted. My brief time in the tent, first with the children, and then with the women as they held up fabrics, vests, shirts, and trousers, was a soothing balm. I felt less like an outsider, and I hoped I could hang on to that feeling.

"It seems foolish to spend money on clothing when there's so much need elsewhere," I said, still questioning the Komizar's loose purse.

"How do you think Vendans go about their everyday lives? They have jobs and professions and mouths to feed. I gave Effiera twice what she would get from anyone else. Making clothing is how she survives."

"Effiera? Do you know every shopkeeper's name in Venda?"

"No. Just hers."

"So you've brought other young ladies to her?"

"As a matter of fact, I have."

He didn't elaborate, and his silence made me wonder who they were. More visitors of the Komizar's or young ladies of his own fancy?

"Why are we going back already?" I asked. "It's still early. I thought you wanted me to see your city. I've seen only a small part."

"The Komizar has some matters for me to look after in the Tomack quarter."

"Isn't that what the quarterlords are for?"

"Not this matter. It has to do with soldiers."

"I could go along with you."

"No."

His reply came hot and clipped and not like Kaden at all. I turned and gave him a long dissecting stare.

"I'll take you back another way," he offered. "Past some of the more interesting ruins."

A compromise, because whatever was in this Tomack quarter, he didn't want me to see it. Again we traveled down narrow lanes, alleyways, and some paths that seemed little more than rabbit trails, jumping over rain-washed gullies and slipping on trampled dead grass. We came at last to a wide, well-traveled street, and Kaden walked me over to a large cauldron bubbling over a fire. There were rough wooden benches scattered in a circle around it, and an old man offered mugs of the brew for a modest price.

"It's thannis," Kaden said. "A tea brewed from a weed." He bought one for each of us, and we sat down on one of the benches. "Thannis is another thing that Venda has in abundance," he explained. "It grows almost anywhere. Ledges, cracks, the rockiest of fields. Sometimes the farmers curse it. Once it takes hold, it's hard to stop it from spreading. Thannis is a survivor, like a Vendan." He said the leaves were purple, sprouting bright above the snows of winter, but in late autumn, for only a few days before seeding, it changed to bright gold. That was when it turned sweet, but also to poison. "A drink of the golden thannis will be your last."

I was glad to see ours was a strange purplish brew and not golden. I took a sip and spit it out. It tasted like dirt. Sour, horrible, moldy dirt.

Kaden laughed. "It's an acquired taste but a tradition in Venda, like the bones worn on our belts. It's said that thannis was all that kept Lady Venda and the early clans here alive those first few winters. In truth, it's probably all that kept me alive more than one winter. When other supplies run out, there's always thannis."

I braved another sip and forced a swallow down, then immediately tried to summon saliva to my mouth to wash the taste away. I was sure it wasn't a taste I'd ever acquire, not even in the bleakest of winters. I glanced up at the old man stirring the cauldron, singing a chant to passersby: *Thannis for the heart, thannis for the mind, thannis for the soul, thannis, live long the children of Venda.* He repeated it over and over, a snaking song with no beginning or end.

Hovering above the steam of the cauldron, I spotted someone standing on a distant high ledge watching me. A woman. Her figure seemed to ripple through the steam, hazy, fading, and then she vanished. She was simply gone. I blinked and looked down at my steaming cup of brew.

"Just what's in this?" I asked.

Kaden smiled. "Only a harmless weed, I promise." He called to the old man and asked him if he had any cream to sweeten my drink. He happily obliged, for though he nearly gave the thannis away, the cream, honey, or spirits to flavor it came at a greater cost. Even with a hefty dosing of cream, the thannis was only marginally palatable. The spirits might have helped more.

We sipped our drinks and watched children chasing after those who passed by, begging to do anything that might bring something in trade.

"They seem so young. Where are their parents?" I asked.

"Most have none, or their parents are on another street corner doing the same."

"Can't you do something for them?"

"I'm trying, Lia. So is the Komizar. But he can butcher only so many horses."

"And raid so many caravans. There are other ways of managing a kingdom."

He glanced at me, a smirk on his lips. "Are there?" His gaze turned back to the street. "When the ancient treaties were drawn and borders established, Venda was not part of those negotiations. The fertile lands of Venda were always few, and each year more fields have fallen fallow. Most of the countryside of Venda is far poorer than what you see here, which is why the city grows. They come searching for hope and a better life."

"Is this how you grew up? On the streets of Venda?"

He swilled down the last of his thannis and rose to return the mug to the old man. "No, I would have been lucky if I had."

"Lucky? Are your parents that bad?"

He stopped mid-step. "My mother was a saint."

Was.

I stared at him, a raised vein snaking at his temple. This was it. His weakness. The buried part of him that he refused to share. His parents.

"We need to go." He put his hand out, waiting for my empty mug. I wanted more answers, but I knew what it was like to ache with memories of a mother and father. My own mother had deceived me, trying to thwart my gift, and my father—

My stomach squeezed.

It was *only a single small notice in the village square.* Walther had told me that as if it might comfort me, but the notice was still a call for my arrest and return for treason, posted by my own father. Some lines should never be crossed, and he proved it when he hanged his own nephew. I still didn't know what role my father had played in the bounty hunter's attempt on my life. Maybe he'd seen it as a convenient way to eliminate a messy court hearing altogether. He knew my brothers would never forgive him if he executed me.

"Lia, your mug?"

I shook off the memory, handing him the mug, and we continued on our way. Here, as in the savanna, ruin and renewal lay side by side, and sometimes it was impossible to discern one from the other. A massive dome that must once have topped a great temple was sunk in rubble, and only a glimmer of carved stone peeked through the earth to reveal that it was more than a mound in the landscape. Next to it stone was piled upon stone, creating a pen for a goat. Animals were carefully guarded here, Kaden told me. They tended to disappear.

We walked on for a long way until Kaden finally stopped at one unassuming ruin, resting his hand on a tree that engulfed one wall like gnarled fingers. "This one used to reach higher than any tower in Venda."

"How would anyone know?" I looked at the partial walls that formed an enormous square. Trees grew atop the remains like twisted sentries. None of the actual remains were more than a dozen feet high anymore, and one wall was almost entirely gone. It seemed a fanciful notion to suppose that it once towered over the entire city. "It may have been only the walls of a manor," I said.

"It wasn't," Kaden said firmly. "It rose almost six hundred feet into the sky."

Six hundred feet? I grunted my disbelief.

"Documents were found that confirm it. As best as they can decipher, this was a monument to one of their leaders."

I didn't really know much about the Ancients' history before the devastation. Little was recorded in the Morrighan Holy Text—mostly just the aftermath. We knew only of their demise, and the scholars had collected the few relics that survived the centuries. Paper documents were rare. Paper was the first thing to crumble away, and according to the Holy Text, when the Ancients were trying to survive, it was the first thing they used for fuel. Survival trumped words.

Ancient documents that had been interpreted were even more rare. The scholars of Morrighan had years of schooling in such things. The Vendans seemed barely able to keep their people fed, never mind educating them in other tongues. How would they accomplish such an enormous task?

I looked back at the monument that had supposedly reached to the sky, now almost totally unrecognizable as anything man-made. Weeds choked every surface. A monument to a leader? Who had the Ancients wanted to immortalize? Whoever it was, the angel Aster, by order of the gods, had wiped it from memory. I thought about the ancient texts I had stolen from the Royal Scholar, still in my saddlebag, which was probably for sale in the *jehendra* by now. I'd probably never see the precious texts again, and I'd had time to translate only a single passage of the Last Testaments of Gaudrel. Were the rest of her words lost to me now? Maybe it didn't matter anymore. But as I gazed at the monument, the few words I had translated rang as clear as if Gaudrel whispered them to me now: *The things that last. The things that remain.* This great monument wasn't one of those things.

"There's another down this way and then we'll go back," Kaden said.

I looked to where he pointed. Great slabs of white shone in the distance. When we reached them, he said tunnels beneath the city had revealed that the ruin was mostly buried. Only the upper portion was exposed. These ruins were not from a tower, but a temple of a different sort. At its center was the enormous sculpted head and partial shoulders of a man. The face was not the perfect face of a god, nor that of an idealized soldier. It was oddly proportioned; forehead too wide, nose too large, protruding cheekbones that made him look starved. Maybe that was why I couldn't turn away—he was like a tribute to a people he would never know, someone from another time chiseled with the same hunger and want as those who lived here now. I reached up and ran my fingers over his cracked cheekbone, wondering who he was and why the Ancients wanted him remembered.

Broken slabs of the surrounding temple lay on the ground near him. One large piece was engraved, but most of the words had been melted away by time. The faint indentations of a few letters survived. I couldn't read it, but my finger traced the grooves, committing the forgotten lines to memory.

F REV R

I was struck with sadness looking at the forlorn figure and lost words. For the first time, I felt a sliver of gratitude for my hours spent studying the Morrighan Holy Text so that truth and history wouldn't be lost again.

"We should go," Kaden said. "We'll take another path, a faster way back."

I stepped away from the monument and looked around, waiting for his lead. We had taken so many turns, I wasn't sure which direction we even needed to go—and then it hit me, like open hands slapped against my shoulders, waking me up.

I stared at Kaden, realizing what he was doing.

He wasn't just kindly obliging me and showing me more of Venda. This had been part of his plan all along. He was deliberately confusing me—and it was working. I had no idea where the Sanctum was from here. He didn't want me becoming familiar with the tangle of streets, so he was taking yet another route back. The twists and turns and alleyways we followed weren't shortcuts—they were obstacles to finding my own way around this maze of a city.

I turned around, looking in different directions, trying to get my bearings. It was impossible. "You still don't trust me," I said.

His jaw was set, his eyes, dark stone. "My problem is, Lia, I know you too well. Like the day you used the bison stampede to separate us. You're always looking for opportunity. You barely made it that day. If you tried something like that here, you wouldn't make it at all. Trust me."

"Swim across the river? I'm not that stupid. What else would I try?"

He looked at me as if he was genuinely puzzled. "I don't know."

There are no rules when it comes to survival, I reminded myself as

I moved toward him. Each step was sharp-edged steel cutting through me, but I took his hand in mine and squeezed it tenderly. Felt his warmth and strength. His uncanny knowing. "Have you considered that maybe I'm trying to view the opportunities right before me," I said softly, "and I'm not looking for anything else?"

He stared at me for what seemed a lifetime and then his hand tightened on my fingers and he pulled me close. His other hand pressed low on my back, holding me snugly against him, only our breath, time, and secrets between us.

"I hope so," he finally whispered, and then, with his face only inches from mine, he released me and said it was time to go back.

CHAPTER FIFTEEN

RAFE

THE WATER IN THE BASIN RAN RED. I SQUEEZED THE RAG
out and lifted it to my mouth again.

It seemed to be Ulrix who hated me the most. I winced as I
dabbed my lip where he had split it, then pressed hard trying to
stop the bleeding. Pain radiated across my face.

After the Komizar bid his farewell to me this morning, he
sent his oversized brute in with some food, but Ulrix and his
henchmen gave me an additional side dish. If every meal came
with a bonus like that, I was in trouble. At least they hadn't aimed
for my ribs again. I was sure at least one was cracked. I couldn't
afford more.

It was ironic that all I had wanted was the chance to prove
myself as a soldier, and now I was forced to play an untrained
and inept emissary when I was matched against brutish clods.

Hand combat wasn't my strongest suit, but I could have taken them down in just a few moves with no one the wiser. Sparing my lip wasn't worth risking the plan, though. Two years ago, when Tavish and I had disobeyed orders and rescued his brother from an enemy camp, we had played drunken, weaponless bumblers. That deception had to work for only a few minutes before we revealed our true purpose. This one would have to last much longer. This time there were no horses waiting. There was no quick escape. My story had given us time, and I had to continue to make them believe it.

The Komizar had bought into it for now. My proposal had played to his ego. He wanted to believe that a powerful kingdom was at last recognizing him as a worthy ally—that the prince was actually coming to *him* to negotiate an alliance. He believed he was finally getting the trembling respect he deserved, and who better to get it from than the future king of Dalbreck? He may have feigned suspicion, but I saw the hunger in his eyes when I laid it out. There was only one thing that someone with great power wanted. More of it.

I knew firsthand.

The marriage alliance with Morrighan hadn't been about protection and strength alone. That may very well have been the least of it. My father and his generals had little respect for the Morrighese army. They considered them weak and favored only by some strategic positions and resources. The alliance had also been a bid for dominance.

My father and his cabinet believed that once we had the beloved First Daughter of Morrighan within our borders, boundaries could be pushed. After acquiring Princess Arabella, the southern port of Piadro in Morrighan was next in their sights, though the cabinet preferred to use the word *dowry*. *Only a small port and a few hills.* But for Dalbreck, having a deepwater western port would increase their power tenfold.

It was also a matter of pride. In another time, the port and surrounding lands had belonged to Breck, the exiled prince of Morrighan, banished from the kingdom for challenging his ruling brother. Though countless centuries had passed since then, Dalbreck still wanted it back—some wounds never healed. They saw Lia as a diplomatic inroad to getting what they believed was rightfully theirs without mounting an outright invasion.

When I mentioned the desire for the port to the Komizar, it rang true for him, not just because he knew the port's value, but because the quest for more power was a hunger he understood. Last night he had fished for details of the court of Dalbreck as if he was already planning for his meeting with the prince. I didn't take him for a fool, though. He wouldn't be misled forever. I knew enough of the reputations of Vendan riders, their swift flight, and the way they slipped through borders with ease. It wouldn't be long before they returned with news of my father's good health. Lia and I had to be gone before then. The brute of a fellow who had identified me was a concern, though. Griz, the Komizar had called him. Had he lied for me, or was he truly confused? Maybe he had seen me up on the dais at a ceremony and mistaken me for one of many dignitaries there. He was a loose end that I didn't feel good about—and he was one mountain of a loose end.

I dropped the rag into the basin and grabbed a dry one. Only a thin smear of blood stained the white cloth when I dabbed my mouth. The flow was stopped, but my lip still throbbed. I walked over to the tall slit of a window, just shy of being wide enough for me to slip through, and I pushed open the shutter. Pigeons fluttered from the wet ledge.

Far below, Venda crawled awake like a lumbering giant. Walls and towers prevented me from seeing much past a few rooftops, but the city appeared to spread for miles. It was far larger than I had expected. I leaned as far forward as the narrow window would allow. Were Sven and the others already slinking down one of those dark streets?

Rafe's plan's going to kill us all.

Orrin may have voiced their thoughts, but none of them hesitated to do as I asked. Tavish even whispered before I rode off, *We've done it before. We can do it again.* But that time we had faced only a dozen, not thousands, and none had been the Komizar.

I turned away and paced the room, trying to think of anything but Lia. I looked down at the cuts across my knuckles, my own stupidity. As soon as they had brought me to my room last night and shut the door, I had punched the wall without thinking.

Reckless actions like that were not part of the plan either. Sven would have reprimanded me for acting with my heart instead of my head and putting a potential weapon, my hand, at risk, but it had been all I could do to sit there and act like I didn't care when Lia kissed Kaden. The only thing that had delayed my reaction was the message I had received loud and clear from Lia—the Komizar watched everything. I knew he was playing us to see how we reacted. Lia's performance had been stunningly believable. The Komizar had nodded approvingly. But how far did she have to go to convince Kaden too? This morning one of the guards took great pleasure in telling me that Lia was no longer wearing the burlap dress, that Kaden had told the Komizar she had earned a whole wardrobe last night. "The little Morrighese bitch has forgotten her frilly emissary already now that she's had a taste of Vendan."

I didn't punch the wall after he left. I pulled myself up from the floor where he had deposited me, tasting the blood pooling in my mouth, and tried to remind myself that Lia hadn't asked for any of this. I reminded myself of the look in her eyes when she first saw me before we crossed the bridge, her gaze that tore me sternum to soul, the one that said we were all that mattered, and I promised myself as I spit blood onto the floor, that one day I would see that look in her eyes again.

CHAPTER SIXTEEN

THE LOCKS AT HOME HAD BEEN CHILD'S PLAY COMPARED to this. I had wrestled with this one for the better part of an hour. How many times had I picked the Scholar's or the Chancellor's doors or—especially fun for me—the Timekeeper's, resetting his clock and timepieces? That had especially angered my father, but I'd only done it hoping it would create an extra hour in his day for me. I'd thought he might even appreciate my resourcefulness. He didn't, but my brothers secretly grinned each time he chastised me. The pride in their faces alone had made it worth it.

But this lock was rusty and stubborn, and a simple hairpin wouldn't budge it, much less this sliver of tinder, which was the only tool I could find. I wriggled it in the keyhole again, this time a little too enthusiastically, and it broke off.

"Damn!" I threw the broken stub to the ground. So the door wasn't an option. There were other ways out of a room, perhaps a little riskier, but not impossible. I went to the window again. The ledge outside was walkable, a good ten inches wide. It was a harrowing drop to the ground, but only a couple of yards away, it connected to the top of a wide wall that branched into two different paths that might lead anywhere. Unfortunately, all three of my windows were in plain view of soldiers in the courtyard below, and they seemed to have an unusual interest in looking up here. I had waved to them twice. Before he left, Kaden had told me, "It will be safer for you to stay here." He had tried to make it sound like he was only trying to keep others out, but it was clear he still didn't trust that I'd stay put.

I flopped down on the bed. He left me with food and water and the promise to return by nightfall. That was hours away, and I still had no information about Rafe. Where was he? I thought about how the guards had beaten him before, but surely they wouldn't beat him now that he'd struck a deal with the Komizar. I hoped. I should have risked asking Kaden. I could have worded it in a casual, disinterested way.

"No," I sighed, and rolled over, nestling into the warmth of the bed. There were only so many things I could safely disguise in my face and voice. For me, Rafe wasn't one of them. It was safer not to talk of him at all. I'd only arouse Kaden's suspicions.

I stared vacantly across the room, wondering what sort of matter could occupy so much of his time, but then I noticed something tucked beside one of the trunks. It hadn't been there before. I sat up, curious. A dusty bedroll? I got up and walked closer. *It was mine.* My bedroll! And beneath it, my saddlebag!

How did they get here? Had Eben also secreted these away before they were sold at market? I grabbed my saddlebag and dumped it out on the bed, the contents flying. The beaded scarf Reena gave me, my brush, my tinderbox, the crumbled remains of the chiga weed—everything—including the ancient texts I had stolen, still tucked in their leather sleeves. My mood transformed from frustrated to jubilant in an instant. Even the simplest item like the string of leather to tie back my hair brought me joy, things that were mine and not borrowed or bought with the Komizar's coin. But especially the books. I quickly tucked them under the mattress of the bed in case anyone thought of taking them back.

I shook out my bedroll and lifted the cloak, still tied up with string, that the vagabond women had given me in case the weather turned. The days and nights had been so warm across the savanna I'd had no need of it except as an occasional pillow. I pulled the string free and threw the cloak around my shoulders, savoring its warmth, but especially cherishing those who gave it to me, remembering the blessings they sent with me, even little Natiya's angry wish for harm to come to Kaden's teeth. I smiled. The cloak felt like their arms around me once again. I grabbed a fistful of fabric and held it to my cheek, soft and the color of a midnight forest—

And the color of dark weathered stone.

There was one more window—the one in the chamber closet. I ran to it. Maybe with the dark cover of a cloak, that one would

be far enough out of view of the guards that I might slip out unnoticed. In my rush, I slid on the braided rug in the tiny room
and fell against the rough stone wall. I rubbed my bruised shoulder, cursing the tear I'd made in Kaden's shirt. I went to the window and peeked out. A guard looked up and nodded, as if he
expected my recurring appearances. Kaden must have warned
them to keep a close eye on *all* windows of his room. I grumbled out a low, angry oath as I smiled and waved back. I stooped
to smooth out the skewed rug and noticed a slightly wider gap
between the floor planks. Cold air seeped through the crack. I
pushed the rug aside and saw that the line continued around in
a perfect square. At one end was an embedded iron ring. *The
Sanctum is riddled with abandoned passageways.*

This was how he did it.

I hadn't slept through the screeching hinges of the door. He'd
made a silent exit this way. My heart hammered as I reached for
the ring. I pulled, and the floor lifted up. Iron levers smoothly
unfolded beneath the planks to reveal a black hole and the barely
visible beginnings of a staircase. Thick air, dusty and ancient,
crawled upward, chilling the small room.

It was an escape. But to what? I leaned over, peering into the
black hole, but the stairs disappeared into oblivion. *Some with
deadly drops.*

I shook my head and started to shut the trapdoor, then stopped.

If Kaden could go down and come out on the other side, so
could I. I hiked up the cloak and swung my feet down to the
first stair. I positioned the heavy rug back over the trapdoor so it
would fall back into place when I closed it, but finding the will

to close it behind me took some time. I finally took a deep breath and let it drop.

The stairs were steep and narrow. My hands glided along the stone walls on either side to help me feel my way down, sometimes passing through what I could only imagine were enormous spiderwebs. I suppressed a shiver and reminded myself of all the webs I had swept away at the inn. *Harmless, Lia. Small, Lia. Compared to the Komizar, innocent little creatures. Keep going.*

Step after step, I saw nothing but deep suffocating black. I blinked, almost unsure if my eyes were open. I sensed the staircase curve, my left foot finding greater purchase on the step than the right, and then after a dozen steps, blessed light appeared. Dim at first, and then blazing. It was only a finger-thin gap in the stone blocks of the outer wall, but in the darkness, it shone like a blessed lantern. It illuminated the path below me, and I was able to move at a faster pace. Some of the stone steps had crumbled away, and I had to carefully ease myself down to a third or even a fourth step. I finally came to a landing that led to a dark passageway and reluctantly stepped into complete blackness again. After only a few steps, I ran into a solid wall. A dead end. *It has to lead somewhere*, I thought, but then remembered the haphazard construction of the entire city. I found my way back to the staircase, down more steps to another landing and dark passageway—and another dead end. My throat tightened. The musty air was suddenly choking me, and my fingers were stiff with cold. What if Kaden hadn't come this way? What if this was one of those closed-up forgotten passageways that I'd never find my way out of again?

I closed my eyes, though it made little difference in the dark.

Breathe, Lia. You haven't made it this far for nothing. My fingers curled into fists. There was a way out, and I would find it.

I heard a noise and whirled around.

A woman stood at the other end of the passage.

I was so shocked I didn't have the sense to be afraid at first. Her face was hazy in the shadows, and her long hair fell in twisted strands all the way to the floor.

And then I knew. Deep in my gut, I knew who she was, though all the rules of reason told me it was impossible. This was the woman I had seen in the shadows of Sanctum Hall. The woman who had watched me from the ledge. The very same woman who had sung my name from a wall thousands of years ago. The one pushed to her death, and the namesake of a kingdom determined to crush mine.

This was Venda.

I had warned Venda not to wander too far from the
tribe.

A hundred times, I had warned her.

I was more her mother than her sister.

She came years after the storm.

She never felt the ground shake,

Never saw the sun turn red.

Never saw the sky go black.

Never saw fire burst on the horizon and choke the air.

She never even saw our mother. This was all she had ever
known.

The scavengers lay in wait for her, and I saw Harik steal her
away on his horse.

She never looked back, even when I called after her.

> *Don't believe his lies*, I cried, but it was too late. She was
> gone.

—*The Last Testaments of Gaudrel*

CHAPTER SEVENTEEN

SHE LOOKED AT ME, HER HEAD ANGLED TO THE SIDE, HER expression unreadable—sadness, anger, relief? I wasn't sure—and then she nodded. Ice crept through my veins. She recognized me. Her lips moved silently, mouthing my name, and then she turned away and the shadows swallowed her.

"Wait!" I called and ran after her. I searched, turning in all directions, but the stairwell and landing were empty. She was gone.

The wind, time, it circles, repeats, some swaths cutting deeper than others.

I braced myself against the wall, my head pounding, my palms damp, trying to explain her away, searching the rules of reason, but it settled into me as true and real as the chorus of cries I'd heard in the heavens the day I buried my brother. The centuries and tears had swirled with voices that couldn't be erased, not even by death, and Venda's was a song that couldn't be silenced, even by being pushed from a wall. It was all as true and real as a Komizar who clutched my neck and promised to take everything.

"The rules of reason," I whispered, a mindless chant that still tumbled from my lips. I didn't even know what it meant anymore.

I took a shaky step forward in the dark, and my boot knocked something exactly where she had disappeared. It made a strange hollow sound. My fingers slid along the wall, and instead of more stone, I found a low wood panel. With a gentle push, I slid it open and found myself under a dark sweep of stairs in the middle of the Sanctum. Bright light splashed the hall in front of me, and I was grateful for a world of hard edges, heavy footsteps, and warm flesh. All things solid. I looked back at the wood panel behind me, questioning my brief descent down the hidden stairway, and wondered what I had really seen. Was it real and true or only terror at being trapped? But the name she had mouthed, *Jezelia*, still juddered through me. Guards walked by, and I slunk back, hiding in the shadows. I had escaped one trap and fallen into another.

This was the busy hallway that led to the tower where the Komizar said he had a secure room for Rafe. I was about to step out when three governors approached and I had to duck back down. All I needed was a free moment to dart out and run up the stairs, and I was certain I could find Rafe's room, but the hall seemed to be a main thoroughfare. The governors passed, then several servants carrying baskets, and finally the quiet held. I pulled my hood over my head and stepped out—just as two guards rounded the corner.

They stopped short in surprise when they saw me.

"There you are!" I snapped. "Are you the ones who were ordered to leave firewood outside the Assassin's room?" I shot them both an accusatory eye.

The tallest of the two glared back. "Do we look like barrow runners?"

"We aren't filthy patty clappers," the other one snarled.

"Really?" I said. "Not even for the *Assassin*?" I put my hand to my chin as if I were memorizing their faces.

One looked at the other, then back at me. "We'll send a boy."

"See that you do! The weather's turned cold, and the Assassin wanted a roaring fire by the time he returned." I turned and walked away in a huff, climbing the stairs. My temples pounded as I expected them to come to their senses, but all I heard behind me was their grousing and shouting at a poor hapless servant down the hall.

After one dead end, two close calls with the wrong rooms, and a quick exit through a hall window, I walked along a ledge that was sufficiently hidden from the view of those below. Peeking through windows rather than opening doors proved to be a safer way to explore, and only a few windows later, I found him.

His stillness struck me first. His profile. He slouched in a chair, looking out an opposite window. The smoldering, calculated stare that had made me uneasy the first time I saw him made me apprehensive again. It breathed menace and frightening reserve, a bow stretched, loaded, aimed, waiting. It was the stare that had made platters in my hand tremble as I set them down before him in the tavern. Even with my slight side view, the ice of his blue eyes cut like a sword. Neither farmer nor prince. They were the eyes of a warrior. Eyes bred with power. And yet last night he'd made them warm for Calantha when she sat close and whispered to him, made them spark with intrigue when the Komizar asked questions . . . made them hooded with disinterest when I kissed Kaden.

I thought of the first time I'd made him laugh as we picked blackberries in Devil's Canyon, how fearful I had been, but then how his laugh had transformed his face. *How it had transformed me.* I wanted to make him laugh now, but here I had nothing to give him that was the least bit amusing or joyful.

I should have revealed myself immediately, but once I knew he was alive and that he had food and water, I was struck with the need for something else—a few seconds to watch him unseen, to view him with the new eyes I had only just gained. What other sides did this very clever prince have?

His fingers tapped a strained beat on the arm of the chair, slow and steady, like he was counting something out—hours, days, or maybe the people who would pay. Maybe he was even thinking about me. *Yes! You were a challenge and an embarrassment.* I thought about all the times we had kissed back in Terravin. Every single time, he had known I was the one who had broken a contract between two kingdoms. And before we had kissed, there were all the times I had looked at him with moon eyes, hoping he would kiss me. Had he felt smug justice watching me leaning on brooms hanging on his every word? *Melons. He told me he grew melons.* The stories he fabricated—just like the ones he'd created last night for the Komizar—flowed out far too smoothly.

I know your feelings about me may have changed.

My feelings had changed, without a doubt, but I wasn't sure how. I wasn't even sure what to call him anymore. The name Rafe was so tightly woven with the young man I thought was a farmer. What should I call him now? Rafferty? Jaxon? Your Highness?

But then he turned. That was all it took. He was Rafe again, and my heart jumped. I saw his bloody lip, and I squeezed through the narrow opening, careless of sound. He leapt to his feet when he heard me, startled and ready for battle, not expecting someone to enter his room through a window and even more surprised that it was me.

"What did they do?" I asked.

He brushed away my hand and questions, and hurried past me to the window. He peered out to check whether anyone had seen me, then turned back, crushing me in his arms, holding me like he'd never let me go, until suddenly he stepped back as if unsure his embrace was still welcome.

Whether it was prudent or not, I didn't care—I burned with his touch. "I suppose if we're going to fall in love all over again, kissing will be part of it." I gently brought his face to mine again, avoiding his split lip, and my mouth fluttered across his skin, kissing the crest of his cheekbone, down to his jaw, across to the corner of his mouth. Every taste of him suddenly new.

His hands tightened around my waist, pulling me closer, and rivers of heat spread through my chest.

"Are you frothing mad?" he asked between heavy breaths. "How did you get here?"

I had known this was coming. This was not part of our plan. I stepped away, pouring myself some water from the flask on a table. "It wasn't hard," I lied. "An easy walk."

"Through a window?" He shook his head, his eyelids briefly squeezing shut. "Lia, you can't go dancing on ledges like a—"

"I'm hardly dancing. I'm sneaking, and I have plenty of practice at it. Some might call me accomplished."

His jaw twitched. "I appreciate your skills, but I'd prefer that you sit tight," he argued. "I don't want to be peeling you off the cobblestones. My men will come. There are military strategies for this kind of situation when the odds aren't in your favor—and then we'll all get out of here together."

"Strategies? Are your soldiers here, Rafe?" I asked, looking around the room. "It wouldn't seem so. But we *are*. You have to accept that they may not come. This is a dangerous land, and they might have—"

"No," he said. "I wouldn't lead my most trusted friends into something I thought they couldn't survive. I told you it might be a few days." But I saw the doubt in his eyes. The reality was setting in. Four men in a foreign land. Four men among thousands of enemies. There was a good possibility they were dead already if they had stumbled into a regiment as Walther and his company had. I didn't even bring up the dangers of the lower river that Kaden had warned me about, and the deadly creatures that inhabited it. There was a good reason that Venda had always been so isolated.

"The guards again?" I asked, returning to the subject of his lip.

He nodded, but his thoughts were still elsewhere. His gaze traveled over my new attire.

"Someone brought me my cloak. It had been wrapped in my bedroll," I explained.

He reached out, pulling the tie at my throat loose, and slowly pushed the cloak back from my shoulders. It fell to the floor. "And . . . these?"

"They're Kaden's."

His chest rose in a deep measured breath, and he walked away, raking his fingers through his hair. "Better his clothes than that dress, I suppose."

No doubt the guards had wasted little time in spreading their sordid tales.

"Yes, Rafe," I sighed. "I earned them. In a sword fight, and that is all. Kaden has a blue goose egg on his shin to prove it."

He turned back to me, relief visible on his face. "And the kiss last night?"

My anger flared. Why wouldn't he let it go? But I realized so much still bubbled near the surface. All the hurts and the deceptions that we hadn't had time to address were still there.

"I didn't come here to be interrogated," I snapped. "What of all your attentions toward Calantha?"

His shoulders pulled back. "I suppose we're both putting on the performances of our lives."

His accusatory tone made my anger spark into a fire.

"Performance? Is that what you call it? You lied to me. Your life's complicated. *That's* what you told me. *Complicated?*"

"What are you dredging up? Last night or Terravin?"

"You act as if it happened ten years ago! You have such an interesting way with words. Your life isn't complicated. You're the blazing crown prince of Dalbreck! You call that a complication? But you went on and on about growing melons and tending horses and how your parents were dead. You shamelessly told me you were a farmer!"

"You claimed you were a tavern maid!"

"I was! I served tables and washed dishes! Have you ever grown a melon in your life? Yet you piled on lie after lie, and it never occurred to you to tell me the truth."

"What choice did I have? I heard you call me a princely papa's boy behind my back! One you could never respect!"

My mouth fell open. "You spied on me?" I whirled around, shaking my head in disbelief, crossing the room, then whipping back to face him. "*You spied?* Your duplicities never end, do they?"

He took an intimidating step closer. "Maybe if a certain tavern maid had bothered to tell me the truth *first*, I wouldn't have felt that I had to hide who I was!"

I matched him step for angry step. "Maybe if a self-important prince had bothered to come see me before the wedding as I had asked, we wouldn't be here now at all!"

"Is that so? Well, maybe if someone had asked with an ounce of diplomacy instead of commanding like a spoiled royal bitch, I would have come!"

I shook with rage. "Maybe someone was too scared out of

her wits to properly choose her words for His Royal Pompous Ass!"

We both stood there, our chests heaving with fury, becoming something neither of us had been with the other before. The royal son and the royal daughter of two kingdoms that had only warily trusted each other.

I was suddenly sick with my words. I hated every one and wanted to take them back. I felt my blood pool at my feet. "I was afraid, Rafe," I whispered. "I asked you to come because I was never so afraid in my life."

I watched his angry flush drain away too. He swallowed and gently drew me into his arms, then tenderly, his lips grazed my forehead. "I'm sorry, Lia," he whispered against it. "I'm so sorry."

I wasn't sure if he was sorry for his angry words or that he hadn't come to me all those months ago when he received my note. Maybe both. His thumb strummed the ridges of my spine. All I wanted was to memorize the feel of his body pressed to mine and erase every word we had just said.

He took my hand and slowly kissed my knuckles one at a time, just as he'd done back in Terravin, but now I thought, *This is Prince Jaxon Tyrus Rafferty kissing my hand*, and I realized it mattered not one whit to me. He was still the person I had fallen in love with, crown prince or farmer. He was Rafe, and I was Lia, and everything else that we were to other people didn't matter to *us*. I didn't need to fall in love with him again. I had never fallen out.

I slid my hands beneath his vest, feeling the muscles of his back. "They'll come," I whispered against his chest. "Your soldiers will come, and we'll get out of this. Together, just like you said." I remembered that he'd said two of them spoke the language.

I leaned back so I could see his face. "Do you speak Vendan too?" I asked. "I forgot to find out last night."

"Only a few words, but I'm catching on to certain ones quickly. *Fikatande idaro, tabanych, dakachan wrukash.*"

I nodded. "The choice words always come first."

He chuckled, and his smile transformed his face. My eyes stung. I wanted that smile to stay there forever, but I had to move on to more urgent but bleaker details I needed to share. I told him there were things I had learned that he and his men would need to know.

We sat down opposite each other at the table that held the basin, and I told him everything, from the Komizar's threats to me after everyone else had left the room, to the stolen cargo down in Council Wing Square, to my conversation with Aster and my suspicion that the patrols were being systematically slaughtered by the Vendan army. They were hiding something. Something important.

Rafe shook his head. "We've always had skirmishes with bands of Vendans, but this does seem different. I've never seen organized troops like the ones we encountered, but even six hundred armed soldiers is something that can be easily quashed by either of our kingdoms once they know what they're dealing with."

"What if there's more than six hundred?"

He leaned back in his chair and rubbed the bristle on his chin. "We haven't seen any evidence of that, and it takes some level of prosperity to train and support a large army."

This was true. Supporting the Morrighese army was a constant drain on the treasury. But even though it brought me some relief to think the army we encountered could be dealt with, I still felt doubt roosting in my gut.

I moved on, telling him about the *jehendra*, the man who put the talisman around my neck, and the women who measured me for clothes. "They were unusually attentive, Rafe. Kind, even. It was strange in comparison to everyone else. I wonder if maybe they—"

"Like you?"

"No. It's more than that," I said, shaking my head. "I think that maybe they wanted to help me. Maybe help us?" I chewed the corner of my lip. "Rafe, there's something else I haven't told you."

He leaned forward, his gaze fixed on me. It reminded me of all the times I swept the inn porches in Terravin and he listened so intently to what I had to say, no matter how large or small it was. "What is it?" he asked.

"When I ran from Civica, I stole something. I was angry, and it was my way of getting back at some members of the cabinet who had pushed the marriage."

"Jewels? Gold? I don't think anyone in Venda is going to arrest you for stealing something from their sworn enemy."

"I don't think the value of it was monetary. I think it was

something they just didn't want anyone to see—especially me. I stole some documents from the Royal Scholar's library. One of them was an ancient Vendan text called the Song of Venda."

He shook his head. "I've never heard of it."

"Neither had I." I told him Venda was the wife of the first ruler and the kingdom was named for her. I explained that she had told stories and sung songs from the walls of the Sanctum to the people below, but she was said to have gone mad. When her words turned to babble, the ruler had pushed her from the wall to her death below.

"He killed his own wife? Sounds like they were as barbaric then as they are now, but how does this matter to us?"

I hesitated, almost afraid to say the words out loud. "On my way here across the Cam Lanteux, I translated it. It said a dragon would rise, one that fed on the tears of mothers. But it also said someone else would come along to challenge him. Someone named Jezelia."

His head shifted slightly to the side. "What are you trying to say?"

"Maybe it isn't chance that I'm here."

"Because of a name mentioned in an old song by a long-dead madwoman?"

"It's more than that, Rafe. I saw her," I blurted out.

His expression changed almost instantly from curious to cautious, as if I'd gone mad too. "You think you saw a dead—"

I cut him off, telling him about the woman I saw in the hall, on the ledge, and finally in the passage. He reached out, his fingers gently tucking a strand of hair behind my ear.

"Lia," he said, "you've been through a horrible journey, and this place—" He shook his head. "Anyone could see things here. Our lives are in jeopardy every minute. We never know when someone will come and—" He squeezed my hand. "The name Jezelia could be as common as air here, and a dragon? That could be anyone. She may have even meant a literal dragon. Have you thought of that? It's only a story. Every kingdom has them. And it's understandable that you might see things in a dark passageway. It might have even been a servant passing through. Thank the gods she didn't expose you to the guards. But you're not meant to be a prisoner in this godforsaken place, of that much, I'm certain."

"But there's something going on here, Rafe. I feel it. Something looming. Something I saw in an old woman's eyes on the Cam Lanteux. Something I heard."

"Are you claiming this is your gift speaking to you?" There was a strange lilt to his tone, a hint of skepticism, and I realized that maybe he didn't even believe I had the gift. We had never talked about it. Maybe the rumors in Morrighan about my shortcomings had spread all the way to Dalbreck. His doubt stung, but I couldn't blame him. Spoken aloud, it sounded ludicrous even to me.

"I'm not sure." I squeezed my eyes shut briefly, angry with myself that I didn't understand my own gift well enough to give Rafe more answers.

He stood and pulled me into his arms. "I believe you," he whispered. "There's something looming, but that's all the more reason why we need to leave here."

I rested my head on his chest, wanting to hold him until—

You think he'd tell you when we were really leaving?

My thoughts froze on Finch's taunt. Kaden wouldn't tell me when he was really returning either. *I don't trust you, Lia.* And he never had, with good reason. This was a game I loathed playing with Kaden.

"I have to go," I said, pushing away, "before he returns and finds me gone." I snatched up my cloak and ran to the window.

Rafe tried to stop me. "You said he'd be gone all day."

I couldn't take a chance, and I had no time to explain. I was only just stepping up on the ledge of the window when I heard the key rattle in the lock and Rafe's door creaked open. I pressed close to the outside wall, but instead of fleeing, I lingered, trying to hear who it was. I heard Calantha's voice, far more accommodating in her tone with him than she was with me. And then I heard Rafe complimenting her on her dress, transforming in a single breath from a prince to a solicitous emissary.

CHAPTER EIGHTEEN

KADEN

I WOVE MY WAY THROUGH THE TROOPS WHO STOOD AT
ease laughing at the bottom of Corpse Call, happy to be relieved
of midday duties. Pockets of soldiers called to me, welcoming
me home. Most of them I didn't know, because I was gone more
than I was here, but they all knew me. Everyone made a point
to know, or know of, the Assassin.

"Heard you brought home a prize," one called.

The bounty of war. I remembered calling Lia the Komizar's
prize myself when Eben aimed to cut her throat. I'd said it without thinking, because it was true. All bounty belonged to the
Komizar to distribute or use for the greatest benefit to Venda. It
wasn't my place to question him when he said, *I'll decide the best
way to use her.* Without a doubt, it wasn't just I who owed him a

great debt—all of Venda did. He gave us all something we hadn't had before. Hope.

I kept walking, nodding; these were my comrades after all. We had a common cause, a brotherhood. Loyalty above everything. Not one of the men I passed hadn't suffered greatly in one way or another, some even more than I had, though I wore the scarred proof on my chest and back. A few coarse remarks from soldiers I could ignore.

Look here.

Another call from somewhere in the crowd.

The Assassin.

No doubt weak from wrestling with his little pigeon all the way across the Cam Lanteux.

I stopped cold and stared at a group of three soldiers, smiles still on their faces. I stared until their feet shifted and their grins faded. "Three of your comrades are about to die. Now's not the time for laughter about prisoners."

They glanced at each other, their faces pale, then melted into the crowd behind them. I walked away, my boots grinding into the wet soil.

Corpse Call was a hillock at the far end of the Tomack quarter. The training camps spread out in a low valley just beyond it, hidden by a thicket of woods. Eleven years ago, when the Komizar came to power, there were no prepared soldiers, no training camps, no silos for storing the grain tithes, no armories for the forging of weapons, no breeding stables. There were only warriors who learned their trade from a father if they had one, and if they didn't, brute passion guided them. Only the local quarter smiths banged out crude swords and axes for the few families who could afford them. The Komizar had done what none before him had, coerced greater tithes from the governors, who in turn coerced greater tithes from the quarterlords in their own provinces. While Venda was poor in fields and game, it was rich in hunger. He beat his powerful message like a war drum, calculating the days, months, and years until Venda would be stronger than the enemy, strong enough so that every belly would be full, and nothing—especially not three cowardly soldiers who had betrayed their oath and run from their duty—would be allowed to undermine what all Vendans had worked and sacrificed for.

I traversed the short trail that led to the top of the hillock, back and forth until I reached the *chievdars* who waited for me. They nodded to a sentry, who blew a ram's horn, three long bleats that hung in the damp air. The troops below quieted. I heard the sobbing of one prisoner. All three were on their knees, wood blocks before them, their hands tied behind, black hoods covering their heads as if they were too repulsive to look upon for long. They were lined up on the crown of the hillock in plain view of all who watched from below. An executioner stood near each one, and the polished curved axes clutched in their hands glinted in the sun.

"Remove their hoods," I ordered.

The sobbing prisoner cried out when the hood was snatched away. The other two blinked as if they didn't quite understand why they were there. Their expressions twisted in confusion.

Make sure they suffer.

I stared at them. Their noses didn't quite fit their faces, and their thin, shivering chests hadn't yet broadened.

"Keep?" the nearest *chievdar* prompted. It was my job as Keep to move the execution forward.

I walked closer and stood before them. They lifted their chins, wise enough to be afraid, wiser still not to ask for mercy.

"You're accused of deserting your duty, your posts, and betraying your oath to protect your comrades. The five you left behind died. I ask each one of you, did you commit these crimes?"

The one who had sobbed broke out in anguished wails. The other two nodded, their mouths half open. Not one of the three was more than fifteen years old.

"Yes," each one said obediently in turn, even through their terror.

I turned to the soldiers below. "What say you, comrades? Yea or nay?"

A unanimous rumble as thick as night rolled in the air.

The weight of the single word pressed down on my shoulders, heavy and final. None of these three had yet seen a razor on his face.

Yea.

Every man waiting below needed to believe his comrades would be there for him, that no fear or impulse would deter him from doing his duty. One of the five who died may have been their brother, their father, their friend.

It was at this point the Komizar or the Keep might have cut a line, not too deep, in the throat of one. Just enough for him to choke on his own blood, to draw out his misery and make the other prisoners retch in fear, just deep enough to sear it into the memory of every witness below. Traitors received no mercy.

The *chievdar* drew his knife and offered it to me.

I looked at the knife, looked out at the soldiers below. If they hadn't seen enough misery by now, they'd have to find it elsewhere.

I turned back to the condemned soldiers. "May the gods show you mercy."

And with a simple nod, before the *chievdar* could protest the quick end, the blades came down and their sobbing ceased.

CHAPTER NINETEEN

THE HALLWAY WAS DARK, AND THE LANTERN I HAD snatched from a hook barely lit my way. I couldn't go back the way I had come. Every turn had been blocked by governors or sentries, and I'd had to make quick unexpected turns to avoid them, slipping down narrow stairways, darting into paths that were little more than tunnels. Now I wandered in this squat hall that showed little promise of leading anywhere. It was empty and bleak, and appeared to be unused.

The walls closed in the farther I went, and the air was musty. I could taste its heavy age on my tongue. I contemplated turning back, but then I finally came to a portal and more stairs that led down. It felt as if I were already in the belly of a deceased creature. The last thing I wanted to do was venture deeper into its bowels, but I stepped down anyway. I worried that Kaden would be back before nightfall and didn't want him to know of my wanderings. He would surely seal the trapdoor.

The stone steps curved, funneling me into more darkness, something I was becoming accustomed to in this hellish city, and then suddenly I heard a rumble and the stair beneath me gave way. I fell, tumbling in the darkness, losing the lantern, my cloak wrapping around me, my hands scraping walls, stairs, anything to try and stop my fall. Finally I landed with a glorious hard thump on a floor. I lay there, momentarily stunned, wondering if I had broken anything.

A cold burst of air washed up from below, carrying the scents of smoke and oil. Faint light revealed an immense root crawling down the wall beside me like a heavy-footed creature. Above me, thin tendrils of other roots hung down like slithering serpents. If not for the light and the scent of lantern oil, I'd have been certain I had fallen into the hellish garden of a demon. I sat up, the cloak still twisted around my shoulders and chest, then rubbed my knee, which hadn't had the benefit of padding. There was a bloody tear in the trousers. Piece by piece, I was shredding Kaden's clothes. How would I ever explain them? I got to my feet, shaking the cloak free, and something hard knocked against my leg. I reached down and squeezed the fabric. There was something rigid sewn in the hem. I ripped it open, and a thin sheaf of leather fell into my hand. A small knife was tucked in it.

Natiya! It had to be. Dihara would never take such a risk. Neither would Reena. But I remembered Natiya's defiant raised chin when she brought the cloak to me. It was neatly rolled up with string around it to secure it. Kaden had grabbed it from her, saying it would have to go in my bedroll.

I turned the knife over in my hands. It was smaller than my own dagger, a three-inch blade at most, and slim. Perfect for Natiya's small hands—and perfect for hiding. It couldn't do much damage if thrown, but at close range it was lethal enough. I shook my head, grateful for her cunning, picturing how nervously and quickly she would have had to work to sew it into the hem with no one the wiser. I slid it into my boot and continued cautiously down the winding staircase. Then, like a gift, with a few more steps, the stairs ended and soft golden light rushed up to meet me.

I stepped out into a room and suppressed a gasp.

It was a vast cavern of white stone, glowing with the warm buttery light of lanterns. Dozens of columns rose up, sprouting into arches across the great expanse. Giant roots like the one I saw in the stairway had bored through the ceiling and snaked down along pillars and walls. Smaller vines dangled between— the whole room looked eerily alive with creamy yellow snakes. The floor was part polished marble, part rough stone, and in some places, piled rubble. Shadows flickered between arches, and in the distance I saw robed figures walking away. I tried to peer after them, but they quickly disappeared into the dark.

Who were they, and what were they doing down here? I hugged my cloak close about me and darted out, hiding behind a pillar. I scanned the cavern. What was this place? *They have elaborate temples built far below the ground.*

A ruin. I was in an excavated ruin of the Ancients.

Three robed figures walked past just on the other side of the pillar, and I pressed closer to the stone, holding my breath. I listened to their shuffling feet on the polished floor, a strange softness to their steps. The sound of reverence and restraint. I stepped out into the light, forgetting caution, and watched the sway of their plain brown robes as they departed.

"Stop!" I yelled, my voice echoing through the cavern.

All three halted and turned. They didn't draw weapons, or maybe they just couldn't because their arms were full of books. Their features were hidden in the shadows of their hoods, and they didn't speak. They simply faced me, waiting. I approached them, keeping my steps steady and assured.

"I'd like to see who I speak to," I said.

"As would we," the one in the middle answered.

My chest clamped tight. He spoke in perfect Vendan, but even in those few words, I heard the difference, the way he formed his words, the erudite air. The foreignness. He was not Vendan. I kept my chin tucked low to keep my face in the shadow of my hood. "I'm only a visitor of the Komizar, and I've lost my way."

One of them snorted. "Indeed."

"Little wonder you keep your face covered," another said, and pushed back his hood. His hair swirled in intricate braids across his head, and a deep line cut between his brows.

"Is this a dungeon of some sort?" I asked. "Are you prisoners down here?"

They laughed at my ignorance, but came forth with the information I fished for. "We're the amply rewarded purveyors of knowledge, and the gut of this beast has much to keep us busy. Now be on your way." He pointed behind me, telling me to take the second stairway up.

Learned men in Venda? I stared at them, my thoughts still racing with the *who* and *why*.

"Go!" he said, as if he were shooing off a one-eared cat.

I whirled around and hurried away, and when I knew they could no longer see me, I ducked behind a pillar and leaned back, my head pounding with questions. Purveyors of *what* knowledge?

I heard footsteps and froze. More of them walked past, a group of five this time, mumbling about their midday meal.

The gut of this beast has much to keep us busy.

A whole army of them prowled through these caverns.

A chill crawled up my neck.

Everything about them was out of place here. What were they being amply rewarded *for*? I dashed out and found the second stairway, taking two steps at a time, the sweet, smoky stench of the cavern suddenly turning my stomach.

CHAPTER TWENTY

I SAT ON THE WALL STARING AT THIN GRAY CLOUDS, strange to me like everything else in this dark city. They striped the heavens like giant claws drawn across flesh, and the pink of twilight bled between them.

The guards below me had, by now, become accustomed to where I sat perched on the wall. I hadn't been able to get back to the trapdoor in the chamber closet, and I'd had to take a chance on getting back in through my window since the door was locked. I had almost made it to the ledge when the guards spotted me. I immediately sat down on the wall, making it appear that it was my destination and I had just come from my window. Their shouts hadn't deterred me, and once they were assured escape wasn't part of my plan, they tolerated my teetering place of refuge.

In truth, I didn't want to go back inside. I told myself I needed air to clear the smoke and sulfur from my nostrils. It seemed to cling to every pore of my body, sickly and pungent. There was something about the strange men down in the caverns that left me dizzy and weak.

I remembered Walther saying I was the strongest of us.

I didn't feel strong, and if I was, I didn't want to be strong any longer. I wanted out. I'd had enough. I wanted Terravin. I wanted Pauline and Berdi and fish stew. I wanted anything but this. I wanted my dreams back. I wanted Rafe to be a farmer and Walther to be—

My chest jumped, and I choked back whatever was trying to shake loose.

Something is looming.

And now, with these strange erudite men in the cavern, it seemed certain.

I felt the loose pieces floating just out of my grasp—the Song of Venda, the Chancellor and Royal Scholar hiding books and sending a bounty hunter to kill me without benefit of trial. And then there was the kavah on my shoulder that refused to fade away. Something had been stirring long before I ran on my wedding day.

I remembered the wind that day I prepared for the wedding. Cold gusts beating against the citadelle, warning whispers winding down drafty halls. It was in the air even then. *The truths of the world wish to be known.* But it was far more than I had believed it to be. The before and after of my life cleaved in two that day, in ways I could never have imagined. My head ached with questions.

I closed my eyes, searching for the gift that I had only just been getting a sense of when I crossed the Cam Lanteux. Dihara had warned me that gifts that weren't fed shriveled and died, but it was hard to feed anything here. Still, I kept my eyes closed and searched for that place of knowing. I forced my hands to relax at my sides, forced the tightness from my shoulders, focused on the light behind my eyelids, and heard Dihara again. . . . *It is the language of knowing, child. Trust the strength within you.*

I felt myself drifting to something familiar, heard the swish of grass in the meadow, the gurgle of a river, caught the scent of meadow clover, felt the wind lift my hair, and then I heard a song, quiet and distant, as delicate as a midnight breeze. A voice I desperately needed to hear. *Pauline.* I heard Pauline saying remembrances. I lifted my voice with hers and sang the words from the Holy Text of the girl Morrighan as she crossed the wilderness.

> *Another step, my sisters,*
> > *My brothers,*
> > > *My love.*
> *The way is long, but we have each other.*
> > *Another mile,*
> > > *Another tomorrow,*
> *The path is cruel, but we are strong.*

I pressed two fingers against my lips, held them there to make the moment stretch as wide as the universe, and lifted them to the heavens. "And so shall it be," I said softly, "for evermore."

When I opened my eyes, I saw a small group gathered below

me listening. Two of them were girls only a little younger than myself, and they searched the sky where I had set my prayers free, their expressions earnest. I looked up again too, scanning the heavens, and wondered if my words were already lost among the stars.

CHAPTER TWENTY-ONE

PAULINE

THREE DAYS AND TWO NOTES LATER, GWYNETH STILL hadn't received a response from the Chancellor. She had convinced me that, while I didn't like or trust either the Chancellor or the Royal Scholar after their treatment of Lia, that also made them the perfect ones for Gwyneth to seek out. They would be the most likely to have secrets about her and, more important, be interested in information about her. It was the unknown players that we had to worry about, and at the current moment, that included just about everyone.

"What difference does it make who we can or can't trust besides the king?"

"Because someone tried to slit Lia's throat when she was in Terravin."

I had sat there in disbelief when Gwyneth told me. Lia had

explained the injury on her throat as a stumble down the stairs while she was carrying an armload of firewood. It grieved me, how much Lia had protected me from during those days just after Mikael had died. I was so wrapped up in my own misery, I hadn't been there for her. This cast everything in a new light. Traitors were always brought back for trial, and certainly the king's daughter above all would receive that small amount of justice. Someone wanted her dead without benefit of even a court hearing. I looked upon the whole court and cabinet now with new eyes.

Gwyneth's third note to the Chancellor, sent early this morning, was answered immediately with an agreement to meet midafternoon. In this note she said she had news of Princess Arabella.

I sat in a dark corner of the pub where no one would notice me, though at this hour, the pub was empty except for two patrons on the far side of the room. My hood shadowed my face, and every last wisp of my blond hair was carefully tucked out of sight. I faced the door and slowly sipped a mug of warm broth. Gwyneth sat at a well-lit table in the middle of the room. I was only to reveal myself if she gave me a signal and we had to resort to our second plan—me confronting the Chancellor. I was certain she wouldn't signal. She was dismayed that I had come along at all, but I would have it no other way. She accused me of not trusting her, and maybe the revelation that she had once been a spy did give me pause, but mostly I was afraid to let a single moment slip past when I might be able to help Lia.

He came alone with no entourage or guard to escort him. I watched him approaching through the pub window and nodded to Gwyneth. She seemed not the least bit nervous, but I was coming to understand that Gwyneth was in many ways like Lia. She hid her fears beneath a practiced veneer of steel, but her fears were there, as sure and shaky as my hands trembling in my lap.

He sauntered across the room and sat down across from Gwyneth. His cloak was plain, and he wore none of the usual finery on his fingers. For once, he didn't want to be noticed. He settled in his chair and looked her over without saying a word. She did the same. I had a clear view of them both. The silence was long and awkward, and I held my breath waiting for one of them to speak, but neither seemed unsettled by the quiet. Finally the Chancellor spoke in a strangely familiar tone, making my skin prickle.

"You look well," he said.

"I am."

"And the child?"

Gwyneth's lips pulled to a straight line. "Stillborn," she answered.

He nodded and leaned back in his chair, breathing out a long sigh, as if relieved. "Just as well."

Her coolness turned frigid, and a single brow arched upward. "Yes. For the best."

"It's been years," he said. "You suddenly have information again?"

"I'm in need of funds."

"Let's see if your information's worth anything."

"Princess Arabella has been abducted."

He laughed. "You'll have to do better than that. My sources say she's dead. She met with an unfortunate accident."

The mug slipped in my hand, and broth sloshed onto the table. Gwyneth steeled her eyes to ignore me. "Then your sources are wrong," she said. "She was taken prisoner by an assassin from Venda. He said he was taking her back to his kingdom, but for what purpose I don't know."

"Everyone knows Venda doesn't take prisoners. You're slipping, Gwyneth. I think we're done here." He pushed away from the table and stood to leave.

"I learned this firsthand from her attendant, Pauline," Gwyneth quickly added. "She witnessed the abduction."

The Chancellor stopped mid-stride. "Pauline?" He sat down again. "Where is she?"

I swallowed, dipping my head lower.

"She's in hiding," Gwyneth said, "somewhere in the north country. A frightened little mouse she was, but she gave me the last of her coin to come here and plead for help for Princess Arabella. She told me to go to the Viceregent, but I came to you instead—since we have a history. I thought I might get a more favorable recompense from you. Pauline promised I'd get an ample reward for my troubles. I'm sure the king and queen desperately want the princess back, regardless of her indiscretion."

He stared at her, the same severe expression I saw him wear in my wanderings at the citadelle, but now it was intensified, as if he were calculating the veracity of every word Gwyneth uttered. He finally reached inside his cloak and threw a small bag onto the table. "I'll speak with the king and queen. Don't mention this to anyone else."

Gwyneth reached out and took the bag in her hand as if weighing it, then smiled. "You have my silence."

"It's good to work with you again, Gwyneth. Where did you say you were staying?"

"I didn't."

He leaned forward. "I ask only because I might be able to help you with more comfortable accommodations. Like before."

"Very generous of you. Let me know what the king and queen have to say, and then we'll discuss my accommodations."

She smiled, fluttered her lashes, tilted her head the way I had seen her do with countless tavern patrons and then, when he left, she sat back and a waxy sheen of sweat lit her face. She reached up and wiped damp strands of hair from her forehead.

I walked over to her. "Are you all right?"

She nodded, but clearly she was shaken. From the moment he'd mentioned the child, I had seen everything about Gwyneth grow tighter. "You had a baby with the Chancellor?" I asked.

Fury swept through her eyes. "Stillborn," she said sharply.

"But, Gwyneth—"

"Stillborn, I said! Leave it, Pauline."

She could say and pretend whatever she wanted, but I still knew the truth. She distrusted the Chancellor so much she wouldn't even tell him about his own child.

―――❖―――

A PACKAGE ARRIVED AT THE INN THE NEXT DAY. IT WASN'T addressed to the messenger service but directly to Gwyneth at the inn. It held a larger bag of coins than the day before and a note.

I've inquired of the parties you mentioned, and they have no interest in pursuing the matter. They both consider it best left as is, with a reminder that the city is still in mourning for Princess Greta and their concerns lie now with Crown Prince Walther, whose company of men has gone missing. This is for your troubles and discretion.

The king and queen had turned their backs on their daughter? *Best left as is?* To be tortured and killed at the hands of barbarians? I shook my head in disbelief. I couldn't believe they would abandon their own daughter, but then the word *mourning* struck me.

I sat on the bed, my strength drained, and guilt overwhelmed me. Mourning I understood. In all my worry for Lia, I had almost forgotten about Greta and the tragedy that set Lia on the road back to Civica in the first place. Walther's haunting expression loomed in front of me again, and the way he had looked as he huddled in the mud behind the icehouse. The horror in his eyes. He hadn't seemed like Lia's brother at all, but a shell of the man he had once been. At least I hadn't seen Mikael killed right before my eyes. Lia had told me only that he died bravely in battle. Now I wondered if a soulless barbarian like Kaden had shot an arrow through his throat too. I cradled my stomach, feeling the grief again.

"We need to leave," Gwyneth said. "Immediately."

"No," I argued. "I'm not leaving just because—"

"Not Civica. This inn. This hamlet. The Chancellor figured out where I'm staying. He must have bribed the messenger. Now he'll either be expecting me to be on my way, or paying me a visit for other favors. It won't be long before he discovers you."

I didn't argue. I'd heard his voice when he asked, *Where is she?* He hadn't asked out of concern for my well-being.

For when the Dragon strikes,
It is without mercy,
And his teeth sink in,
With hungry delight.

—Song of Venda

CHAPTER TWENTY-TWO

BEHIND ME, ASTER, YVET, AND ZEKIAH LAID OUT THE clothes piece by piece. They told me not to look until they were ready. It was easy for me not to peek, because my mind was still occupied elsewhere. I couldn't shake the heaviness in my chest.

It seemed everyone and everything I encountered was laced with deception, from Rafe and Kaden, to the Chancellor and Royal Scholar—even my own mother—and in the Sanctum were strange men hidden away in the caverns who clearly didn't belong here. Was *anything* what it seemed to be? I stared out my window, watching birds flying home to roost. The scaled stone armor of a monster settled into rest, and its jagged back was silhouetted against a darkening horizon. The grimness of night fell on an already grim city.

There was a tug on my trousers, and Yvet told me to come

look. I wiped my eyes and turned. Yvet scampered away to stand between Aster and Zekiah, all three straight-backed like proud soldiers. Aster's grin faded. "What's wrong, Miz? Your cheeks are all splotchy-flushy like."

Their faces stopped me, innocence and expectancy, smudges and bread crumbs, hunger and hope. There was at least something real and true to be found in this city.

"Miz?"

I pinched my cheeks and smiled. "I'm fine, Aster."

She raised her eyebrows and looked over toward the bed. My gaze jumped from bed, to barrel, to trunk, to chair.

I shook my head. "This isn't what I bought today."

"Sure it is! See right there on the chair. A shirt and trousers for riding, just like you asked."

"What about everything else? It's too much. The few coins I gave—"

Aster and Zekiah grabbed my hands and dragged me across the room to the bed. "Effiera, Maizel, Ursula, and a passel of others worked all day to have these ready for you."

A flutter swooped through my chest, and I reached down to touch one of the dresses. It wasn't fancy, and wasn't made of fine fabrics—if anything, just the opposite. It was stitched together with scraps, pieces of soft leathers dyed in the muted greens, reds, and deep browns of the forest, strips of fur, ragged edges hanging loose, some trailing to the floor. I swallowed. It was decidedly Vendan, but it was something else too.

Aster giggled. "She likes it," she said to the others.

I nodded, still confused. "Yes, Aster," I whispered. "Very much." I knelt so I was level with Yvet and Zekiah. "But why?"

Yvet's pale eyes were wide and watery. "Effiera liked your name. She said anyone with a pretty name like that deserved pretty clothes."

Aster and Zekiah shot a worried glance over Yvet's head.

I narrowed my eyes at one, then the other. "And?"

"Old Elder Haragru had a dream a long time ago when he still had a tooth right here," Aster said, tugging on her front tooth, "and he hasn't stopped wagging about it since. He's not quite right in his head with all his piled-on years, but Effiera says he described someone like you, who would come from far away. Someone who should be wearing—"

Zekiah reached behind Yvet and pinched Aster. She pulled her shoulders back, catching herself. "It's only a story," she said. "But Elder Haragru likes to tell it over and over. You know." Aster knocked on her head and rolled her eyes.

I stood and chewed on my lower lip. "I have no way of paying Effiera for all these clothes. I'll have to send them back with you—"

"Oh, no. No, no, no. These can't go back," Aster said, working herself to a worry. "Effiera said they were a gift. That's all. You don't owe her nothing more than a kiss to the wind. And she'd be sorely hurt if you didn't like them. Sorely hurt. They all worked real—"

"Aster, stop. It's not the clothes. They're beautiful. But—" I looked at their faces plummeting from elation to disappointment, and I imagined Effiera's and the other seamstresses' faces doing the same if I refused them. I put my hands up in surrender. "Don't worry. The clothes will stay." Their grins returned.

I looked at the display covering every free surface in the room. One by one, I lifted the garments, running my fingers along fabric and fur, chain and belt, stitch and hem. They weren't only beautiful, they felt *right*, and I wasn't even sure why. I turned back to the first one I had looked at, sewn from leather scraps. It had one long sleeve and the other shoulder and arm were left bare. "I'll wear this one tonight," I said.

ASTER AND YVET HELPED ME DRESS. ZEKIAH BASHFULLY turned around and fiddled with Kaden's wooden swords in the corner. Yvet ruffled the thin strips of trailing fur with her small hands while I attached my single tethered bone around my neck. Aster was just lacing up the back when the lock rattled. We all startled, waiting. The door swung open, and Calantha stepped in. The sword in Zekiah's hand fell to the floor, and he scrambled to Aster's side.

Calantha's single eye glided over me, from shoulder to floor.

She eyed the children next. "Get out," she said quietly. They darted past her and heaved the heavy door shut behind them.

She explained that Kaden had sent her to bring me down to Sanctum Hall. She stepped closer, her hands on her hips, scrutinizing my attire. I lifted my chin, proudly wearing the dress Effiera had made. It fit snugly and perfectly, but Calantha looked at it with a disdainful air.

"The Komizar will *not* be happy about this." A hint of a smile lit her face.

"And that pleases you? You'd like to see his hatred for me inflamed?"

She walked over and touched the dress, rubbing the soft leather between her fingers. "Do you even know what you're wearing, Princess?"

The flutter returned to my chest. "A dress," I said uncertainly. "A beautifully crafted dress, even if it's made of scraps."

"It's the dress of the oldest clan of Venda." She looked at my exposed shoulder. "With a few modifications. It's a great honor to be given the dress of many hands and households." She looked around the room at the other clothes. "You've been welcomed by the clan of Meurasi. That's sure to spark the wrath of many in the Council."

She sighed, the smile playing in her eye again, and gave me one last long look. "Yes, a great many," she mused, and motioned to the door. "Ready?"

CHAPTER TWENTY-THREE

RAFE

"GET YOUR BOOTS ON, EMISSARY. THE KOMIZAR SAYS I have to feed you."

The two of us, alone in my room at last, and my hands were free.

It was a chance I had dreamed about every night as I crossed the Cam Lanteux. I stared at him, not moving. I could be upon him before he even had a chance to draw the weapon at his side.

Kaden grinned. "Assuming you could even disarm me, would it be worth it? Think carefully. I'm all that stands between Lia and Malich and a hundred more like him. Don't forget where you are."

"You seem to have a low regard for your countrymen." I shrugged. "But then, so do I."

He ambled closer. "Malich is a good soldier, but he tends to hold grudges when someone gets the best of him. Especially someone half his size. So if you care about—"

I grabbed my boots and sat down. "I have no interest in the girl."

A puff of air shook his chest. "Sure you don't." He walked to the table and picked up the goblet that Lia had sipped from earlier. He ran his thumb along the smudged rim, eyed me, then set it back down. "If you have no interest, then we have no score to settle, right? You're only here minding the affairs of your prince."

I jerked at the leather pulls of my boot. It was hard to believe we had bunked in the same barn for half the summer. How we had managed not to kill each other then I didn't know, because there had always been tension between us, even from our first handshake at the water pump. *Follow your gut*, Sven always told me. How I wished I had. Instead of cutting in on a dance I should have cut his—

"*Chimentra*. It's a word you might find useful," he said. "There's nothing like it in the Morrighese or Dalbretch languages. Your languages are essentially the same, one kingdom sprang from the other. Our kingdom had to struggle for everything we have, sometimes even our words. It comes from Lady Venda and a story she told of a creature with two mouths but no ears. One mouth can't hear what the other says, and it's soon strangled in the trail of its own lies."

"Another word for liar. I can see why you'd have need of such a word. Not all kingdoms do."

He walked over and looked out the window, unafraid to turn his back on me, but his hand was never far from the dagger at his side. He examined the narrow window as if judging its width, then turned back to me. "I still find it interesting that the prince's urgent message for Venda came right on the heels of Lia's arrival here. Almost as if you were following us. Interesting too that you came alone and not with a whole entourage. Isn't that how you soft courtly types usually travel?"

"Not when we don't want the whole court to know guarded business. The prince is already assembling a new cabinet to replace his father's, but if they get the slightest hint of his plans beforehand, they'll quash it. Even princes have only so much power. At least until they become kings."

He shrugged as if unimpressed with princes or kings. I pulled on my other boot and stood. He indicated with the sweep of his hand that I should exit first. As we walked down the corridor, he asked, "You find the accommodations to your liking?"

The room was basically a boudoir furnished with an oversized bed, feather mattress, netted canopy, rugs, tapestries on walls, and a wardrobe that held thick soft robes. It smelled of perfumed oils, spilled wine, and things I didn't want to think about.

Kaden grunted at my silence. "It's one of his indulgences, and he prefers not to entertain female visitors in his own quarters. I suppose the Komizar thought his frilly emissary boy would be comfortable in it. And it seems you are." He stopped walking and faced me. "My own quarters are much plainer, but Lia seems to be content there. *If* you know what I mean."

We stood chest to chest. I knew what game he was playing. "You think you can goad me into lunging at you so you can slit my throat?"

"I don't need a reason to slit your throat. But I do want to tell you this. If you want Lia to live, stay away from her."

"And now you're threatening to kill her?"

"Not me. But if the Komizar or Council gets even the faintest whiff that the two of you are conspiring together, not even I can save Lia. Remember, your lies might still be found out. Don't bring her down with you. And don't forget, she chose *me* over you last night."

I lunged, smashing him against the stone wall, but his knife was already at my throat. He smiled. "That was the other thing I wondered about," he said. "Though you lost to me at the log wrestling event, your moves were quite practiced, more like a trained soldier than a puff of court confectionary."

"Then maybe you haven't met enough court confectionary."

He lowered his knife. "Apparently not."

We walked in silence the rest of the way to Sanctum Hall, but his words hammered in my head. *Don't bring her down with you . . . the faintest whiff that the two of you are conspiring . . .*

And Kaden already did have a whiff. How, I didn't know, but I'd have to do a better job convincing him and the rest of these savages that there was nothing between us. I hated that his logic rang true—if I was found out, I couldn't bring Lia down with me.

CHAPTER TWENTY-FOUR

WELCOMED BY THE CLAN OF MEURASI.

I knew I should be afraid. The welcome was also going to spark wrath, and further inflaming the Council's hatred toward me was one thing I couldn't afford.

But I had been welcomed. And I felt it. I couldn't turn my back on that either. I felt it with every stitch and scrap of leather that covered me. A strange wholeness. Little Yvet said Effiera had liked my name. Was it possible that outside of the Sanctum walls, there were Vendans who had heard the name Jezelia before, not just in passing but in a forgotten song handed down among families?

I wondered if Calantha was overstating the ire of the Council for her own purposes. I had seen her last night, just as focused on Rafe as the Komizar had been, but surely for very different reasons.

"Go on." Calantha poked at my back, pushing me forward.

I walked into Sanctum Hall. It was noisy and crowded, and I thought I might slip through unnoticed, but then a governor saw me and stopped, choking on his ale, spray flying from his mouth. A *chievdar* cursed under his breath.

My arrival ran through the hall like a loose squealing pig. A ragged path opened up as others caught sight of me. Then, when a group of soldiers stepped aside, Kaden and Rafe saw me. They were at the other end of the hall, seated at the table, but slowly stood as I approached. They both appeared to be confused and cautious, as if something wild had been unleashed in front of them. Rafe couldn't know what this scrap of dress meant, and I wondered why he was looking at me that way too.

I kept moving forward, the soft leather snug against my skin. There were whispers about the kavah on my shoulder, and a few vulgar sounds of approval. I wasn't the filthy royal beast they had seen last night. Now I was something recognizable, someone who looked almost like one of them. I was a piece of their own history that reached back to the oldest clan of Venda.

"*Jabavé!*" Malich and two other Rahtan stepped into my path. "What does the Morrighese bitch wear?" Their knives were curiously drawn as if they intended to cut the dress from me. Or simply cut me.

I steeled my gaze. "Aren't you brave?" I said. "You must approach me with a drawn knife now?" I let my eyes slowly graze Malich's striped face, the trails of my nails still visible across it. "But I suppose your fear is understandable. Considering."

He stepped toward me, but Kaden was suddenly there,

pushing him aside. "She wears what the Komizar ordered her to wear—suitable clothes. You question his orders?"

Malich's knife was tight in his hands, his knuckles white. Orders or no orders, revenge was taut in his eyes. As long as his face was marked by my hand, it would be. The two other Rahtan beside him exchanged a glance with Kaden and sheathed their weapons. Malich reluctantly did too, and Kaden pulled me away toward the table.

"You'll never learn, will you?" he whispered between gritted teeth.

"I hope not," I answered.

"What do you think you're wearing?"

"You don't like it?" I asked.

"It's not what we bought today."

"But it's what Effiera sent."

"For the sake of the gods, sit down and be quiet."

And he, apparently, would never learn either.

I sat on Kaden's left. Rafe was adjacent to him on his right, close enough for Kaden to keep an eye on him, but not close enough for Rafe and me to share even the smallest word without Kaden overhearing. It didn't seem to matter. Rafe's eyes briefly skimmed my Vendan attire, then he looked away and seemed to avoid my gaze thereafter. I should have been glad for his cold dismissal. If Griz could perceive our connection by peering into my eyes, others might too. It was best that we not look at each other at all, but the pull was still there, and the more I avoided him, the more the burn grew in me. All I wanted to do was turn and watch him.

I looked down the length of the table instead. It seated close to sixty, so only half of those present were the Sanctum Council. I guessed the rest were favored soldiers or other guests of the Council.

Kaden spoke with Governor Faiwell of Dorava Province, who sat adjacent to me, and Chievdar Stavik in the next seat, who had slain my brother's platoon in the valley. Just down from them were Griz and Eben. I wanted to thank Eben for my boots, but with the scowling *chievdar* within earshot, I didn't dare.

Servants began bringing in stacks of hammered plates; trays of salted pork snouts, ears, and feet; platters of dark meat that I guessed to be venison; bowls of thick gruel; and pitchers to refill empty tankards. The energy in the hall was different tonight. Maybe it was because the Komizar was gone, or maybe it was just I who was different. I noticed the servants whispering more among themselves. One of them approached me, a spare girl, tall and wispy. She hesitated, then offered a short, awkward curtsy. "Princess, if the ale isn't to your liking—"

Stavik roared, and the poor girl fell back several steps. "Watch your tongue, maid!" he yelled. "There's no royalty in Venda, and she'll sure as hell drink what the rest of us do or not drink at all."

A rumble ran down the table, a growing discord that echoed the *chievdar's* contempt. The unexpected welcome was being challenged as swiftly as a lash to the back. I felt Kaden's hand on my thigh. A warning. And I realized, even as Assassin, he was feeling the edge of what he could control.

I returned the *chievdar's* glare, then spoke to the girl, who was still trembling several steps away. "As Chievdar Stavik so wisely said, I'll drink whatever you serve and be glad for it."

Kaden's hand slid from my thigh. The discord was replaced with uneasy chatter. Baskets of bread were brought to the table. For all their wretched and coarse ways, no one partook prematurely. They all waited for Calantha to offer the acknowledgment of sacrifice.

The same girl who had cowered before the raging *chievdar* just moments earlier now came forward, the platter of bones rattling in her frightened hands as she set it before Calantha.

Everyone waited.

Calantha looked at me, her lone eye narrowing, and then she nodded. The air in the room shifted. I knew what she was going to do before she ever moved. My temples throbbed. *Not now.* This might be the move that killed me. The timing was all wrong. *Not now.* But it was all already in motion. Calantha stood and shoved the platter across the table at me. "Our prisoner will give the acknowledgment tonight."

I didn't wait for dissent, nor for a sword to be drawn. I stood. And before Stavik could utter a word, before Kaden could pull me back to my seat, I sang the Vendan acknowledgment of sacrifice and more. *E cristav unter quiannad.*

The words poured out, hot and urgent, like my chest had been laid open. *Meunter ijotande.* And then more flowed out languid and slow, a wordless language, like that day in the valley, remembrances known only to the gods. I lifted the platter over my head, *Yaveen hal an ziadre.*

I lowered the bones to the table once again and offered the final *paviamma*.

The room was swept silent. No response came back to me.

Seconds ticked as centuries, and then finally a faint *paviamma* echoed back from Eben. The slight tear in the silence opened wider, and more *paviammas* rolled down the table and back again, the brethren looking at their laps. The meal began, food was passed, talk resumed. Kaden breathed an audible sigh and leaned back in his seat. Finally, Rafe looked at me too, but the expression in his eyes wasn't what I wanted to see. He looked at me as if I were a stranger.

I shoved the platter toward him. "Take a bone, Emissary," I snapped. "Or are you not grateful?"

He glared at me, his lip lifted in disgust. He grabbed a long femur and turned back to Calantha without a second glance.

"It seems that if the Komizar doesn't kill them, they might kill each other," Governor Faiwell quipped to Stavik.

"The worst enemy is one that you've slept with," Stavik answered.

They both laughed as if they knew this from experience.

This was our plan, I told myself.

A performance. That was all.

The kind of performance that could rip out a heart a piece at a time. Rafe didn't look at me again for the rest of the night.

CHAPTER TWENTY-FIVE

KADEN WAS SILENT AS HE GOT READY FOR BED, THE KIND of silence that made every other sound grating—his breathing, the weight of his footsteps, the sound of water poured from a pitcher. It was all laced with tension.

He scrubbed his face over the basin, and ran his wet fingers through his hair. His movements were brusque. He crossed the room and pulled his belt from his trousers with a quick yank. "The soldiers told me you sat on the wall outside the window today," he said without looking my way.

"Is that forbidden?"

"It's not advised. It's a long drop."

"I needed fresh air."

"They said you sang songs."

"Remembrances. Just the evening tradition of Morrighan. You remember that, don't you?"

"The soldiers said people gathered to listen."

"So they did, but only a few. I'm a curiosity."

He unlocked his trunk and threw in his belt and scabbard. His knife was placed just under the fur rug where he would sleep—he kept his blade close, even in his own locked room. Was it habit or a requirement of the Rahtan, who always had to be ready? It reminded me that I still had Natiya's knife in my boot and I'd have to be discreet when I removed it.

"Is something wrong? Was it the way I said the blessing?" I asked as I struggled with the laces at my back.

He took off one boot. "You said it fine."

"But?"

"Nothing." He saw me fiddling with the laces. "Here, let me look."

I turned around. "Aster seems to have knotted them," I said.

I felt his fingers fumbling with the task, then finally felt the fabric loosen. "There," he said. I turned to face him. He looked down at me, his eyes warm. "There is something else. When I saw you in that dress, I was—" He shook his head. "I was afraid. I thought— Never mind."

I'd never seen him wrestle so much with his words. Or admit to being afraid. He stepped away and sat on the bed. "Be careful how much you push, Lia." He pulled his other boot off.

"Are you worried about me?"

"Of course I'm worried about you!" he snapped.

I stiffened, surprised by his anger. "I've been welcomed, Kaden. That's all. Isn't that what you wanted?"

"That kind of welcome could also bring a death sentence."

"From the Council, you mean."

"We have very little here, Lia, but our pride."

"And a prisoner's been honored. That's the problem?"

He nodded. "You only just got here and—"

"But, Kaden, the people who welcomed me are Vendans."

His eyes drilled into me. "But they're not the ones who carry lethal weapons."

There was no denying that the tools of Effiera's trade were nothing like Malich's and his cohorts'. I sat down beside Kaden. "What *is* the clan of Meurasi? Why do they matter so much?"

He explained that the city was filled with people from all the provinces. They tended to settle into neighborhoods of their own clan, and each had unique characteristics. One quarter was quite different from another, but the clan of Meurasi represented all things Vendan. Hearty, enduring, steadfast. They honored many of the ways of old that others had forgotten, but from them came the promise of loyalty above all.

"They'll clothe their own, even if they have to piece together scraps to do it. Everyone contributes what they can. Their bloodline reaches all the way back to the only child Lady Venda had. The first Komizar remarried after she died and had many children with other wives, but from Venda, there was only one, Meuras. So yes, it's an honor for anyone to be welcomed to the clan, but a prisoner—" He shook his head as if trying to figure it out then looked at me. "It just isn't done. Did you say something to Effiera in the tent?"

I remembered her expression when Aster told her my name, and then the soft murmurs when I removed my shirt and they saw the kavah on my shoulder. *The ways of old.* Did the Meurasi still pass down the babble of a madwoman? *A pretty name*, Yvet called it. Maybe it was more than that, but given the Council's reaction to my welcome and Kaden's apparent disapproval as well, I decided to keep that card close to my chest for now.

"No," I said. "We only talked about clothes."

He looked at me warily. "Be careful. Don't push it, Lia."

"I heard you say that the first time."

"I don't think you did."

I jumped to my feet. "Why is this *my* fault?" I shouted. "You're the one who took me to the *jehendra* even when I said I didn't need clothes! I bought one thing, and they brought me another. If I had insulted them by refusing the clothes, I'm sure I'd be reprimanded for that too! And tonight did I ask to say the acknowledgment of sacrifice? No! Calantha shoved the platter of bones in my face. What was I to do? Is there anything I can do that's right in your eyes?"

He sighed and pushed against his knees to stand. "You're right. I'm sorry. You didn't ask for any of this. I'm just tired. It's been a long day."

My anger cooled. Maybe it was just part of his training as an assassin not to show it, but Kaden was never tired. He was always alert and ready, but his fatigue was evident now.

I lifted my foot onto the frame of the bed to unlace my boot. "Where were you all day?"

"Duties. Just attending to my duties as Keep."

What kind of duties would take a toll on him like this? Or maybe he wasn't well? He grabbed blankets from the top of the chest and dropped them to the fur rug.

"I'll take the rug tonight," I offered.

"No. I don't mind."

He took off his shirt. His scars always stopped me, no matter how many times I had seen them. They were a harsh reminder of how brutal his world was. He snuffed the lanterns, and once I had changed, he blew out the candle too. Tonight there weren't even dancing shadows to ease me to sleep.

It was quiet for a long while, and I thought he had already fallen asleep, but then he asked, "Was there anything else you did today?"

He wasn't too tired for his mind to still be churning with questions. Did he suspect something? "What do you mean by *else*?"

"Just wondering what you did all day. Besides climb out the window."

"Nothing," I whispered. "It was a long day for me too."

The next day when Kaden had to go out, he had Eben come to keep me company, but I knew it was a ruse to keep an eye on me. Eben was guarding me, just as he had in the vagabond meadow—except that things were different between us now. He was still the trained killer, but now there was a chink in his armor, and a softness in his eyes that hadn't been there before. Maybe it was that I had spared him the burden of killing his own horse. Maybe my whispered acknowledgment of Spirit's name allowed something he had hidden inside to bloom. Just a little. Or maybe it was that we shared a similar grief, watching someone we loved be butchered before our eyes.

On Kaden's orders, Eben was allowed to take me out of my room, but not outside of the Sanctum, not to this wing or that tower, only to a narrowly prescribed area. "For your own safety," Kaden said when I shot him a questioning glare. In truth, I knew he was trying to keep me out of Malich's path and that of certain Council members. By the end of the meal last night, it was apparent that hostility still ran high, more so among a few because of my welcome, but the ever-united Council seemed divided now into two camps, the curious and the haters.

Eben took me on a circuitous route to the paddocks behind the Council Wing. A new foal had been born while he was away. We watched the stick-legged foal frolic in a small corral, jumping for the sheer pleasure of trying out new legs. Eben balanced on the paddock rail trying to restrain a smile.

"What will you name him?" I asked.

"He's not mine. Don't want him anyway. Too much trouble to train." His eyes flashed with every pain he still carried, and his tender years made his denial wooden.

I sighed. "I don't blame you. It's hard to commit to something after—" I let the thought dangle in the air. "Still, he is beautiful, and someone has to teach him. But there are probably trainers who are better at it than you."

"I'm just as good as any old wrangler. Spirit knew what to do with just a twitch from my knee. He—" His chin jutted out and then, in a quiet voice, he added, "He was given to me by my father."

And now I knew the true depth of Eben's grief. Spirit wasn't just any horse.

Eben had never made any mention of his parents. If Kaden hadn't told me that Eben had witnessed their butchering, I'd have thought he was spawned by some impish beast and dropped to earth fully dressed and armed as a small Vendan soldier.

I understood the hole that Eben felt, the wicked depth of it, that no matter how much you wanted to pretend it wasn't there, its black mouth opened up to swallow you again and again.

He shook off the mention of his father in a practiced way, flicking his hair from his eyes, and jumping down from the rail. "We should go back," he said.

I wanted to say something wise, something comforting that would lessen his pain, but I was still feeling that hole myself. The only words that came were, "Thank you for my boots, Eben. They mean more to me than you can know."

He nodded. "I cleaned them too."

I wondered if, like Griz, this was a kindness to wipe out a debt.

"You owed me nothing, Eben. I took care of your horse for me as much as for you."

"I already knew that," he said, and hurried ahead of me.

We walked back through yet another tunnel, but I was getting good at memorizing them now, and I was beginning to understand a pattern to the chaotic layout of architecture. Small avenues, tunnels, and buildings emanated from larger ones. It was as if many large structures within this ancient city had slowly woven together, a graceless animal that grew extra arms, legs, and eyes without regard to aesthetics—only immediate need. The Sanctum was the heart of the beast, and the hidden caverns below, the bowels. No one ever mentioned what stirred beneath the Sanctum, and I never saw the robed figures at meals. They stayed to themselves.

As we walked the last hall to Kaden's room, I asked, "Eben, what are those caverns down below? Aster mentioned them to me."

"You mean the catacombs? Ghoul Caves, Finch calls them. Don't go down there. Only thing in them is stale air, old books, and dark spirits."

I suppressed a smile. It was almost the same description I used for the archives in Civica, only there the dark spirits were Civica scholars.

THE NEXT FEW DAYS PASSED AS THE PREVIOUS, BUT EACH one was shorter than the day before. I learned that time plays tricks when you want more of it. With each day that passed with no sign of Rafe's soldiers, I knew that Vendan riders could be that much closer with news that the Dalbreck king was hale and hearty—a death sentence for Rafe. At least the Komizar would be gone for two more weeks. That would buy us more time for Rafe's soldiers to appear. I tried to hold on to that hope for Rafe's sake, but it was looking more certain that finding an escape was left only to us now.

The weather grew colder, and another icy rain drenched the city. In spite of the cold, each day I climbed out the window and sat on the wall and said my remembrances, searching through them like shuffled papers, trying to find answers, holding on to those that held a glimmer of truth. Each day a larger group gathered to listen, a dozen, two dozen, and more. Many were children. One day Aster was among them, and she called up for a story. I began with the tale of Morrighan, the girl led by the gods to a land of plenty, then told the story of the birth of two of the Lesser Kingdoms, Gastineux and Cortenai. All the histories and texts I had studied for years were now tales that mesmerized them. They were as hungry for stories as Eben and Natiya had been when we sat around the campfire—stories of other people, other places, other times.

These moments at least gave me something to look forward to, because there was no opportunity to talk to Rafe privately. Even when Kaden left me locked alone in his room and I snuck out, I discovered there were now guards posted below Rafe's window too, almost as if they knew he couldn't slip out through the narrow windows but someone smaller might slip in. The evening meal afforded me no greater opportunity for a private moment, and my frustration grew. Here in the Sanctum, we might as well have been separated by a vast continent. I attributed my restless dreams to my aggravation. I'd had another one of Rafe leaving, but it had more detail than before. He was dressed in garb I had never seen, Rafe, a warrior of frightening stature. His expression was hot and fierce, and he wore swords at both sides.

EVENINGS IN SANCTUM HALL WERE LONG AND TIRESOME, not unlike court in Morrighan, but their ways were decidedly louder, cruder, and always seemed on the brink of chaos. The acknowledgment of sacrifice provided a curious quiet moment in stark contrast to their raucous activities. I learned the names of all the Council—the governors, the *chievdars*, and the Rahtan, even though so many of their names sounded alike. Gorthan. Gurtan, Gunthur. Mekel, Malich, Alick. Kaden's name alone seemed to have no close soundalike. The *chievdar* I had met in the valley, Stavik, was sour beyond measure but turned out to be the most civil of the five army commanders.

The governors were the easiest to converse with. Most were glad to be at the Sanctum instead of the desolate homelands they came from, which perhaps lightened their dispositions. Three of the Rahtan were still gone, but the four who were present besides Kaden, Griz, and Malich were, by far, the most hostile of the Council. Jorik and Darius were the ones who had stood by Malich with their knives drawn when they saw my clan dress, and the other two, Theron and Gurtan, seemed to wear sneers like permanent battle paint. I imagined them as the men the Komizar would have sent to finish the job that Kaden had failed to do—and there was no doubt in my mind, they would have finished it without hesitation. They were the very definition of Rahtan. *Never fail.* It was hard for me to reconcile that in some twisted way Kaden had saved my life by bringing me here.

Every evening after the meal, the Council was drawn into games of stones or cards, or they simply drank the night away. The precious Morrighese vintages were swilled like cheap ale. The games of stones were foreign to me, but the card games I recognized. I remembered Walther's first piece of advice to me: *Sometimes winning is not only a matter of knowing the rules, but of making your opponent think he knows them better.* I watched from afar, parsing out the nuances and similarities to the games I had played with my brothers and their friends. Tonight the stakes for one particular game grew, with the largest stack piling up in front of Malich. I watched smugness strut across his face like a barnyard rooster, the same cocky grin he had when he told me that killing Greta was easy.

I stood and walked over to the players. I decided I was in need of some entertainment too.

CHAPTER TWENTY-SIX

KADEN

I WATCHED HER SAUNTER OVER.

It was something about her steps. Her arms crossed in front of her. Her timing. The deliberate casualness of it all.

The muscles in my neck tightened. I didn't have a good feeling about it.

Then she smiled, and I knew.

Don't do this, Lia.

But I really wasn't sure just what she was doing. I only knew no good would come of it. I knew the language of Lia.

I tried to disengage myself from Governor Carzwil, who was intent on sharing every challenge of transporting turnips and bags of lime from his province to Venda. "Lia," I called, but she ignored me. The governor spoke louder, determined to regain my attention, but I kept glancing away. "She's fine," the governor said. "Give her a little rope, boy! Look, she's smiling."

That was the problem. Her smile didn't mean what he thought it did. I knew it meant trouble. I excused myself from Carzwil, but by the time I got to the table, she had already engaged two of the governors. Even though they were two who had warmed to her presence more than the others, I still hovered, sensing something about to spring.

"So, the point is to get six cards with numbers that match? That sounds easy enough," Lia said, her voice light and inquisitive.

Malich spit on the floor next to him, then smiled. "Sure it's easy."

"There's more to it than that," Governor Faiwell said. "The colored symbols must be matched too—if you can, that is. And certain combinations are better than others."

"Interesting. I think I might understand it," Lia crooned. She repeated the basics back to them.

I recognized the tilt of her head, the cadence of her words, the purse of her lips. I knew what she was doing as sure as I still felt the knot on my shin. "Come away, Lia. Let them play their game."

"Let her watch! She can sit on my lap." Governor Umbrose laughed.

Lia looked over her shoulder at me. "Yes, Kaden, I'd like to try my hand at it," she said, then turned back to the table. "May I join you?"

"You have no stake," Malich grumbled, "and no one plays for free."

Lia narrowed her eyes and walked around to his side of the table. "True, I have no coin, but surely I have something of worth to you. Maybe an hour alone with me?" She leaned forward on the table, and her voice turned hard. "I'm sure you'd love that, wouldn't you, Malich?"

The other players hooted, saying that was good enough stake for all of them, and Malich smiled. "You're in, Princess."

"No," I said. "You're not. That's enough. Come away—"

Lia whirled around, her mouth smiling but her eyes lit with fire. "Do I not even have the freedom to make the simplest of choices? Am I the lowliest of prisoners, *Assassin*?"

It was the first time she had ever called me that. Our gazes locked. Everyone waited. I shook my head; not a command but a plea. *Don't do this.*

She turned away. "I'm in," she said and sat down in a chair that was dragged over for her.

She was given a pile of wooden chits, and the game began. Malich smiling. Lia smiling. Everyone smiling but me.

And Rafe.

He stepped up to the outer perimeter with others who had gathered to watch. I turned around, looking for Calantha and Ulrix, who were supposed to be guarding him, but they had joined the crowd too. Rafe shot me a sharp glance, accusing, as if I had let her walk into a den of wolves.

Lia made stupid errors in the very first hand. And the next. She had already lost a third of her chits. Her brows pulled down in concentration. The next hand she lost fewer, but still more than she could afford. She shook her head, rearranging her cards again and again, loudly asking the governor next to her which was more valuable, a red claw or a black wing. Everyone at the table smiled and placed higher bets, determined to win an hour with Lia. She lost more chits, and her face grew dark. She bit the corner of her lip. Malich watched her expressions more than his own cards.

I looked at Rafe. A sheen of sweat lit his brow. Another hand. Lia held her cards close, closing her eyes for a moment as if she was trying to think them into an order that wasn't there. The governors placed their bets. Lia placed hers. Malich topped them all and revealed two of his cards. Lia looked at her cards again and shook her head. She added more chits to the pile and revealed two of hers, the same losing two she had been revealing all night. The governors upped their ante—their final bid of the hand. So did Lia, shoving the last of her chits into the center of the table. Malich smiled, met the ante, and shoved his pile to the center as well. He laid his cards out. A fortress of lords.

The governors threw down their cards, unable to beat him.

Everyone waited, breathless, for Lia to lay her cards out. She frowned and shook her head. Then looked at me. Blinked. A slow blink as long as a thousand miles.

Then back at Malich.

A long sigh, contrite.

She laid out her cards.

Six black wings.

A perfect hand.

"I think this beats yours, doesn't it, Malich?"

Malich's mouth hung open. And then a roar of laughter filled the room. Lia leaned forward and gathered the chits in. The three governors nodded, impressed. Malich stared at her, still not believing what she had done. At last he looked around him, taking in the crowd and the laughter. He stood, his chair flying behind him, his face black with rage, and drew his dagger.

The *shing* of a dozen drawn daggers, including mine, echoed in return.

"Go drink it off, Malich. She beat you fairly," Governor Faiwell said.

Malich's chest heaved, and his glare landed on me, then my knife. He turned away roughly, tripping on the chair behind him, and stormed out of the hall, four Rahtan brothers following on his heels.

Daggers were sheathed. The laughter resumed.

Rafe reached up and wiped the sweat from his upper lip. He had made a swift move toward Lia when Malich drew his knife, as if he intended to block him. Weaponless. Not exactly the behavior of an uninterested court confectionary. Ulrix yanked Rafe away, remembering his duties at last.

I looked back at Lia. She was unruffled, her chin tucked as her eyes still gazed at the now-empty corridor where Malich had exited. Her stare was cold and satisfied.

"Gather your winnings," I ordered.

I escorted her out of the hall and back to my room. When I had shut the door and locked it, I spun toward her.

She was already facing me defiantly, waiting.

"Have you lost your mind?" I yelled. "Did you have to humiliate him in front of his comrades? Isn't it enough that he already hates you with the fire of a thousand suns?"

Her expression was grim. Unfeeling. She was in no hurry to answer, but when she did, her tone held no emotion. "Malich laughed the night he told me that he had killed Greta. He reveled in her death. He said it was easy. Her death cost him nothing. It will now. Every day that I breathe, I will make it cost him something. Every time I see that same smug grin on his face, I will make him pay for it."

She dumped her winnings on the bed and looked back at me. "So the short answer to your question, Kaden, is no. It's not enough. It will never be enough."

CHAPTER TWENTY-SEVEN

RAFE

NOW I UNDERSTOOD WHY SVEN PREFERRED SOLDIERING to love. It was easier to understand and far less likely to get you killed.

I was perplexed when I first saw her walk over to the table where several of the barbarians were playing cards. Then I spotted Malich at the table, and it rushed back to me. *I'll take a game of cards to stitchery any day. My brothers are shrewd, bordering on thieves when it comes to their cards—the best kind of teachers to have.*

Last night it had been all I could do to stand there and not wring her neck myself, but it was harder still to not have a sword in my hand to protect her from Malich.

Yes, Lia, you were and still are a challenge. But damned if I hadn't felt a surge of admiration for her too, even as sweat ran down my neck and I silently cursed her. That was not what I would call sitting tight. Did she ever listen to anyone?

I threw my belt onto the chest. This room was getting on my nerves. The smell, the furnishings, the floral rug. It *was* suited for some pompous court fool. I opened a shutter to let in some of the brisk night air.

It was our seventh day here, and there was still no sign of Sven, Tavish, Orrin, or Jeb. Too long. I was beginning to fear the worst. What if I had led my friends to their deaths? I had made a promise to Lia that I would get us out of this. What if I couldn't?

Don't bring her down with you. . . . If the Komizar or Council gets the faintest whiff . . .

I had tried with every power within me not to look at her. The only time we had spoken in days was in clipped words in Sanctum Hall with too many ears listening to say anything remotely helpful to either of us. I knew she was becoming impatient with my persistent disregard of her, but it wasn't just Kaden who kept a close watch. The Rahtan did too. I sensed that they wanted to catch one or both of us in a lie. Their distrust ran high. And then there was Calantha. I often saw her standing in the shadows in the hall before everyone sat down to eat, scrutinizing Lia, then turning to watch me. There were few women here in the Sanctum, and none seemed to have any position or power—except her. I wasn't sure what the power was or how much she had, because she was always guarded with my inquiries, and no one else would share anything about her, no matter how casual I kept my questions.

That didn't keep her from trying to dig information out of

me, though she tried to make it look like idle banter. She asked me the prince's age and then asked me my own age. *The prince is nineteen,* I had told her, sticking to the truth in case she had knowledge of it, and then I told her I was twenty-five, so it wouldn't invite musings about us being the same age. In truth, I had no personal emissaries. I was a soldier and had no need of messengers or agents to negotiate for me, so all of my answers in regard to an emissary were drawn from a place of greed—a motive the Komizar would understand if Calantha carried our conversations back to him.

I splashed my face with water, washing the sweat and salt from my skin, trying to erase the image of Lia walking off with Kaden to his room.

Three more days. That's what Sven always told me. *When you think you're at the end of your rope, give it three more days. And then another three. Sometimes you'll find the rope is longer than you thought.*

Sven had been trying to teach me patience back then. I was a first-year cadet and kept getting passed over for field exercises. No captain wanted to risk injuring the king's only son. That three days turned into six, turned into nine. Finally it was Sven who lost patience and rode me out to an encampment himself, dumping me at a captain's tent door, saying he didn't want to see my face again until it had a few bruises.

And sometimes you'll find the rope is shorter than you thought.

Here, **I say, pressing my fist to her ribs.**

And here, my hand to her breastbone.

I give her the same instruction my mother gave to me.

> *It is the language of knowing, child,*
>
> *A language as old as the universe itself.*
>
> *It is seeing without eyes,*
>
> *And listening without ears.*

It was how my mother survived in those early years.

How we survive now.

> *Trust the strength within you.*
>
> *And one day, you must teach your daughter to do the same.*

—***The Last Testaments of Gaudrel***

CHAPTER TWENTY-EIGHT

THEY WEREN'T COMING. FROM THE START, I HAD KNOWN their chances were slim, but every time I looked at Rafe's face, I mustered new hope for his sake. These were not just soldiers coming to help free a wayward prince and princess. These were his friends.

Hope is a slippery fish—impossible to hold on to for long, my aunt Cloris would say when I pined for something she deemed childish and impossible. *Then you have to hold harder,* my aunt Bernette would counter to her older sister before ushering me away in a huff. But some things slipped from your grasp no matter how hard you held on to them.

We were on our own. Rafe's friends were dead. It wasn't a whisper in my ear or a prickle at my neck that told me. It was the rules of reason that prevailed, the rules of everything I could understand and see. They said it plainly. This was a harsh land with no forgiveness for enemies.

I watched Rafe each night, stealing a glance when I was sure no one was looking. While my movements within the Sanctum were still closely guarded, his had grown freer, and both Calantha and Ulrix had become less watchful. With calculating patience, he was cultivating their trust. Ulrix, while still a frightening beast of a man, seemed to have given up with his fist, and Rafe suffered no more split lips, almost as if he had judged Rafe an acceptable excuse of a man even though he was enemy swine. Ingratiating yourself with a beast like Ulrix was truly a work of skill.

Rafe drank with the *chievdars*, laughed with governors, spoke quietly with servants. Young maids brushed close, endeared by his stilted attempts at speaking Vendan, eager to refill his mug, smiling at him beneath lowered lashes. But a new identity, no matter how well played, would do him little good once the Komizar discovered he was lying.

It was as if, with the Komizar gone, everyone had forgotten Rafe's looming death sentence, or maybe they just thought it would never come to pass. Rafe *was* convincing. Someone was always pulling him aside, *chievdars* probing about the Dalbreck military, or governors curious about his powerful distant kingdom, for though they ruled their own small fiefdoms here, they had little or no knowledge of the world that lay beyond the great river. They only knew it by way of the Rahtan who spirited past borders, or by Previzi wagons that shared its treasures. The treasures and their abundance—that was what intrigued them the most. The small infrequent loads brought by the Previzi weren't enough to satisfy their appetites, nor, apparently, was the booty of slaughtered patrols. They hungered for more.

I wore my dress of leather scraps tonight. When I entered the hall I noticed Calantha speaking to a maid, and the girl came running over. "It would please Calantha if you would braid your hair." She held up a small strip of leather to tie it with.

I saw Calantha watching us. Every night now, she insisted I say the blessing. It seemed to please some, but heavily rankled others, especially the Rahtan, and I wondered if she was trying to get me killed. When I questioned her motives, she said, "It amuses me to hear you say the words in your odd drawl, and I need no greater reason. Remember, Princess, you're still a prisoner." I had needed no reminder of that.

"You can tell Calantha I have no intention of braiding my hair just to please her."

I aimed a stiff smile at Calantha. When I looked back at the girl, her eyes were wide with fright. It was a message she wasn't keen to deliver. I took the strip of leather from her hand. "But I will do it for you." I pulled my hair over my shoulder and began braiding it. When I was finished, the girl smiled. "Now your pretty picture will show," she said. "Just as Calantha wanted."

Calantha wanted my kavah to show? The girl started to run away, but I stopped her. "Tell me, is Calantha of the Meurasi clan?"

The girl shook her head. "Oh, I'm not to tell, ma'am." She turned and ran away.

Not to tell. I think she already had.

The meal went as all the others before it had. I said the blessing to the humble bowed heads of a few and the scowls of many. The fact that it gnawed at Malich the most made it worth it to me, and I always made a point to slap my gaze on his before I began. But then the words took over, the bones, the truth, the pulse of the walls around me, the life that still dwelled in stones and floor, the part of the Sanctum that was growing stronger in me, and by the time the last *paviamma* echoed back, the scowls mattered naught to me.

Tonight the fare was much the same as every night, thick barley gruel flavored with peppermint leaves, soda bread, turnips, onions, and roasted game—boar and hare. There was little variation, except with the game. Beaver, duck, and wild horse were sometimes served too, depending on what game was caught, but compared to my frequent diet of sand, squirrel, and snake across the Cam Lanteux, it was a veritable feast, and I was grateful for every bite.

I was just dipping my soda bread into the gruel when a sudden sharp clatter roared down one of the hallways that led into the Sanctum. Every man was on his feet in an instant, swords and knives drawn. The ruckus grew louder. Rafe and I exchanged a furtive glance. Could this be his men? With reinforcements?

Two dozen men emerged—the Komizar leading them. He was filthy, spattered with mud from head to foot, but he appeared to relish the squalor. A rare sloppy smile was plastered across his face.

"Look who we ran into on the road!" he said, waving his

sword over his head. "The new governor of Balwood! More chairs! Food! We're hungry!"

The company of men swarmed to the table in all their glorified filth, leaving trails of mud behind them. I spotted the one who had to be the new governor—a young man, both brazen and afraid. His eyes darted around the room, quickly trying to assess new threats. His movements were sharp and his laughter tight. He may have just killed the last governor to gain this position, but the Sanctum was not his homeland. New rules would have to be learned and navigated, and he'd have to manage to stay alive while he did it. His position was not so unlike mine, except I hadn't killed anyone to gain this dubious place of honor.

And then the Komizar spotted me. He dropped his gear to the floor and crossed the room, stopping an arm's length away. His skin glowed with a day's ride in the sun, and his dark eyes gleamed as they traced the lines of my dress. He reached up and fingered the braid falling over my shoulder. "With your hair combed, you only look half the savage." The room erupted in loyal laughter, but his gaze that glided over me told a different story, one that wasn't humorous or amusing. "So, while the Komizar is away, the prisoners will play." He finally turned to Kaden. "This is what my coin bought?"

I prayed Kaden would say yes so the blame would fall to us. Otherwise, Effiera's generous gifts might be repaid with retaliation.

"Yes," Kaden answered.

The Komizar nodded, studying him. "I found one governor. Now it's your turn to find the other. You leave in the morning."

"WHY YOU?" I ASKED, JERKING THE TETHER LOOSE AT MY waist. It clattered to the floor.

Kaden continued to rummage through his trunk, throwing out a long fur-lined cloak and woolen socks. "Why not me? I'm a soldier, Lia. I—"

I reached out and grabbed his arm, forcing him to look me in the eye.

Worry filled his eyes. He didn't want to leave.

"Why are you so loyal to him, Kaden?"

He tried to turn back to the trunk, but I gripped his arm tighter. "No!" I said. "You're not evading me again! Not this time!"

He stared at me, his chest rising in controlled breaths. "He fed me when I was starving, for one thing."

"A charitable act is no reason to sell your soul to someone."

"Everything is so simple to you, isn't it?" Anger flashed across his face. "It's more complicated than an *act*, as you call it."

"Then what? He gave you a nice cloak? A room in the—"

His hand flew through the air. "I was traded, Lia! Just like you were." He looked away as if he was trying to regain his composure. When he looked back at me, the hot fury was still in his eyes, but his tone was slow and cynical. "Except in my case, there were no contracts. After my mother died, I was sold to a passing ring of beggars for a single copper as if I were a piece of trash—with only one caveat—to never bring me back."

"You were sold by your father?" I asked, trying to fathom how anyone could do such a thing.

In seconds, sweat had sprung to his face. This was the memory that mattered, the one he had always refused to share. "I was eight years old," he said. "I begged my father to keep me. I fell to his feet and wrapped my arms around his legs. To this day, I've never forgotten the sickening scent of jasmine soap on his trousers."

He shut the trunk lid and sat down, his eyes unfocused as if reliving the memory.

"He shook me off. He said it was better that way. The *better* was two years with accomplished beggars who starved me so I could bring in more money on street corners. If a day's begging didn't bring enough in, they beat me, but always where it didn't show. They were careful that way. If I still didn't bring in enough, they threatened to take me back to my father, who would drown me in a bucket of water like a stray cat."

His gaze turned sharp, cutting into me. "It was the Komizar who found me begging on a muddy street. He saw the blood seeping through my shirt after a particularly bad beating. He pulled me up on his horse and took me back to his camp, fed me, and asked who had whipped me. When I told him, he left for a few hours, promising it would never happen again. When he returned, he was sprayed with blood. I knew it was their blood. He was true to his word. And I was glad."

He stood and snatched his cloak from the floor.

I shook my head, horrified. "Kaden, it's an abomination to whip a child and just as bad to sell one. But isn't that all the more reason to leave Venda for good? To come to Morrighan and—"

"I *was* Morrighese, Lia. I was a bastard child born to a high-born lord. Now you know why I hate royals. That's who the Komizar saved me from."

I stared at him, unable to speak.

No.

It wasn't true. It couldn't be.

He threw his cloak around his shoulders. "Now you know who the real barbarians are."

He turned and left, the door thundering shut behind him, and still I stood there.

His schooling in the holy songs.

His reading.

His flawless Morrighese.

True.

The scars on his chest and back.

True.

But it wasn't a Vendan who had done this to him, as I had always supposed. It was a highborn lord of Morrighan.

Impossible.

THE CANDLE BURNED OUT. THE LANTERNS DID TOO. I LAY curled in the bed and stared into the dark, reliving every moment, from the time he walked into the tavern, to our long trip across the Cam Lanteux. All the times I marveled at his tender ways that were such a glaring contrast to what he was—an assassin. *All the times.* The way he was so comfortable in the Morrighese world. It seemed perfectly obvious now. He *was* reading the games board. It was Vendan he didn't know how to read, not Morrighese. Pauline and I had both noted how well he sang the holy songs, while Rafe knew none of the words. He had been raised until he was eight as the son of a Morrighese lord.

Kaden's own kind, my kind, had betrayed him. Except for his mother. *She was a saint*, he had said. What had happened to her? It must have been from her that he learned his tender ways. It might be she was the only one in his entire life who had shown him any love or compassion—until the Komizar came along.

It was the middle of the night when he returned. The room was completely black, and yet he moved quietly through it as if he could see in the dark. I heard him set something down, a loud thunk, and then I heard the scant ruffling sounds of clothing being laid out and the soft sigh of his breaths as he lay down on the rug. The room was heavy with silence. Long minutes passed. I knew he wasn't asleep. I could feel his thoughts in the darkness, his stare drilling into the timbers above him.

"Kaden," I whispered. "Tell me about your mother."

Her name was Cataryn. She was very young when she was hired on as governess by a lord and his wife, but soon they discovered she had the gift as well. The lady pressed her daily for thoughts on her own young sons, but soon the lord pressed her for other things. Kaden was born and knew no other way of life. He thought it was normal to live in a cottage on his father's estate. When his mother became ill and her life was quickly withering away, she begged the lord to take Kaden into the manor. The lady would have none of it. A bastard wouldn't be raised with her noble-bred sons, and even though the lord promised Cataryn he would take Kaden, it seemed he had agreed with his wife all along. His mother wasn't even cold yet when Kaden was given to passing beggars without a backward glance.

His mother was beautiful, crystal-blue eyes, black hair that was soft and long. Gentle and slow to anger, she was a teacher above all. She tutored Kaden right along with the lord's sons. At night in the cottage, they looked out the window at the stars, and she whispered the stories of the ages, and Kaden repeated them back to her. He was too young to fully understand why the lord's sons received special privilege, but when he became angry about it, his mother would gather him in her arms and croon against his cheek that he was far richer in the things that mattered because he had a mother who had more love for him than the whole universe could contain.

But then suddenly, he didn't have her. He had nothing. One of his biggest regrets was that he bore his father's white-blond hair and brown eyes. When he looked in a mirror, he at least wanted to see some measure of his mother.

"I see her, Kaden," I said. "I see her in you every day. From the moment I met you, I saw your calmness, your tender ways. Pauline herself told me you had kind eyes. That's more important than their color."

He remained silent except for a low, shaky breath.

And then we both went to sleep.

CHAPTER TWENTY-NINE

HE WAS UP EARLY, BEFORE THE SUN, BEFORE STIRRINGS, before clops or neighs or the first birds of morning. It felt as though we had just gone to sleep. He lit a candle and stuffed his saddlebag.

I stretched in my bed and stood, pulling the quilt over my shoulders.

"I've left some supplies for you in the bag by the door," he said. "I raided the kitchen for what food I could so you can leave the room as little as possible. I arranged for Aster, Eben, and Griz to come check on you each day. With luck, we'll meet the governor on the road and we'll be back by nightfall."

"And if you're not?"

"His province is in the far south of Venda. It'll be a few weeks."

So much could happen in a few weeks. In a few days. But I

didn't say it. I could see the same thought in his eyes. I only nodded, and he turned to leave.

I blurted out a question that burned in me when he reached the door. "Which lord was it, Kaden? Who did this to you?"

His hand paused on the latch and then he looked back over his shoulder. "Does it really matter which one? Doesn't every lord have his bastards?"

"Yes, it *does* matter. Not every lord is a depraved monster like your father. You can't stop believing in the good ones."

"But I have," he said. His voice was empty of emotion, and his resignation tore through me. He turned back to the door as if to leave, but stood there not moving.

"Kaden?" I whispered.

He dropped his saddlebag and walked back to me, cupped my face in his hands, his eyes warm and hungry, and kissed me, his lips soft against mine, then harder, earnest, my mouth meeting his with tenderness. He slowly pulled away and looked into my eyes.

"A real kiss," he said. "That's what I needed, just one more time."

He turned away, grabbed his saddlebag, and left.

And twice in the space of just a few hours, I was breathless as he left the room.

I closed my eyes, hating myself. I found no satisfaction in the fact that I had become as accomplished at deception as Kaden. All I tasted on my lips was my carefully calculated lie.

CHAPTER THIRTY

THE DOOR SHOOK WITH POUNDING FROM THE OTHER SIDE. I knew it wasn't Aster or Eben. Not even Malich. Kaden had said Malich would be occupied with duties all day. It was at night that I had to be watchful. Another impatient knock. I hadn't properly dressed yet or combed my hair. What fool didn't know I was locked in and a key was required to open the door? Griz?

I finally heard the rattle of a key in the lock, and the door opened.

It was the Komizar.

"Most doors in the Sanctum aren't locked. I'm not in the habit of calling someone for a key." He walked in past me. "Get dressed," he ordered. "Do you have anything proper for riding? Or did the Meurasi only clothe you with their dress of rags?"

I hadn't moved, and he turned around to look at me. "Your mouth is open, Princess."

"Yes," I said, my mind still reeling. "I do. Over there." I walked to the chest where they were folded on top and grabbed them from the pile. "I have riding clothes."

"Then put them on."

I stared at him. Did he expect me to dress in front of him?

He smirked. "Ah. Modesty. You royals." He shook his head and turned around. "Hurry up about it."

His back was to me, and Natiya's knife was within reach under my mattress.

Not yet, a voice so deep and buried I tried to pretend it wasn't there. It was the perfect time. His guard was down. He didn't know I had a weapon.

Not yet.

Was this the gift, or was I just afraid of incurring a target on my own back? I *would* be a target. An easy one. A three-inch knife might make short work of an exposed jugular, but it couldn't take on a whole army, and what good would I do Rafe if I was dead? But then thoughts of Walther and Greta pushed aside reason. *Do it.* My fingers trembled. *No mistakes this time, Lia.* Revenge and escape battled within me.

"Well?" he asked impatiently.

Not yet. A whisper as strong as an iron door slamming shut.

"I'm hurrying." I threw off my nightshirt and put on fresh underclothes, praying he wouldn't turn around. Being seen naked should have been the least of my worries right then, and I had never been particularly modest, but I raced gazelle-swift to get them and my riding clothes on, fearful his patience would run out and mildly surprised he was showing any restraint at all.

"There," I said, tucking my shirt into my trousers. He turned and watched as I slipped on my belt, the tether of bones that had lengthened considerably, and finally the long warm vest of many furs, again the revered symbol of the Meurasi.

He had bathed since last night. The mud of the road was gone, and the short sculpted beard once again meticulously groomed. He stepped closer. "Your hair," he said. "Comb it. Do something with it. Don't shame the vest you wear."

I surmised he wasn't taking me out to behead me if he cared about how my hair looked, but it seemed odd that he was even concerned how I looked at all. No, not odd, suspicious. It wasn't about shaming the vest. He sat back in Kaden's chair and watched every move as I brushed and braided it.

Studying me. Not in the lecherous way Malich had ogled me countless times, but in a cool, calculated way that made me guard my movements even more. He wanted something and was devising how to get it.

I tied off my braid, and he stood, grabbing my cloak from a hook. "You'll need this," he said, and he put it around my shoulders, taking his time as he fastened it at my neck. I bristled when his knuckle grazed my jaw.

"What did I do to deserve all these kind attentions?" I asked.

"Jezelia," he said, shaking his head. "Always so suspicious." He lifted my chin so I had to look in his eyes. "Come. Let me show you Venda."

I WAS ASTONISHED THAT IT FELT GOOD TO BE ON A HORSE again. Even though we moved slowly through winding streets, every sway on the back of the horse held the promise of open spaces, meadows, and freedom—that is, if I ignored who rode next to me. He kept his horse close to mine, and I could feel his watchful eye, not just on me but on everyone we passed. Their inquisitive stares were plain. They had heard of the princess prisoner of Morrighan. "Push back your cloak a bit. Let them view your vest." I looked at him uncertainly but did as he asked. He had seemed angry with Kaden about how his coin was spent, but now he seemed absorbed by it.

I was being paraded, though I was uncertain why. Only a little over a week ago, he had marched me through the Sanctum in front of his Council, barefoot and half naked in a burlap sack that could barely be called a dress. That I understood: demean the royal and take her power away. Now it was as though he was giving it back, but I felt in the deepest part of my gut that the Komizar never gave up even the smallest fistful of power.

You have been welcomed by the clan of Meurasi. Was a welcome something even the Komizar didn't know how to navigate? Or maybe it was simply his intent to control it.

We meandered through the Brightmist quarter, which was at the northernmost part of the city. He seemed to be in particularly good spirits as we rode through the streets, calling out to shopkeepers, soldiers, or a patty clapper scooping up horse manure to be patted into fuel, because, as I had learned, even wood was not easy to come by in Venda and dried horse dung burned warmly.

He told me we were headed to a small hamlet about an hour away, but he didn't tell me for what purpose. He was an imposing figure in the saddle, his dark hair ruffling in the breeze, his black riding leathers gleaming under a hazy sky. *He had saved Kaden.* I tried to imagine the person he had been, almost a boy himself when he had lifted a child to his horse and whisked him away to safety. Then he went back to butcher Kaden's tormentors.

"Do you have a name?" I asked.

"A name?"

"One that you were born with. Given by your parents. Besides Komizar," I clarified, though I thought my question was obvious. Apparently it wasn't.

He thought for a moment and answered stiffly, "No. Only Komizar."

We passed through an unguarded gate at the end of the lane. Sparse brown meadowlands spread out before us, and we left the crowded, smoky, mud-soaked avenues of the city behind us.

"We'll have to ride faster," he said. "I'm told you ride well. But maybe that's only when bison are bearing down on you?"

No doubt Griz and Finch had shared their narrow escape—and mine.

"I manage," I said. "For a *royal.*" Though this horse was new to me, I dug in my heels and raced ahead, praying it would respond to my commands. I heard the Komizar galloping close behind me, and I pushed my horse faster. The air was icy crisp, stinging my cheeks, and I was grateful for the fur vest beneath my cloak. He met my pace and pulled slightly in front of me. I snapped my reins, and we ran head to head. I felt my horse still had vast stores of untapped power, and it was as eager as I was to show it, but I slowed just a bit, so the Komizar would think he had bested me, and then when he surged ahead, I returned to a trot. He circled back around, laughing, his face flushed with the cold, his dark-lashed eyes dancing at our small game.

He took his place beside me, and we continued on at a trot with the soldiers keeping pace a short distance behind us. We passed the occasional hovel, the grass so sparse, the way so little traveled, there was hardly a path at all. The small stone houses had scrabbled gardens and swoop-backed horses with not enough meat on their ribs to garner a second glance from a wolf. The landscape was harsh, stark—it was a wonder that anyone was able to scratch out a life here. But there were occasional fingers of forest and slivers of earth that were fertile and green, and as we breached a rise, I spotted the hamlet that was our destination. A nest of thatch-roofed huts huddled into a hillside, and a stand of pines hovered over them. A longhouse stood apart from the huts, and smoke rose in lazy circles from its chimney.

"Sant Cheville," the Komizar said. "The hillfolk in hamlets like these are the poorest but toughest of our breed. The Sanctum may be the heart, but this is the backbone of Venda. Word spreads quickly among the hillfolk. They are our eyes and ears."

I stared at the small cluster of huts. It was the kind of hamlet I could have passed a hundred times in Morrighan and ignored, but looking at it now, something beat within me, a bewildering but urgent need. My horse pranced nervously out of step, as if he felt it too. The breeze swirled around my neck, heavy and cold, and I saw a hole widening, deepening, swallowing me up. *I knew you would come.* I was struck with the same fear and frenzy as on the day I passed the graveyard with Pauline. My fingers tightened on the reins. *We're all part of a greater story too. One that transcends the soil, the wind, time.* I didn't want to be part of this story. I wanted to run back to Terravin. Back to Civica. Back to anywhere but—

This is the backbone of Venda.

I tugged on the reins, stopping my horse, my breath coming in gasps. "Why did you bring me here?" I asked.

The Komizar looked at me, perturbed at the sudden stop. "It serves Venda. That's all you need to know."

He clicked the reins, moving us forward again until we were a dozen lengths from the longhouse. He stopped and turned to the soldiers. "Keep her here. In plain view." He rode down to the hamlet with a soldier following close behind and dismounted, speaking with those who had emerged from their homes. We couldn't hear what was said from where we waited, but it was clear the villagers were happy to see him. He turned and pointed at me, then talked with them again. The people peered at me, nodding, and one man was so bold as to slap the Komizar on the back, a slap that looked a little too much like the Komizar had just met with victory. He left a sack of flour and barley and returned to where we waited.

"Am I to know what you told them?" I asked.

He waved the soldiers to follow, and we moved on past the

hamlet. "The hillfolk are a superstitious lot," he said. "I may disdain such magical thinking, but they still cling to it. A princess of the enemy, with the gift no less, they take as a sign that the gods are favoring Venda. It fills them with hope, and hope can fill their stomachs as well as bread. Sometimes it's all they have through a long bitter winter."

I stopped my horse, refusing to go farther. "You still haven't said what you told them about me."

"I told them you ran from the enemy swine to join our ranks, called by the gods themselves."

"You lying—"

He reached out and grabbed me, almost pulling me from my saddle. "Careful, Princess," he hissed, his face close to mine. "Do not forget who you are when you speak—nor who *I* am. I'm the Komizar, and I'll give them a morsel of whatever they need to fill their growling bellies. Do you understand?" The horses jostled beneath us, and I feared I would fall to the ground between them.

"Yes," I answered. "Perfectly."

"Good, then."

He released me, and we traveled on for several miles until the next hamlet came into view.

"So is this how it shall go all day?" I asked. "Am I never to meet the backbone of Venda, or will I only be pointed at with your long, bony finger?"

He looked down briefly at his gloved hands, and a sliver of satisfaction warmed me. "You're hot-tempered," he said, "and not mindful of your mouth. Could I trust you, or would you slash away at their hope?"

I looked at him, wondering why a man who seemed to feed on sowing fear was now so sensitively concerned with sowing hope in the hillfolk. Was it really just the coming winter that he was trying to prepare them for, or was he bolstering them for something else?

"I know what it means to hold on to hope, Komizar. Many times in crossing the Cam Lanteux, it was all that sustained me. I would not steal their hope, even if it comes at my expense."

He eyed me with suspicion. "You're a strange girl, Lia. Shrewd and calculating, Malich tells me, and adept at games, which I admire. But I do not admire lying." Our gazes were locked, his black eyes trying to read every line of my face. "Do not disappoint me." He clicked his reins and moved on.

As we got closer, the longhouse door opened and an old man limped out, aided by a crooked stick. I had noticed in Venda that there were few stooped adults with white hair. It seemed that the aged were a rare treasure. More people trickled out behind him. The man greeted the Komizar as an equal, not as one of his fearful groveling subjects.

"What brings you?" he asked.

"A few gifts to tide you through the winter." The Komizar signaled a guard, who hefted a large tied bundle onto his shoulder and dropped it near the longhouse door.

"News?" the Komizar asked.

The old man shook his head. "The winds are sharp. They cut both rider and tongue. And the gods promise a hard winter."

"But spring has greater promise," the Komizar said. "And that hope can stave off the talons of winter."

They spoke in riddles I couldn't follow.

The old man looked at me. "And this?"

The Komizar grabbed my arm and pulled me forward so the old man could get a good look. "A princess of Morrighan with the gift. She's run from the enemy swine to join our ranks, called by the gods themselves. Already the enemy scatters. And as you can see," he said, viewing my vest, "she's been welcomed by the clan of Meurasi."

The old man aimed a squinted eye at me. "That so?"

The Komizar's grip on my arm tightened. I looked into the old man's eyes, hoping to convey more with a gaze than my words. "It is as your Komizar says. I am a princess, First Daughter of Morrighan, and I've run from my countrymen who are your enemy."

The Komizar looked sideways at me, a slight smile creasing his eyes.

"And your name, girl?" the old man asked.

I knew you would come.

The voice was as clear as the old man's. I closed my eyes, trying to chase it away, but it only came louder and stronger. *Jezelia, the one marked with power, the one marked with hope.* I opened my eyes. Everyone stared at me, silent and waiting, their eyes wide with curiosity.

"Jezelia," I answered. "My name is Jezelia."

His watery eyes studied me and then he turned to the others standing behind him. "Jezelia, who has been welcomed by the clan of Meurasi," he repeated. They spoke in hushed tones among themselves.

The Komizar leaned close, whispering in my ear, "Well done, Princess. A convincing touch."

It was only a clever sham to him, but clearly more to these hillfolk. The old man turned back to us. "Some thannis to warm you on your way?" he offered.

The Komizar forced a weak smile. Even he thought thannis tasted like sour dirt. "We need to be on our way—"

"We thank you for your graciousness," I interrupted. "We would love some."

The Komizar shot me a dark glare, but didn't balk in front of the old man, as I knew he wouldn't. It would never do to have a newcomer embrace the tradition of Venda more than its ruler—no matter how distasteful it was.

I lifted the proffered mug to my lips. Yes, sour moldy dirt, but not half as bad as wiggling white grubs. I drank heartily and handed my mug to the woman who served it, thanking her for her kindness. The Komizar took twice as long to down his.

He berated me when I didn't offer a "display" of the gift at our next stop.

"You said word passes quickly among the hillfolk. A light touch is better than a heavy-handed performance. Leave them wanting more."

He laughed. "Shrewd and calculating. Malich was right."

"And he is right about so few things."

And so the day went, hamlet after hamlet, the Komizar gaining favor with gifts, sacks of flour and morsels of hope, with me as proof that the enemy was trembling and that the gods were smiling on Venda.

Midafternoon we rested in a valley while the horses drank from a brook. The wind picked up, and the sky grew dark. I held my cloak close about my shoulders, standing apart from the Komizar and soldiers, and looked out at the vista, a land dusky and barren, washed in the colors of a dark pebbled river.

The day had shown me that Venda was an unforgiving place and only the heartiest survived here. A Remnant may have been spared, but only a chosen faithful few had been led by the gods and the girl Morrighan to a land of plenty. Venda was not that land. It had taken the brunt of the devastation. As we rode, we passed forests of stone, rolling hills with only occasional hints of green, fields of burnt red rock, windswept trees twisted into haunting shapes that made them look alive, strips of farmland where small crops were coaxed from hard soil, and distant dead-lands where the Komizar said nothing lived or grew—lands as forbidding as Infernaterr. And yet there was something compelling about the landscape.

All I had seen were people trying to survive, faithful in their own ways, adding a bone at a time to tethers, remembering the sacrifice that put it there and the sacrifices yet to be made, people in barbarian dress, like the clothing I wore now. People who didn't speak in grunts, but in humble notes of gratitude. *I knew you would come.* The words I had heard still bored into me.

A strong gust tore at my clothes, and my hair whipped free of the braid. I pushed the wild strands from my face and stared at the endless landscape and darkening clouds crushing the horizon. With two horses, how far could Rafe and I run? Could we disappear into the emptiness for even a few days? Because three days alone with him now seemed like the gift of a lifetime. I'd do anything for it. We'd been apart for too long.

"So deep in thought."

I whirled around. "I didn't hear you walk up."

"Not wise in this wilderness to be so lost in your reflections that you forget your back. The hyenas prowl this late in the day, especially for little morsels like you." He glanced to where I had been looking, a long horizon and endless dipping hills. "What were you thinking?" he asked.

"Am I not free to own anything? Not even my thoughts?"

"No," he answered. "Not anymore."

And I knew he meant it.

He studied my face as if waiting for a lie, waiting for something. I remained silent. Seconds ticked by, and I thought he might strike me. He finally shook his head. "If you need to take care of personal matters, my men and I will turn our backs for a few minutes. I know how your kind are about your privacy. Be quick about it."

I watched him walk off, wondering at how he had backed down. Wondering about everything. He had saved Kaden, sent food for the hungry, was tireless in knowing his kingdom, from personally retrieving governors to meeting with distant hillfolk. Could I have been wrong about him? I remembered his cruel taunt, *You did well, Chievdar*, when he pulled Walther's baldrick from the captured booty. He knew it would bring me to my knees. But it was more than that that fed my doubts about him. It was his eyes, hungry for everything, even my own thoughts. *Be careful, sister.* My brother's warning burned beneath my ribs.

And yet, when we stopped at the last hamlet and I saw him embrace the elders and leave gifts, saw the hope that he left behind, and remembered it was he who had saved Kaden from the savagery of his own kind, I wondered if anything I felt in my gut really mattered.

nd Morrighan raised her voice,
To the heavens,
Kissing two fingers,
One for the lost,
And one for those yet to come,
For the winnowing was not over.

—*Morrighan Book of Holy Text*, *Vol. IV*

CHAPTER THIRTY-ONE

KADEN

AFTER FOUR DAYS ON THE ROAD, I DECIDED THE GODS WERE against me. Maybe they always had been. No such luck that the governor would be coming my way, half sloshed and late. The brothel in the last town hadn't had the pleasure of his visit yet, and that was a stop he never missed. He was still somewhere on the road from here to there—or he hadn't left yet at all.

Damn Governor Tierny. I'd wring his neck when I caught up with him. Unless someone else had already done that job for me.

The weather was miserable, cold winds by day, cold rain by night. The men who traveled with me were surly. Winter was coming early. But it wasn't the icy winds that were leaving me raw. It was my last night with Lia. I had never told anyone, not even the Komizar, what my mother's name was.

Cataryn.

It was as though I had raised her from the dead. I had seen her again, heard her voice again, as I told Lia about her. Saying her name aloud, something tore inside of me, but then I couldn't stop telling Lia more, remembering how much my mother had loved me—the only person who had ever loved me. That wasn't something I had wanted to share with Lia, but in the dark, once I had said her name, it all poured out, right down to the color of her eyes.

And my father's eyes. That memory stopped me. I hadn't told her everything.

Lia. Like a whisper on the wind.

At first I had thought that was all it was, the wind and long hours riding alone. When Lia had first told me her name in the tavern, it had reminded me of the hush I heard riding across the savanna, *Lia* through the canyons in the desert, *Lia*, the cry of a distant wolf. *Lia* wheedling into my heart before I ever laid eyes on her. And then *Lia* as I stood over her in the darkness of her room, my knife in hand. It was a whisper I finally couldn't ignore, though I had managed to choke it from my life from the moment I met the Komizar. The knowing had only brought me pain.

I had used it the way Lia had. I had told the lady of the manor she was going to die a slow and horrible death, though I had seen no such thing. I was eight years old and angry that it was my own mother who was dying and not the petty one of my half brothers, a woman who had never shown me any kindness. That was when my first beating came. It was at the hands of my father, not the beggars. They only left scars atop the ones he had already laid deep.

Which one was it, Kaden?

His name was one I would never give up, not even to Lia—but it would be my name on his lips as he lay dying. My name would be the one he uttered as he gasped his last breath, knowing he had been betrayed by his own son. It was a thought that had warmed me for years. *Our plans.* That moment had always been implicit in them.

We rounded the pass and had started to make our descent into the valley when we saw them coming toward us. I stopped our procession until I was certain who they were. I sighed and signaled us forward again to meet them. *We must never grow lazy.* But the governor of Arleston had. There would be no neck to wring. He was dead. The squad of men heading our way bore the flags of Arleston, and the man leading them had to be the new governor. A sturdy man, but not young as challengers usually were. I didn't care. He was headed in the right direction, knowing his duty, and that was all that mattered. I could return to the Sanctum now. I could return home to Lia. The last stray governor had been found.

CHAPTER THIRTY-TWO

RAFE

"THAT DOOR," ULRIX GRUMBLED, POINTING AHEAD. "I'LL be back in two hours."

"It won't take me that long to bathe."

"But my duties *will* take me that long. Sit tight until I come back for you."

He stomped off, still angry that I had won a hot bath in a game of cards last night. He claimed he'd let me win because I stank, which may have been true.

As much as I wanted an actual bath, my real purpose was to see more of the layout of the Sanctum, and I knew that the bath chamber was closer to the tower where Lia stayed with Kaden. While I had been given some liberties in my movement, traveling alone to a different part of the Sanctum wasn't among them. I memorized the path we took, asking Ulrix innocuous questions, trying to determine which hallways were the most frequently traveled and where they led. Ulrix, even with his short temper, proved useful.

I opened the door to the bath chamber, and there, as promised, was a tub filled with water. I dipped my hand in. Lukewarm at best, but more than inviting after only being able to wash up with a basin of cold water. There was soap and a towel too. Ulrix must have been feeling generous.

I threw my clothes off and shoved my head in first, scrubbing my face and scalp, then got in and soaked, but the water was rapidly cooling, so I washed and got out before it turned cold. I dried off and was only half dressed when I felt hands on my bare back.

I spun, and there was Lia, pushing me up against the wall. "What are you doing here?" I said. "You can't—"

She drew my face to hers and kissed me, warm and long, her fingers raking through my wet hair. I pulled away. "You have to leave. Someone might—" But then my mouth came down on hers again, hard and hungry, sending a far different message than the one I was trying to convey. My hands slid around her waist, traveled up her back, soaking in all the lost time and days that I had wanted to hold her.

"No one saw me," she said between kisses.

"Yet."

"I heard Ulrix tell you he'd be gone for two hours, and no one will check on me for at least that."

My body molded to hers. I could taste the desperation in her kisses, and she whispered about the distant hills of Venda she had seen, endless hills we could get lost in.

"For a few days if we're lucky," I said. "That's not enough. I want a lifetime with you."

She faltered for a moment, brought back to our reality, then rested her cheek on my chest. "What are we going to do, Rafe?" she asked. "It's been twelve days. And only a matter of a dozen more before riders return with news of the king's good health."

"Stop counting the days, Lia," I said. "You'll drive yourself mad."

"I know," she whispered, and stepped back. Her eyes grazed my bare chest. "You should get dressed before you catch cold," she said.

With her so close, I was anything but cold, but I grabbed my shirt and put it on. She helped me button it, and every brush of her fingers seared my skin.

"How did you get out of your room?" I asked.

"There's an abandoned passageway. It doesn't lead to much, mostly busy hallways, which makes it useless most of the time, but sometimes opportunity presents itself." She didn't seem worried about how she'd get back to her room undetected, though I was. She put her finger to my lips and told me to stop, saying we had precious little time together, and she wasn't going to use it worrying about that too. "I already told you I'm good at sneaking," she said. "I have years of experience at it."

I barred the door and moved empty buckets from a cot to

the floor so we could sit. We updated each other on what little we knew. She nestled in my arms, telling me about traveling through the countryside of Venda and how the people there were just like any others, people trying to survive. She said they were kind and curious and nothing like the Council. I told her what I had learned about the pathways from Ulrix, but I held back on some things I had been doing, particularly the weapons I had managed to hide. I had seen the fire in her eyes when she talked about sneaking one from the barrows in the Sanctum. She had witnessed her brother's brutal death, and I couldn't blame her for wanting revenge, but I didn't want her retrieving a knife or sword before the timing was right.

She pushed on my shoulders to make me lie back, and I pulled her with me, my caution crumbling. I wanted her more than life itself. She looked down at me and traced her finger along my jaw. "Prince Rafferty," she said curiously, as if still trying to grasp who I really was.

"Jaxon is what they call me back in Dalbreck."

"But I'll always call you Rafe."

"Are you disappointed that I'm not a farmer?"

She smiled. "You may learn to grow melons yet."

"Or maybe we'll grow other things," I said, pulling her close, and we kissed again—and again. "Lia," I finally whispered, trying to bring us both back to our senses, "we have to be careful."

She pressed her forehead to mine, silent, then settled back against my shoulder, and we talked, almost as we had on our last night together in Terravin, but this time I told her the truth. My parents weren't dead. I told her what they were like and a little bit about Dalbreck.

"Were they angry when I ran from the wedding?"

"My father was furious. My mother was heartbroken both for me and herself. She was eager to have a daughter."

She shook her head. "Rafe, I am so—"

"Shh, don't say it. You don't owe anyone an apology." And then I told her the rest, that it was never proposed to me as a real marriage and that my father had even suggested I take a mistress after the wedding if the bride didn't suit my tastes.

"A mistress? Well, isn't that romantic?" She leaned up on one arm to look at me. "What about you, Rafe?" she said more softly. "What did you think when I didn't show up?"

I thought back to that morning, waiting in the cloister of the abbey along with the entire Dalbreck cabinet, pulling at my coat. We'd had to ride all night, delayed because of the weather, and I just wanted to get it over with. "When the news came that you had left, I was surprised," I said. "That was my first reaction. I couldn't quite figure out how it could happen. Two kingdoms' cabinets had worked out every detail. In my mind, it may as well have already been chiseled in stone. I couldn't understand how one girl could undo the plans of the most powerful men on the continent. Then, when I finally got past my shock, I was curious. About you."

"And you weren't angry?"

I grinned. "Yes, I was," I conceded. "I wouldn't admit it at the time, but I was furious too."

She rolled her eyes. "Ha! As if I didn't know."

"I suppose it was apparent when I got to Terravin."

"The minute you walked into that tavern, I knew you were trouble, Prince Rafferty."

I wove my fingers through her hair and pulled her closer. "As I did you, Princess Arabella." Her lips pressed to mine, and I wondered if there would ever be a day we didn't have to cut our time together short, but I was getting worried about Ulrix. He'd been gone almost an hour, I guessed, and I didn't want to take a chance in case he returned early. When I pushed her away, she promised to leave in five more minutes. Five minutes is hardly enough time to drink an ale, but we filled it with memories from our time in Terravin. I finally told her she had to go.

I looked out the door first to make sure the hall was clear. She touched my cheek before she left and said, "Someday we'll go back to Terravin, won't we, Rafe?"

"We will," I whispered, because that was what she needed to hear, but as the door shut behind her, I knew if we ever got out of here, I would never take her back to anywhere in Morrighan, including Terravin.

CHAPTER THIRTY-THREE

I TRIED TO STOP COUNTING THE DAYS AS RAFE HAD TOLD me to, but each day that the Komizar took me out to a different quarter, I knew we had one less. Our outings were brief, just long enough to show me off to this elder or that quarterlord and those who gathered around, planting his version of hope among the superstitious. For a man who had little patience for lying, he sowed the myth of my arrival freely, like seed thrown by handfuls in the wind. The gods were blessing Venda.

Strangely, an equilibrium settled in between us. It was like dancing with a hostile stranger. With each of our steps, he got what he wanted, the added devotion of the clans and hillfolk, and I got something I wanted too, though I couldn't quite put a name to it.

It was a strange pull in unexpected ways and times—the glint of the sun, a shadow, the cook chasing a loose chicken down the hallway, the smoke in the air, a sweetened cup of thannis, the brisk chill of morning, a toothless smile, the resonance of *pavi-amma* chanted back to me, the dark stripes of sky as I chanted eventide remembrances. They were all disconnected moments that added up to nothing, and yet they caught hold of me like fingers lacing into mine and drawing me forward.

The advantage of having Kaden gone was that I was left to my own devices at night. In his rush to make arrangements before he left, Kaden had only told Aster to come and escort me to the bath chamber if I requested it and help me with personal needs, but he hadn't defined what those needs might be. I assured her my nighttime request was one of those needs. It turned out she was happy to conspire with me. The Sanctum was far warmer than the hovel she shared with her bapa and cousins. I had asked her if she knew of a way to get to the catacombs without passing through the main hallway. Her eyes grew wide. "You want to go to the Ghoul Caves?" Apparently Eben and Finch weren't the only ones who called it that.

Griz was right. The little urchin knew every mouse trail in the Sanctum—and there were many. In one of them, I had to get down on my hands and knees to crawl through. As we walked through another, I heard a distant roar.

"What's that?" I whispered.

"We don't want to go that way," she said. "That tunnel leads to the bottom of the cliffs. Nothing there but the river, lots of wet rock, and bridge gears." She led me down an opposite path, but I made note of the way. A path that led to the bridge, even though it was impossible to raise, was something I wanted to explore.

We finally emerged into a wider cavelike tunnel, and the familiar sweet smell of oil and dusty air welcomed us. I thought at this hour it would be empty, but we heard footsteps. We hid in the shadows, and when the dark-robed men shuffled past, we followed a safe distance behind. I understood now why it was called Ghoul Caves. The walls weren't just made of broken ruins. Human bones and skulls lined the path, a thousand Ancients holding up the Sanctum, poised to whisper their secrets—ones Aster didn't want to hear. When she saw them and gasped, I clapped my hand over her mouth and nodded reassurance. "They can't hurt you," I said, though I wasn't so sure myself. Their empty-socket stares followed our steps.

The narrow path led in a steep downward slope to an enormous room, one that bore the art and architecture of another time, and I guessed that it might date all the way back to the Ancients. Deep in the ground, and perhaps sealed away for centuries, it was in remarkably good repair, and so were its contents. It wasn't just any room but a roomful of books that would make the Royal Scholar pale—it dwarfed all his libraries put together. At the far end, I saw the robed men sorting books into stacks and occasionally tossing one into a mountain of discards. Similar mountains were scattered throughout the room. Partially hidden from view was a wide curved opening to another room beyond this one. Light poured out of it, bright and golden. I could see at least one figure inside hunched over a table writing on ledgers. This was an extensive organized effort. Passing shadows flickered across the floor. There were others in that room too. Those who sorted the books in the outside room occasionally took one in to them. I desperately wanted to see what they were doing and what the books were that they studied.

"You want one?" Aster whispered.

"No," I said. "They might see us."

"Not me," she answered, showing off how low she was able to crouch. "And it ain't really stealing, because they burn those piles in the kitchen ovens."

They burned them? I thought about the two books I had stolen from the Scholar, both of their leather covers scorched with fire. Before I could stop her, Aster darted out, quiet as a shadow, and snatched a small book from the discards. When she ran back, her little chest heaved with excitement, and she proudly handed me her prize. It was bound differently from any books I had ever seen, razor straight and tight, and I didn't recognize the language. If it was some form of Vendan, it was even older than the Song of Venda I had translated. That's when I knew what they were doing. They were translating ancient languages, which explained why the services of skilled scholars were needed. I knew of three other kingdoms besides Morrighan that had a stable of scholars with any measurable skills—Gastineux, my mother's homeland; Turquoi Tra, which was home to mystic monks; and Dalbreck.

Since they had discarded this book, I knew it wasn't important to them, but at least I knew now what their purpose here was—deciphering a saved tomb of books, the lost books of the Ancients. For a society where few of its people even read, this was an odd scholarly activity. My curiosity burned, but I fought the urge to confront and question them because it would reveal my nighttime wanderings and put Aster at risk as well. I tucked the book under my arm and nudged her toward the pathway of skulls, and we hurried back to my room.

When we closed the door behind us, she giggled nervously at our adventure together. She asked if I could read the book to her, and I told her no, it was in a tongue I didn't understand.

"What about those?" she asked.

I looked to where she pointed. Lying neatly side by side on my bed were the books I had stolen from the Royal Scholar. I hadn't placed them there. I whirled, looking around the room for an intruder. There was no one. Who would enter my room and lay them out like that?

"Aster," I said sternly, "are you playing games with me? Did you put them there before we left?"

But with one look at her anxious expression, I knew it wasn't her. I shook my head so she wouldn't worry. "Never mind. I forgot that I left them there. Come on," I said as I gathered the books up and set them on the chest. "Let's get ready for bed."

She had brought nothing but the clothes on her back, so I dug around for another of Kaden's warm shirts. It fell to her ankles, and she hugged the soft fabric to her skin. When I brushed my hair, I saw her rub her short scruff dreamily as if imagining it long.

"All that hair must keep your neck and shoulders nice and warm," she said.

"I suppose it does, but I have something far prettier that might keep you warm. Would you like to see it?"

She nodded enthusiastically, and I pulled the blue scarf Reena had given me from my saddlebag. I shook out the folds, and the silver beads jingled. I placed it over her head and wrapped the ends around her neck. "There," I said, "a beautiful vagabond princess. It's yours, Aster."

"Mine?" She reached up and felt the fabric, touching the beads, her mouth open in wonder, and I felt a stab that such a small gesture meant so much to her. She deserved far more than what I could give her.

We snuggled on my bed, and I recounted stories found in the Morrighan Holy Text, tales of how the Lesser Kingdoms grew from the chosen one, tales of love and sacrifice, honor and truth, all the stories that made me long for home. The candle burned low, and when I heard Aster's soft restful snores, I whispered Reena's prayer. "May the gods grant you a still heart, heavy eyes, and angels guarding your door."

nd Harik, true and faithful,
Brought Aldrid to Morrighan,
A husband worthy in the sight of the gods,
And the Remnant rejoiced.

—*Morrighan Book of Holy Text, Vol. III*

CHAPTER THIRTY-FOUR

IT WAS ALREADY QUITE LATE, BUT WHILE ASTER SLEPT
with her scarf clutched in her hand, I sat down on the fur rug in
the center of the room and looked at the books that had appeared
on my bed. Somehow they had been laid in plain sight for me to
find, as if I had forgotten them hidden beneath my mattress. In
truth, I was so consumed with the business of staying alive, I almost had forgotten them. I had translated all of the Song of
Venda on my way across the Cam Lanteux, but I'd had time to
translate only one brief passage of *Ve Feray Daclara au Gaudrel*.

I pulled the small book from its sleeve and touched the em-
bossed leather, fingering the burned corner. It had survived the
centuries, a harrowing trip across the continent, and someone's
attempt to destroy it. *Gaudrel.* I wondered who she was, besides
a storyteller from a group of wanderers.

The first passage had seemed to be a fanciful tale told to a child to distract her from her hunger, but even as I had translated it, I knew it had to be more. The Royal Scholar had hidden it away and even sent a bounty hunter to get it back.

I grabbed the vagabond primer from my saddlebag to help me translate, then settled in, puzzling it out word by word, line by line, beginning with the first passage again. *Once upon a time, my child, there was a princess no bigger than you.* It was a story of a journey, hope, and a girl who commanded the sun, moon, and stars. When I went on to the next passage, it was again a child asking for a story, but this time for one about a great storm. It was strangely reminiscent of the Morrighan Holy Text.

It was a storm, that's all I remember,
A storm that wouldn't end.
> *A great storm*, she prompts.
I sigh, *Yes*, and pull her to my lap.
> *Once upon a time, child,*
> *Long, long ago,*
> *Seven stars were flung from the sky.*
> *One to shake the mountains,*
> *One to churn the seas,*
> *One to choke the air,*
> *And four to test the hearts of men.*

Stars flung from the sky. Was it only a story, or was Gaudrel actually one of the surviving Ancients? A mere child herself when

Aster hurtled a star to earth? That would explain why her story had errors. The Holy Text had been transcribed generation after generation by the best scholars in Morrighan, and it was clear that only one star brought on the devastation, not seven. But one or seven, it hardly mattered—for her, it was a storm that wouldn't end. A storm that made the ways of old meaningless. She spoke of sharp knives and iron wills, but I stopped cold when I got to the part about scavengers. Gaudrel and this child were always running from beasts that were as hungry as they were. Were they the mythical pachegos of Infernaterr that the Vendans feared?

Each page was a glimpse of another time, and together they were a chronicle of events from long ago. Gaudrel's history. Some passages seemed to be carefully phrased for a child's ears, but others were brutally raw.

Aster stirred in her sleep, and I quickly skipped forward several pages. I would never get it all translated in one night. The next passage was a story about Gaudrel's father.

> *Tell me again, Ama. About the warmth. Before.*
> *The warmth came, child, from where I don't know.*
> *My father commanded, and it was there.*
> *Was your father a god?*
> Was he a god? It seemed so.
> He looked like a man.
> But he was strong beyond reason,
> Knowledgeable beyond possible,
> Fearless beyond mortal,

Powerful as a—

Let me tell you the story, child, the story of my father.

Once upon a time, there was a man as great as the gods. . . .

But even the great can tremble with fear.

Even the great can fall.

I sat back, staring at the page. It was too eerily close to the Holy Text that said: *They thought themselves only a step lower than the gods.* Two histories swirled before my eyes, mixing like blood and water. Which history came first? The Morrighan Holy Text or the one I held in my hands? Aster rolled over, stretching, mumbling half-asleep, and wondering if I was coming to bed. "Soon," I whispered. I rushed forward through the pages again, searching for more answers.

Where did she go, Ama?

She is gone, my child.

Stolen, like so many others.

But where?

I lift the child's chin. Her eyes are sunken with hunger.

Come, let's go find food together.

But the child grows older, her questions not so easily turned away.

She knew where to find food. We need her.

And that's why she's gone. Why they stole her.

You have the gift within you too, my child. Listen. Watch.

We'll find food, some grass, some grain.

Will she be back?

She is beyond the wall. She is dead to us now.

> *No, she will not be back.*

My sister Venda is one of them now.

Sisters?

I translated the last passage again, certain I had made a mistake, but it was true. Gaudrel and Venda were sisters. Venda was once a vagabond too.

And then I read more.

Let it be known,
They stole her,
My little one.
She reached back for me, screaming,
> *Ama.*

She is a young woman now,
And this old woman couldn't stop them.
Let it be known to the gods and generations,
They stole from the Remnant.
Harik, the thief, he stole my Morrighan,
Then sold her for a sack of grain,
To Aldrid the scavenger.

I closed the book, my palms damp. Stared at my lap, trying to understand. Trying to explain it away. Trying not to believe it.

It wasn't just any child that Gaudrel told this history to.

It was Morrighan.

She was a girl not chosen by the gods, but stolen by a thief and sold to a scavenger. Harik wasn't her father, as the Holy Text claimed. He was her abductor and seller. Aldrid, the revered founding father of a kingdom, was little more than a scavenger who bought a bride.

At least according to this history. I wasn't sure what to believe.

Only one thing felt certain in my heart. Three women were torn apart. Three women who were once family.

CHAPTER THIRTY-FIVE

RAFE

CALANTHA AND ULRIX DRAGGED ME TO THE STABLES. I was to have another ride through their miserable city, the only advantage being that I could search for another way out, though it was looking more certain there were none.

Vendan riders were swift, and the lost days burned in my head. I went through every military strategy Sven had ever drilled into me, but none of those strategies had ever included Lia and the risk to her.

These thoughts were consuming me, so I didn't recognize him at first. He dumped dried patties into a bin near the stables. His clothes were dirty and torn. When I followed Calantha and Ulrix into the stable, my eyes had passed over him, focusing instead on my own horse in the first stall. One of the *chievdars* had claimed him for his own. He was well cared for and groomed, but it goaded me that he would now serve Venda.

Calantha and Ulrix were taking me out on the Komizar's orders. I saw him leaving with Lia as we arrived in the stable yard. I feared for her in the Komizar's company. "She'll be fine," Calantha said. I averted my gaze, saying I was only curious about the purpose of these rides throughout the city. "A campaign of sorts," she told me vaguely. "The Komizar wishes to share our newly arrived nobility with others."

"I'm only a lowly emissary. Not a noble."

"No," she said. "You'll be anything the Komizar wishes you to be. And today you're the grand Lord Emissary of the Prince of Dalbreck."

"For a nation that despises royalty, he seems eager to flaunt it."

"There are many ways to feed people."

As we led our horses from the stable, the patty clapper carted a load in front of the door, tripping and spilling it to its side. Ulrix cursed him for blocking our way. *"Fikatande idaro! Bogeve enar johz vi daka!"*

The patty clapper scrambled on the ground, trying to return the patties as fast as he could to the cart. He stopped and looked up, cowering, spilling out apologies in Vendan. I squinted when I saw him, thinking I had to be mistaken.

It was Jeb. He was filthy, with matted hair, and he stank. Jeb. A patty clapper.

It took every bit of my willpower not to reach down and embrace him. They had made it—at least Jeb had. I looked around the stable yard, hoping to see the others. Jeb vigorously shook his head as he apologized for his clumsiness. He briefly aimed his gaze just at me, shaking his head again.

The others weren't here. Yet. Or did he mean they wouldn't be coming at all?

"Bring some of those up to my room when you're done. North Sanctum Tower," I said.

Calantha exchanged some quick words with Jeb. *"Mi ena urat seh lienda?"*

Jeb shook his head and gestured with his fingers. *"Nay. Mias e tayn."*

"The fool doesn't understand your tongue," Ulrix growled. "And your room gets heated last, Emissary. When the Council is nice and warm, then maybe you'll get some."

Jeb nodded, throwing the last of the patties into the cart. North tower. The fool understood perfectly, and now he knew where to find me. He wheeled the cart out of the way, and Ulrix pushed past us, his patience spent. "I'll meet you there."

"Where is there?" I asked Calantha.

She sighed as if bored. For someone so young, she was jaded beyond her years. As much as I had tried to pry information from her about her position at the Sanctum, she was an icy wall when it came to details about herself. "We're going to the Stonegate quarter with a quick stop at Corpse Call," she said. "The Komizar thought you might find it entertaining."

I HAD BEEN A SOLDIER IN THE FIELD FOR ALMOST FOUR years. I had seen a lot. Men stabbed, maimed, their skulls split wide. I'd even seen men torn apart by wild animals, half eaten. In the Cam Lanteux and on the battlefield, there were no delicate considerations for how a man died. I had learned to expect anything. But the bile rose in my throat when we topped the crest of Corpse Call, and I stifled the catch in my chest as I started to look away.

Ulrix pushed on my shoulder. "Better get a good look. The Komizar's going to ask you what you think of it." I turned back. I looked steady and hard. Three heads on stakes. Flies buzzed on swollen tongues. Maggots roiled in eye sockets. A raven yanked stubbornly on something sinuous from a cheek, like it was a worm. But even through the decay, I could tell they were boys. They were once boys.

"The Assassin took care of these three. Traitors, they were." Ulrix shrugged and walked back down the hillock.

I turned to Calantha. "Kaden did this?"

"Overseeing executions is his duty as Keep. The dressing up on stakes is done by soldiers. They'll stay there until the last flesh falls from the bone," she answered. "That's on the Komizar's orders."

I looked at her, her single pale eye glistening, a weakness to her shoulders that were usually rigid with cynicism.

"You don't approve," I said.

She shrugged. "What I think doesn't matter."

I reached out and touched her arm before she could turn away.

She flinched as if she thought I was going to strike her, and I stepped back.

"Who are you, Calantha?" I asked.

She shook her head, her bored manner returned. "I've been no one for a very long time."

CHAPTER THIRTY-SIX

IT WAS A RARE CLOUDLESS MORNING OF CRISP BLUE SKY. Fresh air was warmed with the fragrance of thannis, for though its taste was sour, its scent was sweet. The brightness of the day helped chase away my exhaustion. As if I didn't have enough to think about, I couldn't get Gaudrel's book out of my head. Through the late night hours, I woke again and again, with the same thought: *They were family. Morrighan was stolen and sold to a scavenger.* Though it might be true that she had the gift and led a people to a new land, those she led were not a noble Remnant chosen by the gods, but scavengers who preyed on others. They had preyed on Morrighan.

"You slept well?" the Komizar called over his shoulder.

I clicked my reins to catch up with him. My sham was to

continue today in the Canal quarter, at the washing grounds opposite the *jehendra*.

"Your pretense warms me," I said. "You care not one whit how I slept."

"Except for the dark circles under your eyes. It makes you less appealing to the people. Pinch your cheeks. Maybe that will help."

I laughed. "Just when I think I couldn't hate you more, you prove me wrong."

"Come now, Jezelia, after I've shown you every kindness? Most prisoners would be dead by now."

While I wouldn't call it kindness, his remarks to me had grown less biting, and I couldn't help but note he did something my father had never done in his own kingdom. He walked among those he ruled, both near and far. He didn't rule from a distance, but intimately and thoroughly. He knew his people.

To an extent.

Yesterday he had asked me what the claw and vine design on my shoulder was. I didn't mention the Song of Venda, and I hoped no one else would either, but I was sure that at least a few of those who had stared at it were digging it up from dusty memories of long-forgotten tales. "A mistake," I had told him simply. "A wedding kavah not properly applied."

"It seems to have captured the fancy of many."

I'd shrugged it off. "I'm sure it's as much a curiosity to them as I am, something exotic from a faraway kingdom."

"That you are. Wear one of your dresses tomorrow that shows it off properly," he had ordered. "That dreary shirt is tedious."

And also warm. Only that was of little concern to him—not to mention, the dresses weren't particularly suited for riding, again, inconsequential in light of his greater plans. I had nodded, acknowledging his demand, but I wore my shirt and trousers again today. He hadn't seemed to notice.

When he wasn't scrutinizing my every movement and word, I enjoyed my interactions with the people. They provided me with a different kind of warmth that I probably needed more. That part wasn't a sham. The welcome of the Meurasi had spread to many clans. The moments of sharing thannis, or stories, or a few sincere words gave me balance, if not a few hours of relief from the Sanctum. My gift rarely came into play. A few times I was gripped with a sense of something large and dark descending. I sucked in a breath and looked upward, truly expecting to see a black clawed thing swooping down upon me, but there was nothing there. Only a feeling that I'd quickly shake off when I saw the Komizar smiling. He never missed an opportunity to turn it into something corrupt and shameful. He made me want to smother the gift instead of listen to it. It seemed impossible to nurture anything in his presence.

We reached a narrow lane and dismounted, handing off the reins to guards who followed us.

"Is it this?" he asked, tugging on Walther's baldrick with his thumb. "Is this what continues to make you so testy?"

I looked at the strap of leather across his chest that I had managed to block from my vision by some magic of will. Testy? By the gods, they had stolen it off my brother's dead body after they had massacred his entire company. *Testy?* I looked from the baldrick into his cool black eyes. A smile swept through them as if he saw every burning thought in my mind.

He shook his head, satisfied with my silent response. "You need to learn to let go of things, Lia. All things. Nevertheless . . ." He slipped his dagger from it, then lifted the baldrick over his head and placed it over mine. His hands lingered on my back as he adjusted it. "Yours. As a reward. You've been proving yourself useful these past days."

I breathed with relief when he finally finished adjusting the baldrick and removed his hands from my back. "Your people already bend at your command," I said. "What do you need me for?"

He reached up, and his hand gently glided over my cheek. "Fervor, Lia. Food supplies are shorter than ever. They'll need fervor to help them forget their hunger, their cold, their fear through this last long winter. That's not too much to ask, is it?"

I looked at him uncertainly. *Fervor* was an odd word choice. It implied something more feverish than hope or determination. "I don't have words to stir fervor, Komizar."

"For now just do what you've been doing all along. Smile, flutter your lashes as if spirits whisper to you. Later I'll tell you the words to speak." His hand slid to my shoulder, caressing it, then I felt the fabric of my shirt pinching me as he gathered it up in his fist. He yanked suddenly, and I winced as the cloth tore free from my shoulder. "There now," he said. "Your tedious shirt is taken care of." His fingers brushed over my shoulder where the kavah now lay exposed, and he leaned close so that his lips were hot against my ear. "The next time I tell you what to do, see that you do it."

WE HEADED TOWARD THE WASHING GROUNDS WITHOUT another word. I garnered stares for both my kavah and my flapping torn shirt. *Fervor. That's not too much to ask, is it?* He was making me a spectacle one way or another. I was certain that in his own mind, the kavah was only something peculiar and exotic, or even backward. He didn't care about the meaning, only that it might help fan this so-called fervor. An added distraction, that's all he wanted, and nothing about it seemed right.

When we reached the washing grounds, I saw three long basins, the pressure of the river skillfully routed through them. Women lined the edges, kneeling to scrub their laundry on the stones, their knuckles split and red from the icy waters. Sickly sweet smoke drifted from one of the many nearby shops that circled the grounds, and the Komizar said he was stepping inside for a moment.

"Talk to the workers, but go no farther than the basins," he said sternly, reminding me I was to do exactly as he said. "I'll be right out."

I watched the women hunched and working, throwing their washed laundry into baskets, but then I spotted Aster, Zekiah, and Yvet across the way, huddled in the shadows of a stone wall and looking at something that Yvet held.

They seemed unusually subdued and quiet, which was

certainly not typical of Aster. I walked across the plaza, calling their names, and when they turned toward me, I saw the bloody cloth wrapped around Yvet's hand.

I gasped and rushed over to her. "Yvet, what happened?" I reached for her hand, but she fiercely clutched it to her belly to hide it from me.

"Tell me, Yvet," I said more gently, thinking I had startled her. "How did you hurt yourself?"

"She won't tell you," Aster said. "She's 'shamed. The quarterlord took it."

I turned to Aster, my face prickling with heat. "What do you mean? *Took it?*"

"A fingertip for stealing. A whole hand if it happens again."

"It was my fault," Zekiah added, looking down at his feet. "She knew I'd been aching fierce for a taste of that marbly cheese."

I remembered the angry swelling stump of Zekiah's forefinger the first time I met him.

For stealing cheese?

Rage descended, so utter and complete that every part of me shook—my hands, my lips, my legs. My body was no longer my own. "Where?" I demanded. "Where is this quarterlord?" Aster told me he was the metalsmith at the entrance to the *jehendra*, then clapped her hand over her mouth. She pulled on my belt, trying to stop me as I stormed away, begging me not to go. I shook her loose. "Stay here!" I yelled. "All of you! Stay here!"

I knew exactly where the shop was. Seeing me fly into a rage, several of the women from the washing grounds followed after me, echoing Aster's words, *don't go*.

I found him standing in the center of his stall, polishing a tankard.

"You!" I said, pointing my finger in his face, forcing him to look at me. "If you ever so much as touch any child again, I will personally cut every limb from your worthless body and roll your ugly stump down the middle of the street. Do you understand?"

He looked at me, incredulous, and laughed. "I'm the quarter-lord." The back of his meaty hand shot up, and though I deflected it with my arm, the force of his blow still sent me sprawling. I fell against a table, tumbling the contents to the ground. Pain exploded through my head where it hit the table, but my blood raced so hot, I was on my feet in seconds, this time with Natiya's knife in my hand.

There was a hush, and the crowd who'd gathered around stepped back. In an instant, the quarrel they had expected to see transformed into something deadly. Natiya's knife was too light and small to throw, but it could certainly cut and maim.

"You call yourself a *lord*?" I sneered. "You're nothing but a repulsive coward! Go ahead! Hit me again! But in the same moment, I'll be slashing your nose from your miserable excuse of a face."

He eyed the knife, afraid to move, but then I saw his eyes dart nervously to the side. Among his wares, on a table equidistant between us, was a short sword. We both lunged for it, but I got to it first, whirling as I snatched it, and the air rang with its sharp edge. He stepped back, his eyes wide.

"Which arm first, quarterlord?" I asked. "Left or right?"

He took another step back but was trapped by a table.

I swung the sword near his belly. "Not so funny anymore, is it?"

There was a murmur from the crowd, and the quarterlord's eyes shifted to something behind me. I turned, but it was too late. A hand clamped down on my wrist and twisted my other arm behind my back. It was the Komizar. He yanked the sword from my hand, threw it toward the quarterlord, and painfully squeezed the knife from my grip. It fell to the ground beside us. I saw him noting the carved handle that was distinctively vagabond. "Who gave this to you?"

I understood Dihara's fear now. I saw the fury in the Komizar's eyes, not just toward me but toward whoever had given it to me. I couldn't tell him that Natiya had hidden it in my cloak. "I stole it," I told him. "What is it to you? Will you cut my fingers off now?"

His nostrils flared, and he shoved me into the arms of the guards. "Take her back to the horses and wait for me."

I heard him yell to the crowd to go back to their business as the guards dragged me away.

He rejoined us only minutes later. His rage was strangely tempered, making me wary.

"Where'd you learn to use a sword?" he asked.

"I hardly used it. I waved it a few times, and your quarterlord wet himself. He's a bumbling coward who's only brave enough to cut off children's fingers."

He glared at me, still waiting for an answer. "My brothers," I said.

"Your quarters will be searched when we return to see if there's anything else you've stolen."

"There was only the knife."

"For your own sake, I hope you're telling the truth."

"That's all you have to say?"

"I'll pardon your threat to my quarterlord this time. I told him you're ignorant of our ways."

"*Me, ignorant?* The cutting of children's fingers is barbaric!"

He stepped closer, pressing me up against my horse. "Starving is barbaric, Princess. Stealing from the mouth of another is barbaric. The infinite ways your kingdom has kept us on this side of the river are barbaric. A fingertip is a small price to pay, but a lifelong reminder. You'll notice we have very few one-handed people in Venda."

"But Yvet and Zekiah are children."

"We have no children in Venda."

ON OUR WAY BACK, WE RETURNED THROUGH THE VELTE quarter.

Again, he greeted those we passed in the street and expected me to nod in kind as if I hadn't just seen a child mutilated by an ogre. He stopped our procession and dismounted to speak with a stout man who stood just outside an open-air butcher shop. I looked at his hands, all his fingers intact, large and stubby with neatly squared nails, and I wondered at how Gwyneth's careful observations about butchers extended all the way into Venda.

"You butchered and distributed the horses I sent with Calantha for the hungry?"

"Yes, Komizar. They were grateful, Komizar. Thank you, Komizar."

"All *four?*"

The man paled, blinked, then stumbled over his words. "Yes. I mean, there was one. Just one that I—but tomorrow I will—"

The Komizar drew his longsword from the scabbard on his mount, and the slow sound of freeing it chilled everything else to silence. He gripped it with both hands. "No, tomorrow you won't." In a move quick and precise, the sword cut the air, blood sprayed my horse's mane, and the man's head toppled to the ground. What seemed like seconds later, his body crumpled next to it.

"You," the Komizar said, pointing to a man gawking in the shadows of the shop, "are the new quarterlord. Do not disappoint me." He looked down at the head. The dead butcher's eyes were still wide and expressive, as if hoping for a second chance. "And see that his head's dressed up where everyone can see him."

Dressed? Like a pig that's been slaughtered?

He got back on his horse, gently clicked the reins, and we moved on without another word, as if we had stopped to buy sausage. I stared at the glistening red drops on my horse's mane. *Justice is swift in Venda, even for our own citizens.* I had no doubt the bloody message was for me as much as it had been for the butcher. A reminder. Life in Venda was precarious. My position was still precarious—and not only quarterlords could be dispatched without so much as a blink.

"We don't steal from the mouths of our brethren," he said, as if explaining his actions.

But I was certain that the quarterlord's deception was the greater crime. "And no one lies to the Komizar?" I added.

"That above all."

When we dismounted in Council Wing Square, he faced me, his face still spattered with blood. "I expect you to be well rested tomorrow. Do you understand? No more dark circles."

"As you command, Komizar. I will sleep well tonight if I must slit my own throat to do it."

He smiled. "I think we're beginning to understand each other at last."

CHAPTER THIRTY-SEVEN

RAFE

THERE WAS NO SIGN OF JEB WHEN WE RETURNED, BUT knowing he was here—looking and sounding more Vendan than ever—helped to ease my mind. Somewhat. I had seen today what could be his fate if he were found out. What could be all of our fates.

"You don't have to do that," Calantha said.

"Habit," I said.

"Emissaries in such a grand kingdom as Dalbreck brush down their own horses?"

No. But soldiers do. Even soldiers who are princes.

"My father bred horses," I said as an explanation. "It's the way I grew up. He said horses return twofold to a rider how they are treated. I've always found it to be true."

"You're still disturbed by what you saw."

The three impaled heads churned in my thoughts. I paused from my brushing. "No."

"Your strokes are long and brisk. Your eyes shine like cold steel when you're angry. I am getting to know your face well, Emissary."

"It was savage," I conceded, "but what you do with your traitors is of no concern to me."

"You don't execute traitors in your kingdom?"

I rubbed the horse's muzzle. "Done, boy," I said and closed the stall. "We don't defile bodies. Your Assassin appears to elevate it to an art." I started to return the brush to the hook but stopped mid-step. Calantha turned to see what I was looking at.

It was Lia.

The shoulder of her shirt was torn, and her face pale. With Calantha there, I had to pretend I didn't care. Lia avoided my gaze and spoke only with Calantha, telling her the Komizar was waiting outside, and she had come to retrieve her cloak, which she had left behind this morning. Had Calantha seen it?

Calantha cast a pointed glance at me, then directed Lia to the back wall of the stable and a row of hooks. "I'll be outside waiting too," she said.

"You don't have to go," I said, but she was already leaving.

Lia walked carefully past me, her eyes averted, and lifted her cloak from the hook.

"We're alone," I whispered. "Your shoulder. Are you all right?"

"I'm fine," she said. "It was just a difference of opinion on clothing choices."

And then I noticed a bruise at her temple. I reached up and pushed her hair away. *"What did—"*

"I tripped against a table," she said hurriedly, brushing my hand away. "Ignore it."

She kept her voice low, her attention fixed on the cloak in her hands. "We have to find a way out of here. When Kaden returns, if I—"

I pulled her into the stall. "Don't tell him anything."

"He's not like the rest of them, Rafe. He might listen if—"

I jerked her closer. "Listen to me," I hissed. "He's as savage as any of them. I saw his handiwork today. Don't say—"

She yanked free and her cloak fell to the ground. "Stop telling me what to do or say! I'm tired of everyone trying to control every word out of my mouth!"

Her eyes shimmered, with fear or rage—I wasn't sure which. *What had happened today?*

"Lia," I said, speaking more softly, "this morning I saw one of—"

"Is the emissary holding you up?" The Komizar stood at the stable entrance.

We both took an awkward step back. "I was just retrieving her cloak. She dropped it."

"Clumsy, aren't we, Princess? But you've had a long, tiresome day." He ambled closer. "How about you? Did you enjoy your tour today, Emissary?"

I worked to keep my voice even and unimpressed. "The Stonegate quarter had some interesting avenues, I suppose." And then for Lia's benefit, "I also saw your Assassin's handiwork. The impaled heads of the boys he executed have grown quite ripe in the sun."

"That's the point. The stench of treachery—it has its own unique aroma—one not easily forgotten."

He reached out and took Lia's arm with a familiarity I hadn't seen before and led her away. I couldn't control the burn in my chest, but I turned back to the horse as if I didn't care, brushing his coat again with long, quick strokes. This was something I'd never been trained for. There were no military strategies or drills to prepare me for the daily torment of not killing someone.

CHAPTER THIRTY-EIGHT

IT WASN'T JUST ONE OR TWO DOZEN, BUT HUNDREDS filling the square. I felt the Komizar's eyes on me from somewhere afar, waiting to corrupt my thoughts. I began with hesitation, trying to find that place of trust he couldn't control. The words came out awkward and self-conscious, a basic childhood prayer.

I tried again, closing my eyes, reaching, breath slow and deep, waiting and waiting, despair creeping in, and then I heard something. Music. The distant faint pluck of a zitarae. My aunts' zitaraes. And then my mother's hum rose above them, with its haunting echo that floated through the citadelle. The music that made even my busy father pause from his duties. I turned my head, listening, letting it strum through me as if it were the first time, and the rote words disappeared.

My remembrances began as utterances, a wordless tune that

followed the music of the zitaraes, each note plucking out the beats of creation, swirling in my belly, a song that belonged to no kingdom or man, only myself and the heavens. And then the words came, an acknowledgment of sacrifices and a girl's long journey, and I kissed two fingers, lifting them to the heavens, one for the lost, and one for those yet to come.

The distant music still seemed to echo off the high stone walls that hemmed me in with the people below. Eventide. A time to be going home, but instead they stayed. A voice called out. "Tell us a story, Princess of Morrighan."

Tell them a story, Jezelia.

There she was, only an arm's length from me, an apparition sitting on the wall, but at the same time solid. Unwavering. Her long hair trailed along the stones, all the way back to another millennium. *Tell them a story.*

And so I did. I told them the story of two sisters.

Gather close, my brothers and sisters,
Listen well,
For there is one true history,
And one true future.
Once upon a time,
Long, long ago,
Seven stars were flung from the sky.
One to shake the mountains,
One to churn the seas,
One to choke the air,
And four to test the hearts of men.

I drew from the words of Morrighan, Gaudrel, and Venda. I drew from Dihara, the wind, and my own heart. I drew from the truth that shivered at my neck.

A thousand knives of light
Grew to an explosive rolling cloud,
Like a hungry monster.
A storm that made the ways of old meaningless.
A sharp knife, a careful aim, an iron will, and a listening heart,
Those were the only things that mattered.
Only a small remnant of the whole earth remained,
But two sisters found grace. . . .

I told the story of the worlds I had seen, whole cities mowed down, no matter how far and wide they spread, and of soaring cities of immense magic that could not withstand a furious storm. I told them of exalted temples that melted into the earth and valleys that wept with generations of blood. But through all this, two sisters remained side by side, strong and loyal, until a beast rose from the ashes and tore them from each other, because even stars thrown to earth could not destroy every last shadow of darkness.

"Where were the gods in this?" someone called.

The gods. I had no answer except, "The gods wept too."

"What were the sisters' names?" another called.

Though I wasn't sure if he could hear me, I saw the Komizar's shadow pass in his tower window.

"It grows dark," I said. "Go home to your suppers. I'll tell you more tomorrow."

THE ROOM SHIVERED WITH EMPTINESS. I SET ABOUT straightening the meager contents, still scattered from the guards' riotous search for hidden weapons. They gave no thought to where they threw things. I longed for the company of the people in the square again. There was more I had wanted to say, and the solitude of the room allowed my doubts to creep back in.

I refolded the rumpled blankets and propped the practice swords back up against the wall. *Impaled heads . . . the Assassin's handiwork.* Rafe's remark was intentional, a warning for me. *What had Kaden done?* I remembered on my first day here that he had an urgent duty regarding soldiers he had to attend to, and his sharp refusal when I asked to go along. Was that where he had gone? *To execute boys?* The difference between children and adults didn't seem to exist in Venda. Had he swung a sword with as little remorse as the Komizar showed this afternoon? I simply couldn't believe it. They might both be Vendan, but they were as different as fire and water. I wondered what the condemned soldiers had done. Stolen food like the butcher? *Starving is barbaric, Princess.* I sat down on the bed. That was why they had no prisoners in Venda. Prisoners had to be fed.

Yet the Council seemed to lack nothing.

I had risen to pour water in the basin and wash up when I

heard footsteps in the hall. A single thump shook the door and then the lock rattled.

It was Ulrix. He cracked the door only a few inches, just wide enough to say, "The Komizar wants you. Wear your purple. I'll wait out here."

He shut the door so I could change. It was too early for the evening meal in Sanctum Hall, and Calantha was always sent to get me. Or the Komizar himself banged on the door. Never Ulrix. *Wear the purple.* Another dress that showed off the kavah, made of scraps of soft buckskin dyed with thannis.

I took the folded dress from the pile on top of the chest and rubbed the soft leather between my fingers. *Something isn't right.* But nothing had been right for so long, I wasn't sure how one more worry mattered.

Ulrix didn't take me to the Komizar's private meeting chamber as I expected, and when I asked where we were going, he didn't answer. He led me to a remote part of the Sanctum, down narrow curving stairs in a wing where I had never been. The stairs emptied into a large, round foyer barely lit with a single torch. There was one small recessed door and hallways on either side that vanished into darkness.

Before we reached the door, it opened, and a handful of quarter-lords, *chievdars*, governors, and Rahtan filed out. This wasn't the Council. Malich was among them, and while I expected a smug grin on his face, they all wore self-assured expressions as they walked past me. When they had disappeared in different directions down the hallways, Ulrix nudged me toward the room. "Go in."

Only a hint of light came through the open doorway, a sub-dued golden flicker. *The gods help me.* I kissed my shaking fingers, lifted them to the air, and moved forward.

A small candle lit a table in the center, leaving the rest of the room cast in black. I saw the faint outline of the Komizar sitting in a chair, his boots propped on the table, leisurely watching me as I entered.

The door slammed shut behind me.

"You wore the purple," he said. "Good."

"How can you tell in the dark?"

I heard the gentle inhale of his breath. "I can tell."

"You hold secret meetings in dark chambers now?"

"Greater plans call for greater privacy."

"But not with the whole Council?"

"I'm the Komizar. I meet with whom I choose, where I choose."

"So I see."

"Come closer."

I stepped forward until I was standing near him. He casually reached out and touched one of the loose scraps cascading from my dress.

"I have some good news for you, Princess. Something that will give you many more freedoms here in Venda. Your status is changing. You're no longer to be a prisoner." He smiled. The candlelight danced along his cheekbone, and his lashes cast a sharp shadow around his eyes.

My dress suddenly felt far too tight and the room sickly warm. "And how did I come by this good news?" I asked.

"It seems that clan elders would like some proof of your intentions. More of a willingness on your part."

"That might be hard to come by."

"Not so hard. And it will serve the fervor."

And then he explained.

His first words froze me; the next ones left me numb. Word by word. I watched his mouth move, admired the careful precision of each syllable, traveled the line of his lips, his facial hair so neatly trimmed across his jaw, the curl of his dark locks against the white of his shirt, his skin clear and warm. I traced the line of a small vein on his neck, listened to the careful pacing of his voice, magnetic, powerful, watched the flickering light play across his forehead. So much to draw my mind away as he laid out detail after detail, but it wasn't enough to block it out completely. Word by word. It was the last thing I expected to roll from his tongue. A turn I hadn't seen coming.

Masterful.

Genius.

Devastating.

You and I will wed.

He looked at me, his eyes hungry, not with lust but with something that ran much colder, gauging my every twitch and breath. I was certain he could see my blood drain to my feet.

"My advisers have seen how the clans have taken to you. You've charmed them. Quite a talent, since clans are tight-knit and can be hostile to newcomers. My advisers believe a marriage will come in useful during the harder times ahead. It will prove your commitment in the clans' eyes.

"And there's an undeniable sweetness for the rest of us if the enemy should find out their Royal First Daughter has not only run away from them but straight into the arms of their adversary. A marriage of her own making, so to speak." He shook his head. "We had quite a laugh over the discord that will sow."

"And you, of course, will make sure they know this."

"The news is already on its way. That was the detail the *chievdars* liked best. It's a victory for all of us. This will also put to rest any notions you may have entertained of ever returning home. If your kin scorned you for treason before, you'll be the most wanted criminal in their kingdom now."

"And what of Dalbreck when they find out about this?"

"What of it? The prince has already voiced his opinion of the thwarted marriage. His dealings are with us now. He won't care if we behead or wed you."

"And if I don't go along?"

"That would be regrettable. My Assassin, it seems, has developed an affection for you. For the greater good of Venda, he'd overlook the new arrangement, but unless he perceives it to be your decision, I'm afraid he could become a problem. I would hate to lose him."

"You'd *kill* Kaden?"

"A measure of passion at last," he said, grinning, and then his eyes went dead. "Yes. As he would me if I did something so stupid as to hinder the greater good. It is our way."

"You mean your way."

He sighed. "If that's not enough to convince you, I think I've glimpsed some lingering fondness in your eyes for the emissary.

I'd hate to break my promise giving him a month for his prince to send a messenger. It would be unfortunate if he began losing fingers prematurely. I'm finding him useful, and I have to admit a certain admiration for his unabashed ambition, but he'd be expendable too, at least pieces of him would be, unless your performance rises to stellar proportions. It's much more efficient to prevent problems than clean them up." He stood and his hands slid up my arms. "Convince them. Convince *me*."

I opened my mouth to speak, but his finger jumped to my lips to silence me. "Shh." His eyes grew dusky. He pulled me close, his lips searing fire against mine, though he barely grazed them as he whispered, "Think, Princess. Choose your next words very carefully. You know I'm true to my word. Think about how you want to proceed from this moment on."

My mind burned with the choice. He had played the winning card on my first day here. "There's always more to take, isn't there, *sher* Komizar?"

"Always, my pet."

I closed my eyes.

Sometimes we're all pushed to do things we thought we could never do. It wasn't just gifts that came with great sacrifice. Sometimes love did too.

Convince him. I relaxed against his touch and didn't turn away when his mouth met mine.

CHAPTER THIRTY-NINE

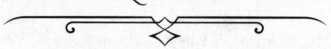

I SAT AT THE HEAD OF THE TABLE NEXT TO THE KOMIZAR. Several of the governors whispered among themselves. They had noticed my new position but said nothing openly. When he walked in with Calantha, Rafe noticed too, pausing for an extra beat as he pulled out his chair. The hall was full tonight, not just the usual Council and soldiers, but elders of the clans too. The Meurasi outnumbered them all, sitting at extra tables that had been brought in. I saw Effiera among them watching me. She tilted her head approvingly at my purple dress of scraps. There were also the quarterlords—the ones I had seen leaving the hidden chamber. Their glances cut not with approval but with stinging victory.

I looked away from Rafe, whose gaze still rested on me. *Don't make a mistake, Lia, not like—* I saw my brother's sightless eyes, the scattered pieces of body in the valley floor, the head of the butcher rolling to the ground. What had made me think I could ever outmaneuver someone like the Komizar? My head still spun with this turn I hadn't seen coming.

While the Komizar was occupied with the *chievdar* to his left, I asked Calantha if she would deliver the acknowledgment of sacrifice tonight. My tongue felt like sand. My head throbbed. I wasn't even sure I could conjure the words from my memory.

"No. It's left to you, Princess," she said. "You will do this."

There was a strange urgency in her tone that made me stop and look more closely at her face. Her pale eye glistened, pinning me to my chair. Insistent.

The platter of bones was set in front of me, and I simply stared at it.

The room grew quiet, hungry, waiting. The Komizar kicked my foot beneath the table.

I stood and lifted the plate of bones and said the blessing in two languages as Kaden had done for me.

E cristav unter quiannad.

A sacrifice ever remembered.

Meunter ijotande.

Never forgotten.

Yaveen hal an ziadre.

Another day we live.

I paused, the platter trembling in my hands. There was stirring, waiting for me to finish, but I added more.

E cristav ba ena. Mias ba ena.

A sacrifice for you. Only for you.

And so shall it be,

For evermore.

Paviamma.

A rumble of *paviammas* returned to me.

The hunger of the Council and guests quickly overtook any notice of the added words, but I knew Rafe had noted it. He was the last to echo back *paviamma* to me as he looked down at the table.

The meal seemed to rush past. I had hardly taken a bite when the Komizar pushed back his seat, satisfied. "I have some news to share with you, Emissary."

The clatter of the meal stopped. Everyone wanted to hear the news. My stomach churned with the small morsel I had eaten. But it wasn't the news any of us expected.

"Riders from Dalbreck arrived today," he announced.

"So soon?" Rafe asked, casually wiping grease from the corner of his mouth.

"Not the riders I sent. These were Rahtan who had already been in Dalbreck."

Rahtan with news. My hand slid to my side, inching down for Natiya's knife in my boot before I remembered it was gone. I eyed the dagger sheathed at Calantha's side.

"It seems there may be some truth in your story. They brought news of the queen's death of a widespread fever, and the king hasn't been seen in weeks, either in mourning or on his deathbed as well. I'll assume the latter until I hear more."

I sat back and stared at Rafe. The queen. *His mother.*

He blinked. His lips half parted.

"You look surprised," the Komizar said.

Rafe finally found his voice. "Are you sure? The queen was in good health when I left."

"You know how those scourges are. They ravage some more quickly than others. But my riders witnessed a rather impressive funeral pyre. Those royals are quite extravagant about such things."

Rafe nodded absently, silent for another long while. "Yes . . . I know."

The pain of my utter helplessness surged through me. I couldn't go to him, couldn't hold him in my arms, couldn't even offer him the simplest words of comfort.

The Komizar leaned forward, apparently noting Rafe's reaction. "You cared for the queen?"

Rafe looked at him, his eyes as fragile as glass. "She was a quiet woman," he answered. "Not like—" His chest rose deeply, and he took a drink of his ale.

"Not like that dried-up bastard she's saddled with? Those are the toughest ones to kill."

I watched the steel return to Rafe's eyes. "Yes," he said, a frightening smile on his lips, "but even the tough ones die eventually."

"Let's hope sooner rather than later, so your prince and I can strike our deal."

"It won't be long," Rafe assured him. "You can count on that. The prince may even help matters along if he has to."

"A ruthless son?" the Komizar said, his words dripping with admiration.

"A determined one."

The Komizar nodded his approval of the prince's pending patricide, then added, "For your sake, I hope very determined. The days do tick by, and my distaste for royal schemes hasn't diminished. I graciously host his emissary, but not without a price that must be paid. One way or another."

Rafe managed an icy grin. "I wouldn't worry. You'll be repaid tenfold for your efforts."

"Very well, then," the Komizar answered, as if pleased with the bounty promised, and motioned for the dishes to be cleared away. In almost the same breath, he ordered more drinks to be poured. The servants came forward with the expensive vintage of the Morrighese vineyards, one never shared beyond personal gifts to the governors. I chewed my lip. I knew what this meant. *No, not now.* Hadn't he shared enough news for one day? Hadn't Rafe heard enough for one night?

But then he twisted it into something even worse—he made me tell them. "Our princess would like to share some news too." He stared at me, his eyes chiseled stone, waiting.

My muscles were loose, wobbly, drained of strength. It felt as if I had already walked a thousand miles, and now I was asked to walk one more. I couldn't do it. I wanted to stop trying and cease to care. I closed my eyes, but a stubborn flame that couldn't be doused still burned.

Convince them. Convince me.

When I opened my eyes, his gaze was still fixed on me, and I met his marble stare. He commanded a marriage, which in his own words meant many more freedoms, but more freedom also meant more power—something he hated to share.

His eyes grew sharp at my delay. Demanding.

And maybe that was the deciding prod in my ribs, as it had always been.

Another mile. For you, Komizar. I smiled, a smile he surely thought was by his order. I'd give him his marriage, but that didn't mean I couldn't turn some fraction of this moment to my advantage, and fractions of moments after that, until they added up to something whole and fearsome, because with my last dying breath, I would make him regret the day he ever laid eyes on me.

I reached out, caressed his cheek, heard the murmurs at the unexpected display of affection, then I pushed back my chair and stood on it. The tables that had been added to accommodate the additional elders and quarterlords at the meal reached to the end of the hall. By standing on the chair, I made certain they could all see and hear me. *Hold my tongue, indeed.*

"My brethren," I called out, my voice loud and overflowing with all the grand flourishes that would please the Komizar. "Today's a great day for me, and I hope when I share my news, you'll agree it's a great day for us all. I owe you all much. You've given me a home. I've been welcomed by you, shared your cups of thannis, been warmed by your fires, your handshakes, and your hopes. The clothes that adorn my back have come from you too. I've received more than I have given, but now I hope to repay your kindnesses. Today the Komizar has asked me to—" I deliberately paused, drawing out the moment, and watched them lean forward, sit taller, their mouths hanging open, breaths held, drinks poised, eyes riveted. I paused just long enough that the

Komizar saw and understood that he was not the only one who knew how to command a room, and finally, when even he edged forward in his seat just a bit, I spoke again. "Today your Komizar has asked me to stand by his side, to be his wife and queen, but I come to *you* first, because before I answer him, I must know that you think my place here will serve Venda. So I ask, what say you, elders, lords, brothers, and sisters? Shall I accept the Komizar's proposal? Yea or nay?"

A breathless hush filled the hall, and then a deafening *Yea! Yea!* Fists lifted to the air; hands pounded on tables; feet stomped the floor; tankards sloshed and spilled in toasts. I jumped down from the chair and leaned over the Komizar, kissing him fully and enthusiastically, which made the hall erupt in more earsplitting cheers.

I pulled back slightly, but my lips grazed his as if we were lovers who couldn't part. "You wanted a convincing performance," I whispered. "You got one."

"A little excessive, don't you think?"

"Listen. Are you not getting the results you wanted? *Fervor,* I think you called it?"

The hall still roared with excitement.

"Well done," he conceded.

And then a question was shouted from an elder in the back.

"When will the marriage take place?"

The advantage was yet mine. Before the Komizar could answer, I called back to the elder, "At the rise of Hunter's Moon to honor the clan of Meurasi." Six days away. Cheers erupted again.

I knew the Komizar had envisioned an immediate execution

of the wedding, but now it was not only announced publicly, it was a date that would honor the clans. The girl Meuras was born under a Hunter's Moon. If he changed the wedding day now, it would be an insult.

The Komizar stood to accept congratulations. Quarterlords and soldiers pressed in, and I lost sight of him, but I saw that at least some of the governors wore wooden smiles, caught off guard by this new development. Perhaps they were unsettled that as Council they hadn't been consulted, or maybe it was something else: that I would be *queen*. The Komizar hadn't even blinked when I said it. If he had balked at anything, I thought it would be that. Vendans do not have royals. But I saw on our hillside rides how he seemed to flaunt it, *a princess of the enemy.*

A tankard was thrust into my hand, and I turned to thank whoever had delivered it. It was Rafe.

"Congratulations, Princess," he said.

We were surrounded, our elbows and backs touching others who mingled in the crowded room, pushing us close together.

"Thank you, Emissary."

"No hard feelings, right?" a nearby governor interjected.

"A mere summer distraction, Governor. I'm sure you've had a few of those," I said pointedly. He laughed and turned to another conversation.

"Just a few days," Rafe said. "That's not much time to get so much ready."

"Vendan weddings are simple, I'm told. A feast cake and witnesses are all that's required."

"How lucky for you both."

The air was brittle between us.

"I'm sorry about your queen," I said.

He swallowed hard, belying his fiery stare. "Thank you."

I could see the rage crackling within him. He was a storm ready to tear loose, a warrior far past the point of holding back—weary of being a compliant emissary.

"Your dress is quite striking," he said. He forced a strained smile to his lips.

The Komizar was suddenly at my side. "Yes, it is. She's becoming more Vendan every day, isn't she, Emissary?" He dragged me away before Rafe could answer.

The night wore long, every elder and quarterlord offering regards to the Komizar, but he received quiet, more devious nods from those who had met with him in his clandestine chambers. It was a strategic move and not a real marriage at all, not even a true partnership as the clans would expect.

I watched him slowly grow irritated with the talkative clan being in the hall. These were not truly his people. They spoke of harvest, weather, and feast cakes, not weapons, wars, and power. Their ways were weak, though he reaped his army from their young. Their only common goal was *more*. For the clans, more food, more future. For the Komizar, more power. For the promises he dangled before them, they gave him loyalty.

It was evident how much he really did need me when he walked away from one elder mid-sentence, his patience spent. He stopped short in front of me, his eyes clouded with wine, and pulled me behind a pillar.

"You must be getting tired. It's time for us to go." He called to Ulrix that we were retiring. It drew laughs from those within earshot.

I saw Rafe watching from a distance as if he might spring. I grabbed a fistful of the Komizar's shirt, yanked him close, and whispered through a razor-tight smile, knowing we were being watched, "I will sleep in my *own* quarters tonight. If this is to be a marriage, it is to be a real one, and you will wait like all good bridegrooms do."

The haze of wine was flushed away by his anger. His eyes cut through me. "We both know there's nothing real about this marriage. You'll do just as I—"

"Now it's your turn to think carefully," I said, returning his glare. "Look around you. See who watches. Which do you desire more? Me or the fervor of your people? Make your choice now, because I promise you—you can't have both."

His expression went cold, and then he smiled, releasing my wrist. "Until the wedding."

He yelled for Calantha to escort me to my room and disappeared back into a circle of drunk soldiers.

CHAPTER FORTY

KADEN

I WAS ALREADY WEARY OF THIS GOVERNOR. HE NEVER stopped talking. At least the small squad of men who accompanied him were mostly silent. It was clear they feared him. If not for his province's crucial importance as a supplier of black ore to the Sanctum, I would have let him trail behind us on the road to choke on our dust.

It was only another day's ride before I could be rid of him. He'd fit in well with the *chievdars*, though. His favorite topic was domination over the enemy swine and all the ways they should be sliced and strung. Wait until he learned we had two enemy swine sleeping in the Sanctum. Neither I nor the men traveling with me had told him, hoping to avoid another tirade.

Most of the time when he spoke, I tried not to listen anyway. Instead I thought of Lia, wondering what had passed in the last eight days. I had charged Eben and Aster with making sure she had everything she needed and called upon Griz to look after her too. He had taken a liking to her, which was not in his nature—but Griz was strong in the old ways of the hillfolk, and the gift had heft with them. With the three of them watching after her, she would be fine, I kept telling myself.

I thought of the taste of our last kiss, the concern in her eyes, the softness of her voice when she asked about my mother. I thought maybe the tide was turning for us. I thought about how much I couldn't wait to return to her and listen to her chant the acknowledgment of sacrifice. *Paviamma.* Every word that—

"And then I said to him—"

"Shut up, Governor!" I snapped. "For three blessed hours, until we set camp, shut up!"

My soldiers smiled. Even the governor's squad smiled.

The governor puffed out his chest and scowled. "I was only trying to break up the monotony of the ride."

"Then spare us. The monotony suits us fine."

I went back to my thoughts of Lia. How could I tell her that I knew in my gut from almost the beginning that we were meant to be together? That I had seen myself growing old with her. That a gift I wasn't even sure she really possessed had told me her name long before I ever laid eyes on her.

CHAPTER FORTY-ONE

PAULINE

BRYN LEANED FORWARD, LOOKING INTO HIS CIDER. HE WAS the youngest of Lia's older brothers, always the cheerful, fresh-mouthed one, who got into as much mischief as Lia. The past several months had sobered him. There were no grins on his face now, no quips on his tongue. "Regan and I secretly cheered when she bolted. We never thought it would come to this."

"Walther too?"

He nodded. "Maybe him most of all. He's the one who left false leads up north for the trackers."

Regan leaned back in his chair and sighed. "We had all voiced our opposition to shipping her off to a stranger and strange land. We knew she'd be miserable, and there are other ways of creat-ing an alliance with a little persistent diplomacy—"

"But apparently, Mother wouldn't hear of it," Bryn interjected, the first hint of bitterness in his tone.

The queen? "Are you sure?" I asked.

"She and the Royal Scholar were the first to suggest they accept the proposal from Dalbreck."

That was impossible. I knew the queen. She loved Lia, I was sure of it. "How do you know this?"

Regan explained that after Lia disappeared, there was a huge row between his mother and father. They were so incensed they hadn't retreated to their private chambers to vent their anger. "Father accused her of undermining him and making him look like a fool. He said that she never should have pushed the matter if she couldn't control her own daughter. They shot the sordid details at each other like they were poison arrows."

"There has to be an explanation for all of this," I said. "Your mother loves Lia."

Regan shrugged. "She refuses to discuss the matter with any of us, including the king. Even Walther couldn't pry anything loose, and he is always able to coax things from her."

Bryn said she mostly stayed in her chamber, even for meals, and he only saw her walking the halls when she was on her way to see the Royal Scholar.

"But the Scholar hates Lia," I said.

Regan nodded in agreement. The animosity between Lia and the Scholar wasn't a secret. "We assume she's seeking comfort and counseling in the Holy Text. He is the expert on such things."

Comfort. Possibly. But I could hear the doubt in Regan's voice.

Bryn downed the rest of his cider. "You're sure she was abducted?" he asked again. His tone was laced with despair. I knew how much he loved his sister, and the thought of her in barbarian hands brought him heartbreaking misery.

"Yes," I whispered.

"We'll confront both Mother and Father," Regan said. "We'll make them listen. We'll get her back."

They left, and my spirits lifted. Regan's resolve gave me a sliver of hope at last. He reminded me so much of his brother. If only Walther were here to stand with them too. I kissed my fingers and prayed for Walther's swift return.

I pushed up from the table to go back to our room. I could see the weariness in Gwyneth's face too as she rose. It had been a long day of waiting and anticipation.

"Well, there you are!"

Gwyneth and I both whirled around.

Berdi stood in the doorway, her hands on her hips. "Blazing balls, I've been to half the inns from here to the lowlands looking for you two! I didn't think you'd be snug up in the middle of town."

I stared at her, not quite believing what I was seeing.

Gwyneth found her tongue before I did. "What are you doing here?"

"I couldn't season a pot of stew to save my life worrying about you two and what happened to Lia. Figured I'd be more useful here."

"But who's watching the tavern?" I squeaked.

Berdi shook her head. "You don't want to know." She wiped

her hands on her dress as if she were wearing an apron, then sniffed the air. "Not much in the way of cooking here either, I see. I may have to poke my head in the kitchen." She looked back at us and raised her brows. "Don't I get any kind of welcome?"

Gwyneth and I both rushed into her wide-spread arms, and Berdi swiped at tears she blamed on the dusty ride. The only thing missing in that moment was Lia.

I hold her back.

> *Be still, child.*

> *Let them take it.*

She trembles at my side,

Fierce with rage.

We watch the scavengers take the baskets of food we have

gathered.

There is no compassion. No mercy.

Tonight we will go hungry.

I see Harik, their leader, among them.

He eyes Morrighan, and I shove her behind me.

Silver knives glitter at his side,

and I am grateful that when they leave,

He does not take more.

—*The Last Testaments of Gaudrel*

CHAPTER FORTY-TWO

CALANTHA ESCORTED ME TO THE BATH CHAMBER. WHILE my door was no longer locked as if I were a prisoner, my new freedoms apparently still required guards posted at the end of my hall *as a precaution*, the Komizar claimed, and I had no doubt they reported back to him every single time I so much as poked my head out the door. I also had escorts, who were essentially guards too, everywhere I went. Last night when Calantha walked me back to my room, she hadn't spoken a word. This morning seemed to bring more of the same treatment.

We entered the dreary, windowless bath chamber, lit only with a few candles, but this time instead of a wooden barrel, there was a large copper tub. It was half full of water, and waves of steam shimmered over the surface. A *hot* bath. I hadn't thought such a thing existed here. The sweet scent of roses filled the air. And *bath oils.*

She must have noticed my steps falter. "A betrothal gift from the clan," she explained flatly, and she sat on a stool, waving me toward the tub.

I disrobed and eased into the scalding water. It was the first hot bath I'd had since leaving the vagabond camp. I could almost have forgotten where I was if not for Calantha's baubled blue eye staring at me and the milky one gazing unfocused into the shadows.

"Which clan do you belong to?" I asked.

That got her attention. Both eyes were focused on me now. "None," she answered. "I've never lived outside of the Sanctum."

This revelation puzzled me. "Then why did you have me braid my hair to show off the kavah?"

She shrugged.

I sank down into the tub. "That's how you solve all your problems, isn't it? With indifference."

"I have no problems, Princess."

"*I* am your problem, that much is certain, but even that's a mystery to me. You both prod me and thwart me as if you can't make up your mind."

"I do neither. I follow orders."

"I think not," I countered and ran a soapy sponge down my leg. "I think you're dabbling with a bit of power, but you're not quite sure what to do with it. You test your strength now and then, bring it out of hiding, but then you shove it away again. All your boldness is on the outside. Inside you cower."

"I think you can bathe by yourself." She stood to leave.

I took a handful of water and threw it at her, splashing her face.

She bristled, and her hand flew to the dagger at her hip. Her chest rose in deep, angry breaths. "I'm armed. That doesn't worry you?"

"I'm naked and unarmed. I'd be a fool not to worry. But I did it anyway, didn't I?"

Her eye blazed. There was no indifference in her face now. Her lip lifted in a condescending sneer. "I was like you once, Princess. Answers were simple. The world was at my fingertips. I was young and in love and the daughter of the most powerful man in the land."

"But the most powerful man in—"

"That's right. I was the daughter of the last Komizar."

I leaned forward in the tub. "The one who—"

"Yes, the one your betrothed killed eleven years ago. I helped him do it. So now you know, I am quite capable of being bold. Arranging someone's death is not so difficult."

She turned and left, and the heavy door rattled shut behind her.

I sat there stunned, not quite sure what to think. Had she just threatened to orchestrate my death? *I was young and in love.* With the Komizar? What did she think when she found out about our marriage? Was that why she had been so silent? Surely she had more reason now to kill me.

I finished my bath, the luxury of it now gone. I rubbed the sponge over my arms, trying to think only of the baths where Pauline scrubbed my back and I scrubbed hers, how we poured pitchers of warm rosewater over each other, the baths where we laughed and talked about love and the future and all the things that friends share—not murder. I couldn't quite absorb it. *Calantha had helped the Komizar kill her own father.*

And yet she hadn't drawn her dagger on me, even though I saw the rage in her eye. I had pushed her just as I intended, but didn't get the answer I expected. Still, much was revealed. In the heartbeat of a second, beneath all the scorn that masked her face, I saw a girl, a younger Calantha, one without an eyepatch, who was terrified. A small glimpse of truth.

She is afraid.

Fear and thannis were two things that seemed to grow easily in this kingdom.

⋯⟨◈⟩⋯

WHEN I CAME OUT OF THE BATH CHAMBER, CALANTHA had left two scrawny smooth-cheeked guards as my escorts in her stead. Apparently she'd had enough of me for one day. I'd had enough of her too. I started to turn one direction, and both guards stepped forward to block me.

"I don't require your escort," I said. "I'm going to—"

"We were told to return you to your room," one of them said. His voice was uneven, and he shifted from foot to foot. The two of them exchanged a wary glance, and I saw a knot of leather at the shorter one's neck peeking from beneath his vest. He wore an amulet for protection. No doubt the other guard did too. I nodded slowly, noting their cautious expressions, and we began walking in the direction they indicated, one on either side of me. When we reached the darkest part of the hallway, I stopped short. I closed my eyes, my hands splayed on my thighs.

"What's wrong with her?" one whispered.

"Step back," the other said.

I grimaced.

I heard them both scramble back.

I fluttered my eyelids open until my eyes were wide and crazed-looking.

Both guards were plastered up against the wall.

I slowly opened my mouth, wider and wider, until I was sure I looked like a gaping cod.

And then I let loose a bloodcurdling scream.

They both ran down the hallway, disappearing so quickly into the shadows I was impressed with their agility.

I turned, satisfied they wouldn't be coming this way again, and went in the opposite direction. It was the first time I had twisted the gift into a sham since I'd been here, but if I wasn't going to be handed my newly earned freedoms, it appeared I would have to seize them. There were secrets just steps away that I had a right to know.

THE CAVERNS DEEP BELOW THE SANCTUM WERE QUIET. Only a little borrowed light from a lantern in the outside corridor helped me navigate. I entered a long, narrow chamber that had clearly been in recent use. A half-eaten loaf of bread was wrapped in waxed cloth. Books lay open on a table. Numbers and symbols that made no sense to me were scribbled on sheets of paper and gave no clue as to where the strange robed men were from. Several tiny sealed flasks filled with clear liquid lined the back of another table. I lifted one and held it to the light. Their own stock of spirits? I replaced it and searched the dim corners but could find nothing.

This chamber hadn't been my intended destination, but as I'd passed its narrow portal, a chill suddenly overtook me. *There.* My flesh crawled. The word pressed heavy against my chest like a hand stopping me. *There.* I was certain it was the gift speaking, an air current within the room that reached out to me, but when I could find nothing, I doubted myself, wondering if it was only one of the drafts in this cavernous underworld.

I took one last long look at the contents of the room and moved on.

ASTER HAD BEEN RIGHT. THIS TUNNEL LED ONLY TO WET rock and gears, the hidden workings of the bridge. The river roared just steps away from me, and I was already wet from its mist. Its power was staggering and frightening, and I wondered how many lives had been lost just trying to construct a way across it.

My spirits sank when I examined the gears. They were part

of an elaborate pulley system with wheels as massive as the one I had seen higher up the cliff at the entrance to Venda. "There's no way," I said to myself. And yet . . .

I couldn't quite bring myself to walk away. The lowest gear was secured into the surrounding rock. It was a slippery ascent, and the churning river below made me check and double-check every foothold, but my short climb revealed nothing of help. If anything, it only confirmed that we wouldn't be leaving by the bridge.

CHAPTER FORTY-THREE

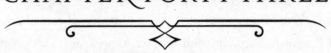

SHE DIDN'T USE THE WORD *LOVE*. MY AUNT CLORIS CALLED it a "confluence of destinies." I thought it was a beautiful word when she said it, *confluence*, and I was certain it had to mean something beautiful and sweet, like a powdered pastry. She said the king of Morrighan was thirty-four and had still not found a proper match when a noble First Daughter of a kingdom under siege had caught a Lord's eye on a diplomatic trip to Gastineux.

Confluence—a coming together by chance, like meandering brooks that join up in a distant unseen gorge. Together they become something greater, but it isn't delicate or sweet. Like a raging river, a confluence can lead to something impossible to predict or control. My aunt Cloris deserved more credit for her astuteness than I had given her. Yet sometimes the coming together, the confluence of destinies, seemed not to be by chance at all.

Today the Komizar had matters that needed his attention in the Tomack quarter, but he'd learned from Calantha that Rafe's family had bred horses that supplied the Dalbreck army. He asked Eben and Governor Yanos to take Rafe to the eastern paddock and stables just outside the city to assess some of his studs and mares.

I had insisted on exercising some of my newly earned freedoms, even if it came with the escort of two well-armed guards, and I went to the Capswam quarter to seek out Yvet's bapa. I gave him half the winnings from my card game with Malich and asked three things of him—that he seek out a healer for Yvet to make sure her hand didn't blacken with infection, to use the remaining coins to buy the cheese she had so dearly paid for already, and to never shame her for the heinous deeds of another. He tried to refuse the money, but I made him take it. And then he cried, and I thought my heart would wrench from my chest.

The guards, two young men who were no more than twenty, witnessed the exchange, and after we left I warned them not to tell Malich where his winnings had gone.

"We're Meurasi," one of them said. "Yvet is our cousin." And though they extended me no promises, I knew they wouldn't tell.

It was midday, and I had just entered the stable yard from the south Sanctum gate, and Rafe from the western gate. My heart lifted as it always did when I saw him, for a brief moment forgetting about the danger he faced and the lies I had to guard. I only saw the scruff of his unshaven face, his hair tied back, the confidence of his posture in the saddle, the same sureness as when he had walked into the tavern the first time. There was an engaging power about him, and I wondered how no one else saw it. He wasn't a conniving lackey to a prince. He *was* the prince. Maybe we all see what we want to see. I had fallen in love with the idea of a farmer, and it hadn't taken much nudging for me to believe it was so.

He was eating an apple, and its red skin shone bright against the drab stable yard. I had seen the treasured fruit arrive this morning with a Previzi caravan and watched Calantha throw him two of the sweet prizes. I hadn't had any fruit since I left the vagabond camp. The closest thing to it here was the root vegetables—carrots and turnips—sometimes served with the Sanctum chickens or wild game. I knew an apple was another reserved luxury delivered to the Council quarters, and I wondered at Calantha's generosity with Rafe.

He swayed easily in his saddle as he approached, biting off another chunk of apple, and our paths met in the middle of the yard. We exchanged a quick glance and dismounted, waiting for teams of horses that were being hitched to wagons to move out of the way. Even though we had an idle moment together and the guards surrounding us were loud with jesting, telling the Previzi drivers to hurry up about their work, there were still too many within earshot. I couldn't take a chance trying to explain last night and how my refusing the Komizar might hasten Rafe's death sentence. He was left to wonder what I was up to. He knew I despised the Komizar. He chewed his apple, his eyes inspecting my dress and the long trails of bones that rattled at my side. I could see every syllable in his eyes: *She's becoming more Vendan every day.*

"If *my friend Jeb* were here," he said, "he'd commend your accessories, Princess. His tastes run on the savage side."

"As do the Komizar's," a guard interjected, a reminder that they were always listening.

I studied Rafe. I wasn't sure if it was a compliment or an insult. His tone was odd, but then something else caught his attention.

I followed his gaze. *A confluence of destinies.*

Not now. Not here. I knew it couldn't go well.

It was Kaden. He was riding toward us with the governor he had sought at his side and what looked like a disheveled squad of men with him.

Rafe began choking, apple flying from his mouth. His eyes watered.

"Chew, Emissary," I said, "before swallowing."

He coughed a few more times, but his eyes remained fixed on the approaching squad.

I saw the visible relief on Kaden's face when he spotted me. He swung down from his horse, and the men with him did the same. Kaden ignored Rafe as if he weren't there, in fact as if no one were there. "You're well?" he asked, not noticing the sudden hush of the soldiers around us. The Assassin was back—the Assassin who had not yet heard the news. The governor stepped up, clearing his throat.

Kaden grudgingly nodded toward him. "This is the new governor of Arleston and his"—he paused, as if searching for the right word—"soldiers."

I understood why it gave him pause. "Soldiers" was a generous term. They were not an impressive lot. No uniforms, their clothes ragged, the poorest of the poor. But the governor was a frightening brute of a man, tall and lean with a broad chest and a vicious scar that striped his face from cheekbone to chin. He had a scowling line between his brows to match.

"And you are?" he said. The sudden forced smile twisting his lips was more wretched than his scowl.

"It's not important," Kaden said. "Let's go—"

"Princess Arabella," I answered. "First Daughter of Morrighan, and this is Rafe, the emissary of Prince Jaxon of Dalbreck."

The governor's smile disappeared. "Enemy swine in the Sanctum?" he said in disbelief.

He glared at Rafe and spit, hitting Rafe's boots. Rafe started forward, but I stepped between them.

"For someone so new to this position, you have an exceptionally reckless tongue, Governor," I said. "Be careful, or you may lose it."

He sputtered with astonishment and looked at Kaden. "You allow your prisoners to speak to you this way?"

"She's not a prisoner anymore," one of the nearby soldiers chided.

And that's when Rafe told Kaden about my new role at the Sanctum.

CHAPTER FORTY-FOUR

KADEN

I THREW OPEN THE DOOR TO THE KOMIZAR'S MEETING chamber, sending it crashing against the wall. Three brethren standing near him drew their weapons. The Komizar remained seated behind a table piled with maps and charts, and our gazes locked. My chest heaved from my flight through the stable yard and the Sanctum.

My Rahtan brethren kept their daggers gripped in their fists.

"Leave," the Komizar ordered. They rightfully hesitated. "Leave!" he yelled again.

They reluctantly sheathed their knives. When they closed the door behind them, he stood and walked around to the side of the table and faced me. "So you've heard the news? I'll assume you're here to offer your congratulations."

I lunged. I knocked him to the floor, and furniture toppled

around us. He pulled my knife from its sheath, but I slammed his hand against the floor, and the knife flew across the room. His other fist caught my jaw, and I fell back, but my knee met his ribs when he came at me again. Glass shattered, papers and maps rained down around us, but my rage finally prevailed, and I pinned him down, holding a shard of his broken lantern to his neck. Blood seeped from my hand as the sharp edge cut into my own flesh.

"You knew! You knew how I felt about her! But everything you already had wasn't enough! You had to have her too! As soon as I turned my back—"

"Then what are you waiting for?" His eyes were fiercely cold. "Slash my throat. Be done with it."

The glass shook in my fist. One slash, and I'd be the next Komizar. It had been expected for years, one Assassin after another rising to power. We sealed our own fates, training our successors far too well in their duties. My hand bled across his neck.

His eyes didn't waver. "That's right," he said. "Think carefully. You always do. That's one thing I've always been able to count on with you. Think about all our years together. Where you were when I found you. Think of all the things we've worked for. All the things you still want. Is a girl really worth it?"

"And yet you marry her? Make her queen? She must be worth it to you! What happened to all your talk of flabby domestic lives? And royals? Venda doesn't have royals!"

"Your anger clouds your judgment. Is that what she's done to you? Poisoned you? My decisions are based solely on what will benefit my countrymen. Where do *yours* come from?"

Only Lia. For me, Venda hadn't existed as I flew into this room.

He looked at me calmly, even with jagged glass at his throat. "I could have had you killed the minute you burst through my door. That's not what I want, Kaden. We have too much history between us. Let's talk."

I glared at him, my lungs burning, heated seconds ticking by, the pulse of his neck steady beneath my hand. Only one small vein separated me from Lia. But it was true—he could have set the Rahtan upon me the second I walked through the door. Even as I came through the gates. He could have been ready with his own dagger. *We have too much history between us.*

I let him up. He threw me a rag to wrap my hand. He surveyed the broken carnage of his study and shook his head.

"You're the one who brought her here. You're the one who said she'd be useful to Venda. You were right. And now the clans have welcomed her. To them she's a sign that the gods have favored Venda. She's a symbol of old ways and promises. We got more than we bargained for, and now we must use it. We have a long winter ahead of us, and most supplies must go to feed our army. But the fervor of the masses won't waver if she feeds their superstitions."

"Why a marriage?" I said bitterly. "There are other ways."

"It was the clan's request, brother, not mine. Think. Have I shown any interest in her before now? The clans welcomed her, but some were wary, thinking it could be another trick of the enemy. They wanted evidence of a true commitment on her part. Marriage to their leader has the permanence they desired. I consulted with the Council. They approved it. You question not just my judgment but that of the entire Council?"

I didn't know what to think. I couldn't believe the Council would approve this, but without me here, why not? Malich was probably the first to call a yea. And from the day the Meurasi welcomed her, I should have known this could become a possibility. The Meurasi did not welcome outsiders.

"Don't worry, things won't change much. I've no interest in the girl beyond what she'll do for our countrymen. You can even keep your pet in your quarters for now if you're discreet around the clans. They must think the marriage is real." He paused as he righted the footed oil lamp. "But I must warn you," he said, turning back to me, "she's developed a genuine kinship with the clans. When I proposed the marriage, she embraced it. She was eager, even. She saw its worth too."

"Embraced? Under threat of her death?" I said sarcastically.

"Ask her yourself. She saw that it afforded her two advantages— greater freedoms and sweet revenge against her father. Certainly you of all people can understand that. Betrayal by one's own kind is a wound that never heals. Use your logic, you smitten ass, and pull yourself together."

I looked at him, my calm returned. "I'll be asking her. You can be sure of that."

He paused as if something had just occurred to him. "Devil's hell, she's not bearing your brat, is she? I hope you're not that stupid."

He assumed, as I had led him to believe, that Lia and I were sleeping together. But the Rahtan were expected to take precautions so as not to be saddled with those flabby domestic lives he so greatly scorned.

"No. There is no brat." I spun and stormed out.

"Kaden," he called as I reached the door, "don't push me too far. Malich would make a fine Assassin too."

SHE LEANED OVER THE BASIN SPLASHING HER FACE, HER shoulders stiffening at the sound of my footsteps behind her.

"Did he force your hand?" I asked. "I know he did. I don't even know why I'm asking." She didn't answer and dipped her hands in the water, washing up to her elbows. I grabbed her arm, spinning her around, and the basin tipped over. It split in two when it hit the floor. "Answer me!" I yelled.

She looked down at the broken halves and the water pooling at our feet. "I thought you already had the answer to your question and didn't require mine."

"Tell me, Lia."

Her eyes glistened. "Kaden, I'm sorry. I'm not going to lie and say I don't want this. I do. You know I don't love the Komizar, but I'm not a foolish dreamy-eyed girl anymore either. The truth is, I've become resigned to the fact that I'm never getting out of here. I need to make a life for myself—the best one I can. Just as you asked me to. And if we're going to be honest"—her voice wobbled, and she swallowed—"the Komizar has something to offer that you don't. Power. There are people here, like Aster, the clans, and others, that I'm actually coming to care about. I want to help them. With a little power, I might. I remember you telling me that you didn't have the choices I thought you did. I understand that now. So like you, I'm taking advantage of the choices I do have. Marriage to the Komizar offers benefits that you can't give me." Her eyes narrowed. "And as an added bonus, the news of the marriage will cut at least my father to the core, if not all of Morrighan. There's some sweetness to that. Believe me when I tell you that my hand was not forced."

"In just a week's time, you decided all that?"

The glisten in her eyes receded as if on cue. "A week is a life-time, Kaden. It can wipe a whole world of people from the face of the earth with the falling of a single star. It can transport a tavern maid living in a seaside village to a scorching desert with ruthless cutthroats as her companions. So in comparison, really, does my small decision to marry a man for his power require more than a week's thought?"

I shook my head. "That's not you, Lia."

Her lip lifted in disgust as if she had suddenly grown weary of being sympathetic. "You're hurt, Kaden. I'm sorry. Truly. But life is hard. Pull your Vendan head out of your ass and get used to it. Didn't you spit out very similar words to me back in Reena's *carvachi*? Well, I get it now. So should you."

Her voice was cold, detached—and what she said was true. Everything sank inside me, falling like she had cut both my breath and muscle loose. I looked at her, even the words on my tongue lost somewhere in the tumble, and I turned away. I walked back out the door, down the hall, not seeing anything as I went, wondering how she'd become so . . . perfectly royal.

CHAPTER FORTY-FIVE

RAFE

I LEANED AGAINST THE PARAPET WATCHING LIA.

I was alone without benefit of guard, Ulrix, or Calantha. Though they let me know often that they were keeping a close watch on me, they were no longer constantly at my side. It seemed all the rules had been relaxed now that the marriage was announced and now that . . .

I rested my head against my arms.

My mother was dead.

It sickened me that her death gained me more credibility.

I should be home. Everyone in Dalbreck was probably searching and wondering—where is Prince Jaxon? Why isn't he here? Why has he shirked his duties? Yes, my father would have Sven's head and mine if we ever got back. That is, if my father was still alive.

Those are the toughest ones to kill.

My father was a tough bastard, just as the Komizar had said. But an old one. Tiring. And he loved my mother, loved her more than his kingdom or his own life. Losing her would weaken him, make him quick prey to scourges he had fought off in better times.

I should be there.

I was back to that again. I lifted my head and looked at Lia sitting on the far wall above the square below. My duty was in Dalbreck, but I couldn't imagine myself anywhere but here with her.

"There were only small gatherings when I left."

I turned. Kaden had come upon me silently. He was hidden in the shadow of a column, watching her too. His was the last company I wanted.

"The numbers have doubled every night," I said.

"They love her."

"They don't even know her, just what the Komizar parades through the streets."

He turned to look at me, his eyes filled with contempt. "Maybe you're the one who doesn't know her."

I looked back at Lia, perched precariously on a high wall. I didn't like anything about it. I didn't want to share her with Venda. I didn't want anything about this miserable land to love her. It was like claws digging in and pulling her into their dark den. But day by day, I saw it. I saw it in the way the bones swung from her hip as she walked, the way she wore their clothes, the way she spoke to them. For her they were no longer the same enemy they had been when we had first walked over that bridge.

"It's not just the remembrances or the stories," I said. "They ask her questions. She tells them about the world past the Great River, a world she'll never see again if she marries your Komizar."

"She's embraced it. She told me."

I snorted. "Then it must be so. We both know Lia always tells the truth."

He looked at me, his eyes dead still, rolling the thought in his head as if he was shuffling through his memory for her past lies. I noticed the bruise on his jaw and his bandaged hand. Those were good signs. Dissension in the ranks. Maybe the Komizar would kill him before I did.

I lifted my gaze, and so did Kaden. We saw them at the same time.

Across the way on the high terraces, governors and guards had come out to observe Lia, and over at the north tower, framed in his window, the Komizar himself watched over it all. He was too far away for us to see his expression, but I saw it in his stance, the ownership, the pride, the strings he surely thought he pulled on his pretty little puppet.

Her words swept through the square, then echoed back from the walls, ringing clear, and a strange stillness crawled across the air. It was all eerily quiet, except for her.

"It's how it was in the valley when she buried her brother," Kaden said. "It stopped every soldier."

For the Kingdoms rose out of the ashes of men and women
and are built on the bones of the lost,

and thereunto we shall return if Heaven wills.
And so shall it be for evermore.

Evermore.

The final word ate through me—the looming permanence if I didn't get her out of here soon. I watched Kaden studying her.

"But he'll be kind to her, right?" I said. "The wedding will be a day for both of us to celebrate. We can wash our hands of her at last. A lot of trouble, isn't she?"

I watched his jaw tighten, the imperceptible flinch of his shoulder. He wanted to jump me for throwing the truth in his face. I almost wished he would. I'd like to have it done with him once and for all, but I had bigger worries to puzzle out and little time to do it. The wedding had shortened my deadline by a week—and now the others were here. I turned to leave.

"You walk freely through the Sanctum now, Emissary?"

"A lot has changed in a week, Assassin, for both of us. Welcome home."

CHAPTER FORTY-SIX

I HAD BEEN HERE FOR SUCH A SHORT TIME, BUT IT already felt like a lifetime. Every hour was wrung with fear, and I had to hold back from what I wanted to do more than anything else. The task seemed rightfully mine, as much as love had seemed mine to find all those months ago when I ran from Civica. My destiny now seemed as clear as words on paper. *Until one comes who is mightier.* A few words with so much promise. Or maybe only a few words of madness.

I took another ribbon from the basket and tied it to a crossbar on the overhead lantern. I had lowered it with the rope so it was within reach, hoping to occupy my mind with something else for a few blessed minutes. Something that took me to a world outside of the Sanctum. But my thoughts kept going back to one thing.

It's harder to kill a man than a horse.

Was it? I didn't know.

But there were hundreds of ways, and they all burned within me. A heavy pot swung into the skull. A three-inch knife plunged into the windpipe. A push from a high wall. Every time I passed an opportunity by, the fire blazed hotter, but the desire burned side by side with a different searing need, to save someone I loved when I had let another down so miserably.

If I killed the Komizar, there would be a bloodbath. I had nothing to offer the governors, Rahtan, or *chievdars*; no alliances, not even a cask of wine to make it worth keeping me alive. My only certain ally on the Council was Kaden, and he alone couldn't erase the target I would inherit on my back. For now, I didn't just want to stay alive for Rafe, I *needed* to stay alive for him. This marriage might not free him, but at least it wouldn't cut his life short. I would always have that to hold over the Komizar—the fervor would end if he harmed Rafe—a marriage bought us both more time. That was all. There were no guarantees beyond that.

I remembered my conversation with Berdi after Greta had been murdered, not caring about guarantees and thinking I'd marry the devil himself if it offered the slimmest chance to save Greta and the baby. Now it seemed that was just who I would be marrying. I leaned on my window ledge, looking up at the heavens. The gods had a wicked sense of humor.

I tied the last ribbon and pulled the rope to lift the chandelier again. A rainbow of color fluttered overhead, and I wondered what Kaden would think when he saw it. Guilt stabbed at me for deceiving him. He'd already been wronged so completely and fully by nobility like me. Loyalty meant everything to him. I understood that now. What else could one expect from a boy who'd been thrown out by his own father like a piece of trash? I sighed and shook my head. *A Morrighese lord.* Now, just like his father, I had betrayed Kaden too. On many levels. I knew how he felt about me, and strangely, I cared for him, even when I was angered by his loyalty to the Komizar. There was a connection between us that I didn't quite understand. It wasn't the same feeling I had for Rafe, but I knew that with our last kiss, I had led Kaden to believe there was more.

There are no rules when it comes to survival, I reminded myself. But I wished there were. The betrayals seemed never to end. Soon the Komizar would ask me to betray those who had welcomed me, to roll my eyes and fill them with the hope he had conjured, and I was sure it would serve him more than the people.

You will hold your tongue and speak the words I give to you.

I sat on my bed and closed my eyes, blocked out the whickering and stamp of horses far below my window, the clank of gates being closed, the screams of the cook chasing after another loose chicken that wished to keep its head. Instead, I was in a meadow with ribbons blowing from trees, mountains above me tinged purple, rose oil being rubbed into my back, breathing in the sweet scent a thousand miles from here.

This world, it breathes you in . . . shares you.

Please share me with Rafe. *I do this for you. Only for you.*

There was a sudden sharp knock at my door. Kaden had left with such disgust painted across his face, I knew he wouldn't be back so soon, if ever. Was it Ulrix with another order from the Komizar? What would it be tonight? Wear the green! The brown! Whatever I command!

An ugly flash of the Morrighese court shot through me. A different setting, but years of the same orders. *Wear that. Be quiet. Sign here. Go to your chamber. Hold your tongue. For the gods' sakes, Princess Arabella, your opinion isn't required. We don't want to hear your voice on this matter again.* I grabbed the flask on the chest and hurled it across the room. Pieces of pottery rained to the floor, and I trembled with the truth—one kingdom wasn't much different from another.

Another knock, this one soft and uncertain.

I wiped my eyes and went to the door.

Aster's eyes were wide. "You all right in here, Miz? 'Cause I can scoot this fetcher away and come back another time, but Calantha told me to bring him and his cart here, and it's mighty loaded, but that don't mean you have to be letting him in your room right now, because you're looking plenty warm with your cheeks all flushed, and—"

"Aster, who are you talking about?"

She moved aside, and a young man stepped timidly into view. He slipped his hat from his head and clutched it to his stomach. "I'm here to leave fuel for the hearth."

I looked back over my shoulder at the bin near the fireplace. "I still have wood and patties. I don't need—"

"The weather's turning colder, and I got my orders," he said. "The Komizar says you'll need more."

The Komizar concerned about my warmth? Not likely. I

looked at him—a rumpled patty clapper—but something about him didn't seem quite right. The pale brown of his eyes was a bit too sharp. An unbridled energy simmered in them, and even though his clothes were filthy and his face unshaven, his teeth were even and white.

"Calantha told me to come right back, Miz," Aster said. "Can I leave this fetcher here with you?"

"Yes, that's fine, Aster. Go along." She ran off, and I stepped aside, waving the young man to the bin by the hearth.

He rolled his cart into the room but stopped in the middle and turned to face me. He looked at me curiously, then bowed deeply. "Your Highness."

I frowned. "Are you mocking me?"

He shook his head. "You might want to close the door."

My mouth fell open. He spoke these last words in Morrighese and had switched tongues without missing a beat. The majority of Vendans outside of the Sanctum didn't speak the language, and those within—the Council and some of the servants and guards—spoke it with a heavy broken tongue if they spoke it at all.

"You speak Morrighese," I said.

"We call it Dalbretch where I'm from, but yes, our kingdoms' languages are almost identical. The door?"

I sucked in a shocked breath, quickly slamming the door, and whirled back to him. Tears sprang to my eyes. Rafe's friends weren't dead.

He dropped to one knee and took my hand, kissing it. "Your Highness," he said again, this time with greater emphasis. "We're here to take you home."

WE SAT ON MY BED AND TALKED FOR AS LONG AS WE dared. His name was Jeb. He told me the journey into Venda had been a tricky one, but they had been in the city for a few days now. They were working out preparations. He asked me questions regarding the Council Wing and the layout of the Sanctum. I told him every hall and path I knew of, especially those least traveled, and the tunnels in the caverns below. I told him who the most bloodthirsty Vendans of the Council were, and about those who might be helpful, like Aster, but that we couldn't do anything that might put her at risk. I also mentioned Griz and how he had covered for Rafe, but I suspected it was only as a payback to me for saving his life.

"You saved his life?"

"I warned him about a bison stampede."

I saw the question in his eyes. "I can't control or summon it, Jeb. It's a gift, something passed down through the surviving Ancients, that's all. Sometimes I don't even trust it myself—but I'm learning to."

He nodded. "I'll nose around and see if I can figure anything out about this Griz fellow."

"The others," I asked, "where are they?"

He hesitated. "Hidden in the city. You won't see them until it's time. Either Rafe or I will give you warning."

"And there are four of you?" I tried my best to sound optimistic, but the number said aloud had a gravity of its own and spoke for itself.

"Yes," he said simply, and moved on as if the odds were a gulf that they would somehow navigate. He wasn't sure exactly when they'd be ready to move, but they hoped details would be worked out soon. They were still investigating the best way to accomplish their task, and there were a few supplies they were having difficulty acquiring.

"The *jehendra* in the Capswam quarter has just about every kind of shop there is," I said.

"I know, but we have no Vendan money, and it's far too busy there to steal anything."

I leaned over and felt for the leather pouch under my bed. It jingled as I placed it in Jeb's hands. "Winnings from a card game," I explained. "It should buy just about anything you might want. If you need more, I can get it." Nothing could have given me greater satisfaction than knowing Malich might play a role in our escape.

Jeb felt the weight of the pouch and assured me it would be more than enough. He said he'd remember never to play me in a game of cards. From there, he spoke in gentle positives the way a well-trained soldier would, saying they would be acting as quickly as they possibly could. A soldier named Tavish was the coordinator of all details, and he would give the signal when everything was ready. Jeb downplayed the dangers, but the words he avoided rippled beneath the surface—the risk and possibility that we might not all get out.

He was young, only Rafe's age, a soldier not unlike any of my brothers. Beneath the ragged clothes and dirt, I saw a sweetness. In fact, he reminded me of Bryn, a smile always tugging at the corner of his mouth. Maybe a sister waited at home for him to return.

I blinked back tears. "I'm sorry," I said. "I am so very sorry."

His brow creased with alarm. "You have nothing to be sorry for, Your Highness."

"You wouldn't be here if it weren't for me."

He placed both his hands gently on my shoulders. "You were abducted by a hostile nation, and my prince called me to duty. He's not a man prone to folly. I would do anything he asked, and I see his judgment was true. You're everything he said you were." His expression turned solemn. "I'd never seen him so driven as when we raced across the Cam Lanteux. You need to know, Princess, he didn't mean to deceive you. It tore at him."

It was those words that undid me, in front of Jeb of all people, a near perfect stranger, and I finally broke down. I fell into his shoulder, forgetting that I should be embarrassed, and sobbed. He held me, patted my back, and whispered, "It's all right."

I finally pushed away and wiped my eyes. I looked at him, expecting to see his own embarrassment, but instead I only saw concern in his eyes. "You have a sister, don't you?" I asked.

"Three," he answered.

"I could tell. Maybe that's why I—" I shook my head. "I don't want you to think I do this a lot."

"Cry? Or get abducted?"

I smiled. "Both." I reached out and squeezed his hand. "You have to promise me something. When the time comes, watch Rafe's back before mine. Make sure he gets out, and your fellow soldiers. Because I couldn't bear it if—"

He put his finger to his lips. "Shh. We'll all watch one another's back. We'll all get out." He stood. "If you see me again, pretend not to know me. Patty clappers are not memorable."

He gathered his cart, tossing a few patties into the hearth box, and flashed me a mischievous smile over his shoulder as he left, glib and cocky, shrugging off the dangers. So much like Bryn. This patty clapper was one I would never forget.

terrible greatness
Rolled across the land,
A tempest of dust and fire and reckoning,
Absolute in its power,
Devouring man and beast,
Field and flower,
All that dared to be in its path.
And the cries of the snared
Filled the heavens with tears.

—*Morrighan Book of Holy Text*, Vol. II

CHAPTER FORTY-SEVEN

SANCTUM HALL WAS DECIDEDLY QUIETER TONIGHT. I could sense it even from a distance as we walked down the corridor. The revelry usually rolled across the stone floor to meet us. Not tonight.

I wanted to fish and see if Calantha had any suspicions of who she had sent up to my room, but she said nothing, so neither did I. I didn't want to raise questions and mistrust where there was none.

As we got closer to the hall, the silence was palpable. "They fought, didn't they?" I asked.

"That is the word," Calantha answered.

"I saw a cut on Kaden's hand."

"And everyone's waiting to see how the Komizar fared," she said. I stole a sideways glance at her. She chewed on her lower lip.

"Why wouldn't the Komizar kill him for that?" I asked. "He seems to tolerate no rebellion and holds the threat of death over everyone else."

"Assassins are dangerous. It's in his favor to keep Kaden alive. No one knows that better than he does."

"But if Kaden's dangerous—"

"He could be replaced by someone more dangerous. Someone not as loyal. There's a strong bond between them too. They have a long history together."

"As do you and the Komizar," I said, digging and hoping for more.

She only replied with a curt "Correct, Princess. As do we."

The quiet was awkward as I entered Sanctum Hall. Without the usual din, the whole room seemed emptier, or maybe that was just because tonight the clans, quarterlords, and other special guests weren't filling every available corner. It was only the Council and servants. Rafe was standing at the far end of the table in the center of the room, talking to Eben. It was apparent that neither the Komizar nor Kaden had come in yet.

And then I spotted Venda.

She moved through the room, solid as any of us, her hand running along the table as if she were wiping crumbs from it, as if centuries and a push from a wall were inconsequential to her purpose. No one else seemed to note her presence, and I wondered if they mistook her for a servant. I walked closer, unable to tear my eyes away, fearing she would vanish into mist if I blinked. She smiled when I stopped on the opposite side of the table from her.

"Jezelia," she said, as if she had said my name a hundred times, as if she had known me from the time I was an infant and the priests lifted me up to the gods.

My eyes stung. "Did you name me?" I asked.

She shook her head. "The universe sang your name to me. I simply sang it back." She walked around the table until she was just an arm's length from me. "Every note hit me here," she said, and she put her fist to her breastbone.

"Did you sing the name to my mother?"

She nodded.

"You sang it to the wrong person. I'm not—"

"It is a way of trust, Jezelia. Do you trust the voice within you?"

It was as if she could read my thoughts. *Why me?*

She smiled. "It had to be someone. Why not you?"

"For a hundred good reasons. A thousand."

"The rules of reason build towers that reach past the treetops. The rules of trust build towers that reach past the stars."

I looked around, wondering if anyone else was listening. Every eye in the Sanctum was riveted on me, glazed with an awe bordering on fear—even Rafe's eyes. I turned back to Venda, but she was gone.

Me and frightening madness. That was all they witnessed, and I questioned my own sanity. I saw several soldiers pull amulets from beneath their shirts and rub them. *It had to be someone.* I leaned against the table for support, and Rafe stepped toward me, forgetting himself. I quickly composed myself, standing rigid.

A servant girl shuffled forward timidly. "What did you see, Princess?"

Three *chievdars* stood just behind her, glaring at the girl for acknowledging any power I held that they did not. Without the clans here, they didn't need to pretend. I phrased my words carefully, for fear the girl would suffer for her earnest question. "I saw only the stars of the universe, and they shined upon all of you."

My vague answer seemed to appease the naysayers and believers both, and they went back to their quiet conversations, still awaiting the appearance of the Komizar.

Rafe's eyes remained on me, and I saw the worry in them. *Look away*, I prayed, because I couldn't tear my own gaze free, but then I glanced at his hands, the ones that had gently cradled my face. *It would be unfortunate if he began losing fingers prematurely. Convince them.*

With everyone watching, I had a large audience to convince. I looked away just as the Komizar entered the hall. "Where's my betrothed?" he called, though I was plainly in his sight. A servant rushed to fill his hand with a mug, and both Rahtan and governors stepped aside as he walked toward me. "There she is," he said, as if his eyes had just landed me. I saw the small cut on his neck, and no doubt everyone else did too. "Don't be concerned, my love," he said. "Only a nick from shaving. I was perhaps a little too earnest in my desire to be presentable to you." His eyes danced with warning even as he smiled at me. *Say something*, was the command I saw in them. *Say just the right thing.*

"No need to risk your flesh. You're always presentable to me, *sher* Komizar."

"My sweet little bird," he said and reached out, placing his hand behind my head, drawing me toward him. He whispered against my lips, "Make this good."

Who was he trying to fool? The Council already knew the marriage was a sham and I was only a tool for his gain, but then I realized it was for another purpose. He wanted to show he was not thrown by the Assassin's attack and that he still had a firm grip on power.

Kissing him when it served me was one thing, but when it served him, it was quite another. I braced myself as his lips met mine, surprised that he was gentle, tender even, but perfunctory on every level. It was an accomplished performance, but then at the last moment, his hand curled into my hair and his lips pressed harder, passionately. I heard the crude laughter around us and felt the color rise at my temples. He finally let go of me, and instead of cold calculation, I saw unsettled desire spark in his eyes. It was the last thing I wanted to see there. I willed the color from my face.

He turned away as if exhilarated and bellowed, "Where's the food!"

Servants scurried, and we took our seats, but the conspicuous absence of the Assassin hung in the room like a poisonous cloud and kept the normal banter in check. I said the blessing, but before I passed the plate of bones, I took one to keep my hands and eyes occupied, even though my tether already jingled heavy with their weight.

It was a small bone, bleached and dried in the sun as they all were after the cooks buried them in a barrel of meal with beetles so that every scrap of flesh and marrow was eaten away. The larvae of the beetles were used for fishing on a river inlet, which in turn yielded more bones. It was an endless cycle of sacrifice upon sacrifice. I fiddled with the bone, wishing I could wipe away the taste of the Komizar from my lips. I was afraid to look up and meet Rafe's gaze, because I knew what I would see, the strain spreading like a feverish stain across his face. If I had to watch him day after day kissing a maid or being pulled into her embrace, I would truly go mad.

"You're not eating, Princess," the Komizar said.

I reached out and took a slice of turnip and nibbled it to appease him.

"Eat up," he insisted. "We have a big day ahead of us tomorrow. I wouldn't want you to grow faint."

Every day was a big day for the Komizar. No doubt for me it meant more parading through the city or countryside. Curiously, there was only one quarter he hadn't taken me to—the Tomack quarter in the southernmost part of the city.

The sudden tramping of footsteps echoed through the hall, and much to the Komizar's dismay, the meal paused—no one wanted to miss the entrance of the Assassin, and all were eager to see if he bore the evidence of a brawl. Everyone present quickly took note that there were multiple footsteps coming toward us. Their hands went from plates to the weapons sheathed at their sides. Protected by the impassable Great River, they surely didn't fear the enemy without, so they must always be ready for the enemy within. Bloodbaths, as Kaden called them.

Kaden entered from the eastern passageway. Everyone saw what they wanted to see, the evidence of a brawl, if not a challenge. A blue bruise darkened his jaw, and his hand was wrapped in a bandage, but he had no weapon drawn, and they eased back in their seats. It appeared the Komizar had fared better than his Assassin. The odious new governor and his personal guard walked beside Kaden. There was muffled laughter from the end of the table where Malich sat with his smug circle of Rahtan. Kaden made a determined straight shot to the Komizar. "The new governor of Arleston, as you requested," he said, as if depositing a box of cargo at the Komizar's feet. He turned briskly to the governor. "Governor Obraun, this is your sovereign. Bend your knee and pledge your allegiance now."

The governor did as he was told, and before the Komizar could respond, Kaden stepped over between us and leaned with one arm against the table. He seethed fury, and though he whispered, it was still loud enough that those seated near us could hear him. "And you, *royal*, will sleep in my quarters tonight," he hissed. "The Komizar said there's no reason you will not serve us both— and after my long journey, I wish to be served. Do you understand?"

I said nothing, but fire raced across my cheeks. I hadn't seen him this angry since the night he flung me into the *carvachi* for attacking Malich. No, tonight he was far more enraged. I had betrayed him personally. I represented every noble of Morrighan meeting all his low expectations, but now, with a few words, he had met mine too. I did not take those kinds of orders from anyone.

I looked at the Komizar and he nodded, indicating he approved this shared arrangement. His eyes smoldered with satisfaction, pleased with his Assassin's rage directed at me. Kaden pushed away from the table and found an empty seat in the middle across from Rafe. The tension that always sparked between them magnified, their hot gazes fixed on each other for far too long. Rafe couldn't have heard what Kaden said to me, but maybe my flushed face was all he needed to see. Chairs were slid aside so the new governor and his guard could sit near his sovereign.

The Komizar and governor seemed to connect immediately, but for me their conversation became a blur of sound, disconnected words, laughter, and the clinking of mugs. I watched the governor's lips move, but Kaden's words were what I heard. *And you, royal, will sleep in my quarters.*

"And now you'll marry enemy swine?" My gaze darted to the governor's arrogant beady eyes.

I stood and seized a fistful of his jacket, jerking his face close to mine. "If you say 'enemy swine' one more time, I will tear the flesh from your face with my bare hands and feed it to the hogs in the stable yard! Do you understand me, Governor?"

The Komizar grabbed my arm and yanked me back to my seat.

Both the governor and his wide-eyed guard looked at me in startled amazement.

"Apologize, Princess," the Komizar ordered. "The governor

is a new loyal member of the Council and has had little time to adjust to the idea of the enemy walking on Vendan soil."

I glared at him. If my supposed newfound freedoms were to be of any use to me at all, I would have to chip away and snatch them a small piece at a time. "He calls your betrothed swine!" I argued.

"It's a common phrase we use for the enemy. *Apologize.*" His fingers dug into my thigh beneath the table.

I looked back at the governor. "I beg your forgiveness, Your Eminence. I would not truly feed your face to the hogs. It might make them *sick*."

There was audible sucking of breath, and time seemed to stop, as if these were to be my last seconds on earth, as if I had at last pushed too far. The silence stretched thin and taut, but then, midway down the table, Griz snorted. His boisterous laugh cut through the shocked hush, then Eben and Governor Faiwell joined in with laughter too, and soon the prevailing doom of the moment was washed away by at least half of those at the table joining in at my "jest."

Governor Obraun, as if he sensed he was caught in the middle of a swift, unexpected squall, laughed too, assuming the insult to be a joke. I smiled to assuage the Komizar, though inside I still raged.

For the rest of the meal, the governor made an exaggerated point to call me the Komizar's *betrothed*, which drew more laughter. His guard remained quiet, and I learned he was mute—an odd choice for a guard who might need to sound an alarm—but perhaps he was deaf as well and was the only one able to endure the governor's ceaseless prattle.

My toes clenched and unclenched inside my boots, and the fires on either end of the hall seemed to burn too hot. Everything inside me itched. Maybe it was knowing that somewhere in this city Jeb and his fellow soldiers were working to find a way out for all of us. Four. It was a number I had scoffed at, but now it seemed like the precious split-second chance I had taken in the face of a stampeding herd of bison. Risky but worth it.

I thought the evening couldn't get worse, but I was wrong. As they began clearing the platters and I was hoping to leave, a parade of barrow runners began pushing carts into the room.

"Here at last," the Komizar said as if he knew they were coming. I saw Aster among the runners, struggling with a cart loaded with armor, weapons, and other booty. My stomach dropped. Another patrol had been massacred.

"Their loss, our gain," the Komizar said cheerfully.

The small bit of turnip I had swallowed seemed stuck in my chest. It took a moment for me to truly focus on the contents, but when I did, I saw the blue and black colors of Dalbreck emblazoned on shields and banners—and the lion—whose claw I bore on my back. The haul was almost as great as the one from my brother's company, and even though these weren't my countrymen, I felt my grief anew. Around me, greed glowed in the *chievdars'* and governors' faces. Even this action by the Komizar was not just about booty, but again about fervor. Another kind. Like the scent of blood given to a pack of dogs.

As the last barrow runners set down their goods, Rafe's chair screeched back and toppled behind him as he stood. The sudden crash turned every head toward him. He walked over to a cart, his chest heaving, looking at the contents. He pulled a long sword from a pile, and the sound of steel rang in the air.

The Komizar slowly stood. "You have something you wish to say, Emissary?"

Rafe's eyes blazed, their blue ice cutting through the Komizar. "These are my countrymen you've slaughtered," he said, his tone as frigid as his gaze. "You have an agreement with the prince."

"On the contrary, Emissary. I may or may not have an agreement with your prince. Your claim hasn't yet proven true. On the other hand, I definitely do not have an agreement with your king. He's still my enemy, and he's the one sending patrols out to attack my soldiers. At the moment, everything is still status quo between us, including your very tenuous position." He held a hand out toward a guard, and the guard threw the Komizar a sword.

He looked back at Rafe, casually testing the sword in his grip. "But maybe you're only wishing for some sport? It's been a long time since we have had any entertainment within these walls." He took a step toward Rafe. "I wonder just how good a swordsman a court emissary might be."

Snickers rolled through the room.

Oh, by the gods, no. Put the sword down, Rafe. Put it down now.

"Not very good," Rafe answered, but he didn't put the sword down. Instead he tested the grip in his hand with as much threat as the Komizar.

"In that case, I'll pass you on to my Assassin. He seems eager for sport as well, and not as accomplished as I am with this particular weapon." He tossed the sword to Kaden, and with lightning reflexes, Kaden stood and caught it. He was more than accomplished.

"First blood," the Komizar said.

I found myself out of my seat, moving toward them, but then was caught in the iron grip of Governor Obraun. "Sit down, girl," he hissed, and he shoved me back into my seat.

Kaden stepped toward Rafe, and all the young barrow runners scrambled to the outer reaches of the hall. Rafe glanced at me, and I knew he saw the pleading in my eyes—*put it down*—but he wrapped both hands securely around the grip and stepped forward anyway, meeting Kaden in the middle of the room.

The long-repressed animosity between them was thick in the air. My mouth went dry. Kaden raised his sword with both hands, a moment's pause as each assessed the other, and then the fight was on. The fierce clang of steel on steel reverberated through the hall, blow after blow. It seemed nothing like a match intended to draw only a drop of blood.

Rafe's swings were powerful, deadly, more like a relentless battering ram. Kaden met the blows, but after a few strikes began to lose ground. He deftly sidestepped, whirled, and swung, nearly slicing Rafe in the ribs, but Rafe expertly blocked the blade with amazing speed and threw Kaden back. I could feel the fury flying off Rafe like fiery sparks. He swung, and the tip of his sword caught Kaden's shirt, ripping it open on one side, but no blood.

Kaden advanced again, fast and furious, and their clanging blows chattered through my teeth.

The onlookers were no longer quiet. The dull roar of their commentary accompanied each ringing assault, but the governor suddenly shouted out above them all, "Watch your step, emissary swine!" and then laughed.

"Shut up!" I yelled, afraid it would distract Rafe, and then he did seem to falter, his blows not coming as fast or as strong, until at last Kaden backed him up to a wall, and fumbling under a series of strikes, Rafe lost hold of his sword, and it clattered to the floor. Kaden pressed the tip of his sword just under Rafe's chin. Both of their chests heaved with exertion, and their gazes were locked. I was afraid to say anything, for fear my voice alone would cause Kaden to plunge the sword into Rafe's throat.

"First blood. *Farmer,*" Kaden said, and he swiped his sword downward, nicking Rafe's shoulder. A bright red stain spread across Rafe's shirt, and Kaden walked away.

There were shouts of victory among Kaden's comrades, and the Komizar congratulated them both for an entertaining match. "Strong start, Emissary. Weak finish. But don't feel too bad. It's what I'd expect of court puffery. Most of your worries and battles are momentary and don't require Vendan endurance."

I fell back against my chair. My brow was damp, and my shoulders ached. I saw the governor and his guard studying me, no doubt thinking I had been rooting for my fellow swine. I glared at them both. The Komizar told Calantha to see to the cut on Rafe's shoulder, not wishing his emissary to die of blood poisoning just yet, and he lifted a mug to Kaden. I saw a smug, knowing glance pass between them. Whatever quarrel had recently passed, it was now mended. I would *serve them both*.

In hell I would.

A practice sword could bash his skull in as easily as a steel one. This time I wouldn't be aiming for his shin. I stood and left, my assigned escorts trailing on my heels.

CHAPTER FORTY-EIGHT

KADEN

I SAW HER LEAVE. THE EVENING BETWEEN US WAS FAR FROM over. I tried to follow, but everyone wanted to gloat with me about my easy victory over the emissary.

Easy.

The thought made my blood boil all over again.

By his third swing, I knew I wasn't fighting an emissary. By his fifth, I knew he wasn't even an average soldier. By the tenth strike, I knew I was going to lose. But suddenly his attack softened, and he made stupid mistakes. He didn't lose. He let me win. Preserving his identity as a foppish emissary was more important to him than parting my head from my shoulders—and I knew that was a prize he very much desired.

I swilled back a last gulp of ale and left Chievdar Dietrik mid-sentence, following after Lia. The corridor echoed with my footsteps. I reached my chamber and threw the door open. She was standing there, ready for me, a practice sword in her hand and battle in her eyes.

"Put it down!" I ordered.

She lifted it high in the air, ready to strike. "Get out!"

I stepped closer and said each word slowly, so there was no mistaking the threat in them. "Put the sword down. *Now.*"

Her stance remained defiant. She would kill me before she set it aside. "So I can *serve* you?" she sneered.

I wasn't going to let her off that easy. I was going to let her reel and stew and feel just as shattered as I had been. I took another step, and she swung, barely missing my head. My rage bubbled over, and I lunged at her, catching the wooden blade with my hand as she swung again. We fell to the ground and rolled, grappling for the sword. I finally squeezed her wrist until she cried with pain and dropped it. I tossed it across the room. She lurched to roll away, but I slammed her back down and pinned her.

"Stop it, Lia! Stop it now!"

She stared at me, her breaths heavy and furious.

"Don't you hurt her, Master Kaden! Let her up! Because I know how to use this!"

Lia and I both looked toward the door. It was Aster, and her eyes were wild with fear.

"Get out!" I yelled. "Before I skin you!"

Aster raised the sword higher, standing her ground. Her arms trembled with the weapon's weight.

"Listen to you!" Lia said. "Threatening a child. Aren't you the brave Assassin?"

I let go of her and stood. "Get up!" I ordered, and once she got to her feet, I pointed at Aster. "Now tell her to leave, so I don't have to skin her."

Lia glared at me, expecting me to back down. I reached for my dagger. She grudgingly turned to Aster, her expression softening. "It's all right. I can handle the Assassin. He's all bluster, no bite. Go on now."

The girl still hesitated, her eyes glistening. Lia kissed two fingers and lifted them to the heavens in a silent command to Aster. "Go," she said quietly, and the girl left reluctantly, shutting the door behind her.

I thought Lia had calmed down, but as soon as she turned back to me, her wrath had returned. *"Royal? You will sleep in my quarters tonight, royal?"*

"You know I'd never force myself on you."

"Then why did you say it?"

"I was angry," I said. "I was hurt."

Because I knew everything she had said to me about the Komizar and wanting power was a lie, and I wanted to call her bluff. Because I wanted the Komizar to believe there was an irreparable change in our relationship. Because I was trying to keep her here in my room and safe for one more night. Because everything was flying out of control. Because she was right— I wanted to trust her but I didn't. Because when I left a week ago, she had kissed me.

Because I so stupidly loved her.

I saw the tempest in her eyes, the waves of calculation crashing and cresting, weighing every word of what she could and couldn't say. Tonight there would be no honesty within her.

"It's a dangerous game you're playing, Lia," I said. "And it's not a game you'll win."

"I don't play games, Kaden. I wage wars. Don't make me wage one on you."

"Those are brave bold words that mean nothing to me."

Her lips parted, ready for a biting comeback. "I'm not—" But she caught herself and refused to go on, almost as if she didn't trust herself to say more. She turned away and grabbed a blanket from the barrel and threw it to me. "I'm going to sleep, Kaden. You should too."

She was done. I could almost see the weight on her shoulders. Her lids were heavy with weariness, as if no fight was left in her. She didn't bother to change. She lay on the bed and pulled the quilt over her shoulders.

"Can we—"

"Good night."

We went to sleep without another word, but as I lay there in the dark, I replayed our earlier conversation in my head. She had hit every note when she explained her decision to marry the Komizar: the resignation, bitterness, throwing my own words back in my face, the regret, the glistening eyes, every single note as if she was singing a practiced song. Her performance was near flawless, but it had none of the genuine weariness that I had just seen now. *I'm not going to lie, Kaden.*

But she had. I was certain. I remembered her bitter words to me as we left the vagabond camp when I said she was a poor liar. *No, actually, I can be a very good one, but some lies require more time to spin.*

And now, as I retraced the past days, her claim of trying to build a new life here, her kiss, I wondered . . . just how long had she been spinning one?

CHAPTER FORTY-NINE

RAFE

"HAVE YOU TAKEN LEAVE OF YOUR SENSES?" I HISSED.

I sat in a dark storeroom off the kitchen that smelled of onions and goose grease. Calantha had left me here to wait while the cook boiled up a poultice for my wound.

"It was an opportunity that dropped into our laps. We can't all show up as patty clappers and emissaries. How's the shoulder?"

I pushed his hand away. "It's crazy. How long can Orrin play the mute? What were you thinking? And who are all those other soldiers that showed up with you?"

"Terrified boys, mostly. As far as they know, I truly am the new governor of Arleston. We ambushed them on the road. Easy pickings. The governor was as soaked as a fish. Nasty fellow. Barely knew what hit him. His so-called guards fairly handed us their weapons in one breath and pledged their new allegiance in the next."

I shook my head.

"Come on, boy. This is a plum position. I don't have to slink about, and I can carry weapons without raising a brow."

"And spit in my face."

"On your boots," he corrected. "Don't malign my aim." Sven chuckled. "I thought you were going to choke when you saw me."

"I did choke. I still have a piece of apple stuck in my throat."

"Most of our way here, I wasn't sure we'd even find you alive. I prodded that Assassin for miles, but he's a tight-lipped fellow, isn't he? Wouldn't let loose with anything, and the soldiers with him weren't much better. I finally overheard one of them talking around the campfire about the foppish emissary of the prince."

Orrin, standing by the door to the kitchen keeping an eye out for the cook, whispered over his shoulder, "That Assassin is the first one we'll take out."

"No," I said. "I'll take care of him."

Sven asked about the details of my arrival, and I told them about my proposal to the Komizar, and how I had played on his greed and ego.

"And he bought it?" Sven asked.

"Greed is a language he understands. When I told him our stake was a port and a few hills, it rang true."

Sven's expression darkened. "You knew about that?"

"I'm not deaf, Sven. It's what they've wanted for years."

"Does she know?"

"No. It doesn't matter. I'd never allow it to happen."

Sven peeled back the blood-sodden tear in my shirt and grunted. "It was a stupid move you made tonight."

"I pulled back."

"Only thanks to me."

I knew he'd point that out. *Watch your step.* If they suspected I was anyone other than who I claimed to be, it wouldn't bode well for any of us—especially Lia. We'd end up dead, but she'd end up married to one animal and serving another at his bidding. The wedding was three days away. We had to move fast.

"Where's Tavish?" I asked.

"Still working out the details of the raft. He's acquiring the barrels to tether together."

Barrels. In a split-second passing today, Jeb had briefly whispered the escape would be by raft, but I'd hoped I had heard him wrong. I shook my head. "There has to be another way."

"If there is, you tell us what it is," Sven said. He told me they had already looked at other options and confirmed the bridge was definitely not one of them. It required too many men to raise and drew too much attention. Traveling on land for hundreds of miles to the lower river wasn't an option either. We'd be hunted down before we reached the calm waters, and there were beasts in that part of the river that did their own kind of hunting. Orrin had already gotten a taste of that. His calf had been shredded before Jeb and Tavish managed to kill the monster that had latched on to his leg.

They insisted a raft was the only option. Tavish had studied the river. He said it would work. Though the drop and rushing waters sent up a powerful mist, that same mist provided concealment, and there were slower eddies on the western bank. The raft just had to be maneuvered into one at just the right point. It was possible. The other advantage to the river was that it would sweep us out of Vendan reach so swiftly, we'd be miles away before they even managed to get the bridge raised to try to follow, and then they'd have no idea where we had exited the river. Orrin said they had left their horses and some of the Vendan horses we had captured roped off in a hidden pasture some twenty miles downriver. It was the perfect plan. So they said. If the horses were still there. If a hundred other things didn't go wrong. I tried to remind myself that Tavish had always been the architect of details. I had to trust him, but I'd have felt better if I could see the certainty in his eyes for myself. I didn't know if Lia even knew how to swim.

"How's your leg?" I asked Orrin.

"Tavish sewed me up. I'll live."

"But it needs a dressing too," Sven said firmly.

Orrin lifted his pant leg and shrugged. The dozens of stitched lines showing above the top of his boot were red and festering, which explained his slight limp. But it had given Governor Obraun and his injured guard a good excuse to join me here. Sven had told Calantha his guard had been attacked by a panther while hunting and was in need of a poultice too.

While we were whispering, Jeb snuck in from another door. "Anyone here need a crap cake?"

I smiled, surveying him head to foot. He was the only one among us who cared about the season's latest fashion and whether his buttons were polished. Now he was dressed in rags, his hair filthy, and he fully looked the role of a patty clapper. "How'd you get stuck with that job?" I asked.

"Everyone's happy to open the door for a patty clapper making a delivery. Happy at least for a few seconds." He made a clicking sound out the side of his mouth, like the snapping of a neck. "We may need to take a few out quietly in their rooms before we make our move."

"And he speaks Vendan like a native," Sven added.

Jeb was like Lia, gifted at languages. He seemed to enjoy their exotic feel on his tongue as much as exotic fabrics on his back. But Sven had learned Vendan the hard way—a few years into his service, he was imprisoned, along with two Vendans, in a Lesser Kingdom. They were captured for slave service, as he called it, working for two years in their mines until he and the Vendans finally hatched an escape.

"I gathered that you're somewhat conversant now too?"

"I get by," I said. "I don't speak it well, but I can understand a fair amount. As you saw, the Komizar and some of the Council speak Morrighese, and Lia helped me with some phrases."

Jeb stepped forward, cracking his knuckles. "I talked to her," he said.

He had our undivided attention now, including Orrin, who looked back at us over his shoulder. Jeb said he saw her just before the evening meal in Sanctum Hall. He'd managed to make a delivery to her room. "She knows we're here now."

"All four of you?" I said. "She wasn't impressed by our numbers when I told her."

"Can you blame her? I'm not impressed either," Jeb answered.

Orrin snorted. "It only takes one person to skewer—"

"The Assassin's mine," I reminded him. "Don't forget that."

"She gave me useful information," Jeb continued, "especially about paths in the Sanctum. The place is crawling with them, but some are dead ends. I've already been stuck in a few and almost fell down one. She also gave me her winnings from a card game for supplies."

"That's what she called it? Winnings?" I said. "More like what she swindled. I lost five pounds of sweat that night."

Sven rolled his eyes. "So she's good at cards and tearing off faces."

"Certain faces." I looked back at Jeb. "Did she say anything else?"

He hesitated for a moment, rubbing the back of his neck. "She said your mother was dead."

The words hit me again. My mother was dead. I told them what the Komizar had said, and his claim that the funeral pyre had been witnessed by Vendan riders. Sven balked, saying that was impossible, that the queen was hearty and wouldn't succumb so easily or quickly, but the truth was we had all been away for so long we had no idea what was happening at home, and a new wave of guilt hit me. They all refuted the story, saying it was only a Vendan lie to torment me, and I let them hold on to that thought—maybe I wanted to hold on to it too—but I knew the Komizar had no reason to lie. He didn't know she was my mother, only my queen, and telling me had helped strengthen my claim.

"One other thing," Jeb said, then shook his head as if thinking better of it.

"Go ahead. Say it," I said.

"I like her, that's all. And I made promises to her that we'd all get out. We damn well better keep them."

I nodded. I couldn't consider any other option.

Orrin blew out a puff, ruffling his straggled hair. "She scares me," he said, "but I like her too, and hang me, she's—"

"Don't say it, Orrin," I warned.

He sighed. "I know, I know. She's my future queen." He went back to the door to watch for the cook.

We caught Jeb up on other details, including the loss of Dalbreck soldiers, the match between me and the Assassin, and how Sven's face was almost fed to the hogs.

"It was a sealed kettle ready to explode in there," Sven said. "But it's safer that she genuinely hates us for now—safer for her and us—especially since Orrin and I are so visible. Let's keep it that way for a while." Sven ran his hand along his scarred cheek. "She's only seventeen?"

I nodded.

"She carries a lot on her shoulders for someone so young."

"Does she have any other choice?"

Sven shrugged. "Maybe not, but she came close to revealing her hand tonight. I had to shove her back in her chair."

"You shoved her?" I said.

"Gently," he explained. "She started across the room to come between you and that Assassin."

I leaned forward, raking my fingers through my hair. She

acted impulsively because I did. The strain was making us both careless.

"Here she comes," Orrin whispered and sat back on the bench next to me.

The door swung open, and the cook eyed the roomful. She mumbled a curse and plopped down a pair of tongs and a steaming bucket at the end of the bench. She pulled a stack of rags from under her arm and dropped them next to the tongs. "Five layers. Leave it on overnight. Bring back the cloths when you're done. Clean."

She pushed back through the door, her charming instructions complete, and we were left with the suffocating fumes of the yellow-green mixture filling the room. Jeb noted that the stench of horse manure was preferable to the poison the cook had brewed. How it would help a wound, I wasn't sure, but Sven seemed confident. He took a hearty whiff of the putrid substance.

"I'd rather have a dose of your red-eye," I said.

"So would I," he said longingly, "but the red-eye's long gone." He took great pleasure dipping the pieces of cloth into the hot liquid and placing them over my gash and Orrin's festering leg wounds.

"For dragging her all the way across the Cam Lanteux, that Assassin seemed none too fond of her tonight," Sven observed.

"He's more than fond of her. Trust me," I said. "He's just incensed that she agreed to marry the Komizar while he was away. I know she had no choice. The Komizar's holding something over her—I just don't know what it is."

"I know," Jeb said. "She told me."

I looked at him, dread flooding through me, waiting.

"You," he said. "The Komizar said if she didn't convince everyone that she had embraced the marriage, you'd start losing fingers. Or more. She's marrying him to save you."

I leaned back against the wall and closed my eyes.

For you. Only for you.

I should have known when she added those words to the prayer. They had haunted me ever since she said them.

"Don't worry, boy, we'll have her out of here before the wedding."

"The wedding's in three days," I said.

"We'll be sailing down the river by then."

Sailing.

On barrels.

CHAPTER FIFTY

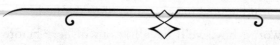

THE BIG DAY THE KOMIZAR PROMISED ME BEGAN WITH A fitting for a wedding dress. I stood on a block of wood in a long, barren gallery not far from his quarters. A fire roared in the fireplace at the end of the room, chasing some of the chill away. Every day had grown colder, and a puddle of water on my window ledge from last night's rain had turned to ice.

I watched the flames lick the air, hypnotized. I had almost told Kaden last night. I came close, but when he said it was a game I wouldn't win, I feared he was right. All it took was one misstep.

A confession was on the tip of my tongue but then the smug exchange between Kaden and the Komizar at the end of the evening had flashed through my mind. *There's a strong bond between them. They have a long history together.*

I could almost admire the Komizar for his brilliance.

Who better to have as his Assassin than Kaden, so intensely loyal, so loyal he would never challenge the Komizar? So loyal he would set aside a knife even in a fit of rage. Kaden was forever in his debt, an Assassin who couldn't forget the betrayal of his own father and who would never repeat his treachery even if it cost him his own life.

"Turn," Effiera instructed. "There, that's enough."

The army of dressmakers were a welcome distraction. Though a special dress was not customary in Vendan weddings, the Komizar had ordered one, and he wished to supervise the fitting as it progressed. He would issue his approval before final work was begun. It was to be a dress of many hands to honor the Meurasi clan, but he had specified the color was to be red, which Effiera and the other dressmakers had clucked about all morning, trying to find just the right mix of fabrics, and seeming satisfied with none. They pieced together scraps of velvets, brocades, and dyed buckskin.

They pushed and prodded with their pieces, and a dress finally took form on me as they pinned and unpinned, a labored nervousness to their work. They were used to crafting dresses from their tents in the *jehendra* and not under the supervision of the Komizar.

Every time he said "Hmm" and shook his head, one of the dressmakers would drop her pins. But his comments weren't harsh or angry—he actually seemed preoccupied with something else. It was a side to him I hadn't seen. We were all grateful when Ulrix called him away to attend to a matter, but he promised to return soon. They worked quickly while he was gone to finish the long snug sleeves—this time I at least had two—but my shoulder was still carefully left bare to show off the kavah.

"What do you know of the claw and vine?" I asked.

The women all fell silent. "Only what our mothers told us," Effiera finally said quietly. "We were told to watch for it, that it was the promise of a new day for Venda—the claw, quick and fierce; the vine, slow and steady; both equally strong."

"What about the Song of Venda?"

"Which one?" Ursula asked.

They said there were hundreds of songs of Venda, just as Kaden had told me. The written songs were all long destroyed, but that didn't keep her words from living on in memory and story, though there were few now who remembered them. At least they knew of the claw and vine, and the clans I'd met on the fens and uplands knew of the name Jezelia too. An anticipation ran through them. Pieces of Venda's songs were alive, in the air, and rooted in some deep part of their understanding. They knew.

All the written songs destroyed. Except for the one I possessed. And someone had tried to destroy that one too.

The door opened, and they all startled, expecting to see the Komizar, but it was Calantha.

"The Komizar's been delayed. It may be a while. He wishes the dressmakers to wait in the next chamber until he's ready for them again." The women wasted no time in following the instructions and scurried off with armfuls of fabric into the next room.

"What about me?" I asked. "Am I supposed to wait, stuck in a dress full of pins until he decides to come back?"

"Yes."

I grumbled a seething breath.

Calantha smiled. "So much hostility. Isn't an uncomfortable wait worth it for your beloved?"

I looked at her, tired of her sarcasm, and formed a biting reply, but it suddenly stalled on my lips as I stared at her. She was always trying to hate me. My own words circled back to me. *I think you're dabbling with a bit of power.* A power she was afraid to exert. She was like a wildcat circling a hole, trying to find a way to get the bait without falling into the trap.

She turned to go abruptly, as if she knew I had glimpsed her secret.

"Wait," I said, jumping down from the block. I grabbed her wrist, and she stared at my hand as if my touch burned her. I realized that, other than a stiff poke to my back, I had never seen her touch anyone.

"Why did you help the Komizar kill your own father?" I asked.

As pale as Calantha already was, she blanched. "That's not for you to ask."

"I want to understand, and I know you want to tell me."

She yanked her wrist loose. "It's an ugly story, Princess. Too ugly for your delicate ears."

"Is it because you love him?"

"The Komizar?" A small laugh escaped her lips. She shook

her head, and I could almost see something large and numbing jar loose inside her.

"Please," I said. "I know you've both helped and hindered me. You're battling something. I won't betray you, Calantha. I promise."

The air was taut. I held my breath, afraid the slightest move would push her away from me again.

"Yes, I love him," she admitted, "but not in the way you're thinking." She walked across the room and stared out the window for a long time, then finally turned and told me. Her voice was detached, vacant, as if she spoke of someone else. She was the child of Carmedes, a member of the Rahtan. Her mother had been a cook in the Sanctum who died when she was small. When she was twelve, Carmedes seized power and became the 698th Komizar of Venda. He was a suspicious man with a heavy hand and short temper, but she managed to mostly avoid him. "I was fifteen when I fell in love with a boy from the Meurasi clan. He told me clan stories of other times and other places that made me forget my own miserable life. We were careful to keep our relationship a secret and managed that feat for almost a year." Her chest rose in several slow breaths before she went on. "But one day, my father caught us in the servants' stable together. He had no reason to be angered. He cared little about me, but he flew into a rage."

She sat on one of the dressmaking stools and told me that back then our current Komizar was the Assassin. He was a young man of eighteen, and he had found them both bleeding into the straw. The boy was dead, and she was half dead. The Assassin scooped her up and called for a healer. "The bruises faded, the bones mended, the torn patches of hair grew back, but some things were gone for good. The boy and—"

"Your eye."

"My father came to see me once during the weeks that I lay bedridden. He looked down at me and said if I ever did anything like that again, he would take out my other eye and my teeth as well. He wanted no more bastards running through the Sanctum. When I could walk again, I went to the Assassin, opened his palm, placed the key to my father's private meeting chamber in it, and pledged my loyalty. Forever. The next morning my father was dead."

She stood, pulling back her shoulders, looking drained.

"So if you see me both prod and thwart, Princess, it's because some days I see the man the Komizar has become, and some days I remember the man he was."

She turned and walked toward the door, but I called after her just as she opened it.

"Forever is a long time," I said. "When will you remember who you are, Calantha?"

She paused briefly without responding, then closed the door behind her.

I HAD BEEN WAITING SO LONG I HARDLY NOTICED THE door easing open. It was the Komizar. His gaze landed on the dress first, then rose to my face. He closed the door and took another long look.

"It's about time," I said.

He ignored my remark, taking his time as he approached. His eyes skimmed over me, touching me in ways that made my cheeks grow hot.

"I think I chose well," he said. "The red suits you."

I tried my best to make light of it. "Why, Komizar, are you actually trying to be kind?"

"I can be kind, Lia, if you'll let me be." He took a step closer, his eyes molten.

"Shall I call the dressmakers back in?" I asked.

"Not yet," he said, strolling closer.

"It's not easy to move in a dress held together with pins."

"I don't want you to move." He stopped in front of me and ran a gentle finger down my sleeve. His chest rose in a deep controlled breath. "You've come a long way since the burlap dress you wore on your arrival."

"That wasn't a dress. It was a sack."

He smiled. "So it was." He reached up and pulled a pin from the dress. The fabric at the shoulder fell loose. "Is that better?"

I bristled. "Save your charming seductions for our wedding night."

"I was being charming? Shall I take out another pin?"

I took a step back, which I was loath to do, for fear it would encourage him. I tried to change the subject and noticed he had changed into riding clothes. "Isn't there something you should be doing right now? Somewhere you need to be?"

"No."

He stepped forward, reaching for another pin, but I hit his hand away. "Are you trying to seduce me or force yourself on me? Since we've agreed to be honest with each other, I'd like to know up front so I can decide how to proceed."

He grabbed my arms, and I winced at the prick of pins in my flesh. He pulled me close and pressed his lips to my ear. "Why do you shower the Assassin with your affections and not your betrothed?"

"Because Kaden has not demanded my affections. He has earned them."

"Have I not been kind to you, Jezelia?"

"You were kind once," I whispered against his cheek. "I know you were. And you had a name. *Reginaus.*"

He pulled away as if I'd thrown cold water on him.

"A real name," I continued, feeling a rare advantage. "A name given to you by your mother."

He stepped toward the hearth, his ardor vanished. "I have no mother," he snapped.

It was evident I had opened one of the few veins of warm blood in his body.

"It would be easy enough for me to believe that was true," I said. "It seems more likely that you were spawned by a demon and an available knothole. Except that I spoke to the woman who held you as your mother grunted you onto this earth. She said your mother named you with her last breath."

"There's nothing special about that, Princess. I'm not the first Vendan whose mother died in childbirth."

"But it's a *name*. Something she gave to you. Why do you refuse to be called by the last word that left your mother's lips?"

"Because it was a name that meant nothing!" he lashed out.

"It gave me nothing! I was only another filthy brat on the streets. I was nothing until I became the Assassin. That name meant something. There was only one name better. Komizar. Why settle for Reginaus, as common as dirt and just as useful, when there's a name that only one can bear?"

"Is that why you killed the last Komizar? Only for a name? Or to avenge Calantha's cruel beating?"

His fury waned, and he peered at me cautiously. "She told you?"

"Yes."

He shook his head. "That's not like Calantha. She never speaks of that day." He threw another log onto the fire and stared into the flames. "I was only eighteen. Too young to become the next Komizar. I hadn't built enough alliances yet. But I hungered for it. Every day. I imagined. *Komizar.*" He turned and sat down on the raised hearth. "And then Calantha happened. Most of the Council was quite fond of her. She was a pretty little flower then, but they didn't dare go near her for fear of the Komizar. She was ruined by the beating, scarred inside and out, but many of the Council favored me after that for saving her life. When Calantha pledged her loyalty to me, many of the Council did too. The ones who didn't I eliminated. I had learned then that alliances are not just offered, they have to be carefully devised." He stood and walked closer to me. "To answer your question, one purpose simply served another. Avenging her beating also brought me a name that I desired."

He gave the dress a cold perusal. "Tell the dressmakers that one will do," he said, offering his final approval. "And, Princess, just so you know, if you bring up the name Reginaus again, I'll have to pay a visit to the midwife with the loose tongue. Do you understand?"

I dipped my head in a single nod. "I know of no one by that name."

He smiled and left.

And I spoke the truth. It was clear that the boy named Reginaus was long dead.

CHAPTER FIFTY-ONE

"I'll be moving you to a room near my quarters tomorrow. Servants will come to gather your things. This will make it more convenient once the wedding is behind us."

Convenient. My skin prickled. I knew what convenient meant.

It was strange that I should find comfort in Kaden's quarters, but I did. I knew Kaden was at least trustworthy in certain things—even when he was stinking drunk. His quarters also had a secret passage. I doubted my new chamber would.

We left our horses with the guards on the outer edge of a thicket of trees, and the Komizar guided me through the woods. The trees were thin-trunked and close together, but I could see where a path had been worn through them. This was an oft-visited destination. He called it his own personal shortcut. After only a few minutes of walking, the line of trees stopped and we emerged on a bluff that overlooked a vast valley. I stared, not quite sure of what I was seeing.

"It's magnificent, isn't it?"

I looked at him, his face glowing. This was where his passion lay. His gaze floated over the valley. It was a city, but nothing like the one we had just left.

It was a city of soldiers. Thousands. He didn't notice that I hadn't answered him or even spoken, but he began systematically pointing out the regions of his city in listlike fashion.

There were the breeding grounds.

The smelteries.

The forges.

The armories.

The barracks.

The fletcher shops.

The cooperages.

The granaries.

The testing fields.

He went on and on.

Everything was plural.

The city stretched to the horizon.

I didn't need to ask what it was for. Armies served only two purposes—to defend or attack. They weren't here to defend anything. Nobody wanted into Venda. I tried to see just what was going on at the testing grounds, but it was too far away. I squinted and sighed. "All I see from here is a sprawling city. Can we get a closer look?"

He happily led me down a twisting trail to the valley floor. I heard the riotous ping of iron being hammered on anvils. Many anvils. The hum of the city surrounded me, a hum of single-mindedness and purpose. He walked me among the soldiers, and I saw their faces, boy and girl alike, many as young as Eben.

He walked briskly so I couldn't stop to talk to any of them, but he made sure they knew who and what I was—a sign that the gods favored Venda. Their young faces turned in curiosity as we passed.

"There are so many," I said stupidly, more to myself than the Komizar.

The immensity of it was staggering.

The patrols were being slaughtered. They were hiding something. Something important.

This. An army twice as large as any one kingdom's.

He brought me to a level knoll that looked out over another stretch of valley. Trenches and ramparts surrounded it. I watched soldiers wheel large devices to the middle of the field, but the contraptions gave no hint of their purpose until they began using them. Arrows flew at dizzying rates, a blur in the air as a soldier turned a crank. A wall of arrows were all being shot by one man. It was like nothing I had ever seen.

After that came another testing field. And another. These weapons had a sophistication that didn't match the spare, crude life of the Vendans.

He pulled me along in his zeal, and it was the last field that froze me with terror. "What are they?" I asked. I stared at golden striped horses twice the girth of other horses and at least twenty hands high, their black eyes wild and their nostrils breathing fierce steam into the cool air.

"Brezalots," he answered. "They have nasty dispositions and aren't good for riding, but they run straight and true when prodded. Their hide is thick. Nothing will stop them. Almost nothing."

He hailed a soldier for a demonstration. The soldier strapped a small pack to the horse's back, and then struck his hindquarters with a sharp prod. Blood spurted from his rump, but the horse ran straight and true, just as the Komizar said he would, and even though soldiers along the side of the field pelted him with arrows, they didn't penetrate his thick hide, and he didn't stop. He headed straight across the field, directly between hillocks of hay, and then there was a deafening noise and a blinding fireball. Burning hay rained down. Splinters of wood along with pieces of the horse thudded to the ground. It was like a pot of oil had exploded in a fire but with a thousand times more power. I blinked, too shocked to move.

"They're unstoppable. One horse can take down a whole squad of men. It's amazing what the right combination of ingredients can do. We call them our Death Steeds."

Ice crept down my spine. "How did you learn the right combination of ingredients?" I asked.

"It was right beneath our noses all along."

He didn't need to say more. *The purveyors of knowledge.* That was why they skulked in the caverns and catacombs. They were unlocking the secrets of the Ancients and giving the Komizar the recipe for Morrighan's destruction. What had he promised them in return for their services? Their own piece of Morrighan? Whatever the prize, great or small, it could never be worth the lives that would be lost.

WE MOVED ON TO MORE FIELDS, BUT NOW I HARDLY SAW them, trying to imagine how any army could stand up to what I'd already seen. Finally we stood at the base of five towering granaries with walls of polished steel that were blinding in the sun. These were enormous stores of food on the edge of a city in want. "Why?" I asked.

"Great armies march on their stomachs. Men and horses must be fed. There's almost enough here to march a hundred thousand soldiers."

"March where?" I asked, hoping that by some grace of the gods, I could be wrong.

"Where do you think, Princess?" he asked. "Soon Vendans will no longer be at the mercy of Morrighan."

"Half of these soldiers are children."

"Young, but not children. Only the Morrighese have the luxury of pampering fresh-cheeked babies. Here they're muscle and sweat like everyone else, doing their part to help feed a future for us all."

"But the *loss*. You'll still lose people," I said. "Especially the young ones."

"Probably half of them. But the one thing Venda doesn't lack is people. When they die, they'll be glad for the cause, and there are always more to replace them."

I stood there, stunned, taking in the enormity of his plans. I had guessed they were planning something. An attack on an outpost. *Something.* But not this.

I searched for something to say, but I knew my plea was futile before it ever left my tongue. Still, the words spilled out, weak and already vanquished. "I might be able to plead with my father and the other kingdoms. I've seen how Venda struggles. I could convince them. There's fertile land in the Cam Lanteux. I know I could find a way to make them let you settle it. There's good land to farm. Enough for all of you to—"

"You, plead with anyone? You're a hated enemy of two kingdoms now, and even if you could convince them, I have far greater aspirations than to be dragged by a yoke and harness. What is a Komizar without a kingdom to rule? Or many kingdoms? No, you'll plead for nothing."

I grabbed his arms, forcing him to look at me. "It doesn't have to be this way between the kingdoms."

A faint smile lit his face. "Yes, my princess, it does. It is how it's always been and always will be, only now it will be us wielding power over them."

He pulled away from my grip, and his gaze returned to his city, his chest puffing, his stature growing before my eyes. "It's my turn now to sit on a golden throne in Morrighan and dine on sweet grapes in winter. And if any royals survive our conquest, it will give me great pleasure to lock them up on this side of hell to fight over roaches and rats to fill their bellies."

I stared at the consuming power glistening in his eyes. It pumped through his veins instead of blood, and beat in his chest instead of a heart. My plea for compromise was babble to his ears, a language long erased from his memory.

"Well?" he asked.

A terrible greatness rolled across the land.

A new terrible greatness.

I said the only thing I could say. What I knew he wanted to hear. "You've thought of everything, *sher* Komizar. I'm impressed."

And in a dark and frightening way, I was.

CHAPTER FIFTY-TWO

RAFE

I HOVERED NEAR THE FIREPIT IN HAWK'S PAVILION pretending to warm my hands. Ulrix had given me changes of clothing, but they hadn't included any gloves. It was just as well. It gave me an excuse to stand here with Sven, who had also "forgotten" to wear his gloves to the pavilion. We watched the keeper training the hawks. Orrin stood opposite us as a lookout for anyone who might approach.

"He has eight barrels in a cave down by the river," Sven whispered, even though the nearest guards stood far behind us on the other side of the court. "He says he only needs four more."

"How is he getting them?"

"You don't want to know. Let's just say Vendan justice would leave him fingerless."

"His thievery better be flawless, because he's going to need every finger to secure that raft."

"He did acquire the rope honestly, thanks to the princess and the money she gave him. The kind of rope he needed can only be had in the *jehendra*, which would be far more difficult to lift things from, so thank the gods she's good at cards."

I thought about the card game and the blood I had sweat watching her play. *Yes, thank the gods and her brothers, she is good.*

"Jeb used patties to cover the rope up in the bottom of his cart and sneak it out to Tavish." Sven held his hands closer to the flames and asked me about the Sanctum routines.

I told him more of what I had learned in these past weeks—what times the guards changed at the entrances, how many could be found in hallways at any given moment, when Lia was most likely not to be missed, the governors who were more amiable than others, those who tipped their mugs heavily, the Rahtan and *chievdars* he didn't dare turn his back on, and where I had hidden weapons—three swords, four daggers, and a poleaxe.

"You pilfered weapons right under their noses? *A poleaxe?*"

"It just takes patience."

"You? Patience?" Sven grunted.

I couldn't blame him for his cynicism. I was the one who rode off with only a half-assed plan to guide us. I thought about the last several days and all the times I'd had to restrain my natural impulses, the agonizing waiting when all I wanted to do was act, weighing the satisfaction of a victorious moment against a lifetime with Lia, calculating every move and word to make sure it gave her and us the best possible chance. If there was a torture in hell crafted specifically for me, this was it.

"Yes, *patience*," I said. It was a scar as painfully won as any in battle. I told him that Calantha and Ulrix were my primary guards and that Calantha missed nothing, so I had little opportunity around her, but after laying me flat several times and finding that I offered only a weak fight, Ulrix had grown satisfied that the emissary was not one to waste much worry over. Opportunities arose, and slowly I slipped one mislaid weapon after another into dark forgotten corners, to be retrieved and moved to another dark corner until I had them where I was sure no one would find them.

"No one missed them? Not even the poleaxe?"

"There are always a few swords set aside during late nights and card games in the Sanctum. When losers get nervous, they drink, and when they drink, they forget things. In the morning, servants return mislaid weapons to the armory. The poleaxe was luck. I saw it propped up against the sow pen for the better part of a day. When no one seemed to miss it, I tossed it behind the woodpile."

Sven nodded with approval as if I were still his charge in training. "What about last night? Have you gotten any whiff of suspicions about the sword fight?"

"I fumbled. I lost. My shoulder drew first blood. By now that's all they remember. Any skill with the sword is lost in the shadow of Kaden's victory."

We saw Orrin on the other side of the fire signaling us that someone was approaching, and we stopped talking.

"Morning, Governor Obraun. Feeding mice to the falcons?"

We turned. It was Griz. He spoke in Morrighese, which he had claimed he didn't know. I looked at Sven, but he wasn't responding. Instead the old curd had paled.

Orrin and I both knew something was wrong. Orrin began to draw his sword, but I waved him back. Griz wore two short swords, and his hands gripped the hilts of both. He stood too close to Sven for us to make a move. Griz grinned, soaking in Sven's reaction. "After twenty-five years and that trophy crossing your face, I didn't recognize you right off. It was your voice that gave you away."

"Falgriz," Sven said at last, as if he were looking at a ghost. "Looks like you've gained an ugly trophy up top too. And a sizable gut down below."

"Flattery won't get you out of this."

"It did the last time."

A smile creased the giant's eyes in spite of the scowl that crossed his scarred brow.

"He's the one who lied to the Komizar for me," I said.

Griz whipped his gaze at me. "I didn't lie for you, twinkle toes. Let's get that straight right now. I lied for *her*."

"You're a spy for her kingdom?" I asked.

His lips curled back in disgust. "I'm a spy for you, you blasted fool."

Sven's eyebrows shot up. This was obviously a new development for him too.

Griz jerked his head toward Sven. "All those years stuck with this lout gave me a little knowledge about courts, and a lot of knowledge about languages. I'm no traitor to my own kind, if that's what you're thinking, but I meet with your scouts. I carry useless information from one enemy kingdom to another. If royals want to throw their money away for the tracking of troops, I'm happy to oblige. It keeps my kinfolk from starving."

I looked at Sven. "This is who you were stuck with in the mines?"

"For two very long years. Griz saved my life," he answered.

"Get it right," Griz snarled. "You saved my neck, and we both know it."

Orrin and I exchanged a glance. Neither one seemed pleased about his spared life or in agreement over who saved whom.

Sven rubbed his stubble, studying Griz. "So, Falgriz. Do we have a problem?"

"You're still a dense bastard," Griz answered. "Yes, we have a problem. I don't want her leaving, and I assume that's what you're here for."

Sven sighed. "Well, you're partially right." He nodded toward me. "I'm here to spring this knucklehead, and that's all. You can keep the girl."

"What?" I said.

"Sorry, boy. King's orders. We've got an escort waiting just on the other side of the river."

I lunged at Sven, grabbing him by his vest. "You lying, filthy—"

Griz yanked me off Sven and threw me to the ground. "Don't be messing with our new governor, *Emissary*."

Sanctum guards began running over after seeing me jump Sven.

"Not much of a guard, are you?" Griz said to Orrin, who hadn't moved to protect Sven. "At least *look* like you know what you're doing, or you won't last long around here." Orrin drew his sword and held it menacingly above me. Griz cast another warning scowl at me. "Just so we all understand each other. I don't care if you all drown in the river or beat each other senseless, but the girl stays here." And then just to Sven, "The stitchery's an improvement."

"As is the needlework on your skull."

Sven and I eyed each other. We had a problem. Griz stomped off, telling the approaching guards to go back to their posts, the matter was settled, but as I watched him walk away, I noticed the Assassin standing in the shadow of the colonnade. He stood there with no apparent destination. Just watching us. And even after Griz had long passed, he continued to look in our direction.

CHAPTER FIFTY-THREE

IT HAPPENED WHEN I TOOK MY BOOTS OFF. THE HEAVY clunk of the heels hitting the floor. *The shoes.* The whisper. The memory. The knowing chill that had settled across my shoulders the first time I heard their footsteps. *Reverence and restraint.*

It hit me suddenly and violently, and I thought I was going to be sick.

I leaned over the chamber pot, a damp sweat springing to my brow.

They had changed everything but their shoes.

I swallowed the salty sick taste on my tongue and fanned my anger instead. It flamed to a rage and propelled me forward. I bypassed the guards and used the hidden passage. Where I was going, I could not have an escort.

THIS TIME WHEN I STRODE THROUGH THE CATACOMBS AND then down into the cavern where piles of books waited to be burned, I gave no care to the loudness of my footsteps. When I got there, no one was in the outer room sorting books, but the far room was dimly lit. I saw at least one robed figure within, hunched over a table.

The inner room was almost as large as the first, with several piles of its own waiting to be hauled away and burned. There were eight robed figures within. I stood at the entrance watching them, but they were so consumed with their tasks they didn't notice me. Their hoods were drawn, as was their practice, supposedly a symbol of humility and devotion, but I knew the purpose was as much to block out others so they could remain focused on their difficult work. Their deathly work.

The priest I had met with back in Terravin had sensed something was amiss, even if he hadn't known exactly what it was. *I wouldn't speak to the other priests of this matter. They might not all agree where loyalties lie.* I realized now that he had tried to warn me, but if the Komizar had coaxed these men here with promises of riches, I might be able to sway their greedy hearts with greater treasures.

I looked down at their shoes, almost hidden by their brown robes. They seemed out of place here instead of tucked behind polished desks.

I had grabbed a large volume from one of the piles of discards as I walked in, and now I threw it to the ground. The loud smack echoed through the room, and both the seated and standing scholars turned to see me. They showed no alarm, not even surprise, but the seated scholars left their chairs to stand with the others.

I stopped in front of them, their faces still hidden in the shadows of their hoods. "I would expect at least a cursory bow from subjects of Morrighan when their princess addresses them."

The tallest one in the middle spoke for them all. "I was wondering how long it would take you to find us down here. How well I remember your wanderings in Civica." His voice was vaguely familiar.

"Show your traitorous faces," I ordered. "As your lone sovereign in this wretched kingdom, I command it."

The tall one stepped forward. "You haven't changed a bit, have you?"

"But you most certainly have. Your new attire is decidedly plainer."

He sighed. "Yes, I do miss our embroidered silk robes, but we had to leave those behind. These are much more practical here."

He pushed back his hood, and my stomach turned with nausea. He was my tenth-year tutor, Argyris. One by one, the others pushed back their hoods too. These weren't just any scholars from remote regions. These were the elite inner circle, trained by the Royal Scholar himself. The Royal Scholar's second assistant, the lead illuminator, my fifth- and eighth-year tutors, the library archivist, two of my brothers' tutors, all scholars who had left their positions, presumably for other work in Sacristas throughout Morrighan. Now I knew where they had really gone, and maybe worse, I had known early on that they weren't trust-worthy. Back in Civica, I had felt agitation in their presence. These were the scholars I had always hated, the ones who filled me with dread, the ones who wrestled the Holy Text into our heads with all the grace of a bull, and with none of the tenderness or sincerity I heard in Pauline's voice as she sang remembrances. These before me shredded the text into torn pieces of history.

"What did the Komizar promise to make it worth turning your back on your countrymen?"

Argyris smiled with the same arrogance I remembered from the days when he looked over my shoulder, berating me on the spacing of my script. "We're not exactly traitors, Arabella. We're simply on loan to the Komizar by order of the Kingdom of Morrighan."

"Liar," I sneered. "My father would never send this kingdom anything, much less court scholars, to—" I looked at the piles of books around us. "What new menace are you working on now?"

"We're merely scholars, Princess, doing what we do," Argyris answered. He and the other scholars exchanged smug grins. "What others do with our findings is not our business. We simply uncover the worlds these books hold."

"Not all the worlds. You burn pile after pile in the Sanctum ovens."

He shrugged. "Some texts are not as useful as others. We can't translate them all."

The way he couched his words and distanced the scholars from their treachery made me ache to rip his tongue out, but I restrained myself. I still needed answers. "It wasn't my father who loaned you to Venda. Who did?" I demanded. They only looked at me as if I were still their impetuous charge and smirked.

I pushed past them, shoving them out of the way, ignoring their indignant huffs, and went to the table where they'd been working. I shuffled through books and papers, trying to find some evidence of who had sent them. I opened one of the ledgers, and a roughly garbed arm reached past me and snapped the tablet shut.

"I think not, Your Highness," he said, his breath hot on my ear.

He pressed so close, I could barely spin to see who it was. He pinned me against the table and smiled, waiting for recognition to wash over my face.

It did.

I couldn't breathe.

He reached up and touched my neck, rubbing the small white mark where the bounty hunter had cut me. "Only a nick?" He frowned. "I knew I should have sent someone else. Your sensitive royal nose probably smelled him coming a mile away."

It was the driver from the stable yard. And now I was certain, the tavern guest Pauline had mentioned to me. *You didn't see him? He walked in right after the other two. A thin, scruffy fellow. He shot plenty of sideways looks your way.*

And also the scruffy young man I had seen one night with the Chancellor.

"Garvin, at your service," he said, with a mock-genteel nod. "It's lovely to watch the wheels spin in your head."

There was nothing about him that would stand out. Medium build, ashy uncombed hair. He could blend in with any crowd.

It wasn't his appearance that had left an impression on me. It was the startled expression of the Chancellor when I stumbled upon him and two scholars in a dark nook of the eastern portico. Guilt had flooded their faces, but I hadn't registered it then. It was the middle of the night, and I had just snuck in from a card game and was so concerned about my own detection that I hadn't questioned their odd behavior.

I glared at him. "It must have been such a disappointment for the Chancellor to learn I wasn't dead."

He smiled. "I haven't seen him in months. As far as I know, he thinks you are dead. Our hunter has never failed us before, and the Chancellor had gotten word that the Assassin was on your trail too. There was little doubt that one of them would finish you. Wait until he finds out the truth." He chuckled. "But the spin of your greater betrayal to Morrighan in marrying the Komizar may serve his purposes even better. Well done, Your Highness."

His purposes? I thought of all the jeweled baubles that graced the Chancellor's knuckles. *Gifts*, he had called them. What else was he getting in return for delivering wagons of wine and the services of scholars to the Komizar? A few sparkling ornaments for his fingers could hardly be worth the cost of treason. Was it a ploy for more power? What else had the Komizar promised him?

"I would tell the Chancellor not to spend his riches before they're in his greedy palm. I'll remind you, I am not dead yet."

Garvin laughed, and his face loomed closer to mine. "Here?" he whispered. "Yes, here you're as good as dead. You'll never be leaving again—at least not alive."

I tried to push past him, but he tightened his grip on the table.

He was not a large man, but he was wiry and tough. I heard the snickers of the scholars, but I could see only the stubble on Garvin's chin and feel his thighs pressing close to mine.

"I'll also remind you, though I may be a prisoner of the Komizar, I'm his betrothed as well, and unless you'd like to see your thin, sour hide served on a platter, I would suggest you move your arms now."

His smile disappeared, and he stepped aside. "Be on your way, and I'd advise you not to come this way again. These catacombs have many forgotten and dangerous passages. One could easily get lost forever."

I brushed past him and the scholars, tasting the bitterness of their betrayal, but when I was a few yards away, I stopped and slowly scrutinized them.

"What are you doing?" Argyris asked.

"Memorizing each of your faces and how you look in this moment—and imagining what you'll look like a year from now as you face death. Because as you all well know, I do have the gift, and I've seen every one of you dead."

I turned and left, and heard not a shuffle nor a whisper in my wake.

It was the second time in less than an hour I had perpetrated a sham.

Maybe.

Because in a brief cold second, I saw every one of them hanging from a rope.

CHAPTER FIFTY-FOUR

I SAT ON A WOODEN BENCH NEAR THE SERVANTS' STABLES, staring at a feather stirring on the ground, my feet and fingers numb, my thoughts jumping from rage to disbelief. Secrets at home, secrets in the caverns. Deceit knew no boundaries.

Secrets. That was what I saw in Argyris's startled eyes and felt pressing on my chest when I passed through the cavern. A dangerous secret.

Movement in the distance caught my eye. He walked toward me.

The ultimate betrayer.

He stopped several feet away, noting that something was off. "Where are your escorts?"

I didn't answer.

"I've looked everywhere for you," he said. "What are you doing out here? It's freezing."

So it was.

"Can we talk?" he asked.

I studied Kaden, his eyes warm and searching. Kaden wanting a truce. Make everything better, like we were walking in a meadow after one of his drunken tirades. Kaden bringing me a basket of crabapple dumplings. Kaden holding me as I watched my brother die, saying how sorry he was. Kaden with his steady eyes. His deceptive calm. *His devastating betrayal.*

He stared at my jiggling knee.

It wasn't I who had betrayed him.

"Lia?" he said as if testing the waters. *Lia, is it safe to approach you?*

"You knew," I said. My knee bounced. My hands trembled. "All along you knew."

He took a cautious step forward. "What are you—"

I flew at him, slapping at him, beating at him as he retreated, step after step, trying to dodge my blows. "Don't pretend you didn't know! All along you played games, telling me you were trying to save my life while you planned to exterminate every last person I love! Walther and Greta weren't enough? Now it's my other brothers? Berdi? Pauline? Gwyneth?" I stopped advancing on him and glared. "You want to kill every last person in Morrighan!"

His shoulders pulled back. "You saw the army."

I returned his passionless stare. "I saw the army."

He was quiet for only a moment and then he lashed out, his hand sweeping the air as if that could dismiss my accusation. "What of it? Morrighan and Dalbreck have their armies too. Ours isn't going to kill everyone. Only those who suppress us."

I looked at him in disbelief. Did he really believe that?

"And I'm sure that includes your father, a highborn lord. He's probably first on your list."

He didn't answer, but his jaw clenched.

"So that's what it's been about all along. Vengeance. You're so consumed with hatred for your father that you want to kill every last breathing person in Morrighan."

"We're marching on Morrighan, Lia. We're removing those in power, and that includes my father, and yes, he may die."

"May?"

"I don't know what will happen. I don't know what kind of fight we'll face. With our numbers, they would be wise to lay down their arms, but if not, yes, he and many others will die."

"By your hand."

"You're a fine one to talk about vengeance. Ever since Walther's and Greta's deaths, you've chased after revenge, telling me no matter what you did, it would never be enough. Your eyes glow with vengeance every time they fall on Malich."

"But I don't plan on killing a whole kingdom to get it."

"It's not going to happen that way. The Komizar and I have agreed that—"

"You have an agreement with the Komizar?" I laughed. "How wonderful for you. Yes, we all have our agreements with him. The Chancellor, the emissary, me. He seems very good at striking agreements. You once ridiculed me for not knowing my own borders. I was shamed by that truth, but my ignorance pales in comparison with yours. I'm sure Berdi, Gwyneth, and Pauline would be so relieved to know that *you* have an agreement."

I spun and walked away.

"Lia," he called after me, "I promise you, I won't let any harm come to Berdi, Pauline, and Gwyneth."

I paused. Without turning around, I accepted his promise with a single nod, then continued on my way, and though I wasn't sure he could make any such claim, I held on to that small bit of hope. Even if Rafe and I didn't make it, maybe Kaden would remember his promise to me.

On my way back to my room, I made a side trip to the caverns. *There.* Sometimes it takes a while to understand the truth whispering at your back. It felt like old times, slipping into the Royal Scholar's study. Only this time when I took something, I didn't leave a note.

nd so Morrighan led the Remnant across the wilderness,
Listening to the gods for the path of safety.
And when at last they came to a place
Where heavy fruit the size of fists hung from trees,
Morrighan dropped to her knees, shedding tears,
Giving thanks, and uttering remembrances,
For all who were lost along the way,
And Aldrid fell down beside her,
Thanking the gods for Morrighan.

—*Morrighan Book of Holy Text, Vol. V*

CHAPTER FIFTY-FIVE

ONCE AGAIN I WAS ALONE AND FREEZING, THE FIRE IN THE
gallery long turned to cold ash. I heard them calling outside,
Jezelia. A story, Jezelia. The room grew pink with dusk.

He had laid it all out quite clearly.

It's time now. You will say my words. See these things. Do these things.

I would be his pawn.

His army city swam in my vision and then Civica, destroyed,
in ashes, the ruins of the citadelle rising like broken fangs on the
horizon, plumes of smoke clouding the sky, my own mother a
puddle in the midst of rubble, weeping, alone, and tearing her
hair from her scalp. I blinked again and again, trying to make
the images vanish.

She's coming.

The words nestled full and warm beneath my ribs.

I heard Aster's footsteps. They had a weight I knew, a sound that danced with need and hope, a sound as ancient as the ruins around me. *She's coming. They are coming.* But now there were more footsteps, urgent. Too many. My chest tightened, and I sat down on the hearth, looking at the floor, trying to discern where the sounds were coming from. The hall? The outside walkways? It seemed as if they surrounded me.

"Miz? What are you doing in here? What happened to the fire? You'll catch your death in here without your cloak."

I looked up, and the gallery was full. Aster stood just a few feet away, but behind her a hundred, a thousand milled, a city of another kind spread out. The gallery had no walls, no end, a never-ending horizon, thousands drawing close, watching, waiting, generations, and standing among them, only an arm's length behind Aster, was Venda.

"They're waiting for you, Miz. Outside. Don't you hear them?"

My hair lifted from my shoulders; wind breezed through the gallery, swirling, tickling at my neck.

Siarrah.

Jezelia.

Their voices rose, cutting through the wind, the lamentations of mothers, sisters, and daughters of generations past, the same voices I heard in the valley when I buried my brother, remembrances that rent distant heaven and bleeding earth. Prayers not woven of sounds alone but of stars and dust and evermore.

Yes, I hear them.

"Aster," I whispered, "turn around and tell me what you see."

She did as I asked, then shook her head. "I see a mighty big floor in need of a stiff broom." She stooped and picked up a scrap of red cloth left behind by the dressmakers. "And this here remnant."

She brought the scrap to me, placing the ragged threads in my hands.

And then the gallery was a gallery again, the walls solid, the thousands gone. I held the fabric in my fist.

All ways belong to the world. What is magic but what we don't yet understand?

"You all right, Miz?"

I stood. "Aster, would you fetch my cloak for me? The gallery terrace will give me a better view of the square."

"Not that wall, Miz."

"Why not?"

"That's the wall they say"—her voice dropped to a whisper—"they say that's the one the lady Venda fell from." She looked around as if expecting to see her spirit lurking.

This revelation made me hesitate, and I pushed open the door to the terrace. The hinges squealed with their own warning. The wall beyond was thick and low, just like any other in the Sanctum. "I won't fall, Aster. I promise."

The beads on Aster's scarf jingled as she nodded and then she raced out the door.

I WRAPPED MY CLOAK SNUG ABOUT ME AS I SETTLED ON the wall. The gallery terrace was wide and jutted out over the square. I said my remembrances first.

Lest we repeat history,
the stories shall be passed
from father to son, from mother to daughter,
and to all my brothers and sisters of Venda,
for with but one generation,
history and truth are lost forever.
Hear the stories of the faithful,
The whispers of the universe,
The truths that ride the wind.

I sang of braveries and sorrows and hope, seeing without eyes, hearing without ears, the ways of trust and a language of knowing buried deep within them, a way as old as the universe itself. I told them of the things that last, the things that remain, and of a dragon that was waking.

For we must not just be ready,
for the enemy without,
but also for the enemy within.
And so shall it be,
Sisters of my heart,
Brothers of my soul,
Family of my flesh,
For evermore.

A low *evermore* from the crowd rose up to meet me, and they began to disperse to the warmth of their homes. "And may the gods keep the wicked far from you," I whispered to myself.

I had gathered my cloak to get down from the wall when suddenly the breeze calmed. The world grew strangely silent, muffled, and white flakes began to fall from the sky. It dusted the parapets, the streets, and my lap with a sparkle of white as it floated down in lazy circles, magical. *Snow.* It was a soft, cool feather brushing my cheek, exactly as Aunt Bernette had described. As the gentle flakes fell into my outstretched palm, a heavy ache grew in my chest for home. Winter was here. It felt like a door was closing.

CHAPTER FIFTY-SIX

KADEN

I WALKED WITH THE KOMIZAR ALONG THE WALL WALK of Jagmor Tower. Malich, Griz, and two brethren, Jorik and Theron, trailed behind us. Now that the whole Council was present, our first official session would convene tomorrow, but the unofficial sessions had already begun. The Komizar had gathered the Rahtan together privately to make sure that tomorrow we sat next to the governors who were likely to balk. The Rahtan was his inner circle, the ten who never failed in our duty or wavered in our loyalty to one another and Venda. It wasn't just duty; it was a way of life we all embraced, a belonging that never had to be doubted. Our footsteps, our thoughts, everything about us presented a unified force that made even the *chievdars* measure their words.

Still, the vast army was taking its toll on the provinces. One more winter, the Komizar said, just one more to secure the plans, the supplies, and the weapons that the armories were fashioning and stockpiling. The Komizar and *chievdars* had calculated exactly what was needed. Losing two governors in one season spoke of discontent, though, and several of the other governors mumbled among themselves. The Rahtan was to split them up, calm their fears, remind them of the rewards to come, and if that didn't sway them, remind them of the consequences. But the deciding game piece was Lia. She was a fresh strategy, one that caught their attention, an inroad to encourage the same populace the governors had to squeeze blood from to give just a little more. If the clans were soothed, so also were the governors, and they saw the targets on their own backs shrinking.

The Komizar was bringing me back into the fold, and second chances were not his way. My mad attack on him was already diminished by my easy victory over the emissary—proof that I was Rahtan to the marrow and I followed his orders by reflex. No one mentioned my verbal attack on Lia, but I knew that was as much responsible as anything for the dismissal of my transgression, not just by the Komizar but my brethren as well. When troubles arose, the Assassin ultimately knew where his loyalties lay. The sound of our combined footsteps on the stone walk was a comforting rumble, purposeful and strong—and lately I'd had precious little comfort.

As we approached Sanctum Tower, the Komizar spotted Lia sitting on the gallery wall.

He grinned. "There's my Siarrah now, just as I ordered. And look how the crowds in the square have grown."

I had already noted the size.

"The numbers are twice those of yesterday," Malich said warily.

"The air is bitter, and yet they still come," Griz added.

The Komizar's face set with satisfaction. "No doubt due to this evening's vision."

"A vision?" I asked.

"You think I'd let her spew her nonsense forever? Remembering long-dead people and forgotten storms? Not when we have our own magnificent storm brewing. Tonight she tells them of a vision of a battlefield where Venda is victorious. She tells them of a lifetime of spring and plenty to be gifted to the brave Vendans by the gods, making all their sacrifices worth it. That should ease the governors' and the clans' concerns." He lifted his hand to the crowds and called out to them as if to take credit for this turn of fortune, but none turned his way.

"They're too far away to hear you," Jorik said. "And a murmur grows among them."

The Komizar's expression darkened, and his eyes scanned the mass of people, for the first time seeming to assess the vast numbers. "Yes," he said. His eyes narrowed. "That must be it."

Jorik tried to soothe the Komizar's ego further by adding that he couldn't hear Lia's words either, because of the distance.

But I could hear her plainly—her voice carried on the air—and she wasn't speaking of victories.

CHAPTER FIFTY-SEVEN

I DIDN'T FEEL THE PAIN RIGHT AWAY. I STARED AT THE floor, a blurry sideways view, my cheek still pressed to the stone, the stench of spilled ale rising up to me. Then I heard the Komizar yell for me to get up.

It was mid-morning, and I had been taking a late breakfast in Sanctum Hall due to last-minute early morning fittings. Calantha and two guards were there with me when we heard sharp footsteps coming down the south corridor. The Komizar stormed in and ordered everyone else out.

I tried to get my bearings, to focus on the tilting room.

"Get up! Now!" he ordered.

I pushed up from the floor, and that's when the pain hit. My skull throbbed like a giant fist was crushing it. I forced myself to stand and steadied myself against the table. The Komizar was smiling. He stepped forward, gently touched the cheek he had just struck, then hit me again. I braced myself this time and only stumbled, but my neck felt as though it were snapping in two. I faced him, squaring my shoulders, and felt something warm and wet trickle on my cheek.

"Good morning to you too, *sher* Komizar."

"Did you think I wouldn't find out?"

I knew exactly what he was talking about, but I feigned confusion.

"I told you precisely what to say, and yet you told stories of dead sisters and dragons waking from sleep?"

"They like to hear stories of their kingdom's namesake. It's what they wanted to hear," I answered.

He grabbed my arm and yanked me toward him. His eyes danced with fury. "I don't care what they *want*! I care about what they need to hear! I care about my orders to you! And I don't care if the gods themselves hand delivered their words to you in golden goblets! All your drivel about listening without ears, seeing without eyes doesn't matter. The guards laughed out every word to me—but not one mention of battles and victory! That is what matters, Princess! That is *all* that matters."

"I beg your forgiveness, Komizar. I was carried away in the moment by the kindnesses of the people and their earnest desire for a story. I'll be sure to tell yours next time."

He looked at me, his chest still heaving. He reached up and wiped my cheekbone, then rubbed the blood between his fingers.

"You'll tell Kaden you tripped on the stairs. Say it."

"I tripped on the stairs."

"That's better, my little bird." He rubbed the blood on his finger across my lower lip, and then bent to kiss me, pushing the salty taste of my own blood onto my tongue.

CALANTHA AND THE GUARD DIDN'T SPEAK AS THEY LED me back to my room, but before she turned to leave, she paused to eye my face. A short while later, a basin of water with herbs floating on top was delivered to my room by a servant. The girl also brought a slice of soft, fleshy root. "For your face," she said beneath lowered lashes and hurried away before I could ask who sent it, but I could guess it was Calantha. This offense had hit a little too close to home.

I dipped a soft cloth in the water and dabbed it to my cheek to clean the wound. I winced at the sting. I had no mirror, but I could feel the bruise and the burning scrape from hitting the floor. I closed my eyes and held the soaked fabric to my skin. *It was worth it. Every word I spoke was worth it.* I couldn't leave them without some kind of knowing of their own. I saw it in their faces, weighing my words and what they might mean. I had pushed as far as I dared, for not everyone in the square had come to hear what I had to say. Some were there to report it. I had seen the Sanctum guards and the quarterlords not only scrutinizing me, but also watching those who had gathered to listen.

I picked up the piece of root the girl had brought and sniffed it. Thannis. Was there nothing this lowly weed couldn't do? I held it to the wound and felt it soothe the throb.

Across the room, my gaze landed on the wedding dress laid across Kaden's trunk. It had been finished with little time to spare. Hunter's Moon was tomorrow. The wedding was to begin at twilight as the moon rose over the foothills. There would be no processions, no flowers, no priests, no parties, none of the fanfare that accompanied a wedding in Morrighan. Vendan wedding traditions were simple, and witnesses were the greatest requirement. It would take place on the eastern wall walk overlooking Hawk's Pavilion. A volunteer chosen by the Komizar would tie our wrists together with a red ribbon. When we raised our tied hands before them displaying our union, the witnesses would call back a blessing—*bound by earth, bound by the heavens*—and that would be it. The feast cake of dried fruits that would follow was the greatest luxury, but the simplicity didn't make the anticipation any less feverish. The Hunter's Moon and my extravagant red clan dress were embellishments that added to the fervor. I walked over and touched the gown, so carefully pieced together, a dress of many hands and many households. A dress of welcoming, not of good-byes. A dress of staying, not leaving.

Was this to be my end? Forever a hostage of one kingdom and despised by the others? I wondered if Vendan riders were already in Morrighan spreading the news of my ultimate betrayal to my countrymen. I pictured those who would curse me—the cabinet, the Royal Guard, my mother and father. I closed my eyes trying to hold back tears. *But certainly not my own brothers or Pauline.* A sob jumped to my throat.

This wasn't the story I had written for myself. Not the story of Terravin and salty breezes and love. I crushed the fabric in my fist and held it to my face, staining the hem with the deeper red of my own blood. With Pauline's image still looming in my thoughts, a more horrible worry overtook me—no one in Morrighan would be considering my traitorous act for long because they would either be on this side of hell scrabbling for roaches and rats to fill their bellies or they would be dead.

The Komizar's success seemed assured—unless I could somehow get word to them. Kaden's promise to protect Berdi, Gwyneth, and Pauline was not enough. All of Terravin wasn't enough. There were so many more in Morrighan, and none of them deserved this end. The Komizar had mentioned one last winter. That must mean they wouldn't march until after that? When? Spring? Summer? How much time did Morrighan have? Not much more than I did.

I jumped when I heard a knock at my door. I wanted no more surprises, and cautiously cracked it open.

It was Calantha. "I have another towel for you." She moved aside. "And I brought this."

Rafe stepped into view.

Blood pooled cold at my feet. Was this a trap?

"I may have only one eye," Calantha said, "but I perceive far more with one than most do with two. I've dismissed the guards at the end of the hall to see to another matter, and the Council is still in session. You have fifteen minutes before the guards return to their post. No more. I'll be back before then." She set the towel she had brought down on my bed and left.

Rafe's eyes immediately went to my cheek, and I saw icy rage pass through them.

"It wasn't Kaden. He didn't touch me. I'm all right," I pleaded. "We only have a few minutes." I didn't want to waste it on anger and accusations. Rafe and I hadn't been alone with so much as a private word in days.

He swallowed his anger as if he could read my thoughts. He started to speak, but I stopped him. "Kiss me," I said. "Before you say anything else, just kiss me and hold me and tell me it was worth it, no matter what happens."

He brushed the hair from my face. "I promised you I'd get us out of this, and I will. We're going to have a long life together, Lia." His arms slid around me, pulling me to him as if nothing could ever come between us again, and then his mouth came down on mine, gentle, hungry, the sweetest taste I had ever imagined, all my dreams held tight and alive again in one short kiss.

We reluctantly stepped apart, because time was so short. Rafe spoke quickly. "Wear your riding clothes in the morning. Say your remembrances from Blackstone Terrace. Do you know where it is?"

I nodded. Blackstone Terrace was one of many that overlooked the square, but it was rarely used because access to it was more complicated.

"Good," he said. "Say them just after first bell. By then, the Council will be thick in their sessions. Stick to your routine so guards who watch from the square aren't alerted. When you leave, take the outside staircase down to the second level and go through the portal there. It's a deserted path that only a few servants use. I'll be waiting there for you with Jeb."

"But how—"

"Do you swim, Lia?"

"*Swim?* You mean the river?"

"Don't worry. We have a raft. You won't need to swim."

"But the river—"

He explained to me why it was the only way, that the bridge was impossible to raise without a small army, and the lower river was too far away. "Tavish has it worked out. I trust him."

"I can swim," I said, trying to calm my heart. *A raft. Tomorrow morning.* I didn't care if it was the craziest plan in the world. We'd be leaving before I had to marry the Komizar. He asked if there was anything I needed to take. He'd give it to Jeb now to secure on the raft, because there wouldn't be time tomorrow. I grabbed my saddlebag and stuffed a few things in it, including the Ancients' books. I grabbed his arm. "But, Rafe, if things don't go as planned, if you have to leave without me, promise me you will."

I could tell he was about to protest but then he paused, chewing his lip. "I will," he said, "if you promise to do the same."

"You're a terrible liar."

He frowned. "And I used to be so good at it. You're my downfall. But you still have to promise me."

I'd never leave without him. Without me as leverage, he'd be going home to Dalbreck in pieces. He could probably already see the lie on my tongue. "I will," I answered.

He sighed, and his lips grazed mine again, whispering against them. "I suppose we'll both have to get out, then."

"I suppose we will," I whispered back.

My body molded to his, and the seconds ticked by. All I wanted was more time with him. His lips traveled to my neck.

"It was worth it, Lia," he said. "Every mile, every day. I'd do it all again. I'd chase you across three continents if that's what it took to be with you."

I heard a small sigh, and he pulled away. "There may be one snag in our plan, though," he said. "Griz."

"Griz? He seems like the least of our worries. He already covered for us once."

A crease deepened between his brows as if Griz made his head ache. "He knows who I am, and it seems he's well acquainted with one of my men too. When Griz spotted him, he figured something was in the works, and he made it clear he doesn't want you to leave. He's one of the clanspeople and expects you to stay here. My soldier explained he was only here to get me out, and Griz seemed to buy it, but he's keeping a close watch on us."

I shook my head in disbelief. "Let me understand this correctly. He doesn't care that Dalbreck soldiers are on this side of the river or about conspiracies and escape plans, just so long as he gets to *keep* me?"

"That's right. We plan on taking him out silently in his quarters if we have to, but as you may have noticed, he's a big brute—it might not be easy."

My blood simmered. *Keep me.* Like a boy with a frog in his pocket. "No," I said. "I'll take care of Griz—"

"Lia, he's too—"

"I'm trusting *you*, Rafe. You need to trust me on this. I will handle Griz."

He opened his mouth to argue.

"*Rafe*," I said firmly.

He sighed and nodded grudgingly. "Tonight in Sanctum Hall, be sure to talk about future plans. What will happen a week from now and a month from now. Ask about the weather, anything so it looks like you expect to be here. It's not just the Komizar who misses nothing. The Rahtan, the *chievdars*, and especially Griz note every word."

There was a light tap at the door. Our time was up.

"Your shoulder," I said. "How is it healing?"

"Just a nick. The cook gave me a foul poultice to treat it." He bent down and lightly kissed the cut on my cheekbone. "Look at us," he said. "We're quite a pair, aren't we?" But then one kiss led to more, as if he'd forgotten he had to go.

"No one would recognize us," I answered. "We're hardly a proper prince and princess anymore."

He laughed mid-kiss and leaned back to look at me. "You were never a proper princess." His hands cradled my face, and his smile faded. "But you're everything I want. Remember that. I love you, Lia. Not a title. And not because a piece of paper says I should. Because I do."

There was no more time for words or kisses. He grabbed my saddlebag and hurried to the door.

"Wait!" I said. "I have something else to give you." I went to the chest and took out a small sealed flask of clear liquid. "It's a little something I lifted in my travels," I said. "It might buy us more time." I told him exactly what to do with it.

He grinned. "Not a proper princess at all." He carefully tucked the flask into my saddlebag and left.

CHAPTER FIFTY-EIGHT

LIGHT FLURRIES OF SNOW BEGAN TO WHIRL ON THE WIND, but it wasn't enough to stop me. I found Griz in the paddock with Eben and the foal.

I jumped up on the railing and down into the paddock.

"What happened here?" Griz asked, clumsily motioning to a place on his own cheek that mirrored mine. His hair flew wild in the wind.

I glared at Griz but didn't answer, instead turning to Eben. "How's the training going, Eben?" I asked.

Eben looked at me warily, sensing something was amiss and not just because of my bruised and cut face. "He's a fast learner," he answered. "He'll walk on a lead now."

Eben rubbed the horse's muzzle, and the young horse calmed at his touch. Their connection was already evident. *The way of*

Eben, Dihara had called it. *There is a knowing between them, a way of trust, mysterious but not magical. . . . A way that requires a different kind of eye and ear.* I reached out and stroked the star on the foal's head.

Griz shifted impatiently from foot to foot.

"Have you named him yet?" I asked.

Eben hesitated, glancing at Griz.

"Don't listen to the counsel of fools, Eben." I pressed my fist just below my ribs. "If you feel it here, then trust it."

"Spirit," Eben said quietly. "I gave him the same name."

Griz's patience was exhausted, and he motioned toward the rail. "You should be going—"

I lit into him, my voice loud and sharp. "I'll leave when I'm ready to leave, do you understand?"

"Eben," Griz said, "leave us alone for a minute. The princess and I—"

"Stay, Eben! You need to hear this too, because who knows what other nonsense these fools have filled your head with."

I walked up to Griz and poked him in the chest. "Let me make this perfectly clear to you. Though some might seek to make it appear otherwise, I am not a bride to be bartered away to another kingdom, nor a prize of war, nor a mouthpiece for your Komizar. I am not a chip in a card game to be mindlessly tossed into the center of the pot, nor one to be kept in the tight fist of a greedy opponent. I am a player seated at the table alongside everyone else, and from this day forward, I will play my own hand as I see fit. Do you understand me? Because the consequences could be ugly if someone thought otherwise."

Eben looked at me with mouth agog, but Griz stood there, in all his hulking, menacing mass, looking more like a chastised schoolboy than a fierce warrior. His lips twitched, and he turned to Eben. "Let's run some circles with Spirit."

I saw the surprise on Eben's face that Griz had called his horse by name.

I guessed that Griz had gotten my message. Now if he would only remember it.

BY THE TIME I GOT BACK TO THE SANCTUM, THE WIND was howling and the flurries had turned to driving snow that pelted my face. It was again just as Aunt Bernette had described, the cruel burning side of snow. I kissed two fingers and lifted them to the heavens for my aunt, my brothers, and even for my parents. It wasn't so hard for me to believe anymore that snow could have such different sides. So many things did. I pulled my cloak close about me as it tried to whip free. Winter was marching in with a vengeance. There would be no remembrances on the wall this evening.

Upon my return, a guard was waiting for me with a message. *Wear the brown.*

Even with all the busyness of his Council meetings, the Komizar still managed to send a message. No detail was too small or great for him to control.

I knew why he chose the brown. It was the plainest of my dresses, certainly drab in his eyes, but all the better to contrast and showcase the red he'd have me wear tomorrow. I had no doubt he'd ordered the snow itself as the perfect backdrop, and surely he'd ordered the sun to shine in the morning so as not to deter the crowds.

I dressed as he instructed, but there was more to put on besides the plain brown dress.

I lifted Walther's baldrick to my lips, the leather soft and warm against them, the ache in me as full as the day I had closed his eyes and kissed him good-bye. I put it on and pressed it against my chest.

Next came the tether of bones, full and heavy with gratitude. I wore my hair loose and flowing about my shoulders. There was no need to show off the kavah tonight. By now, everyone in the Sanctum knew it was there.

I put on the amulet bought in the *jehendra*, a ring of pounded copper that had been offered by the Arakan clan, a belt of dried thannis woven by a girl on the high plains of Montpair. The welcome of Venda came to me in so many ways, each gift heavy with hope.

There was nothing I wanted more than to leave this place, to disappear with Rafe into a world of our own and pretend Venda had never existed, to pretend these last few months had never happened, to start our dream afresh—to have the better ending Rafe hoped for. I ached for home in a way I hadn't thought possible, and I knew somehow I had to get there to warn them. But I couldn't deny a stirring in me too. It caught me in unexpected moments—when a servant girl, ashamed, fluttered her lashes downward, when I caught a rare glimpse of Eben the child, when Effiera echoed her mother's words—*the claw, quick and fierce; the vine, slow and steady.* When a tentful of women measured, fitted, and embraced me with their clothes, and I felt the expectation sewn into them. *They'll clothe their own, even if they have to piece together scraps to do it.*

And maybe the stirrings overtook me the most when I was with Aster. How had I come to love her in such a short time? As if on cue, she tapped on my door and entered. She had a cart and her chosen army with her—Yvet and Zekiah. They were too small to be barrow runners but were able to earn a meal in the kitchen by doing other tasks.

"We're supposed to gather your things for you, Miz, and haul them over to your new quarters. If that's all right with you, that is. But I think it has to be all right, because the Komizar ordered it, so I hope you don't mind if we fold up your clothes and put them in this here—" Her face flooded with worry, and she rushed toward me. "What happened to your cheek?"

I reached up, touching my cheekbone. I found it hard to lie to Aster, but she was too young to be drawn into this. "It was only a clumsy fall," I answered.

She frowned as if unconvinced.

"Please," I said, "go ahead and move my things. Thank you."

She clucked like an old woman, and they went about their work. If all went well, I'd be in my new quarters for only one night. They gathered the belts and underclothes that Effiera had given me first, then went on to the dresses. Aster grabbed the towel on the bed that Calantha had brought, but as she lifted it, something heavy fell from it and clattered to the floor.

We all sucked in quick breaths. My jeweled knife. The one

I'd thought was gone forever. Calantha had had it all along. Aster, Yvet, and Zekiah gawked at the knife, took a step back, then looked at me. Even in all their innocence, they knew I shouldn't possess weapons.

"What should we do with *that?*" Aster asked.

I knelt hastily, scooping it up as I grabbed the towel from Aster. "It's a wedding gift from the Komizar," I said and wrapped it up again. "He wouldn't be happy that I was so careless with it. Please don't mention this to him." I looked up at the three wide-eyed faces. "Or to anyone."

They all nodded, and I shoved it into the bottom of the cart. "When you take these things to my room, please unload the knife carefully and place it under all my clothes. Can you do that?"

Aster looked at me, her expression solemn. She wasn't buying any of it. None of them were. Their innocence and childhoods had been stolen long ago like Eben's. "Don't worry, Miz," Aster said. "I'll be careful and put it in a real good place."

I started to stand, but Yvet stopped me and leaned forward to kiss my injured cheek, her little lips moist against my skin. "It won't hurt for long, Miz. Be brave."

I swallowed, trying to answer without turning into a blathering fool. "I'll try, Yvet. I'll try to be as brave as you."

Betrayed by her own,
Beaten and scorned,
She will expose the wicked,
For the Dragon of many faces
Knows no boundaries.

—Song of Venda

CHAPTER FIFTY-NINE

KADEN

I SAT AT THE COUNCIL TABLE, LISTENING, NODDING, TRYING to add a word when I could, but once again Lia had commandeered my thoughts. With every drop of blood within me, I was certain I needed her here. That she needed to be here. But it seemed almost impossible now.

I had known.

I knew what he was planning, and I said nothing because it was everything I thought I wanted—"the steps to justice," he called them—and I wanted justice. That's what I had called it too. But I knew we were twisting words. It was vengeance, pure and simple. It was all that mattered. I was certain that the day I looked into my father's eyes and eased him into his last breath, my own breaths would grow fuller. That the scars I bore would miraculously disappear and be forgotten. Any price seemed worth that prize. *Innocents die in war, Lia.* I had said those words countless times to myself as justification, even when I learned of Greta's death. *Innocents die.* But now I pictured Berdi dishing out extra helpings of stew, myself dancing in the streets of Terravin with Gwyneth and Simone . . . and there was Pauline, as kind and gentle a girl as it was possible for any earthly being to be. They had names now. Their faces were sharp and clear, while the face of justice had grown dim.

At the same time, I couldn't forget the people of Venda who had taken me in either. They had adopted me as one of their own. Nourished me. I *was* Vendan now, and I knew their need was great. We were a kingdom that struggled every day at the hands of those who showed no compassion. Didn't this land deserve some measure of justice? And the answer to that I knew was an undeniable yes.

I won't let any harm come to them.

I had made a promise to Lia I wasn't sure I could keep.

The meetings were running long. Governor Obraun was remarkably easy to sway, agreeing to double the loads from his mines in Arleston. Almost too agreeable. The other governors balked, claiming they couldn't squeeze blood from a stone. The Komizar assured them they could.

You have an agreement. How wonderful for you.

"Nothing to say, Assassin?"

I looked up, and Malich smirked at me from across the table, delighting in catching me in other thoughts.

"We all have practice at squeezing blood from stone. We've done it for years. We can do it through one more winter."

His smile faded while the Komizar's grew, pleased that I had pushed the cause. He nodded, our long-held understanding reestablished.

CHAPTER SIXTY

PAULINE

WE WERE WAITING ON THE FRINGE OF THE CITADELLE plaza for Bryn and Regan, hanging in the shadows of the towering spruce, when a soldier galloped wildly past us. He fell from his horse at the foot of the steps, appearing half dead. A sentry rushed to his side, and the soldier said a few words we were too far away to hear, and then he passed out. The sentry disappeared into the citadelle as two guards lifted the soldier and carried him inside.

A crowd began to gather as word spread of the soldier. He had been identified as being from Walther's platoon. Minutes passed and then an hour, and there was still no sign of Bryn or Regan.

By the time anyone emerged from the citadelle again, the square was full. The Lord Viceregent came out and stood at the top of the steps, his face stricken. He smoothed back his white-blond hair as if trying to compose himself—or perhaps wishing to postpone what he had to say. His voice cracked in his first few words, but then he gathered his strength and announced that Crown Prince Walther of Morrighan was dead, along with his platoon, butchered by the barbarians.

My knees weakened, and Berdi grabbed my arm.

Silence choked the crowd for a moment and then mother after mother, sister, father, wife, brother, fell to their knees. Their anguished wails filled the air, and then the queen appeared on the steps, thinner than I remembered, her face ashen. She walked into the crowd, and she wept with them. The Viceregent tried to offer comfort, but there was no consoling her or anyone else.

Finally I saw the brothers emerge and stop at the top of the steps. Their expressions were grim, their eyes hollow. There was no sign of the king, but then the Chancellor appeared on their heels. Gwyneth and I both tugged on our hoods to be sure we were thoroughly covered. The Chancellor's face wasn't stricken, but severe. He told everyone there was more bad news he had to share—news that would make their grief twice as hard to bear.

"We have news of Princess Arabella." A hush fell, and sobs were choked back as everyone waited to hear what had become of her. "When she shirked her duty as First Daughter, she put us all in peril, and we see the fruit of that treachery with the death of Prince Walther and thirty-two of our finest soldiers. Now word comes that her betrayal runs even deeper. She is creating a new alliance with the enemy. It was part of her plan all along. She has forsaken us and announced her plans to marry the barbarian ruler to become the Queen of Venda."

There was a collective sucking in of breaths. Disbelief. *No, it wasn't possible.* But I looked at Bryn and Regan. Standing like statues, they made no attempt to defend their sister or discredit the Chancellor.

"It is declared," he continued, "that from this moment forward, she is the most reviled enemy of the Kingdom of Morrighan. Her name will be stricken from all records, and if the gods should deliver her into our hands, she will be executed on sight for her crimes against the chosen Remnant."

I couldn't breathe. It wasn't possible.

Regan made eye contact with me at last, but his gaze was empty. He made no effort to show he didn't believe it. Bryn's head drooped, and he turned and walked back into the citadelle. Regan followed.

They were grieving for Walther. That had to be it. Surely, in their hearts, they knew it was a lie. She'd been abducted. I told them myself. I know what I saw and heard.

We walked back to our inn in shocked silence.

"She wouldn't do it," I finally said. "Lia would never join forces with the enemy against Morrighan. Never."

"I know," Berdi said.

My abdomen cramped, and I bent over, clutching myself. Berdi and Gwyneth were immediately at my sides, holding me in case I fell. "The baby's just stretching," I said and took a deep, calming breath.

"Let's get you back to the inn," Gwyneth said. "We'll sort this out about Lia. There has to be some explanation."

The cramp eased, and I straightened. I still had two months to go. *Don't come early, child. I'm not ready.*

"Do you need to rest?" Berdi asked. "We can stop in this tavern and get you a bite to eat."

I looked at the nearby tavern. It was tempting, but I only wanted to get back to—

I froze.

"What's wrong?" Gwyneth asked.

Something caught my eye. I shook off their assistance and walked closer to the tavern, trying to get a better view through the window.

I blinked, trying to refocus again and again.

He's dead.

Lia had told me. I heard her words as clearly as if she were saying them to me now. She had stared at her feet, and her words had run together in a quick, nervous string. *His patrol was ambushed. The captain of the guard buried him in a distant field. His last words were of you—tell Pauline I love her. He's dead, Pauline. He's dead. He isn't coming back.*

But her eyes had darted away from mine time and again.

Lia had lied to me.

Because there he was, plain as day. Mikael was sitting in the tavern, an ale on one knee and a girl on the other.

The world spun, and I reached out to a lantern post to steady myself. I wasn't sure what hit me harder, that Mikael was alive and well or that Lia, whom I had trusted like a sister, had deceived me so completely.

Berdi was at my side gripping my arm. "Do you want to go in?" she asked.

Gwyneth was there too, but she was looking through the window where I still stared. "No," she said quickly. "She doesn't want to go in. Not right now."

And Gwyneth was right. I knew where to find him when I was ready, but I wasn't ready now.

CHAPTER SIXTY-ONE

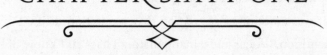

THE GUARDS WERE ESCORTING ME DOWN THE CORRIDOR to Sanctum Hall when we heard footsteps coming our way. Hurried footsteps. Kaden rounded the corner into our hallway and stopped.

"Wait for her at the stairs," he said, dismissing the guards. "I need to speak to the princess."

They did as they were ordered, and he pulled me into a narrow dark passage. His eyes grazed over my cheek.

"It was only a clumsy fall, Kaden. Don't make more of it than it is."

He reached up, gently running his thumb beneath my cheekbone. His jaw clenched. "How long are we going to go on like this, Lia? When are you going to be honest with me?"

I saw the earnestness in his eyes, and I was surprised that

my chest ached with wanting to tell him everything, but Rafe and I were too close to freedom now for the luxury of honesty. I still didn't know what Kaden might do. His devotion to me was obvious, but his loyalty to Venda and the Komizar was proven.

"I'm not hiding anything from you."

"What about the emissary? Who is he?"

It was more of an accusation than a question. I lifted my lip in revulsion. "A liar and a manipulator. That's all I know of him. I promise."

"You give me your word."

I nodded.

He was appeased. I saw it in his eyes and by the relieved breath rising in his chest. He believed for now that I wasn't conspiring with the emissary. But his confidence in me was fleeting. He moved on to other suspicions.

"I know you don't love the Komizar."

"I already admitted that to you. Are we going to go through this again?"

"If you think marrying him will bring you power, you're wrong. He won't share it with you."

"We'll see."

"Dammit, Lia! You're spinning a lie. I know you are. You told me you would, and I believe you. What are you up to?"

I remained silent.

He sighed. "Don't do it. It won't go well. Trust me. You are going to be staying here."

I tried to show no response, but the way he said it made my

blood stop cold in my chest. There was no anger in his tone or taunting. Just fact.

He stepped away, raking his fingers through his hair, then leaned back against the opposite wall. His eyes burned with need. "I heard your name," he explained. "It floated on the wind, whispering to me before I ever got to Terravin. And then that day on the tavern porch when you bandaged my shoulder, I saw us, Lia. Together. Here."

My mouth went dry. He didn't need to say more. With those few words, it added up—our time across the Cam Lanteux when he seemed to sense things before they happened, my mother's own words racing back to me when I had asked her about sons having the gift. *It's happened, but not to be expected.*

Kaden had the gift. At least some small degree of it.

"Have you always known you had it?"

"It's part of the reason why my father gave me away. I used it against his wife in anger. I've denied the gift ever since, but there are times—" He shook his head. "Like when I was coming for you. I knew it was the gift, even if I didn't want to admit it. And then I saw us. Here."

My heart jumped when I thought of my own dreams of Rafe leaving me behind. They seemed to confirm what Kaden thought he saw.

We had to be wrong. It wasn't what I felt in my heart.

"And we are here," I said breathlessly. "For now. Seeing us here together isn't much of a revelation."

"Not now. I saw us a long time from now. I had a baby in my arms."

"And I had a dream last night that I could fly. It doesn't mean I'll grow wings."

"Dreams and knowing are two different things."

"But sometimes it's hard to tell the difference. Especially when you haven't nurtured the gift. You're as inexperienced at this as I am, Kaden."

"True," he said, and stepped closer. "But I know this with certainty. I love you, Lia. I will always love you. Remember that tomorrow when you bind your life forever to the Komizar's. . . . I love you, and I know you care for me."

He turned and left, and I closed my eyes. My head pounded with my deceits and lies, because the gods help me, I knew I shouldn't, but I cared about Kaden too—only not in the way that he so desperately wanted me to. Nothing, not even time or a gift, could change that.

I saw us, Lia. Together. Maybe he just wanted to see us and conjured an image in his own mind, the way I had daydreamed about one boy or another countless times back in Civica. I opened my eyes, staring at the opposite wall. I wished that love could be simple, that it was always given and returned in the same measure, equally and at the same time, that all the planets aligned in a perfect way to dispel all doubts, that it was easy to understand and never painful.

I thought of all the boys I had chased in the village, longing for some hint of affection from them, the stolen kisses, the boys I was sure I was in love with, of Charles, who led me on but ultimately had no feelings for me. And then Rafe came along.

He changed everything. He consumed me in a different

way—the way his eyes made everything jump inside of me when I looked into them, his laughter, temper, the way he sometimes struggled for words, the way his jaw twitched when he was angry, the thoughtful way he listened to me, his incredible restraint and resolve in the face of overwhelming odds. When I looked at him, I saw the easygoing farmer he could have been, but I also saw the soldier and prince that he was.

We've had a terrible start—it doesn't mean we can't have a better ending.

The way he filled me with hope.

But I couldn't ignore the rocky path of love either. I thought of my parents, of Pauline, of Walther and Greta, even Calantha, and I wondered if love ever ended well. I knew only one thing with certainty—it couldn't end the way Kaden hoped it would.

CHAPTER SIXTY-TWO

THE WIND MOANED THROUGH CREVICES AND BATTERED doors and shutters like a giant fist. *Let me in.* It was the kind of storm that sounded like it would never end. *I'm here for you.* This was snow. This was winter.

Two fires roared in Sanctum Hall, one at either end, but cold drafts still swirled at our feet. I watched for Venda, for a reassurance that I wasn't mad, that Rafe's plan of crossing the river wasn't insanity itself, but the shadows were only shadows.

Rafe sat just a few seats down from me, and we all waited for the Komizar and the Rahtan to arrive. The *chievdars* bellowed among themselves as usual, but the absence of the Rahtan seemed to set the governors on edge. They were unusually subdued. None mentioned my cheek, but I saw them looking at it. "It was the stairs," I finally blurted out, then caught myself, repeating more quietly, "I fell on the stairs." I wanted no scenes, no words, nothing to raise the ire of the few governors who had been kind to me. Governor Faiwell shot me a brief, questioning glance. The low, stifled conversations resumed. Governor Umbrose sat staring into his mug, looking slightly dejected—or drunk. Was it their Council meetings today that had dampened their usual revelry? And then we heard the faint echo of footsteps.

I had never heard the Rahtan all approaching together. There was an ominous rhythm to their steps and a chilling ring to the weapons at their sides. It wasn't that they walked in unison but with a deliberate demanding beat. *Never fail.* That's what I heard.

"What's this?" the Komizar asked as they entered. "Has someone died?"

There was an effort to fill the quiet pall. Instead of sitting in clusters as they usually did, the Rahtan spread out, dragging seats between governors. Kaden sat adjacent to me, and the Komizar took his place on my left. He didn't bother with the pretense of a kiss—other matters seemed to occupy his thoughts. He called for ale and food, and the servants began bringing platters to the table.

Calantha sat at the other end of the table, almost as if she wanted to distance herself from Rafe and me. Was she already regretting her acts? Was she seeing the Komizar with the eyes of yesterday again? And more important, would she expose her transgression? Maybe she had already removed the knife from my room. I prayed Aster had hidden it well. Only when it was time for me to go would I dare to carry it.

The platter of bones was set before me for the blessing. I nearly spilled it as I lifted the heavy tray.

"Wedding jitters, Princess?" the Komizar asked.

I pasted on my most serene face. "On the contrary, *sher* Komizar. I'm eager for tomorrow. My fingers are only numb from the cold. I haven't yet grown accustomed to your climate."

I held the bleached sacrifice over my head for what I hoped was the last time and stared at the sooty ceiling of the Ancients. In an instant, I saw the sky and stars beyond, a universe spreading wide, with a long memory—and that's when I heard the cries. Across time, thin as blood swirling in a river, I heard the cry of death, the grieving howls of mothers falling to their knees, the weeping of my own mother. *They knew.* The news had reached Morrighan. Their sons were gone. The grief stole my strength, and I thought my knees would buckle.

"Be done with it," the Komizar snapped impatiently under his breath. "I'm hungry."

The platter shook in my hands, and I wanted to bash it into his head. Rafe leaned forward, catching my gaze, and I saw the strength in his eyes, the restraint, the message—*hold on, we're almost there.*

I said the acknowledgment of sacrifice, and when I set the tray down, I kissed two fingers and lifted them to the gods, my mother's cries still ringing in my ears. *We're almost there.*

The rest of the meal was uneventful, for which I was grateful.

Each quiet step brought us closer to tomorrow. But it was almost too quiet.

Kaden had hardly spoken a word of consequence through the whole meal, but as I started to push away from the table, he grabbed my hand. "What did you see, Siarrah?"

It was the first time he had ever called me that.

The Komizar snorted, but everyone at the table waited to hear my response.

"What do you mean?" I asked.

"Your lashes fluttered before the blessing. You gasped. What did you see?"

The truths may wish to be known, but now was not the time. Instead I twisted lies into something golden and glorious that I knew Kaden wanted to hear. Something I hoped would stop him from searching for the truth.

I looked at him warmly and smiled. "I saw myself, Kaden. Here. Many years from now."

I let my gaze linger on his for a few moments more, and though I didn't say the words aloud, I know he heard, *I saw myself here with you.*

Relief shone in his eyes. I forced the warmth to remain on my face for the rest of the evening, even as my lie twisted into a dark, cold knot inside of me.

The Komizar walked me to my new quarters. "I think you'll find it warmer than Kaden's drafty room."

"His quarters were fine. Why not just leave me there?"

"Because if you're still poking your head out a south tower

window after the wedding, instead of being over here with me, the clans might wonder why. We want to at least give them the appearance of a true commitment, don't we, my dove? But Kaden can come visit you here in the late hours. I'm a generous man."

"So considerate of you," I answered. I had been in this tower before. It was where Rafe's chamber was located, but I had never been on this floor. The Komizar led me to a door opposite his and opened it. The only light came from a small candle that glowed on a table. The first thing I noted was the walls. They appeared to be solid.

"There aren't any windows," I said.

"Of course there are. But they're small, which helps keep it warmer. And look, there's a nice large bed—enough room for two as the need arises."

He stepped closer and gently caressed my face where he had struck it. His dark eyes glowed with power. He seemed invincible, and I wondered just how hard it would be to kill him, or if it was even possible. I heard my mother's admonition. *Taking another life, even a guilty one, should never be easy. If it were, we'd be little more than animals.*

"Tomorrow is our wedding day, Princess," he said and kissed my cheek. "Let's make it a fresh start." There was no one to see this performance just now, and I wondered at his gentle peck.

As soon as he left, I inspected the room. I thought the shadows would lead to something, a closet perhaps, but the small cramped space was all there was. The four windows were little more than shuttered peek holes six inches across, and the whole room was barely larger than the holding cell he had thrown me into when I first arrived. The chest and bed took up most of the space. This showed a commitment and fresh start? I was more like a tool thrown into a nearby shed.

I began searching through the clothes that Aster, Yvet, and Zekiah had delivered. The candle offered little light, but as I searched every fold and pocket, I began to despair, thinking Calantha had already come and retrieved it. It wasn't here. I went through everything again, hoping that in my haste I had missed it, but it wasn't in my clothes or any corner of the chest. I searched under the mattress and found nothing. *I'll be careful and put it in a real good place.* Aster knew all the best secret places. A place she was sure—

I ran to the opposite corner, where a lidded chamber pot was nestled on a low stool. I lifted the lid and reached into the dark hole, and my fingers wrapped around something sharp. Aster understood the ways of the Sanctum far too well.

And though the wait may be long,
The promise is great,
For the one named Jezelia,
Whose life will be sacrificed
For the hope of saving yours.

—*Song of Venda*

CHAPTER SIXTY-THREE

JUST AS I SUSPECTED, THE MORNING WAS QUIET, ABSENT of storm and wind, and I was certain the Komizar had somehow made an agreement with an unknown god of weather. No doubt it was the god who would pay dearly at some point for the bargain he'd struck.

I had tossed all night and wasn't sure I'd slept at all. I slid aside one of the shutters, and a blast of cold air hit me. Blinding light poured through the small opening. Once my eyes adjusted, I was stunned by what I saw. Every roof, parapet, and inch of ground in the square below was covered in a thick layer of white. It was both beautiful and frightening. How much would traveling through snow slow us down?

There was a tap on my door, and when I opened it, I saw a tray of cheese and bread on the floor and heard the scurrying footsteps of whoever had delivered it, apparently afraid to be anywhere in the vicinity of the Komizar. I ate every morsel, knowing it might be my last for a while, and then I began to dress, putting on my trousers and shirt as Rafe had instructed. Besides being more suited to riding than a dress, my trousers were far warmer. My shirt still flapped loose from where the Komizar had torn it. I smoothed the fabric up over my shoulder and used Walther's baldrick to keep it in place.

I heard the early stirrings of the city outside. *Say your remembrances from Blackstone Terrace . . . just after the first bell.* The terrace was close to these quarters, in view from the fist-sized windows of my chamber. I judged by the sun that the first bell would ring in an hour or less. By now the Council was probably settled into the talks that I assumed were not going smoothly, judging by some of the governors' faces last night. Were they balking at the plenty in the Komizar's silos while their own citizens suffered with growling bellies? Discontented subjects could lead to more challenges and shorter lives. It seemed that the promise of my visions was a way to douse the fires of discontent. The Siarrah, sent by the gods, would see a victory at hand. That would fill the bellies of those in the far-flung provinces for a while.

I put on the furred vest of the Meurasi, pieced together by sacrifice, and my stomach squeezed. They weren't all my enemies. The word *barbarian* was gone from my lips, except to describe a savage few, and it seemed at least one lord of Morrighan was among those few.

I'd started to retrieve the knife from beneath the mattress

where I'd hidden it when I heard the door rattle. I dropped the mattress and spun around.

It was the Komizar. I stared at him, trying to quickly compose my expression to one of indifference. "You have no Council meetings this morning?"

He scrutinized me, taking his time to answer. "Why are you wearing your riding clothes?"

"They're warmer, *sher* Komizar. With the snow on the terrace, I thought them a better choice for saying my morning remembrances."

"There'll be no more performances unless I'm with you." He angled his head to the side, mocking me like I was a dim-witted mule. "I think I need to be there to help you remember exactly what you're supposed to say."

"I'll remember," I said sternly.

We stood there, both of us hearing the faint chants of *Jezelia*.

"You won't be addressing them without me by your side," he repeated.

I saw it in his eyes. I heard it in his tone. It was all about power, and he couldn't relinquish even the smallest fistful that had inadvertently passed to me. The pockets of clans throughout the city who gathered in the square had grown and called for *me*, not him, something he hadn't anticipated, though he had all but orchestrated it. Compared to the vast numbers in the city and his staggering army, their numbers were few, but he still wanted to control every last one of them and be certain where their loyalties lay.

"They call for me, Komizar," I said gently, hoping to soften his countenance.

"They can wait. All the better to augment their fervor before the wedding. I have a more important task for you."

"What task is more important than increasing their fervor with visions of plenty?"

He looked at me suspiciously. "Bolstering the governors who will be going home to their provinces in a week's time."

"Is there a problem with the governors?" I asked.

He grabbed the red dress I was to wear for the wedding from the chest and threw it on the bed. "Put it on. I'll be back to take you to the Council session later today. At my signal, you'll give the governors their own private performance, where you'll conveniently flutter your lashes and spew words of victory. The right words this time."

"But the dress is for our wedding this evening."

"Put it on," he ordered. "It would be wasteful to save a dress for a few dim hours."

I hoped to quickly quell his growing agitation so he would leave. "As you wish, *sher* Komizar. It's our wedding day, after all, and I wish to please you. I'll be dressed by the time you return." I grabbed the dress from the bed and waited for him to leave.

"Now, my pet. I'll be taking your riding clothes with me. You'll have no need of them, and I know how wedding jitters can make some brides impulsive, especially you."

He stood there waiting. "Hurry. I don't have time for your feigned modesty."

Neither did I. I needed him to return to the Council Wing as soon as possible. I quickly shed my vest, belt, and boots, then turned around to take off the rest. I could feel his eyes drilling into my back, and I quickly wriggled into my dress. Before I could turn around, his hands slid around my waist and his lips traced the kavah on my shoulder. I grabbed my shirt and trousers from the bed and turned, shoving them into his stomach.

He laughed. "Now, that's the princess I know and love."

"You've never loved anything in your life," I said.

His expression softened for a brief moment. "How very wrong you are." He turned to leave, but just before he closed the door behind him, he added, "I'll be back in a few hours." His lip lifted in distaste, and he whirled his hand in the air. "Do something with your hair."

He shut the door, and I ruffled my hair into a ragged mess of frustration. And then I heard a growling *thunk*.

I ran to the door and tried the latch. It didn't budge. I pounded with my fists. "You can't lock me in! That's not our agreement!" I pressed my ear to the door, but the only answer I got was the faint sound of his footsteps receding.

Agreement. I almost laughed at the word. Unlike Kaden, I knew the Komizar honored nothing unless it served him. I looked around the room for something that could pick the lock. I took a bone from my tether, used my knife to split it into a thin sliver, and prodded at the small keyhole to no avail. Every piece of metal in this wretched damp city was stiff with rust. I tried another bone and another, and heard the chants outside growing louder. *Jezelia.* When would first bell ring? I ran to the windows, but they were too small and too deep for me to call to anyone. And then I heard a light knock.

"Miz Lia?"

I ran to the door and fell against it. "Aster!" I said, relief flooding through me.

"They're calling for you," she said.

"I hear them. Can you unlock the door for me?"

I heard her jiggling keys in the lock. "None of these work."

My mind raced, trying to think what would take the least time. Fetch Calantha? She had a key to everything in the Sanctum. But whose side would she be on today? I took a chance and told Aster to get her. She left and I sat on the floor, leaning back against the door. Time crept by in agonizing beats, marked by the calls of *Jezelia*, and then I heard first bell. My heart sank, but then the rush of footsteps clattered through the hall, and I heard Aster's panting breaths at the door.

"I looked everywhere, Miz. I couldn't find her. No one knows where she is."

I tried to calm the panic rising in me. Time was slipping away. *I'll be waiting.* Was he still there?

The Komizar's room. There. "Search the Komizar's room!" I yelled. It was just across the hall. "He's gone to the Council Wing. Hurry, Aster!"

I grabbed the baldrick from the bed and slipped my knife into its sheath. Next I added my tether of bones and finally my cloak to conceal the knife. If I did get out of this room, I had to look as I always did to the guards who might see me. Minutes passed. I sat on the bed. *Leave without me, Rafe. You promised.*

"I got it!" Aster called through the door. I heard the heavy bolt slide and the door opened. Her face beamed with her accomplishment, and I kissed her forehead. "You *are* the saving angel Aster!"

She rubbed her clipped locks. "Hurry, Miz!" she said. "They're still calling."

"Stay here," I told her. "It might not be safe."

"Nothing's safe around here. I'm going to see you get there!"

I couldn't argue with her logic. It was true. The Sanctum was anything but a sanctuary. The only thing it harbored was constant threat. We ran down halls, steps, and little-used passages, up steps and down steps again. The short distance suddenly seemed like miles. It was not an easy terrace to get to. I prayed I wasn't too late, but at the same time, I hoped Rafe had left without me and was already safe across the river. We passed no one, thankfully, and finally reached the portal that led to the terrace.

"I'll wait here and whistle if anyone comes."

"Aster, you can't—"

"I can whistle loud," she said, her chin set in the air.

I hugged her. "I'll know if someone's coming. Now, go. Get back to the *jehendra* and your bapa and stay safe there." She reluctantly turned away, and I hurried through the long portal to the terrace. It was covered with a thick layer of snow, and I walked to the north wall, knowing I was already late. There would be no stories this morning, only the shortest of remembrances so the guards in the square would suspect nothing, and then I'd be on my way, but when I reached the wall, a pervasive silence spread through the crowd. It spread to me, like hands reaching out, taking mine. *Tarry, Jezelia. Tarry for a story.* I alone possessed the last surviving copy of the Song of Venda. It wasn't my story to keep. Whether babble or not, I had to give it back to them before I left.

"Gather close, brothers and sisters of Venda," I called out to them. "Hear the words of the mother of your land. Hear the Song of Venda."

AND SO I SAID IT, VERSE AFTER VERSE, HOLDING NONE OF it back. I spoke of the Dragon feeding on the blood of the young, drinking the tears of their mothers, his cunning tongue and his deadly grip. I told them of hungers of another kind, ones that were never sated or quenched.

I saw heads nod in understanding, and puzzled guards looking at one another, trying to make sense of it. I remembered Dihara's words, *This world, it breathes you in . . . shares you. But there are some who are more open to the sharing than others.* For the guards and many who stood below, my words were only babble, just as Venda's had been so long ago.

As I spoke, a breeze circled around. I could feel it inside me, stretching, reaching, then moving on again, traveling over the crowd, through the square and down the streets, through the valleys beyond and across the hills.

> *For the Dragon will conspire,*
> *Wearing his many faces,*
> *Deceiving the oppressed, gathering the wicked,*
> *Wielding might like a god, unstoppable,*

Unforgiving in his judgment,
Unyielding in his rule,
A stealer of dreams,
A slayer of hope.

Until one comes who is mightier,
The one sprung from misery,
The one who was weak,
The one who was hunted,
The one marked with claw and vine,
The one named in secret,
The one called Jezelia.

A murmur ran through the crowd, and then Venda was there, standing beside me. She reached out and took my hand. "The rest of the song," she whispered, and then she spoke more verses.

Betrayed by her own,
Beaten and scorned,
She will expose the wicked,
For the Dragon of many faces
Knows no boundaries.

And though the wait may be long,
The promise is great,
For the one named Jezelia,
Whose life will be sacrificed
For the hope of saving yours.

And then she was gone.

I wasn't sure if I was the only one who had heard her, or even seen her, but I stood there dazed, trying to grasp the enormity of what she had said. In an instant, I knew those were the verses ripped from the last page of the book. I braced against the wall, steadying myself with this revelation. *Sacrificed.* The murmur from the crowds grew louder, but then movement caught my eye and my gaze jumped up to a high wall across the way. *Chievdars,* governors, and Rahtan were watching me. I drew in a startled breath. Their meeting had adjourned early.

"Miz?"

I turned. Aster stood in the middle of the terrace. The Komizar stood behind her with a knife held to her chest.

"I'm sorry, Miz. I just couldn't leave you like you told me. I—" He pressed the tip of the knife against her, and she blanched with pain.

"Dear gods, no!" I cried, locking my eyes onto the Komizar's. I pleaded with him, delicate, desperate, and slow, stepping closer, trying to bring his focus back to me. I held on to him fiercely with my eyes and smiled, trying to somehow dispel this madness. "Please, let her go, *sher* Komizar. You and I can talk. We can—"

"I told you, without me, there would be no more performances."

"Then punish me. She has nothing to do with this."

"You, my little bird? At the moment you're far too valuable. She, on the other hand . . ." He shook his head, and before I could even fathom what he was doing, he plunged the knife into her chest.

I screamed and ran toward her, catching her as she slipped from his arms. "Aster!" I fell to the ground with her, cradling her in my lap. "Aster." I pressed my hands to the wound in her chest, trying to stop the flow of blood.

"Tell my bapa I tried, Miz. Tell him I'm no traitor. Tell him we—"

Her last words lay frozen on her lips, her crystal eyes bright, but her breath still. I pulled her to my chest, rocking her, holding her as if I could defy death. "Aster, stay with me. Stay!" But she was gone.

I heard a small chuckle and looked up. The Komizar wiped his bloody knife on his trouser leg and slipped it back into its sheath. He towered over me, his boots dusted with snow. "She got what she deserved. We have no room in the Sanctum for traitors."

Numbness washed through me. I looked at him, incredulous. "She was only a child," I whispered.

He shook his head, clucking. "How many times do I need to tell you, Princess, we don't have such luxuries. Venda has no children."

I gently slid Aster from my lap onto the snow and got to my feet. I stepped closer to him, and he looked into my eyes with all the smugness of a victor. "Do we understand each other at last?" he asked.

"Yes," I said. "I think we do." And in the turn of a second, the smugness was gone. His eyes widened in wonder.

"And now," I said, "Venda has no Komizar either."

A swift act. One that was easy.

I pulled my knife from his side and plunged it in again, twisting for good measure, feeling the blade cut through his flesh, ready to plunge it in again and again, but he stumbled back several paces, finally comprehending what I had done. He fell against the wall near the portal, staring at the red stain spreading across his shirt. Now he was the one who was incredulous. He drew his knife from its sheath, but he was too weak to step forward, and it spilled from his hand. His sword remained useless at his side. He looked back at me in disbelief and slid to the ground, his face twisted in pain.

I walked closer and stood over him, kicking his knife away. "You were wrong, Komizar. It's much easier to kill a man than a horse."

"I'm not dead yet," he said between labored breaths.

"You will be soon. I know about vital organs, and though I'm certain you have no heart, your guts are in pieces now."

"It's not over," he gasped.

I heard shouts and turned. Though the people below couldn't see what I'd done, those on the high wall on the far side of the square had seen. They were already running, trying to find the quickest route to the terrace, but Kaden and Griz charged through the portal first. Griz pushed both halves of the heavy portal door shut behind him and wedged a bar through the iron pulls.

Kaden looked at the blood on my hands and dress, and the knife still in my grip. "By the gods, Lia, what have you done?" And then he spotted Aster's lifeless body lying in the snow.

"Kill her," the Komizar yelled with renewed energy. "She

won't be the next Komizar! Kill her now!" he demanded, choking on his breaths.

Kaden stepped over to him and knelt on one knee, looking at his wound. He reached across and pulled the Komizar's sword from its scabbard and faced me.

Griz's hand went warily to one of the swords at his side.

Kaden held the weapon out to me. "You might need this. Somehow we're going to have to get you out of here."

"What are you doing?" the Komizar screamed. He slumped further to the ground. "You owe me everything. We're Rahtan. We're brothers!"

Kaden's expression was as grieved as the Komizar's. "Not anymore," he answered.

Even as he lay dying, the Komizar continued to issue demands, but Kaden turned back to me, ignoring him—and then we heard the trampling of heavy boots on steps. Rafe appeared at the head of the stairs where I was supposed to have fled already. Jeb and another man stood behind him.

They walked toward us, taking in the scene, and slowly Rafe drew his sword. His men did the same. Kaden looked from Rafe to me. His eyes flooded with understanding. He knew.

"I'm leaving, Kaden," I said, hoping to avoid a clash. "Don't try to stop me."

His expression hardened. "With him."

I swallowed. I could see it in every twitch of his jaw. He had already guessed, but I said it anyway. "Yes. With Prince Jaxon of Dalbreck." There was no turning back now.

"You always meant to."

I nodded.

His gaze faltered. He couldn't hide the pain of my betrayal.

"Step away from her," Rafe warned, still cautiously advancing.

Suddenly Griz grabbed my arm, dragging me to the wall where the crowds still waited. He raised my hand to the sky before them. "Your Komizar! Your queen! Jezelia!"

The crowds roared.

I looked at Griz, horrified.

Kaden's face was equally shocked. "Are you mad?" he yelled at Griz. "She'll never survive! Do you know what the Council will do to her?"

Griz looked out at the cheering crowds. "This is bigger than the Council," he answered.

"She'll die just the same!" Kaden said.

Rafe pulled me from Griz's grip, and then the world seemed to explode. The portal doors burst open, the iron bar flying loose, and Rahtan flooded in, governors following on their heels. The first blows came from Malich, who focused all his energy on Kaden, brutal and hungry. Kaden deflected his first strikes and advanced, the fierce clang of metal on metal juddering in the air. Theron and Jorik came at Griz, their assault relentless and violent, but Griz was a giant wielding two swords, and he met them blow for blow, driving them back.

Rafe felled one guard after another, fighting shoulder to shoulder with Kaden against the onslaught.

Governor Obraun advanced toward me, and I lifted my sword to strike when he suddenly turned and dealt a death blow to

Darius. The governor was fighting on our side? His own mute guard fought beside him, but now he was yelling with a voice that was loud and clear, warning Jeb of someone charging from the side. Governor Faiwell battled beside Jeb, as did two of my assigned guards. None of it made sense. Who fought against whom? The melee of screams and clattering swords was deafening. In one swing, Rafe brought down Gurtan and Stavik and moved on to more. He was frightening in his power, a force I didn't even recognize.

The grunts of battle and the sickening crunch of bone filled the air. They had hemmed me in behind their backs. I was clearly the target of those advancing. My own sword was useless. I tried to break through to help, but Griz pushed me back.

Malich's expression was wild as he attacked Kaden, driven by more than just duty. A scream pierced the air when Griz finally thrust his sword between Theron's ribs, but Jorik swung, and his sword sliced Griz's side. Griz fell to one knee grasping his ribs and Jorik raised his sword to finish the job. Before he could plunge it into Griz, I threw the knife still in my hand. It hit Jorik dead center in the throat, and he stumbled backward. He was dead before his body ever hit the ground. Griz managed to get back to his feet, still wielding one sword while he held his injured side. Blood was everywhere, and the snow was a slushy red. A bloodbath.

The onslaught slowed, and at last the numbers seemed in our favor.

"Get her out of here!" Kaden yelled. "Before more come!"

Rafe yelled to the not-so-mute guard to clear the stairs and ordered me to follow, then laid a deathblow on Chievdar Dietrik, who had charged toward him, determined not to let me go.

"This way, girl!" Governor Obraun grabbed my arm and pushed me toward the stairs. Another man ran with us. I heard Jeb call him Tavish, and the mute guard, Orrin. Rafe followed behind, guarding our backs. I looked back and saw Kaden, Griz, Faiwell, and the two guards holding off those remaining on the terrace. Gods help them when more came. Surely all of the soldiers' barracks had been alerted by now.

We hurried down the stairs to the second level and turned into the portal, the plan gone horribly off course. As soon as we passed through the heavy door, it slammed shut, and I looked back to see Calantha bolting it.

"Calantha," I said, stunned.

"Hurry!" she yelled.

"You can't stay now. Come with us."

"I'll be all right," she answered. "No one knows I'm here. Go."

"But—"

"This is my home," she said firmly.

There wasn't time to argue with her, but I saw a resolve in her face that hadn't been there before. We exchanged a last knowing nod, and I ran.

Rafe now led the way with me just behind him. It was a long dark corridor, and our footsteps echoed through it like thunder, but then the sound doubled and we knew we had guards charging toward us from the opposite direction.

"Down here!" I shouted, turning toward a path I had

traveled with Aster. "It will take us to the catacombs." I led them on the twisting path and then down a long flight of steps. When we reached the bottom, I heard loud shuffling. I put my finger to my lips and mouthed, *Someone's coming.* Jeb pushed past me. I tried to stop him, but Rafe nodded to let him go.

He stepped out from the landing into the light, and I saw him transform back into the patty clapper. He smiled and a guard came into view, asking him if he had seen anyone run past. When Jeb pointed in one direction, the guard turned, and in a lightning-quick motion, Jeb snapped his neck.

"It's clear," he called to us. "He was the only one."

We ran through the narrow catacombs and down trails that led us through the caverns. We were so deep in the earth I knew the scholars had no way of knowing that a war had been un-leashed above them. The few who saw us running past were stunned into silence, confused over what was going on. They only conjured wars; they didn't fight them. I turned at the path-way of skulls. "This will take us to the river," I said. When we heard the roar of the falls, the one called Tavish pushed in front to lead us to the raft. About a hundred yards down, we stepped out of the tunnel into the mist from the river. The ground was slick and icy.

"This way!" Tavish called over the din, but then four soldiers emerged from another tunnel that emptied onto the river and a new battle ignited. Rafe, Jeb, Obraun, and Tavish ran forward to intercept the assault. Orrin and I took on more guards who ran toward us from the tunnel we'd just left. I stepped to the side, hidden from view, and when the first came through, I swung, catching him in the neck. Orrin took the next one, and we both downed the third. I caught him in the ribs, and when he stumbled forward, Orrin gored his back.

Rafe yelled for us to get to the raft, that they would catch up, and Orrin pulled me along a bank and down a trail of rocks, with Tavish following close behind. We came to an outcropping of rocks, and panic gripped me. I saw no raft, but Tavish jumped. I thought he'd gone straight into the river, but then I saw him on the raft nearly hidden by mist and rock.

"Jump!" he ordered.

"Not without Rafe!" I said.

"He'll be here! Jump!" The raft strained against the ropes that secured it to the bank. Orrin gave me a nudge, and we both jumped.

"Stay low!" Tavish said, and told me to grab one of the knotted ropes to hold on.

The raft pitched and rolled, even in the calmest waters near the shore. I stayed low as Tavish ordered, gripping the rope to stabilize myself. Even through the mist, I could see the high cliffs above us, guards and soldiers traversing the trails downward. They seemed to multiply like feverish insects determined to swarm over us. Everywhere we looked, we saw more coming. They spotted us as well and arrows began flying, but they fell short and landed on the shore. Jeb and Obraun arrived and jumped down with us. "Rafe's coming!" Jeb said. "Get ready to lift the ties!" His shoulder was bleeding, and blood drenched Obraun's arm. Orrin and Tavish reached for the ropes securing the raft.

"Not yet!" I said. "Wait! Wait until he's here!"

The soldiers scrambling down the wall of rock to the river were getting closer, their arrows falling dangerously near, but suddenly arrows started flying in the other direction, toward them. I turned to see Orrin letting loose a firestorm of arrows. Soldiers tumbled from ledges. Orrin managed to slow their assault, but there were always more to replace the men he took down.

We heard a terrifying scream through the mist and every drop of blood in me burned with fear. I saw Jeb and Obraun exchange an anxious glance.

"Free the ropes," Obraun ordered.

"No!" I cried.

But just then, Rafe broke through the haze and was running toward us. "Go!" he yelled, and Tavish set the ropes free. A powerful explosion ripped through the air. Rafe leapt to the raft as it was already moving from shore, barely crossing the expanse, and pieces of rock rained down around us. He grabbed the knotted rope I shoved in his hand. "That should keep the bridge out of commission for at least a month," he said. It was more than I had expected of the small flask of clear liquid.

We were rapidly swept into the current, and the raft pitched and jumped in the violent waters. With Obraun and Jeb both injured, Tavish and Orrin took over the rudder and somehow managed to steer the bobbing barrels through the treacherous current, away from shore. But we weren't far enough away yet. I spotted Malich perched on a boulder, easily within range. *Dear gods.* What had happened to Kaden?

Malich's bow was loaded and aimed at Rafe's back. I jumped forward to push Rafe down as the raft spun in an eddy and I was tossed to the side. A fiery pain jolted my thigh. Even through the violent rocking, I saw Malich smile. It wasn't Rafe he was aiming at. It was me.

"Lia!" Rafe shouted, and scrambled toward me, but not before another arrow hit my back. It burned like a glowing ember searing into my flesh. I couldn't catch my breath. Rafe's hand grabbed my arm, but I still tumbled backward as the raft rolled and pitched. I plunged into the icy water. Rafe's hand held tight, fiercely digging into my arm, but the current was strong and my heavy dress quickly became weighted with water like an anchor pulling me down. I tried to kick it away, but it circled around my legs, binding them as tightly as rope. The river was numbing and wild, water rushing into my face, choking me, and the current was too much for Rafe's grip. The fabric of my sleeve began ripping loose. I tried to lift my other arm, but it wouldn't move, as if the arrow had pinned it to my side. Two sets of hands were grappling at my arm and shoulder, trying to get a better hold in the wild swirl of water, but then a quick suck of gushing water pulled me free from them. I was swept into the icy waters away from the raft. Rafe jumped in after me.

We tumbled through the current, his arms reaching me again and again but being pulled away as many times, the water covering our heads, both of us gasping for air, with the raft nowhere in sight. He reached me at last, his arm circling my waist, trying frantically to rip the dress off. "Hold on, Lia."

"I love you," I cried, even as I choked on water. If there were to be last words he heard from me, I wanted it to be those. And then I felt us sliding, tumbling, the world turning upside down, and I lost sight of him, lost sight of everything, the wretched dress the Komizar had made me wear pulling me under as if he were tugging at me from beneath the water himself, getting the last say, until finally I couldn't fight against its weight any longer, and my icy world went black.

CHAPTER SIXTY-FOUR

RAFE

I HAD WALKED THE RIVERBANK FOR MILES, SEARCHING everywhere. I wouldn't accept that she was gone. I was numb with the cold and uncertain how much time had passed. I never caught sight of the raft again and wondered if the others had made it. With every step, I retraced the events, trying to understand how everything had gone wrong. I saw the child, Aster, again, her body lying in the snow, and the knife in Lia's hand. I saw the Komizar too, slumped against the wall and bleeding. There hadn't been time to put the pieces together then, and I still couldn't.

My thoughts just kept going back to Lia. *I'd had her.* I'd had her in my arms and then we were tumbling in the falls and she slipped from my grasp. *I'd had her, and the river ripped her away.*

The current was fast and relentless. I wasn't sure how I had made it to shore myself. By the time I did, I was miles down-river, and my limbs were frozen. Somehow I had dragged my-self up on the bank and forced my legs to move, praying she had done the same. I couldn't accept anything else.

I slipped on an icy rock and fell to my knees, feeling my strength fading. That was when I spotted her ahead, facedown on the bank, settling into the earth as if she were already a part of it, her fingers lifeless in the mud and snow.

Blood stained her back where the arrow had entered. Only a broken stub remained. I ran and dropped to her side, gently turning her and pulling her into my arms. Her lips were blue, but a soft moan escaped them.

"Lia," I whispered. I brushed the snow from her lashes.

Her eyelids fluttered open. It took her a moment to see who I was. "Which side of the river are we on?" she asked, her voice so weak I could barely hear her.

"Our side."

A faint smile creased her eyes. "Then we made it."

I looked up, surveying our surroundings. We were miles from anywhere, without horses, food, or warmth, and she lay badly injured and bleeding in my arms, her face the color of death.

"Yes, Lia, we made it." My chest shook, and I leaned down and kissed her forehead.

"Then why are you weeping?"

"I'm not. It's only—" I held her closer, trying to share what little warmth I had. "We should have stayed. We should have—"

"He would have killed me eventually. You know that. He

was already weary of the little power he shared with me. And if not the Komizar, his Council would have done the job."

With each word, her voice became fainter.

"Don't leave me, Lia. Promise you won't leave me."

She reached up and wiped the tears from my face. "Rafe," she whispered, "we made it this far. What's another thousand miles or two?"

Her eyes drifted closed, and her head lolled to the side. I put my lips to hers, desperately searching for her breaths. They were shallow and weak, but still there.

We made it this far. I didn't even know where we were. We were lost on a riverbank with miles of dark forest surrounding us, but I scooped one arm under her knees and the other carefully behind her back and stood. I kissed her one more time, my lips gently resting on hers, trying to bring back their color. And I began walking. A thousand miles, or two, I would carry her all the way to Dalbreck if I had to. No one would pry her from my arms again.

We already had three steps behind us.

"Hold on, Lia," I whispered.

Hold on for me.

ACKNOWLEDGMENTS

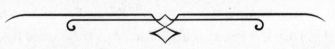

WOW. ANOTHER BOOK IS DONE? MY HEAD IS STILL SPINNING from the publication of the first book. More than ever I know the birth of this book is by some miracle and the help and support of so many.

First, bloggers, tweeters, booktubers. Oh my. ARCs for *The Kiss of Deception* came out quite early and you jumped on it. You blogged, tweeted, squealed, spread the word, and encouraged me enormously. And pestered for the next. That kind of pestering rocks. Your belief in Lia's story bolstered my own. You kept me going.

Librarians and teachers. You shouted out and began immediately booktalking it to your patrons and students. One librarian even contemplated getting a claw and vine kavah on her shoulder. Maybe she has! All your enthusiasm helped me reach the finish line.

I feel so lucky to be part of the Macmillan king- and queendom. Every single person on staff deserves a crown—and that's about five thousand crowns. It doesn't take just a village to make a book, but a whole dedicated city. Special thanks go to Jean Feiwel, Laura Godwin, Angus Killick, Elizabeth Fithian, Katie Fee, Caitlin Sweeny, Allison Verost, Ksenia Winnicki, Claire Taylor, Lucy Del Priore, Katie Halata, Ana Deboo, and Rachel Murray for your tremendous support. I lift a cup of thannis to you all! Sweetened, of course.

The magic of Rich Deas and Anna Booth continues to entrance me, from gorgeous covers to title graphics to fonts that the font geek in me can swoon over. Their talent is staggering. Also, thanks to Keith Thompson, who made the world of the Remnant Chronicles come to life in a map that is too beautiful for words.

I already mentioned her in the dedication, but she deserves accolades and more here too—my editor, Kate Farrell. We've been across the Cam Lanteux and back. I never would have made it without her. She guides me when I can no longer see the way— and she does it with patience, wisdom, and a smile. She is truly a rare gift.

For support in myriad ways, I'm grateful to YA writers Marlene Perez, Melissa Wyatt, Alyson Noel, Robin LaFevers, and Cinda Williams Chima. Whether it was helping me find a word that escaped my clutches, a wrestling match with ideas, wise counseling, much-needed laughs, or helping to spread the word, I thank you deeply. Karen Beiswenger and Jessica Butler suffered through early drafts that sometimes had more blanks than words—and they always asked for more. Fearless. I owe you both.

I am ever thankful to my friend, wise counselor, advocate, and agent, Rosemary Stimola. She never ceases to amaze me. She is balance, grace, and a bit of lion personified. (Okay, sometimes a lot of lion.)

My family is the best—my rock and foundation—Jess, Dan, Karen, Ben, and Ava and Emily. They cheerlead and center me at all the right moments. I am the luckiest mom and ama in the world.

Throughout the long days of writing this book, my husband, Dennis, fed me. Literally and figuratively. He was my prince and assassin rolled into one, protecting me and saving me from the ravages of hunger, fatigue, and sometimes slobbering dogs demanding dinner. He pulled up the slack and offered hugs and back massages. He continued to help out with the kissing logistics too. I think he wants this series to never end. *Enade ra beto.*

Lia's strength and determination didn't come out of thin air. Besides all the strong women I work with, and those I have long admired from afar, I am blessed with so many in my personal life who awe and inspire me. Kathy, Susan, Donna, Jana, Nina, Roberta, Jan, and a multitude of others, hooking arms with you. Sisters in blood and spirit, you are my army.

GOFISH

MARY E. PEARSON

Which kingdom do you think you would belong to if you were a character in the Remnant Chronicles?
That's a tough one. There are twelve kingdoms altogether, but of the major kingdoms, I'd probably want to be in Morrighan, and specifically, I would settle in Terravin. Ocean breezes and a quaint little fishing village? What is not to love? Especially with Berdi's tavern and her fish stew. Though I would also love to travel with the vagabonds and see all the lands of the continent—and it would be pretty cool to have a purple carvachi too.

Readers are introduced to Venda (considered the barbarian kingdom by many characters) in this book. What was your process for coming up with the Vendans' culture and language?
It was a long, evolving process as the story unfolded. A lot of their culture comes from the harshness of land they live in. Venda suffered the worst of the devastation, so even when they rebuilt their cities, they had to use whatever scraps they could scavenge. The haphazard city construction itself illus-

trates how every scrap and stone was used to build shelter. Their beginnings were desperate, and because of this, a strong bond developed among the people. They are loyal to a fault because they depend on each other to survive. The language has a certain harsh sound to it too—utilizing more hard consonants, as compared to the Vagabond language, which was more free-flowing and melodious. I wanted each language to have its own distinct sound.

The Komizar is also introduced in this book. What was your inspiration for this character, and how did you go about writing such a complex, fascinating villain?
In creating a villain, I always remember the old saying, "Even the villain is the hero of his own story." It is all about point of view, and I think keeping this in mind helps to create a complex villain that at times you can relate to even as you hate or fear them—which makes them all the more compelling. I loved writing the Komizar. He is magnetic in so many ways. He loves a good game, has a sense of humor, and at times is even caring and heroic—but he is also fueled by an insatiable hunger, which means there is no line he won't cross. Nothing is sacred to him. For me, it was fascinating to see a very intelligent and calculating man use what appears to be kindness to get what he wants.

Throughout both *The Kiss of Deception* and *The Heart of Betrayal*, there are selections from The Last Testaments of Gaudrel, Song of Venda, etc. Can you tell us a little about the challenges of storytelling in this way?
In the Remnant Chronicles, the foundation of Lia's world is based on certain truths—and truth is a recurring theme throughout

the trilogy. There are three ancient texts sprinkled throughout the novels that bring new light to these revered truths and open up Lia's eyes to new possibilities. These texts really show the power of story in our world, how it shapes us, sometimes even feeds us, and how quickly the truths story holds can be lost to the generations. It was a challenge to fuse these histories with how they affected the characters of subsequent generations, and also to show how much of history is lost to us forever.

What can we expect from *The Beauty of Darkness*? (No spoilers, please!)

Lia survives the daring escape from Venda only to find herself injured and in the wilderness with Rafe while being hunted down by Rahtan seeking vengeance.

With war on the horizon, Lia has no choice but to assume her role as a soldier and leader. As she hurries to reach Morrighan to warn them about the coming threat and also about traitors in their midst, she finds herself at crossed purposes with Rafe and suspicious of Kaden, who has tracked her down.

Lia must make heartbreaking sacrifices in order to save the kingdoms, even as she is forced to face those who have betrayed her the most deeply.

What was the world-building process like?

I had to imagine a world built on myth, ruin, and the ashes of a bygone world. That took me in a lot of different directions physically, spiritually, politically, and ecologically, and even though it is all fictional, it still led me to a lot of research. I keep extensive notes and maps to keep it all straight. Especially for creating the various languages! Everything is based on coming from a prior culture.

Tell us about your writing process. Where do you write? When? What do you eat/drink while crafting a story?

Ah, it always comes back to food, doesn't it? I am not much of a snacker—usually the only thing you will find sitting on my desk is a glass of water—but I do admit that at certain times of the year when I have really good dark chocolate in the house, I will freely set it next to my keyboard when I am gnashing my teeth over a scene or deadline, and indulge at will. And of course it is all medicinal, so I can do it guilt-free, right? As far as the writing itself goes, when I begin a project, I open a file, give it a working title, and from that point on the file is open on my computer. Except for a power outage, it's never closed. And then from morning until I go to bed, I write. Not continuously, of course. I will sit down in the morning, reread what I wrote the day before, rewrite a bit, and then try to make progress with new territory, go take a shower, go back to write more that came to me while in the shower, and so it goes throughout the day. I have daily goals of so many words—the ones I call keepers. In one day I may write 3000 words to end up with 250 that I feel are right.

As for where I write, I have a bedroom in my house that has been converted to an office. It is the darkest, quietest corner of the house, with a pretty view out the window of trees in my yard, and very often I have birds outside my window, looking in. Maybe that's why birds have made appearances in my last two books.

When did you realize you wanted to be a writer?

I think it was in high school. Before that I had always loved writing, but the actual "job" of being a writer hadn't occurred to me. I remember reading *The Outsiders,* my first book that really seemed like it came from my generation, and I thought, this is the kind of book I could write. Before that, while I had loved the literature I had read, it always seemed like it was from another time—authors long dead, the classics and such—so joining those ranks seemed distant and unattainable.

How did you celebrate publishing your first book?
When "the" call came, I still remember jumping up and down in the kitchen with my daughters squealing. That was all the celebration I needed.

Which of your characters is most like you?
When I finished *The Miles Between,* I thought that one of the secondary characters, Mira, was a bit like me. She is perky and cheerful and always trying to make everyone get along, but beneath that perky exterior she has some more serious motivations. I've known for years that I have a "peacemaker" personality, so I was a bit surprised to see some of those qualities emerge in Mira.

As a young person, who did you look up to most?
My sister. I was five years younger and I tagged along behind her incessantly, and she was always nice to me and always included me. Of course, during our teen years we had a few arguments—mostly over the bathroom—but other than that we have always gotten along great. She is a strong, even-tempered, salt-of-the-earth kind of person, and I still look up to her.

What was your worst subject in school?
Math. I am not a numbers person. I can barely remember how old I am—which is sometimes convenient.

What was your best subject in school?
English, but not when it came to dissecting sentences. I hated

that part. I think because I was an avid reader I internalized what made a sentence correct, rather than memorizing the "rules" of proper sentence structure. I think rules and memorization are for left-brainers, and I am an intuitive right-brainer all the way.

Are you a morning person or a night owl?

Definitely a morning person, but I am married to a night owl, so I have learned to sleep in a little more. But my body clock still tries to wake me at the first sign of dawn.

What do you want readers to remember about your books?

There's a hundred different answers to that depending on the book and the reader, but a few thoughts . . . I hope that perhaps they will remember seeing themselves and feeling less alone, or remember stretching to ponder new ideas or viewpoints, or remember walking in someone else's shoes and gaining a new perspective, or perhaps simply remember a fond few hours where they were able to escape into a different world where they shared a journey with me.

What was your favorite book as a teen?

I loved poetry—Dickinson, Frost, Cummings, Yeats—anything I could get my hands on. A few books that I loved and reread many times were *The Outsiders* by S. E. Hinton, *A Tree Grows in Brooklyn* by Betty Smith, and *The Good Earth* by Pearl S. Buck. As a younger teen I remember loving anything written by Ruth M. Arthur. A while back I managed to get my hands on an old copy of *Requiem for a Princess,* which has long been out of print. I reread it and was happy to see that I was as impressed with her writing now as I was then.

What would your readers be most surprised to learn about you?

That I love to laugh. I can be very serious and my books tend to be on the very serious side, but laughter is the necessary balance to it all. My husband makes me laugh every day, and when I get together with my sister, I become impossibly silly.

LIA AND RAFE HAVE ESCAPED VENDA,
and the path before them is winding and dangerous—
what will happen now?

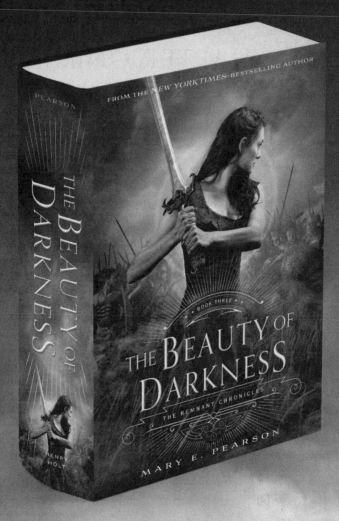

KEEP READING FOR AN EXCERPT!

CHAPTER ONE

DARKNESS WAS A BEAUTIFUL THING. THE KISS OF A SHADOW. A caress as soft as moonlight. It had always been my refuge, my place of escape, whether I was sneaking onto a rooftop lit only by the stars, or down a midnight alley to be with my brothers. Darkness was my ally. It made me forget the world I was in and invited me to dream of another.

I sank deeper, searching for its comfort. Sweet murmurs stirred me. Only a sliver of golden moon shone in the liquid dark, floating, rocking, always moving, always out of my reach. Its shifting light illuminated a meadow. My spirits lifted. I saw Walther dancing with Greta. Just beyond them, Aster twirled to music I couldn't quite hear, and her long hair flowed past her shoulders. Was it the Festival of Deliverance already? Aster called out to me, *Don't tarry now, Miz*. Deep colors swirled; a sprinkling of stars turned purple; the edges of the moon dissolved like wet sugar into black sky; the darkness deepened. Warm. Welcoming. Soft.

Except for the jostle.

The rhythmic shake came again and again. Demanding.

Stay.

The voice that wouldn't let go. Cold and bright and sharp.

Hold on.

A broad hard chest, frosty breaths when my eyes rolled open, a voice that kept pulling the blanket away, pain bearing down, so numbing I couldn't breathe. The terrible brightness flashing, stabbing, and finally ebbing when I could take no more.

Darkness again. Inviting me to stay. No breaths. No anything.

When I was halfway between one world and another, a moment of clarity broke through.

This is what it was to die.

LIA!

The comfort of darkness was stripped away again. The gentle warmth turned unbearably hot. More voices came. Harsh. Shouts. Deep. Too many voices.

The Sanctum. I was back in the Sanctum. Soldiers, governors . . . the Komizar.

My skin was on fire, burning, stinging. Flesh wet with heat.

Lia, open your eyes. Now.

Commands.

They had found me.

"Lia!"

My eyes flew open. The room spun with fire and shadows, flesh and faces. Surrounded. I tried to pull back, but searing pain wrenched my breath away. My vision fluttered.

"Lia, don't move."

And then a flurry of voices. *She's come to. Hold her down. Don't let her get up.*

I forced a shallow breath into my lungs, and my eyes focused. I surveyed the faces staring down at me. Governor Obraun and his guard. It wasn't a dream. They had captured me. And then a hand gently turned my head.

Rafe.

He knelt by my side.

I looked back at the others, remembering. Governor Obraun and his guard had fought on our side. They helped us escape. Why? Beside them were Jeb and Tavish.

"Governor," I whispered, too weak to say more.

"Sven, Your Highness," he said, dropping to one knee. "Please call me Sven."

The name was familiar. I'd heard it in frantic blurred moments. Rafe had called him Sven. I looked around, trying to get my bearings. I lay on the ground on a bedroll. Piles of heavy blankets that smelled of horses were on top of me. Saddle blankets.

I tried to rise up on one arm, and pain tore through me again. I fell back, the room spinning.

We have to get the barbs out.

She's too weak.

She's burning with fever. She's only going to get weaker.

The wounds have to be cleaned and stitched.

I've never stitched a girl before.

Flesh is flesh.

I listened to them argue, and then I remembered. Malich had shot me. An arrow in my thigh, and one in my back. The last I remembered I was on a riverbank and Rafe was scooping me into his arms, his lips cool against mine. How long ago was that? Where were we now?

She's strong enough. Do it, Tavish.

Rafe cupped my face and leaned close. "Lia, the barbs are deep. We'll have to cut the wounds to get them out."

I nodded.

His eyes glistened. "You can't move. I'll have to hold you down."

"It's all right," I whispered. "I'm strong. Like you said." I heard the weakness of my voice contradicting my words.

Sven winced. "I wish I had some red-eye for you, girl." He handed Rafe something. "Put this in her mouth to bite down on." I knew what it was for—so I wouldn't scream. Was the enemy near?

Rafe put a leather sheath in my mouth. Cool air streamed onto my bare leg as Tavish folded back the blanket to expose my thigh, and I realized that I had little on beneath the blankets. A chemise, if that. They must have removed my sodden dress.

Tavish mumbled an apology to me but wasted no time. Rafe pinned down my arms, and someone else pressed down on my legs. The knife cut into my thigh. My chest shuddered. Moans escaped through my clenched teeth. My body recoiled against my will, and Rafe pressed harder. "Look at me, Lia. Keep your eyes on me. It'll be over soon."

I locked onto his eyes, the blue blazing. His gaze held me like fire. Sweat dripped down his brow. The knife probed, and I lost focus. Gurgled noises jumped from my throat.

Look at me, Lia.

Digging. Cutting.

"Got it!" Tavish finally shouted.

My breath came in gulps. Jeb wiped my face with a cool cloth.

Good job, Princess, from whom I didn't know.

The stitching was easy compared to the cutting and probing. I counted each time the needle went in. Fourteen times.

"Now for the back," Tavish said. "That one will be a little harder."

I WOKE TO RAFE SLEEPING BESIDE ME. HIS ARM RESTED heavily across my stomach. I couldn't remember much about Tavish working on my back except him telling me the arrow was embedded in my rib and that probably saved my life. I had felt the cut, the probe, and then pain so bright I couldn't see anymore. Finally, as if from a hundred miles away, Rafe had whispered in my ear, *It's out.*

A small fire burned in a ring of rocks not far from me. It illuminated one nearby wall, but the rest of our shelter remained in shadows. It was a large cave of some sort. I heard the whicker of horses. They were in here with us. On the other side of the fire ring I saw Jeb, Tavish, and Orrin asleep on their bedrolls, and just to my left, sitting back against the cave wall, Governor Obraun—*Sven*.

It hit me fully for the first time. These were Rafe's four men, the four I'd had no confidence in—governor, guard, patty clapper, and raft builder. I didn't know where we were, but against all odds they had somehow gotten us across the river. All of us alive. Except for—

My head ached, trying to sort it all out. Our freedom came at a high cost to others. Who had died and who had survived the bloodbath?

I tried to ease Rafe's arm from my stomach so I could sit up, but even that small movement sent blinding jolts through my back. Sven sat upright, alerted by my movement, and whispered, "Don't try to get up, Your Highness. It's too soon."

I nodded, measuring my breaths until the pain receded.

"Your rib is most likely cracked by the impact of the arrow. You may have cracked more bones in the river. Rest."

"Where are we?" I asked.

"A little hideaway I tucked into many years ago. I was thankful I could still find it."

"How long have I been out?"

"Two days. It's a miracle you're alive."

I remembered sinking in the river. Thrashing, then being spit up, a quick gust of air filling my lungs and then being pulled under again. And again. My hands clutched at boulders, logs, everything slipping from my grasp, and then there was the fuzzy recollection of Rafe leaning over me. I turned my head toward Sven. "Rafe found me on the bank."

"He carried you for twelve miles before we found him. This is the first sleep he's had."

I looked at Rafe, his face gaunt and bruised. He had a gash over his left brow. The river had taken its toll on him too. Sven explained how he, Jeb, Orrin, and Tavish had maneuvered the raft to the planned destination. They'd left their own horses and a half dozen Vendan ones they had taken in battle in a makeshift paddock, but many had escaped. They rounded up what they could, gathered the supplies and saddles they had stashed in nearby ruins, and began backtracking, searching the banks and forest for us. They finally spotted some tracks and followed them. Once they found us, they rode through the night to this shelter.

"If you were able to find our tracks, then—"

"Not to worry, Your Highness. Listen." He cocked his head to the side.

A heavy whine vibrated through the cavern.

"A blizzard," he said. "There will be no tracks to follow."

Whether the storm was a blessing or hindrance, I wasn't sure—it would prevent us from traveling too. I remembered my aunt Bernette telling me and my brothers about the great white storms of her homeland that blocked out sky and earth and left snow piled so high that she and her sisters could venture outside only from the second floor of their fortress. Dogs with webbed feet had pulled their sleds across the snow.

"But they will try to follow," I said. "Eventually."

GASTINEUX
CANDORA
CORTENAI
INFERN
KINGDOM OF
MORRIGHAN
TRIBE OF GAUDREL
CAMLAN
CIVICA
TERQUOI TRÁ
CITY OF
DARK MAGIC
TERRAVIN
AZENTIL
PIADRO
SAFRAN SEA
GITOS
M
D